URBAN ALLIES

URBAN ALLIES

Ten Brand-New Collaborative Stories

EDITED BY

JOSEPH NASSISE

HARPER Voyager
An Imprint of HarperCollins Publishers

URBAN ALLIES. Individual pieces copyright © 2016 by their respective author as noted above. All rights reserved. Printed in the United States of America. No part of this book may be used or reproduced in any manner whatsoever without written permission except in the case of brief quotations embodied in critical articles and reviews. For information address HarperCollins Publishers, 195 Broadway, New York, NY 10007.

HarperCollins books may be purchased for educational, business, or sales promotional use. For information please e-mail the Special Markets Department at SPsales@harpercollins.com.

FIRST EDITION

Harper Voyager and design is a trademark of HarperCollins Publishers L.L.C.

Designed by Paula Russell Szafranski
City illustration © by 21/Shutterstock, Inc.

Library of Congress Cataloging-in-Publication Data has been applied for.

ISBN 978-0-06-239134-6

16 17 18 19 20 ov/rrd 10 9 8 7 6 5 4 3 2 1

CONTENTS

Ladies' Fight

CAITLIN KITTREDGE AND JAYE WELLS

AVA

I watched delicate fingers of mist uncurl as Leo's car rolled silently down the highway between Baton Rouge and New Orleans. We were passing through a nowhere pocket of swamp country, the road raised up on a causeway between the thick tangle of mud, grass, and cypress that filled the windows.

The sun was barely up, and aside from a heron we startled with our passing, it was like we were the only two people left on earth.

"You hungry?" Leo said at length, his thin tattooed fingers tapping the steering wheel. "I think I saw signs for a diner a few miles up."

I shook my head. I still wasn't used to this. Just the two of us, sitting in a car gliding through Louisiana like we were on a road trip. "I'm fine," I said.

Leo sighed. The car was so quiet I could practically hear his heart beating. His annoyance sounded like a hurricane.

"You and me are gonna have to actually talk to each other sooner or later," he said. "I think we've said maybe six words that weren't bickering between here and Nevada. That's gotta be some kind of record."

I stayed quiet. If he thought this was me being recalcitrant he hadn't seen anything yet.

"Fine," Leo said. "I'll talk for both of us. 'Gee, Leo, it's been weird since you died and woke up a Grim Reaper.' It sure as shit has, Ava, but I'm glad that I've got you around to have my back."

I ran a hand across my throbbing forehead. "It's not about that," I said finally.

"She speaks," Leo exclaimed. "Welcome back, kid."

"Listen," I said. "I've been there. I died and I woke up as a monster. It's not you and me. It's everything else."

Leo reached over and squeezed my hand. His hands were delicate and long-fingered, like a musician's. If it weren't for the Russian tattoos inking every joint you'd think he was a piano player and not a hardened killer. "If I learned one thing from growing up the way I did, it's that gangsters are always going to fight and the best thing people like us can do is keep our heads down and move forward when the dust settles."

"If some cranky Russians were all we had to contend with, I wouldn't be worried," I grumbled. I didn't say what I was really thinking—that the "gangsters" fighting were angels and demons. That both Leo and I were game pieces being pushed around a board by the sort of creatures whose main purpose was to make life miserable for everyone around them.

"So we'll go to NOLA, get the Grim Reaper's Scythe and then you really won't have to worry," Leo said with that easy grin he could muster even in situations like this. I would have kind of hated it, if I didn't like him so much.

By the time we hit the outskirts of New Orleans, the fog had cleared off, just a low coating of it clinging to the Mississippi as we crossed the bridge. I'd gone back to being silent. The misgivings I had about the whole Scythe thing were a fight Leo and I had already had, repeatedly, on the way from Nevada.

Scythes were a reaper's tool for taking souls, when the warlock or mage they'd made the deal with ran out the clock. Every one was different, and at first Leo and I assumed his was the sweet ride we currently inhabited. What else could you think about a muscle car that ran completely silent and never needed gas?

But it was just a steed, not a weapon. The Grim Reaper's Scythe wasn't like the Scythe that had belonged to Gary, the reaper who'd made me into a hellhound. It was something as ancient and primeval as the Grim Reaper himself. And since Leo was the first Grim Reaper in almost a thousand years, his Scythe was lost somewhere in the metaphysical attic of space and time, under almost a millennium of demon meddling and reaper politics that kept his office vacant so any demon could swoop in and use the reapers as their own personal servants—with a side of heavy muscle.

So now we were heading to New Orleans on a tip from a friend of a friend of a scumbag warlock that Leo'd dealt with when he was alive and just a plain old necromancer.

Leo exited the highway in the Garden District and slowed, crawling through streets just beginning to wake up. My breath fogged the window as I looked out and I rubbed the spot away. The last time I'd been here the streetlamps had been gas and I'd been alive, barely twenty years old and in love with the man who'd eventually betray and murder me.

"After we pick up the Scythe we should go for breakfast," Leo said. "I could really go for some of those tiny donuts. You know. They're called something French."

"Beignets," I murmured as we slowed, parking across the street from a mansion that was, by anyone's standards, extremely fancy. Even if I weren't really just a hillbilly from Tennessee at heart, I would have thought the place was swank.

"Yeah, those," Leo said. He swung his door open and looked at me when I hesitated. "You coming or what? Boyd said that the owner's a vamp, and daylight is the way to go if we're going to be in and out."

"I can't believe we're breaking into the house of somebody who clearly has enough money to see we're sent to a deep dark hole if we get caught," I said. "Never mind breaking in on the advice of somebody named *Boyd*."

"Hey, Boyd may be a scumbag but he's a scumbag who loves having somebody owe him a favor," Leo said. "He's not gonna screw us over."

"And the owner," I said, refusing to cross the street just yet. "Vamps tend more toward dank basements and caves, not beautifully restored Greek Revival mansions. You know that, right?"

"Yeah, about that." Leo rubbed his chin in the gesture I recognized as him lying his ass off. "I don't think she's strictly a vamp in the venomous, blood-drinking crackhead sense you and I understand it. I mean, until a couple weeks ago I thought demons were a creepy bedtime story, so maybe we don't know every critter in the Monster Manual just yet."

"Did you just use Dungeons and Dragons to convince me to fight off some kind of super-vamp collector of magical artifacts who basically lives in a fort?" I said, folding my arms.

Leo shrugged. "Did it work?"

"Fuck you," I said, heading across the street. "If we get thrown in jail, I'm leaving you there."

The house wasn't as fortress-like as it appeared from the outside, but it was still big and fancy and had a really nice non-magical security system in place. A camera whirred at me and I turned quickly, stepping behind a thick oleander bush to hide my face.

"Don't worry about it," Leo said. "Boyd gave us the security code."

"Boyd is just a magical helper elf when it comes to getting in good with the Grim Reaper, isn't he?" I grumbled.

Leo turned on me, his good mood draining out like a drunk's piss into a Bourbon Street gutter on a Saturday night. "Ava, we need the Scythe if we have a chance of making this work. I'm not going to be caught with my dick out when I run up against the next demon."

I shut up. After almost a century of living with Gary, who had a temper that would make the average rabid dog look cuddly, I knew when to play the quiet game. Besides, Leo was right. He'd been a powerful necromancer and the demon who killed him had still sliced through his magic like a hot knife and planted said knife between his ribs up to the hilt.

Leo punched in the security code, and the side door we'd found popped open. But I grabbed him by the shoulder before he could step over the threshold.

"Magic," I said quietly. Leo really was desperate if he'd ignored a barrier spell. It smelled like burning trash wafting across the wind, hot and sharp, ready to knock back anyone it didn't read as friendly. It wasn't blood conjuring, though, or dark magic. And I didn't think light magic could pack that kind of punch.

All of that was a story for another day. For now, I had to stop Leo from frying himself.

"Hold on," I said, standing back a bit and rolling my shoulders. Usually when I became the hound it was on the fly, my adrenaline was pumping and it wasn't a big deal. I'm always in both states—there's no breaking bones and wolfman shit going on. I'm both a human and a hound, always. I try not to think too much about how that's possible—discussing pocket dimensions and string theory isn't usually my idea of fun.

Now, though, the shift was more of a whisper than a scream. I opened my eyes and I was at knee height to Leo, staring at the world through the red-tinged vision of a hound. I could see the spell dancing in front of all the doors and windows, crisscrossing the house like a laser show. I took a deep sniff and stepped forward, tentatively putting one foot over the threshold. The spell hissed and crackled, but didn't tear me apart or set off alarms. For whatever reason, it didn't react to me in hound form at all.

I looked back at Leo, who held up a hand to indicate he'd stay where he was. With his other hand he slid a sheet of paper through the barrier with Boyd's crappy hand-drawn map on it. I memorized the way to the library, where the Scythe supposedly was, and padded down the hall. It smelled a little damp and of dry rot, like most old homes in New Orleans. There were pictures on the walls, but I didn't bother to check them out—I could tell by the smell of old paint and wood that they were expensive, but I was much more focused on where I was headed.

The library was indeed stuffed full of magical crap. I still wasn't convinced that Boyd wasn't punking Leo—it seemed way too easy. Break into the house of a sleeping vamp during the day, with nary a bodyguard in sight? Find something as significant as the Scythe just sitting around?

Maybe they didn't know what they had, I reasoned as I nosed through a few of the dusty shelves, letting out a sneeze.

"What the *hell*!" a voice exploded from behind me. I jumped and spun, baring my teeth. The figure in the chair, who appeared to be one of those freaky hairless cats, just extra large and, well, *talking*, also bared its teeth, letting out a scalding hiss. "Damn!" it shouted, jumping to its feet. "What in the fuck are you supposed to be—Cujo Junior?"

I opened my mouth to say I wasn't there to hurt anybody, even though on four legs I could only speak in the hellhound's native language of mostly growls and grunts, but before I could, the "cat" started to scream like a broken siren. A puff of purple smoke exploded and when it cleared, a seven-foot-tall green-scaled demon had taken the cat's place. Before I could react, it started screaming again.

"Sabina! SABINA! Get in here!"

SABINA

Something woke me from the sleep of the dead. At first, I thought it was Adam's hand, which was snaking over my hip and curving toward my chest. But then a shout from downstairs broke through my sleepy haze. I jackknifed upright.

"Hmm," Adam groaned.

"Shh!" I cocked my head to listen. The mage I loved didn't have my preternatural hearing, so he probably hadn't heard anything. "Something's wrong. I think—"

"*Sabina!*"

I leapt out of bed, threw on my robe, grabbed my gun from the bedside table, and zapped out of the bedroom. I reappeared downstairs in the foyer. Adam flashed in a split second later. I started off, but he grabbed my arm.

"Wait," he whispered. "What the hell?"

A volley of shouts—two male and one female—from the direction of the library answered the question for me. Our gazes met for a split second before we both took off down the hall. As we ran, the air sizzled as Adam called up his magic. I gripped my gun tighter and mentally ran through possible scenarios. Things had been really quiet lately in New Orleans. The Dark Races Council had been getting along, and there hadn't been any threats from enemies in months.

We burst through the library's wooden double doors to find the largest dog I'd ever seen, a sketchy-looking dude, and a very naked and pissed-off demon.

The dog growled and the hackles on its back rose like spikes.

I pointed my gun at the male, who had one pointed right back at me. "Call off the mutt." The male wasn't giving off any of the typical physical clues a dark race being might—no lavender smell that would indicate he was a faery, no copper penny scent of a vamp, and, while I detected some traces of magic, it wasn't the sort of power I'd expect from a mage. There was a chance he might be a werewolf, but it was hard to tell if the dirty dog smell came from him or from the actual dog.

In response to my command, the dog growled again, as if it could understand me. I moved the gun's aim from the dude to the dog. I didn't plan on shooting the mutt. These two were hardly threats to the combined power of a mage, a Mischief demon, and the Chosen of the Dark Races.

"What the hell is going on here?" Adam asked.

Giguhl spoke first. "I'll tell you what's going on! I was sitting here minding my own business when these two snuck in through the side door."

I frowned. "How is that possible?"

Instead of answering my question, the guy said, "Where's the Scythe?"

"What Scythe?" I glanced at Adam, who shrugged back. Giguhl shook his head to indicate that he, too, was in the dark. "Look, dude, you've obviously made a big fucking mistake here. I don't own a Scythe, but I have a variety of other weapons I would be happy to introduce you to." I flashed my fangs and hissed a little to see how he reacted.

He didn't react to the fangs, but he kept shooting sideways glances at Giguhl. I couldn't blame him. Most humans have never seen a demon. He might spend part of the time in a hairless kitty body, but when he was full demon, he was a scary son of a bitch.

"Ava?" the dude said. I assumed he was addressing the dog. Ava seemed like a really weird name for a dog that big and ugly.

But before I could continue judging his weird taste in pet names, the dog's body started vibrating and writhing. I wondered if I was going to have to clean a dead dog off of my carpet, but instead it was like the lights had flicked off for a second, and in that blink the figure changed from a dog to a petite, dark-haired woman with a Bettie Page bob and a pissed-off look on her face.

"What the fuck?" I'd seen werewolves shift before, so I wasn't too impressed by the display. What did unsettle me was that this chick wasn't a werewolf. She was clearly a human who had some sort of magic ability to shift into the form of a dog, sort of like how Giguhl could shift into cat form without being a were-being. But it made no sense for a Daughter of Adam to have these abilities. "Who are you people?"

"Where's the Scythe?" The female's voice was hoarse but her tone was surprisingly demanding.

Giguhl put his hands on his naked hips. "It's right here, sweetheart."

Her eyes dipped and widened before she quickly looked away. Her cheeks didn't redden, like mine had the first time I got an unwanted eyeful of the demon's forked . . . scythe.

"The reaper's Scythe," the guy said. "We were told you have it and we're not leaving without it."

"Reaper? Like the Grim Reaper?" I said, not bothering to hide the amusement in my voice. "Look, I don't know what you two have been smoking, but there is no Scythe in this house, reaper or otherwise."

The chick tossed a look at her partner in crime. I didn't know her, but I certainly was familiar with the what-the-hell-have-you-gotten-us-into glare known the world over by women who hang out with men who are trouble. Judging from the Russian gang tats and the stink of mundane magic coming off that guy, he wasn't just trouble, he was Big Trouble—capital B, capital T. He met her look with an untroubled one of his own. "Boyd said it's here, so it's here."

Adam held up a hand. "Boyd? Boyd who?"

"Shut the fuck up," the Russian said.

Unperturbed by his rudeness, Adam soldiered on. "You're not talking about Boyd Rothrock, are you?"

The Russian stilled. "What if I am?" He squinted, trying to look all tough, but I noticed the hint of uncertainty that crept into his posture.

Adam crossed his arms and shook his head. "Unbelievable." It was my turn to hold up a free hand. "Who's Boyd Rothrock?" Even though I was the head of the Dark Races on the mortal plane, it's not like I knew every vampire, faery, were, mage, or demon alive.

"He's a Recreant," Adam said, referring to a type of mage who'd been disavowed by the Hekate Council because they refused to follow the rules of conduct. "He's also a major asshole."

"It's true," the Russian admitted. "He is an asshole. But being an asshole doesn't make him a liar."

"No, what makes him a liar in this case is that he's been gunning for me for decades," Adam said.

"Why?" I asked.

"Because I am kind of to blame for him being kicked off the council."

I nodded. Adam's old job was being a Knight of Pythias for the mage Hekate Council. Acting as a sort of special ops mage, he'd had the opportunity to make lots of enemies in his past. But now wasn't the time to rehash the past. We'd get to that. For now, we had more pressing issues.

"Okay, so what we have here is a problem. Several of them, actually. But first, let's dispense with the formalities." I pointed to myself. "I'm Sabina Kane, the Chosen of the Dark Races." They both blinked at me, as if I'd just spoken a foreign language. I sighed. "That means I'm sort of the queen of all the non-humans on earth. I'm also part vampire and part mage."

"We call her a *magepire*," Giguhl said.

Ignoring my smart-assed sidekick, I nodded toward Adam. "That's my partner, Adam. He's a mage." I tipped my head the opposite way. "That's Giguhl, he's a fifth-level Mischief demon and the son-in-law of the King and Queen of the Dark Races underworld."

Both of their eyes widened. For some reason they were both way more worried about being in a room with a demon than they were knowing there was also a vampire and a mage in the place.

"Your turn," I prompted.

They exchanged a look. It was obvious the guy was in favor of telling me to fuck off, but the chick, who seemed the more rational of the two, shot him a look that threatened bodily harm if he didn't pull his head out of his ass. I liked her despite the fact she'd tracked her muddy paws all over my rug. Finally, she won and spoke first.

"I'm Ava and that's Leo."

"You're a . . . weredog?" I asked.

She snorted. "Hellhound."

Giguhl made a dismissive sound.

"What are you looking at?" Ava said. "You're some sort of weird demon-slash-mole-rat shifter."

The demon's black lips sputtered with indignation. "I—I—mole-rat? I can't even." He waved a claw to indicate I needed to defend his honor.

"Not a mole-rat," I said. "A hairless cat."

"Really?" She tilted her head. "That's weird."

"Whatever, were-bitch."

I stepped forward before Ava could make good on the threat in her eyes. "Anyway, we've established what everyone else is. How about you, Leo?"

"I'm a reaper," he said, as if it was the most obvious thing in the world.

"Where's your robe, hotshot?" Giguhl said over a snicker.

Leo's eyes narrowed but he clearly was uncomfortable being around the demon, so he didn't respond.

"Wait," Adam interjected, "I'm confused. If you're the Grim Reaper, does that mean someone stole your Scythe?"

He shook his head. "No, it's not like that. I'm not *the* Grim Reaper. That's just a job title. I'm in charge of a lot of other reapers. The Scythe we're looking for is a special weapon that allows reapers to drain the souls of their target, trap the soul, and transport it to Hell. It's pretty self-explanatory."

"We obviously don't have it since we didn't even know reapers were a thing. We know why Boyd wanted to screw us over, but what does he have against you guys?"

Leo's eyebrow shot up. "That's exactly what I'm going to ask him while I'm kicking his ass."

I sighed and shot a look at Adam. "This is gonna be a real shit show, isn't it?"

He smiled. "Yup."

Ava asked Leo, "Do you know where he is?"

Leo shook his head. "We talked on the phone. He didn't tell me where he's staying."

Adam smiled. "Oh, I have a pretty good idea where we can find him."

"Okay, since we're all on the same side here, let's stash our weapons and take this to the kitchen so we can figure out our next steps, because I sure as shit could use a drink," I said.

"Amen, sister," Giguhl said.

I shook my head at the demon. "No drink for you until you find some pants, Mr. Giggles."

AVA

It didn't take long to decide that Leo and Adam should stay put and try to hunt for Boyd with scrying while Sabina and I went to visit a contact she had at a bar off Bourbon Street.

The place was one of those dives that tries a little too hard to pretend it's still Prohibition, just a red neon sign hanging over a flat black door to indicate there was anything except apartments behind the vine-covered brick walls. I sighed as Sabina pressed the buzzer, and she gave me the sharp look I was starting to recognize as her stink-eye.

"Problem?"

"You really think this guy of yours knows Boyd?" I said as an answering buzz from the interior let us inside.

"Probably," she said. "If anyone in the city does." She strode ahead as the darkness of the bar closed in around us, down a narrow hall and into a low musty room with a water stained ceiling. A jazz combo composed of guys who looked almost as old as the building was playing on what could only charitably be referred to as a stage. Most of the bottles behind the bar were dusty as tombstones.

Sabina took a seat on a bar stool, positioning herself so she could see the whole room and both the kitchen and the front doors. I sat down and faced her, so I could cover the corners she couldn't see. She nodded approvingly at me.

"Leo teach you that?"

"A hundred years of hanging around crappy speakeasies taught me," I said.

Sabina twirled one finger at the bartender, a guy wearing one of those straw hipster hats who was the only person under sixty in the joint. Her hair gleamed molten in the low light, and her pale skin managed to look even more flawless. I glanced in the cloudy mirror over the bar and discovered that sexy, discreet lighting just made me look dead.

"So you and Leo," she said. I grimaced as the bartender ambled over.

"It's really not a girl-talk-style story."

"I'm not interested in girl talk," Sabina said. "I'm interested in if your feelings for each other will screw this up."

"You'd have to ask Leo," I said as the bartender leaned over to get our order. "I don't do feelings."

Sabina opened her mouth and I cut her off. "Any feelings."

"What can I get you, Ms. Kane?" the bartender asked her, and I dropped my eyes from hers, hoping my lie was convincing. It was easier than admitting that Leo and I couldn't feel those things, even if we wished our situation could be different.

"The usual." Sabina slid a folded piece of paper with Boyd's name across the sticky bar. The bartender opened it, read the name, and then shook his head.

"Sorry, Ms. Kane."

He went to make her drink and Sabina sighed, pulling out her cell phone to call her pet mage.

"That's it?" I said. Sabina shrugged.

"If they've never heard of him, they've never heard of him."

I nudged her arm as I turned on my stool. "Watch the bartender," I said quietly. Sabina frowned.

"You have some kind of power to tell when people are lying? There's no way Boyd could have convinced anyone in this place to lie for him. I told you—I'm the Chosen of all of the world's Dark Races."

"I have the power of meeting a lot of liars," I said. So what if I didn't have perfect hair and a fancy title? The bartender was acting so squirrelly he might as well have been chewing acorns.

I slid off my stool and started down the bar, but the guy saw me coming and backed up, pushing into a rear room through a swinging door. I caught a glimpse of a guy I figured was Boyd before it slammed shut in my face, and I heard a dead bolt click.

"Move."

Sabina was behind me, and when I shifted to the side she put her foot to the door, shattering the wood around the lock. We were just in time to see Boyd go out the window. He moved faster than a man should be able to, and I figured he was juiced with magic. Great.

"Go around front!" I hollered at Sabina as I pulled myself onto the sill. "Try to cut him off!"

The bartender cowered in the corner, holding up his hands as Sabina gave him a snarl in passing. "He made me! He threatened my family—I had no choice!"

"Whatever helps you sleep at night, dude," I said, and then my boots hit the ground ten feet below the window and I was running through the dense air of Bourbon Street, trying to keep the mage in sight.

SABINA

Bourbon Street is thirteen blocks long, and on the average weekend night, it is packed with thousands of humans in various states of sobriety. The air smells of cigarette smoke, vomited daiquiris, and raging hormones. But there was also an undeniable energy to all those vulnerable bodies gathered together to dance and sing like there was no tomorrow. It was the one thing I envied about humans. It was the curse of immortality that time never felt precious, so life never felt worth celebrating.

However, it's one thing to wax poetic about mortals celebrating being alive and another thing entirely to have to dodge puddles of vomit and piss and staggering frat boys while you're chasing an asshole mage.

Boyd didn't have much of a head start, but he wove in and out of groups of stumbling humans like he'd been doing it his entire life.

"Should I change?" Ava asked. She was asking about switching into her hellhound form. "Can't risk it," I said. "Too many people with smartphones and cameras."

"So?"

"So, I can't risk being the reason humans find out paranormal beings are real."

She shook her head and kicked up her speed a notch. I shook my head and easily caught up with her. Truth was, if I ran at my full speed—or used my magic to flash through the crowd—Ava wouldn't have been able to keep up with me, hellhound or not. But if there's one thing I've learned through the years, it's that impatience complicates things. We had no idea what motivated Boyd to set up Adam and Leo. Chasing him down like prey might feel good but it might not get us any answers. So I was content to follow him and see what happened.

Music spilled out of bars as we ran past, creating a sort of mix tape of disco, rap, and country music. Flashing lights and neon signs of naked women winked against the dark sky.

Up ahead, I saw Boyd's stupid hat bobbing and weaving above the crowd. We were nearing the end of the busy part of Upper Bourbon, where the cops blocked the road off from cars at night. Once he got out of the crowd, he'd be easy picking because Ava and I could bring some of our magical favors to the party.

"Once he's past the barricades, you can change," I called to her.

She nodded and dodged a couple who were painted silver from head to toe. The guy wore a pair of running shorts that had been spray-painted to match his skin. The lady wore a pair of silver panties, and two fleur-de-lis stickers covered her nipples. As we passed, the guy lifted his lady friend and put her legs over his shoulder so he could pantomime cunnilingus for the crowd. I rolled my eyes and kept running. Almost there. Boyd had maybe a block left before the crowd gave way to a shadowy street beyond.

"Shit!" Ava said.

I pulled my eyes from the silver people and looked in time to see Boyd cut a hard right on Orleans. "Godsdammit."

We turned to follow him. At the end of Orleans, the cathedral loomed. Lit from the front, a statue of Jesus with his arms spread wide cast an ominous silhouette on the cathedral's façade. If Boyd made it past the cathedral to Jackson Square, it would be almost impossible to catch him. There were too many side streets and alleys to keep up without the help of magic.

Ava hit my arm and pointed with her other hand. On the left side of the street, Boyd was scaling a gate. "Got you, asshole," I said under my breath. Once we were off the street, all bets were off.

Ava and I beelined for the gate. She made a running jump for the top of the gate. I reached to help boost her up, but she kicked at me. "I got it."

With my brows raised, I backed away and crossed my arms. I used to be like that. Never wanted help from anyone. Needed to prove I could do it all on my own. Maybe one day Ava would learn that asking for help didn't make you weak. But it wasn't my lesson to teach her. I just hoped when she learned it, it wasn't the hard way.

Her fingers gripped the upper ledge and she grunted as she pulled herself up. She kicked out her leg and swung it over the top. Perched there, straddling the top, she took a moment to glance back at me to flash a victorious look.

I shook my head and started to open my mouth to tell her to quit screwing around, but a movement beyond the gate caught my eye.

"Ava!" I yelled. But I was too late. Before the word even left my mouth, a ball of black light hit Ava. Her mouth dropped open in a silent scream as her eyes rolled back in her head.

I leapt forward in time to catch her before she hit the concrete.

Boyd watched her fall. Holding her too-still body, I glared at the asshole.

"Tell Lazarus I said hi."

I started to lower Ava to the ground so I could rise to shoot this bastard between his eyes with a spell that would make his balls shoot out through his head. But before I could, Ava gasped and her body began convulsing in my arms. At the same moment, a flash of light accompanied Boyd's exit from the courtyard beyond.

"Fuck!"

Ava's eyes opened. Thin veins of black webbed across the whites of her eyes.

My phone rang with Adam's tone in my pocket. Using my free hand, I grabbed it. "Adam—"

"Sabina! You need to back off on Boyd. We just found out he's into some serious dark necromancy."

"No shit," I said. "He blasted Ava. I'm bringing her home."

The black veins were spreading across her pale face now. Her mouth opened and closed like a carp's as she gasped for air.

"And Adam? Be ready to go." I looked down at Ava. Her body felt limp, as if the burden of staying alive was becoming too heavy. "She's barely hanging on."

AVA

I didn't remember much after Boyd hit me with the curse. It felt like taking a power line to the chest—everything went cold and smooth and black, and I floated down through the layers of gauzy darkness until I felt something hitting me on the cheek—not hard, exactly, but not gentle either. Like I was being slapped by a baby, repeatedly.

My eyes fluttered open and I saw that damn hairless cat leaning over me. "Well, shit," it said. "You're alive after all."

Everything was too bright and too hot, now that I was back in the land of the living. I didn't try to move—I wasn't so much of a badass that I was going to stand up only to keel over again.

"Did Boyd get away?" I rasped. My throat felt like I'd been doing shots of Tabasco sauce.

Sabina nodded, coming to stand next to her demon cat. "I

had to let him go or let you die. Don't tell me you're pissed off at my choice."

"Far from it," I said, offering her a weak smile. "I'd buy you a drink, if I had money. Or could walk."

"Sabina, Leo, and I managed to combine our powers to draw the death magic out of you. Luckily there were three of us because that shit was nasty," Adam said. "You might feel some residual effects of the curse for a few hours, but mainly I'm concerned about the fall you took."

I waved him off. "I'm fine." It wasn't a lie, exactly. I figured Sabina's Amazon moves had kept my skull from cracking open, but the entire right side of my body was a knotted, bruised wreck from where Boyd's spell had hit me. I wriggled everything and figured I had a few cracked ribs, maybe a torn rotator cuff, but I'd had worse.

Leo appeared, holding a bottle of water, and I shoved his hand away when he offered it to me. His face twisted in a frown. "You concussed or something?"

"I'm right, is what I am," I snarled. "I told you it was a bad idea to come here on the say-so of some rando who probably has it out for you just as much as he does Adam." I did struggle up then, turning my back on him as recrimination and blame exploded behind me, everyone from Leo to the demon cat yelling about whose fault it was we had to deal with Boyd's sorry ass.

"I don't mean to be rude, but Ava's the one who actually let him get away," Adam said, which made Leo growl.

"Blame her for this again and I'll kick your ass!"

"Touch him and I'll make sure there's nothing *left* of your ass," Sabina snapped.

Giguhl sighed. "Can we all please stop saying *ass* so much?"

I felt in my pocket for a tissue, or maybe a knife to jam into my ear canal so I didn't have to listen to the fight, and my fingers closed around the scrap of fabric I'd grabbed from the top of the fence when Boyd had caught himself on the sharp iron spikes. Served him right—what kind of respectable human man ran around in cargo pants anyway?

I held the sticky fabric to my nose and breathed in the smell of dirty pennies. Boyd had cut himself—not badly, but there was enough blood for my purpose. My only purpose, really at least when I was a hellhound.

"Leo," I said, turning back around. "GUYS," a little louder, when they all just kept swearing at each other. I held up the bloody scrap. "I can find Boyd. I can track him."

SABINA

I'd fought battles with demons and any manner of nasty dark races and beasts. I'd conquered Irkalla and become a demi-goddess despite incredible odds. But nothing had prepared me for the embarrassment of walking through the French Quarter at 2:00 A.M. holding leashes for a hellhound and a hairless demon cat.

"Watch it," the cat hissed after I'd jerked the leash for the umpteenth time.

"Stay on the sidewalk then," I snapped. "And quit pissing on everything."

As it was, I was having trouble keeping up with Ava's hound form as she zigzagged through the streets trying to pick up Boyd's scent. Unlike Giguhl, she couldn't speak when she was in her animal guise, so I had to pay attention to her body language and growls to understand what she was doing.

At that point, we'd scoured the area around Orleans where Boyd had disappeared. Finally, Ava took off toward Congo Square. A half hour later, we'd wandered all over Louis Armstrong Park, stopping six times for Giguhl to piss on various statues and benches and—before I could prevent it—a homeless man.

Finally, just before I was about to bring Ava to heel and call the search off, she stopped. Her hackles prickled and her nose rose to the sky. A low growl of warning rumbled from her mouth.

"What is it, Lassie?" Giguhl said. "Is Timmy in the well again?"

"G, stop it," I said. "Ava, is it Boyd?"

The hellhound whined and pulled against the leash.

"All right, let's go." I picked Giguhl off the ground and put him on my shoulder a split second before Ava took off like a bullet. As we ran, I reached into my pocket and called Adam.

"Hey, we have a bead on him."

"Where?"

I looked ahead in the direction Ava was running and realized she was headed straight for the cemetery that lay next to Interstate 10. "St. Louis Cemetery," I said. "Meet us near the front wall."

"Yes, ma'am," he said. "Don't go in before we're there, Red." I could tell from the tension in his voice that he was imagining me getting hit by the same spell that had almost taken down Ava.

I snorted. "I'm a chthonic demigoddess, Adam. It's gonna take more than a necromancy spell to bring me down."

By that point, Ava had reached the cemetery's white walls. Over the top, I could see the roofs of the hundreds of above-ground tombs that made up New Orleans' most famous City of the Dead.

"I'd prefer not to have that . . ."

One second Adam was speaking into my ear through the phone. The next, he appeared to my left. ". . . theory tested."

I shook my head at him. "Show-off."

He smirked at me and kissed my forehead. Behind him, Leo wasn't looking so hot. His complexion was greenish and he swayed into the wall.

"You all right?" I whispered.

Before he could answer, the hellhound moved toward him and pressed into his side, as if to steady him. His hand rested on the dog's back for a moment as he regained his composure. "Next time give a man some warning, mage."

"Sorry," Adam said, sounding genuinely chastened. "I forget not all beings have traveled magically before."

Leo shook his head. "No worries." Absently, he patted the hellhound's head and took a deep breath. "Okay, where are we?"

The three of us knelt down next to the wall with the hellhound and the cat watching our backs as we strategized. "St. Louis Cemetery," I said. "It's famous for being the place where the voodoo queen, Marie Laveau, is buried."

"It's also known as the most dangerous cemetery in the city at night," Adam added. "Lots of junkies and criminals."

"And asshole necromancers, apparently," Leo concluded. "Makes sense he'd come here. The death energy in this place is off the charts. After his run-in with you two, he'd need to recharge."

Adam nodded and looked at me. "So how are we going to play this?"

"We need to take him alive."

Leo snorted. "Like hell. He almost killed Ava. I say we take him down." Beside him, the hellhound snorted her support of Leo's plan.

"I get it, but what if he's working for someone else? If we kill him, we lose the chance of finding out if there's a larger conspiracy at play here."

"Who would he be working for?" Leo asked.

The list of enemies from my past was long but not very distinguished. Adam had plenty of his own, as well. And judging from what I'd seen of Leo and Ava, they'd hardly been candidates for sainthood. "Anyone, Leo. He could be working for anyone. But we'll never know that unless we catch him alive."

"He's gonna throw some serious shit at us. We may not have the choice of taking him alive."

I paused to consider the truth of that statement. Finally, I nodded. "Okay, fine. We try to take him alive until that option isn't possible anymore." I looked Leo and the hellhound in their eyes. "But if either of you take him out before that time comes, you will have to answer to me. Trust me when I say that is not a conversation either of you will enjoy."

Leo snorted as if he'd heard his fair share of people bluffing power they didn't possess. "You talk tough."

I touched his hand. A purple flash of magic shot up his arm and straight into his head, where it filled his brain with images of the sorts of things I could do to him if he pissed me off. It was just a flash of images—like a movie in fast-forward, but by the time it was done a couple of seconds later, his eyes were wide like a spooked horse's and his skin was milky pale.

The hellhound whined next to him and pressed its head into his shoulder. Leo shook himself and swallowed hard.

"Do we understand each other?"

He nodded but wouldn't quite meet my eyes. "Got it. Leo lives until that's not an option."

"All right," I said, dismissing the tension. I wasn't going to hold a grudge against Leo for doubting my power. But I didn't miss the look Adam shot me. He clearly felt my little display was overkill. I ignored him and got down to business. "Let's move in. Ava, I think you should be in your human form. Let's keep the hellhound a surprise."

"What about me?" Giguhl asked while Ava shifted back. The demon cat was sitting on the ground on his hip with his head cocked at me.

"I want you at full strength when we go in there. If he starts zapping us with necromancy spells, you're the only one who will be totally immune."

Giguhl nodded and changed back into his demon form. The shift from cat to demon brought with it a puff of purple smoke and the stench of brimstone. Unlike Ava, the demon didn't arrive fully clothed when he shifted. Belatedly, I pulled a pair of running shorts out of my knapsack and handed them to him. "Cover yourself, dude."

He grinned at me. "If you want to intimidate this Boyd guy, it'd be better if I were naked."

"We want to intimidate him, G," Adam said. "Not make him laugh."

That earned the mage a middle claw. "Bite me, mancy."

Ava looked at me like she was having second thoughts about being seen with us.

She shook her head and turned to check her weapons.

I shrugged and went back to checking my own ammo. It had been a while since I'd had the chance for a good fight and I found myself looking forward to it. I just hoped Boyd didn't have any more nasty surprises up his sleeve.

AVA

Usually, I had to admit, doing a big group outing to fight a mage who could kill you with a touch was my nightmare. The last time I'd tried to do a group activity involving magic I'd wound up the surprise human sacrifice of the night, and then I'd gotten turned into a hellhound for my trouble.

But as we walked down the main avenue of the cemetery, I found myself tapping my fingers against my leg, worried about Leo and Adam and even that weird cat demon. Sabina could take care of herself, I figured. She seemed more pissed off than worried.

Fog started to curl around our ankles, black as pitch and smelling twice as bad as that stuff that the demon gave off when he changed shapes. Leo groaned.

"I hate overdramatic mages. Just come out and fight like a man."

Adam grunted his agreement. I thought that given another ten or twenty years those two might almost sort of get to be friends.

"Ask and you'll receive," Boyd rasped from up ahead. He was standing in an open area, mausoleums on three sides, a little conjured fire burning for flare around his feet. That was what gave off the noxious smoke. It started to blur my vision, my eyes watering.

"You like that?" he called to me. "A little spell to confuse your senses. Breathe enough of it and you'll be on the worst trip of your life." He grinned at all of us. "Or you could just leave. Avoid being poisoned, avoid dying. Let me do my business and get gone from your fair city."

"Hey, asshole," Leo said. "If we came all the way out here, clearly we're not leaving."

"Give it up, Boyd." Sabina's voice cut through the crackling of the flames. "You have nowhere to run."

Boyd's grin got wider, and every hair on my neck stood up. I couldn't even yell at Sabina to look out, it happened that fast—he threw a spell at her that cut through the air like a freight train. Adam let out a yell, and tried to push her out of the way. The spell exploded between them, and they both went down. Adam fell way harder than Sabina, and she scrambled to cover him with her own body as he panted.

I glanced at them as Leo faced Boyd, feeling an unexpected pang. Nobody had ever come close to doing that for me, not even Leo. Not that I wanted him to. I was a lot tougher than he was, even as a reaper.

"Cute," Boyd said. The smoke was really fucking with my eyesight and my balance, and I coughed as Leo slung a spell at Boyd. He missed, chipping a chunk out of the mausoleum behind Boyd's head. "Not so cute," Boyd tsked. "Just sad."

I tried to block a spell from hitting Leo, I really did, but I wasn't fast enough. Leo wheezed under me, pushing at my arm to try to get me off him. "I'm okay, Ava," he rumbled in my ear. "I'm okay."

I looked back at Boyd as he advanced, flames parting before him, coming to stand over me. I really hoped that this would work.

"And you?" he said, giving me a light kick before he stepped back, spreading his arms. "What could you possibly do to me all by yourself, little girl?"

I gathered the last of my strength. I was going to have to time this just right. "You're right," I croaked. "I give up."

Boyd nodded. "Then walk away, bitch."

I gritted my teeth as I got up, leaving Leo where he was. I walked far enough to get away from the worst of the smoke, then stopped. "On second thought," I said, as I shifted back into the hound on the fly. "I think I'll stop you here and now."

I ran full tilt at Boyd, ignoring the acid burn in my lungs, hit him in the chest with my paws hard enough that I felt one of his lungs collapse, and took him to the ground. I locked my jaws around his amulet and yanked once, twice. The flames sputtered around us, his magic interrupted for a split second. Boyd was screaming invective, but I didn't listen. When I was the hound, humans all sounded the same.

SABINA

The instant the hellhound rolled off Boyd with the necklace in her mouth, the rest of us hauled ass. The impact with Ava had knocked the wind out of Boyd, but he wasn't down for long. By the time we reached him, he was up on his feet, albeit a bit unsteady. Seeing the hound with his necklace hanging from her sharp teeth, he lunged. The hound's head lowered and emitted a feral growl that had the mage pausing. Then, as we watched, the hound tossed back her head and tossed the necklace down her wide throat. A loud gulp acted like an exclamation point at the end of the move.

"Give it up, Boyd," Adam called. His voice sounded a little weak, which only made me angry all over again.

"You're all idiots," he said. "That necklace isn't the source of my powers. It boosted them, but I can still fight without it." As if to prove his point, he lifted his hands and waggled them. Blue energy arced across his fingertips.

"Oooh, super scary jazz hands," I said. "Whatever will we do, boys?"

As if we'd prearranged the move, Leo and Adam fell in beside me. I took Adam's hand in my left. With my eyes on Boyd, I groped the air, searching for Leo's hand, but instead I got a handful of hellhound fur. I dragged my gaze from Boyd to smile down at the dog. At the same moment, a shock of magical energy zoomed up my right arm.

Apparently, swallowing the amulet had given Ava some of the necromancy powers Boyd had held. On the other side of Ava, Leo placed his free hand on Ava's coat and jerked his hand back as the energy hit him too. "I'll be damned," he whispered. The hellhound made a low growl, which sounded like a curse. More gingerly, Leo touched her again. This time, when the energy hit him, he grinned at the canine.

Boyd stood in the center of our circle with his arms crossed. "You can't do shit to me," he said. "I've got powerful friends."

I laughed. "I can assure you that my friends are way more fucking powerful than anyone you know, magic boy."

He squinted. "You're as big of a bitch as Clovis said you were."

Adam's hand contracted on mine. I froze. "Hold on a damned minute. Do you mean to tell me that your 'powerful friend' is Clovis Trakiya?" I threw back my head and laughed.

Boyd's confidence faltered. "He hired me to send Leo after you two. Said it would kill two birds with one stone."

Years earlier, Clovis had tried to create a war between the Dark Races using Adam and me as pawns. At the time, I'd let him live because I'd yet to come into my full powers. It was one of my biggest regrets. I almost wanted to thank Boyd for giving me the excuse to correct that mistake.

"I know why Clovis wants us out of the way, but why Leo?" Adam asked. He glanced at Leo, who shrugged.

"I don't know. He said he owed a favor to some reapers or something. Look, it's not my business. I only did this to get the amulet." Before the last word left his mouth, he raised his hands and shot a zap of magic at Adam.

I leapt in front of him to block the shot. My chthonic magic rose so fast it made me a little light-headed, but it blocked Boyd's magic. He was right. His magic was still pretty strong, but it definitely lacked the kick it had with the amulet.

Before he could renew his energy, I regained my original position. I grabbed Adam's hand and Ava's fur. Giguhl and Leo closed the circle around Boyd as I called up the rest of my power.

The magical circuit connected almost instantly. Unused to managing so much energy, the hellhound yelped beside me, but I held on tight. The wind whipped up around us, creating a cyclone effect. In the center of the circle, Boyd's wild gaze darted about. Blue energy danced around his body as he tried to gather enough strength to defeat all of us.

But the combined power of Adam's magic, my chthonic powers, the amulet in Ava's belly, Giguhl's demonic energy, and Leo's impressive necromancy created a shimmering plasma dome that surrounded all of us. The magic didn't hum—it screamed. Bracing myself against the pressure, I managed to shout, "Now!"

The power we'd raised coalesced into a throbbing ball of energy over Boyd's head. He fell to the ground with his hands raised in vain. The ball dropped. It engulfed Boyd and tore open a rift in the fabric of the mortal realm. Boyd disappeared into the wormhole.

Releasing power is always tricky. It feels a little like licking an electrical socket. One second, the four of us were holding the power of millions of megawatts of magical energy, and then the next it whooshed from our bodies. I stumbled back into a tomb, Adam bent over with his head in his hands, and

Leo stumbled a couple of steps before vomiting. Giguhl just slapped his claws together and said, "Good riddance," but his green skin looked a few shades paler than usual. While the rest of us had practice adjusting to the sudden shift in magical barometric pressure, Ava did not. That's why when I regained my footing it took me a moment to realize that the hellhound had collapsed onto the grass.

"Shit, Adam, help me!" We lunged toward the too-still canine. She didn't appear to be breathing.

"What do we do?" he asked.

I shook the massive chest of the unconscious dog. Nothing.

At that moment, Leo pulled himself together and came over. "What's—" He finally saw Ava lying on the ground and fell to his knees next to her large body. "Ava?" He shook her just as I had, and still nothing happened. He looked up wildly. "Help her!"

I didn't have time to think about what I was doing. Using my fangs, I ripped at the soft flesh of my inner wrist. Without being asked, Adam opened the hellhound's massive maw.

"Wait!" Leo began but it was too late. Blood flowed down the dog's throat. After a few moments, I removed my arm and placed a hand over the wound. Ever since I became a demigoddess I could heal myself with just a thought, so the wound closed instantly.

"Now what?" Leo said, sitting back on his haunches and looking defeated.

"Now we wait," I said quietly.

"No," he shook his head. "Will she become a vampire?"

Before I could answer, a loud whine escaped the hellhound's mouth and the massive body reared up and fell into Leo, pinning him. "Ava!" he yelled, wrapping his arms around the animal. The hound trembled and whimpered, but her eyes were open and I could have sworn I saw Ava looking back at me.

She struggled to be free of Leo's hold, and he let her go with great reluctance. Four paws as big as saucers stumbled across the grass. I rose to follow just in case she needed help, but before I could reach her, a sound like a demon escaped the shuddering body.

The hellhound's massive head lowered. The teeth ratcheted open and ropes of drool spilled onto the matted grass.

"What did you do to her?" Leo yelled. He started to run toward her, but Adam held him back.

In the next breath, the dog's mouth opened all the way and a stream of brackish bile spewed from that gaping maw.

"She's turning, isn't she?" Leo said. "Oh God!"

"Dude, chill," I said. "Her body is just cleansing itself. She's not going to become a vampire. It doesn't work like that."

Just when I thought she was done, a large item lurched out of the hellhound's mouth and plopped into the puddle of vomit. The amulet. "Well, that sure beats the alternative exit," I said. I looked at the guys, grinning. They didn't seem as amused. I guess not everyone has the stomach to watch a hellhound vomit vampire blood and magical amulets.

Before I could tell them to lighten up, Ava suddenly shifted back into human form. She lay on the grass, blinking, until Leo skidded over to kneel beside her. "Ava?" He touched her face. "Are you okay?"

She spit onto the ground, wiped her hand across her lips, and said, "I need a fucking drink."

An hour later, we sat around a table in the courtyard of my favorite bar, Lagniappe. Some nights it served as New Orleans' best drag club, and that night was half-price beers, so we ordered two buckets of ice-cold Abita Ambers.

"So Boyd was working for Clovis all along?" Giguhl asked between licks of his own bowl of beer. Since we were in public he had to be in his hairless cat form.

I took a long, cold pull from my beer before answering. Defeating rogue necromancers is thirsty work. "It appears so."

"I could get in touch with Valva." He glanced at Ava and Leo, who'd both started at the name. "That's my wife. She's in Irkalla with the kids to visit their grandma and grandpa." He didn't mention that "Grandma and Grandpa" were the King and Queen of the Dark Races underworld. "Anyway, I could have her ask around, but she'll probably nag for like an hour." He winked at Leo. "Women, am I right?"

Leo cleared his throat and took a sip of beer while avoiding the cat demon's eyes.

"Thanks, Giguhl. I'm overdue for a visit to Irkalla, anyway."

"So what are you going to do about him?" Ava asked.

"Clovis?" I shrugged. "I'll figure something out. First I need to talk to my twin sister, Maisie, who lives in the underworld. She might be able to tell me where he is."

Ava squinted at me. "You have a sister who lives in the underworld?"

I laughed. "Who among us has an uncomplicated family?"

Ava saluted me with her beer. "Touché."

"How about you two?" Adam asked. "Where will you go now?"

Ava and Leo exchanged a glance. In my opinion, it was not the shared glance of two platonic friends, but the intimate glance that communicated a world of information without a word being spoken. But I wasn't about to point that out, since those two seemed about as ready for a healthy relationship as I'd been when I'd met Adam so many years ago.

Leo answered for them. "We're going to head up to Minnesota. Got a line on a thing."

I didn't question him despite his cagey language. My life had had plenty of those moments where the less anyone knew about my activities the safer everyone was. "Well, if you ever come our way again, you've got a place to crash," I said. "Just call ahead next time." I reached out and clinked my beer bottle with Ava's.

She smiled back. "Trust me, we will. I don't think I could handle stumbling on Giguhl in his birthday suit again."

The cat looked up from his bowl of beer. "You know when you're in dog form everyone can see your butthole, right?"

Ava's cheeks flamed immediately. "Maybe so, but at least I'm not a pussy, Mr. Giggles."

"You know what?" Giguhl said. "You're not half-bad for a bitch."

I braced myself for Ava's reaction to that comeback, worried it might spark a real shit show of a fight between the two.

"Same goes." Ava leaned forward and frowned at the demon. "And for the record? We can see yours, too."

There's really no laughter like the kind shared over a round of beers following a battle. We were all warriors in our own right, but there's real satisfaction in teaming up with other fighters. That night, I think we all learned a thing or two about teamwork. As we finished our drinks and said our goodbyes, I wasn't sure if we'd ever see Ava and Leo again. But one thing was for sure. If I ever needed someone to have my back in a fight, I'd be giving them a call.

Tailed

SEANAN McGUIRE AND KELLEY ARMSTRONG

VERITY

A low-rent motel on the outskirts of Albany, New York

MARCH 2012

"I hate everything," announced Sarah, voice muffled by the pillow covering her face. She was sprawled across one of the two beds in our shabby budget motel room, her arms and legs akimbo. The fact that she was using her outside voice when she was this exhausted told me how the Pet Expo had been for her. Normally, if she's too tired to stay on her feet, she goes straight to telepathic communication, and forget any illusions I might have about privacy. Sometimes life with telepaths means never getting to say "That's a secret."

We'd been in a warehouse packed to the gills with people for two days now, and it was getting to her. Not *just* her; it was getting to me too, although with less "psychic migraine" and more "urge to start stabbing people who invade my personal space." The upstate New York Pet Expo was proving to be more challenging than I'd expected. It had looked so *simple* on paper. Put on practical shoes and a brown wig, stick close to Sarah, and go looking for exotic animal poachers among the stalls of guinea pigs, fancy rats, and interestingly colored ball pythons. Piece of cake.

Sarah, in addition to being telepathic, was a natural ambush predator; most people tended to forget she existed five minutes after meeting her, and if I was with her, the effect sometimes extended to me. It helped if I wore drab clothing and didn't smile too much. She had a lot of survival advantages, mostly because everyone who met a member of her species wound up wanting to kill them. It was a matter of evolutionary necessity.

"Come on, you can't hate *everything*." I pulled off my wig, plucking the bobby pins out of my short-cropped blonde hair. "You like gravity."

"No. Hate it."

"You like ketchup."

"Hate it."

"You like calculus."

Sarah lifted her head and glared at me. "No fair bringing religion into this."

"Love you too," I said, blowing her a quick kiss. "I'm sorry you had to spend the day surrounded by filthy human minds."

"You *should* be." She rolled onto her back, staring mulishly at the ceiling. "Some of the things they were thinking about doing to each other were horrifying. Murder things, sex things, credit card fraud things—um, that reminds me, the guy who was selling tarantulas near the hot dog stand? We should probably call in a tip about him to the local police. He's like, *way* into identity theft."

"The world is a panoply of wonders," I said. Our motel room was small enough that the bathroom was more of a closet with a shower tucked into the corner. The sink and mirror were at the back of the sleeping area, in an arrangement I was sure the architects considered "discreet," and I thought was actually sort of gross. I drifted that way and peered at my reflection before reaching for the makeup remover. Without the wig, this much eyeliner was not a good look for me. "No one was thinking about poaching?"

"Everyone was thinking about poaching. Half the snakes we saw were wild-caught, and don't get me started on the lady with the sugar gliders. One of the rabbit vendors also breeds jackalopes, but he didn't bring any to the expo."

"Selling jackalopes isn't illegal," I said, wiping the left side of my face clean. The antlered lapines were far from critically endangered, and if he was breeding his own and not selling them to scientific research facilities, he wasn't my concern. "What else did you get?"

"You mean apart from the migraine and the desire to go full-cuckoo and wipe out the human race?" Sarah sighed. "Nothing. I got nothing."

I paused in the act of wiping away my makeup, looking at her reflection in the mirror. I didn't say anything. Neither did she.

The human race has a tendency to think that just because we have all the good toys—thumbs and knives and cable television—we're at the top of the food chain, and we try to ignore the fact that we only hold that precarious position because we killed almost everything that could challenge us. The dragons, the giants, all the competitors for the top-dog spot; we built an empire on their bones, consigned them to legend, and forgot about them. But the others, the things we *didn't* kill . . . they didn't forget about us. The reality of what we'd done was the world they had to live with every day.

Most people don't know that humanity isn't alone. That's an inconvenient truth they were swift to forget. Others, like the Covenant of St. George—assholes—remember and do their best to finish the purge of anything they don't consider "natural." And then there's me, and people like me. We're cryptozoologists and monster social workers and conservationists, trying to make up for the murder in our family trees by protecting what's left of the preternatural world. But that sword cuts both ways, and when something most people don't believe in becomes a danger to humanity, we have to make sure that no one gets hurt.

No one innocent, anyway.

Sarah was my cousin, thanks to the wonders of adoption. She was my friend, thanks to the fact that she was funny, smart, and usually willing to go along with whatever bizarre scheme I'd hatched. But she was also a telepathic ambush predator from a species of killers, and the fact that she was usually content to read comic books and do Sudoku puzzles didn't mean she wasn't potentially a danger. We all knew that one day things could change.

"Sorry," said Sarah in a small voice.

I finished wiping the makeup off. "Have you been following my internal monologue again?"

"You think loudly sometimes. It's not like I can help it." She propped herself up on her elbows and gave me a wry look. "I wouldn't wipe out the human race. There's no X-Men without the human race."

"We are saved by the strangest things." I turned away

from the mirror and crossed to the dresser. I hadn't gone to the expo unarmed—I was undercover, not stupid—but there was a difference between the kind of weapons I was willing to carry into a crowd and the kind I wanted in the woods. "Look. You stay here, chill out, watch some cable, drink some ketchup, and try to refrain from getting overly murder-y. I'm going to wander around the woods and see if I can figure out where the local tailypo are nesting."

"You really think we have a poacher?"

"There's someone selling 'long-tailed raccoons' on Craigs-list. Either we have a poacher, or we've had a small nuclear spill and no one thought to tell the locals." I felt better with half a dozen throwing knives in my pockets. Every girl has her own version of the security blanket. "They weren't at the expo today, but they'll be here. I just need to find the adults before this asshole comes along and scoops up all the local juveniles."

Tailypo don't breed well in captivity. Tailypo don't do *anything* well in captivity. They're essentially the raccoon version of the lemur, and they don't enjoy being held against their will. People were going to get hurt if they insisted on keeping tailypo as pets, which was inevitably going to lead to the tailypo being identified as a "new species," and there was nothing good at the end of that chain of events. Looking too hard at the tailypo would lead to looking for their habitat, and there were things that tended to cohabitate with our long-tailed friends that we wanted to keep hidden, at least for a little while longer.

"Okay," said Sarah. She flopped back down onto the bed. "Don't get dead. Your parents would never forgive me."

"I won't," I promised, and slotted my gun into its holster before leaving the room. Sarah would be on the computer before I made it to the trees, sending a chat request to our cousin Artie in Oregon and wailing about her day. It would be good for the both of them.

My family is weird, but we get by, and we're good at what we do. The forest spread out in front of me like a homecoming, and I stepped into the welcoming gloom.

ELENA

When Clayton and I decided to have kids, there'd been only one issue I was very clear on—that our children would be properly socialized into the human world. That's obvious to most people, but not so obvious to werewolves, who prefer the insular company of their Pack. Also really not obvious to Clay—the former child werewolf who'd spent most of his early school years growling in a corner, counting down the minutes until he could go home to Jeremy and escape the clutches of human children who might do something unbearable, like talk to him.

So our children were being integrated into the human community. They went to a normal school . . . well, okay, a private one, when the other didn't quite work out. They were enrolled in normal childhood activities . . . well, swimming and art and other independent pursuits, after the preschool-soccer fiasco. They were encouraged to have friends . . . well, *a* friend, please, Kate, just one, and no, your brother doesn't count.

At eight years old, the twins' socialization was still a work in progress. A serious work in progress for Kate. Logan accepted it, but "accept" was the key word. "Humoring his mother" might be a better way of putting it.

The biggest problem, though? Good parenting is about teaching by example, and since Clay sure as hell wasn't tackling this one, it was down to me. Which meant signing up as a parent chaperone on this overnight trip to Albany. I'd further encouraged the twins to use this opportunity to make new acquaintances, starting by choosing bus seatmates they didn't know well. So, of course, I had to do the same.

I shared my seat with a mother who began by announcing she was into "scrapping." Conversation had seemed much more promising when I thought that she meant she liked to fight. But apparently "scrapping" was her term for scrapbooking, and I didn't really understand what *that* was, so she proceeded to explain . . . for the entire two-hour trip. The moment the bus pulled into the parking lot, I bolted from my seat with a murmured, "Need to check on the kids."

The aisle was already jammed with eight-year-olds equally eager to escape forced confinement. Kate was off the bus, probably first in line. I spotted Logan, still seated, carrying on an intense conversation with his seatmate . . . another parent chaperone. Apparently, I'd needed to specify that I meant "sit with another child."

We disembarked, and I joined the growing cluster of parents and children at the head of a forest path. The class trip would begin with a science project—a late afternoon "scavenger hunt" in the woods. I was actually looking forward to this part, as were the twins, and as soon as I stopped at the crowd's edge, Kate zipped over, her worksheet in hand. Logan joined us a moment later.

"Elena," said a voice behind me, and I turned to see MaryAnne, one of the mothers I knew less well—by choice. Her BFF, Charlene, followed. "I barely even recognized you without your husband at your side."

"He *is* very attentive," Charlene said. "He never seems to let you out of his sight. I must admit, I do find that . . . troubling."

"Yeah," Kate said. "He keeps her locked in the cage in our basement, but we know where he hides the key."

"Oh, Kate," MaryAnne said with a chuckle. "You are something, aren't you?"

Charlene's snort said my daughter was indeed something. My hackles rose, but MaryAnne continued, murmuring, "Now, personally, I wouldn't mind being locked in a cage with your—"

"We should get closer," I cut in. "So we can hear the teacher."

"Bitches," Kate muttered as we walked away.

"*Kate*," I said. "Language."

"Note that she's objecting to the profanity of the word choice," Logan murmured. "Not the meaning."

Kate snickered. I gave Logan a look. He turned wide blue eyes on me. "I'm agreeing with you, Mom. Kate shouldn't call them that. It's an insult to real bitches."

I growled under my breath. He gave me a rare grin, and we continued over to the teachers.

After giving us final instructions, the teachers told us to break into groups. I started looking around.

"Here," Logan said, taking his sister's worksheet and giving her another page. "I got an early copy and reorganized the items, classified by object type, subclassified by—"

"Serious?" Kate said. "You're such an old man, Lo."

His eyes narrowed. "Do you want to test how *old* I am? Remember the last time—"

"Enough," I said. "We need to find another group to join."

"No, we don't," Kate said. "They'll just slow us down."

Before I could argue, Logan said, "She has a point, however tangentially. If we team up with others, in the excitement of the hunt, we may forget to hide the fact we can smell better and hear better. Our scent may also send wildlife into a panic, which will raise questions. It's safer if we do this by ourselves."

"Uh-huh."

"I'm just thinking of the Pack," he said. "Minimizing an exposure threat, which is everyone's job." He looked at me. "Especially the Alpha's."

I rolled my eyes but waved them into the forest, and we took off before anyone could stop us.

It had been unseasonably warm for March, and after a half hour of hiking, we'd shed our jackets and tied them around our waists. We'd also knocked off most of the scavenger hunt items. This part of the class trip was intended for urban kids, who'd be lucky to have a stand of trees behind their neighborhood playground. We had acres of forest in our backyard, and the twins seemed to spend half their lives there, endlessly exploring. Finding acorns and silver birch and even cranberry bushes wasn't exactly difficult for them.

The best part of a forest, though, is the wildlife. Not surprisingly, that's what fascinates Kate and Logan most. Unlike their father at their age, they don't see tracking and studying animals as developing predatory skills. To them it's pure interest, the expression of a kinship with nature that's wondrous to see.

We were peering into a hollowed-out log, watching a fox and her newborn kits while the mother slept, wrapped around her babies. One had wriggled free of its littermates and was trying to explore, more rolling than walking.

The twins watched the kit, and I watched them, the delight in their faces, my "babies" who had not been babies in far too long, growing up surrounded by adults. Here, though, even Logan's eyes glowed in childlike wonder.

When the mother fox seemed to realize one kit had wandered, she opened her eyes and we moved away quickly, before we alarmed her.

"Can we come back tomorrow, Momma?" Logan asked as we walked to the path. He used to call me that when he was little. It's rare these days and every time it makes me smile.

"The hotel is only a couple of miles away," he continued. "And we'll have time when the other kids go to the pet show."

"Since we aren't going," Kate grumbled.

Her brother shot her a look, and she acknowledged it with an apology. I'd told the teacher they have allergies, but that's a lie. They really *can't* go, and that isn't me being an overprotective parent—it's the animals I'm protecting, the ones who'd go nuts at our scent.

"I'd just like to see the dogs," Kate said. "The different breeds. In case . . . you know."

When Logan gave her another look, she said, "What? We *could* get puppies. Reese did. He said as long as you start when they're little, they'll get used to our scent."

"Can we discuss this later?" I asked.

"That depends," she said. "Is this your kind of discussing it later or Dad's? Because yours means you're hoping we'll forget."

Unfortunately true, though I was trying to break the habit, now that they were old enough to call me on it. "It's your father's kind. The honest one. Which doesn't mean you can expect a puppy anytime soon but, yes, we can discuss—"

I stopped as I caught an unfamiliar scent. An animal zipped past us. It looked like a cross between a cat and a raccoon, and had an incredibly long tail, which kept going across the path even after the animal itself had disappeared.

As the creature flew up a tree, Kate darted forward to get a better look. Logan ran after her, and they both stood at the base of the tree, craning their necks as they squinted.

I hurried over in time to see that impossibly long tail through the leafless branches. When the creature sprang to the next tree, the kids and I followed on the ground, but the animal was faster, and soon disappeared.

"What was that?" Kate said. When even her brother shrugged, she fished the phone from my pocket.

"Umm . . ." I said. "You could ask to use that."

"You could buy us cell phones."

"We probably should have them," Logan said. "For emergencies."

"Like this," Kate said. "It's a curiosity emergency, which is the most important kind."

She held up the phone and cursed under her breath. Then she stuffed it into her pocket and started scaling the nearest tree. Logan and I waited until she found a suitable branch, crawled out, held up the phone and gave a crow of victory. A few moments later she started coming down, calling, "Tailypo."

"What?" I said.

"It's a tailypo," she said. "From American folklore. It's believed to be the evolutionary link between raccoons and Maine Coon cats." She paused. "Which I think is impossible."

"It is," Logan said as his sister seated herself on the lowest branch, her legs swinging. "As suggested by the 'American folklore' part. It's a legend. In other words, not real."

"Looked pretty real to me."

He sighed and climbed up to sit beside her as she handed him the phone. "Yes," he said finally. "It did resemble this, but there's no such thing as a tailypo."

"There's no such thing as werewolves either," she said.

He opened his mouth in a retort, but a voice cut him off. It was MaryAnne, coming down the trail with Charlene and their kids, swatting at mosquitoes.

"Did I hear someone talking about werewolves?" Mary-Anne asked.

"Kate was saying they don't exist," Logan said as he hopped from the tree.

"Well, duh," said one of their boys.

"Actually . . ." Kate jumped down beside her brother. "I'm

pretty sure I just spotted one." A sideways look at Logan and me. "Maybe more than one."

"Oh, Kate," MaryAnne said. "You really are something!"

"She sure is," the boy muttered.

Kate flipped him the finger behind her brother's back. I grabbed her hand before the boy noticed and said, "So, how are you guys doing?" and led the group off, but not before casting a slow look around the forest and mouthing to Kate that we'd come back, as soon as we ditched the muggles.

VERITY

Growing up in a private compound in the Oregon woods— with "private compound" being the polite way of saying "inside a big box of survivalist granola, complete with nuts, flakes, and the occasional Incubus"—had equipped me with the survival skills to handle basically anything the forests of North America could throw at me. I had bargained with Bigfoots, squabbled with Sasquatch, and run like hell when a herd of Peryton sniffed out my position. There was nothing in the woods that I was not prepared for.

Nothing save for the mosquitoes of New York, which had apparently been feeding on the blood of something giant, radioactive, and mutation-triggering. The damn things were big enough to bite *through* the fabric of my shirt, raising welts the size of pennies.

"Fuck, *fuck*, fuck, *fuck*, fuck," I swore as I scaled the nearest tree, taking refuge in juvenilia. It wasn't making the mosquitoes stop biting, but it was making me feel better, if only because there was something satisfying about spoiling my day's PG rating without getting naked. I had mosquito repellant in my pack. I just hadn't been expecting to *need* it. Back home the mosquitoes mostly ignored me, probably because my brother was delicious, and I was too stringy to be worth biting.

The tree was silent as I hauled myself hand-over-hand into the branches and wedged myself into the highest spot that I could be sure was safe. That was the weirdest thing about this particular forest for me: no frickens. That probably explained a lot about the local mosquito population. Frogs did a lot to keep biting insects at bay. Frickens, with their stubby feathers and ability to glide short distances, did even more. A mosquito that escaped the ground-dwelling frogs might still find itself the victim of death from above when there were frickens around.

But there *should* have been frickens here. According to the field guides, this was prime territory; not too dry, not too wet, exactly suited to the life cycle of the world's only remaining feathered amphibians. There hadn't been any mass die-offs or new pollutants introduced to the water table; the local papers would have noticed. While dead frickens tended to get written off as sparrows or starlings or whatever the local L.B.B. (little brown bird) happened to be, they *would* have been noticed. And the area was replete enough with aging hippies and environmental crusaders that pollution would have been noticed even faster.

"What the hell is going on out here?" I muttered, digging the rosemary cream from my bag. Rosemary is one of the best mosquito repellants nature has going, and has the convenient added bonus of smelling like, well, a plant. Because it *is* a plant. It doesn't disturb the wildlife the way chemical repellants can, and I've never heard of anyone being attacked by a bear because they smelled like a delicious casserole. (I *have* heard about some guy getting treed by wolves for wearing too much Axe body spray into the woods, which is proof that wolves have pretty good taste. Although I bet he didn't taste very good.)

The tree didn't answer me. I finished slathering the cream over my exposed skin and put the tube away before dropping soundlessly down to the ground and stalking deeper into the woods. I needed to find some mud.

Mud is one of those things that thrive in a good forest. Even when the area isn't swampy—and too few areas are, which is a real pity; I love a good swamp like I love little else that doesn't come with sequins—it's usually possible to find someplace mucky and yucky and full of all the delightful things that live in soft earth.

I found what I was looking for about a quarter of a mile from the spot where I'd entered the woods. A stream cut through a clearing that was overhung with branches so that direct sunlight never reached the ground. The lack of light had kept the underbrush from getting a good rooting in the area, and the earth dissolved into glorious mud a few feet from the water. I squelched my way into the middle of it, letting the mud cake on my boots, and crouched down to start scanning the bank of the stream for holes.

There are a lot of things that like to burrow in mud. Venomous snakes, for example. Some species of frog. It's never possible to be *sure* what made a given hole, since all holes look pretty much the same, but it's possible to make an educated guess. I spotted a likely hole, leaned forward, and rammed my arm into it up to the elbow.

You don't make it in my family if you're squeamish about a little mud.

Feeling around in the sludge and sediment of the bank, my fingers hit something slick and strong that felt like a length of intestine wrapped in sandpaper. I grabbed it and hauled, yanking until my arm popped back out of the bank, bringing a worm a foot and a half long along for the ride. It was flailing wildly, sawtoothed mouth gaping and making little sucking gestures, like it thought it could disgust its attacker away. I grabbed it just below the mouth with my free hand, keeping it from latching onto me. Bloodworms are relatively harmless, but that didn't mean I wanted to be bitten by one if I could help it. Even harmless things can have a *lot* of teeth.

"Hello, new friend," I said, leaning closer. "What can you tell me about the local ecosystem?"

The bloodworm hissed. Being non-sapient members of the family that gives us such natural wonders as "the leech" and "that other kind of leech, oh God, get it off me," they tend not to be great conversationalists.

That doesn't mean they don't have anything to say. The bloodworm's skin was a smooth, rich shade of chocolatey brown under the mud, which meant it was getting plenty to eat; no malnourished limbless horrors here. Its teeth were sharp and unbroken, which meant it hadn't been forced to go after prey beyond its usual assortment of fish, frogs, and the occasional foolish snake. A bloodworm that hadn't been finding the right kind of food would attack just about anything, including cattle or hikers. That did a number on their teeth, since they weren't really adapted to go after that sort of prey.

I flipped the squirming bloodworm upside down, giving its belly a critical look. The scaling there was as healthy and unbroken as the top had been, and its tiny, thorn-like claspers—an example of parallel evolution, since it shared that particular feature with snakes—were still intact. It was a breeding-age male, and had seen no environmental reason *not* to get on with the business of making more bloodworms.

"So there's nothing in the water, and there's nothing contaminating the ground," I muttered, frowning at the still-squirming bloodworm. "There should be frickens here. Where the hell are all the frickens?"

The bloodworm hissed. I sighed.

"You're right, this isn't your problem. Sorry about that." I lowered the bloodworm gently back to the mud and let go. It squirmed away, burrowing into the bank and disappearing. Bloodworms aren't very smart; since I'd released it without eating it, it would assume it was safe now, and stay exactly where it was. I could come back for it later.

And that was why so many cryptozoologists used bloodworms as bait, and why only the fact that they bred like, well, bloodworms had kept the species from going extinct years ago. Bloodworms were incredibly talented when it came to making more bloodworms.

I'd known going in that someone was poaching tailypo from the local woods. That was the sort of thing that threw up a lot of red flags within the cryptid community, and hence within the cryptozoological community. But no one had noticed that someone was also taking the frickens. Frickens were small. Frickens only attracted attention in their absence, when they stopped singing from the trees.

Someone was out here harvesting supposedly impossible things and taking advantage of the fact that what wasn't acknowledged by science wasn't protected by the law, and while I didn't know how long it had been going on, I knew that it was long enough for the frickens to have gone silent. This wasn't good. This wasn't good at all.

I was deep enough in the woods to be outside of Sarah's normal broadcast range. Maybe if I'd been a cuckoo, too— but if I'd been a cuckoo, the odds were good that I would have been a serial killer who thought the suffering of others was funny, so it was probably for the best that I was human. Besides, humanity had something almost as good as telepathy. I wiped the mud off my hands onto my jeans before digging the cell phone out of my pocket.

"Take that, evolutionary lack of telepathy," I said, raising the phone.

No service.

I blinked at the screen before standing up straight, as if a difference of a few feet would change anything. It did not, in fact, change anything. The phone remained stubbornly disconnected from the network, deadweight instead of a useful communications tool.

"This is why we do not taunt the universe," I muttered, shoving the phone back into my pocket and turning to begin the long, irritating process of walking back to the hotel. Sarah would want to know that things were more complicated than we'd originally believed, and I was going to want her to come back into the woods with me. What was the point of having a telepath if you weren't going to use it?

Here's the thing about poachers, especially ones who aren't overly concerned with whether their traps hurt somebody: they're assholes, and like all assholes, they're happy to cut corners. I worked my way out of the swamp and onto solid ground, crunching through the dead leaves and underbrush that had fallen to cover most of the forest floor. Maybe I should have been paying closer attention to the patterns the leaves made on the ground, but I was too busy looking at the trees, searching for a flash of feathers or for the long, stripy tail of a tailypo. The poachers couldn't have captured them all, and these were the sorts of trees that tailypo preferred.

Halfway across a clearing, I finally spotted a flash of striped brown fur in the branches overhead, moving fast enough that it would have been impossible to tell tailypo from raccoon, if not for the meter-long tail that followed after the initial motion. I stopped, cupping my hands above my eyes like it would somehow enable me to see farther.

And the false ground beneath my feet gave way, dumping me ingloriously into the waiting pit trap.

ELENA

We ditched MaryAnne and the others easily enough. I may have slipped Kate's blank scavenger hunt sheet from Logan's pocket. I may have surreptitiously circled three of the thirty items. I may have then shown it to MaryAnne and said, "We've found these. How about you guys?" Kate may have piped in with, "We could team up. We'll use your list." That may have been the point at which they realized they'd already finished this area and had to skip over to another and they'd love to combine forces, but they really should let us finish this section on our own.

"That was pretty smart, Mom," Kate said as they walked away.

I handed her back the sheet. "I didn't make Alpha on my looks, you know."

"No, you made it because no one else wanted the job."

"We heard you say that to Dad once," Logan said. "If you weren't suitable as Alpha, though, Jeremy would never have stepped down. So it's not entirely true."

"Thank you. So much." I ducked under a spiderweb strung across the path. "How many more items *do* we need to find?"

"We've completed the basic and the intermediary lists. The rest are bonus items, and we've found half of those."

"We can keep looking," I said. "Or cut out early and find food. I heard stomachs grumbling."

Normally, the answer would be food. It was always food, especially with Kate. But she glanced into the forest and said, "I'd really like to get the bonus items," and I knew what she meant was, "I'd really like to get another look at that creature." I reached into my jacket and passed out granola bars.

"The list it is," I said. "After dinner, we'll—"

I stopped as a scent hit me. I tilted my head, teasing it out. The twins did the same. While only male children inherit a werewolf's genes, both of our kids show secondary characteristics, like enhanced senses and strength, and they seem to have had them all their lives, which isn't normal. But neither is having two bitten werewolves for parents.

The smell I picked up on the wind was human, and no one I recognized from the class. Before I could say anything, the breeze changed and brought a very different scent. We all looked up . . . to see the creature from earlier on a tree branch over our heads, its own nose working hard as it tried to figure out *our* scents.

No one moved. The twins didn't even seem to be breathing. They stared. No, they studied, taking in every part of the creature they could see. Kate backed up for a better look from a fresh angle, and the beast inched along the branch, following her. I zeroed in on its gaze as I watched for the slightest sign of imminent attack. It might look cute, but it was the size of a small dog, and those fangs told me it was no herbivore. It didn't seem to be readying to spring, though, just following Kate, and as curious as she was.

She continued moving to the trunk of the tree. Then she put up one tentative hand to start climbing. The creature just watched her. She shimmied to the first branch, about three feet under the beast. Its muscles tensed, but seemingly for flight rather than attack. I got into position, though, ready to let out a snarl if it made any aggressive move. It didn't. As Kate moved into a crouch, it leaned down until their heads were less than six inches apart. Then a noise startled it—the sound of someone moving through the forest.

The beast lifted its snout, sniffed, and took off, flying through the trees. Kate jumped down and followed on ground level, her brother at her side. After about ten running steps, I caught two human smells—one male and one female—from different directions.

I was about to call the kids back when a crash resounded through the forest, followed by a yelp and a thud, and I kicked it into high gear. Ahead, I saw what looked like a pit, partially covered in branches. A trap. I remembered that high-pitched yelp of surprise and raced toward it.

Logan stepped into my path, his arms out to stop me as he whispered, "We're fine, Mom."

I skidded to a halt as Kate joined him. I looked toward the trap and caught the same smell from a few minutes ago, that of the strange woman who was now at the bottom of the pit.

I motioned for the kids to stay where they were and coupled it with a look that said that wasn't Mom giving the order—it was their Alpha. They understood that instinctively and stood their ground, not even craning for a better look. I eased forward until I could see the captive without being spotted. She was short, blonde, and dressed like a hunter, wearing almost as much mud as she did khaki.

I backed up and waved for the kids to follow until we were out of human earshot.

"She's fine," I whispered. "But there's someone else here. A man, I think."

They didn't point out that there were lots of people out here—a whole class of them. They knew that's not what I meant, and they sampled the air, sniffing. Then Kate nodded and said, "Something spooked the tailypo. It wasn't just scared. It was freaking out."

I didn't question this any more than they'd questioned me about the stranger in the forest. My daughter has an innate ability to read emotions. I don't know if it's an actual power or no different from a human with an extraordinary sense of smell. If she said the creature was panicked, it was.

"If we do have a tailypo in this forest"—Logan caught his sister's look—"and, yes, it seems we do, it would be valuable. Very valuable. Which suggests that trap could be for it."

"*Could* be?" Kate said.

"Presumption is a dangerous logical leap," he said calmly. "But it certainly could be. And if the man's scent spooked the tailypo, it could be connected. Which means we should investigate."

"And the chick in the pit?" Kate said.

"She seems calm enough."

"She's pissed off. But I'd be, too. We can leave her there." Kate looked up at me. "Okay, Mom? Is that the right move?"

I smiled. "It is. She's fine, and for all we know, she's with that man, and she stumbled into her own trap. She can wait. Let's see what's going on here."

VERITY

One thing that will snap me instantly out of being pissed that I've been dumped down a pit trap: the sound of running feet. Bipedal, whatever it was, and either child-sized or actually a child. No one who wasn't related to me was going to bring a kid this far into the forest, so I was voting "small adult." I tensed, waiting for whoever it was to approach. They didn't.

That left me with two options. Option one, they had no idea the pit trap was here, and hadn't felt the need to investigate the strange hole in the forest floor. Unimaginative, but not outside the realm of possibility. Option two, they knew they'd caught something human, and were going to get a bigger gun. Something that would kill or sedate most of the pit trap–able animals in this forest wasn't going to do a damn bit of good against something the size of me.

Our poachers, whoever they were, were going after tailypo and cleaning out the local fricken population. I had to assume that larger animals were also on the menu. When something doesn't officially exist, it doesn't have many people rushing to protect it. We were in prime jackalope migration territory, and mature bucks would have been more than large enough to trigger the deadfall. Ditto igneous scorpions—and after spending a day at the pet show, with its many creepy, crawly options, I had absolute faith that there was a buyer for even something as unpleasant and inclined to sting as an igneous scorpion.

The steps were not repeated. I glared at the slice of sky visible at the top of the pit trap for a moment before pulling the knives out of my shirt and jamming them into the dirt a bit above eye level. Time to get the hell out of here!

Years of free-running and parkour have left me with a degree of upper body strength entirely out of proportion with what most people would assume from looking at me. Even so, I was swearing steadily by the time I reached the lip of the pit trap and hauled myself back onto solid ground. I paused long enough to reach back down and snatch my knives from the pit wall. These asshole poachers had stolen half an hour of my time and a layer of skin off my knees.

I'd be damned before I was going to give them two of my favorite throwing knives.

Oh, who was I kidding? All throwing knives were my favorite throwing knives. If there was a support group for people who had an unhealthy fondness for bladed weapons, I would have been their poster girl. And I still didn't have cell service.

I paused. At this point, there was definitely a poacher out here, and whoever it was needed to be stopped before they damaged the local ecosystem beyond repair. But they were using purely human tactics, and they were unlikely to have any special tricks up their sleeves. Hidebehinds didn't need to set pit traps. Cuckoos didn't need to set traps at all. Did I really need Sarah to deal with one little poacher? No, I did not. After the day she'd had, she deserved a few hours alone in the room to watch basic cable and chat with Artie. She would definitely be easier to deal with during the drive home if I let her chill for a while.

"I can handle this," I said, trying to sound positive. It almost worked. I clung to that attitude as I made for the nearest tree, grabbed a branch, and began to climb.

Tailypo are arboreal. Given their choice in the matter, they only touch the ground to raid trashcans and chitter menacingly at tourists. I scanned the branches as I climbed, finally spotting signs of tailypo passage about two-thirds of the way up. That was good. That meant we still had tailypo running free in the area, and that there might be time for me to get in the poacher's way. I followed the scratches on the bark to the end of the tree, dropped down to the ground, and began making my way through the woods, this time scanning my surroundings for additional traps.

I found two: a second pit trap, and a snare sized perfectly for adult jackalope. I took perverse pleasure in triggering them both from a distance, rendering them useless for poaching purposes. That would teach them to put a pit trap where I was walking.

The deeper I went into the woods, the darker it became. Not just because the afternoon was stretching toward evening, although that was a factor; the trees here were closer together, their branches more tightly interwoven, until they blocked almost all the available light. It wasn't really a surprise when I stepped through a veil of bushes and found myself looking at a small hunting cabin, tucked away into the brush and effectively camouflaged by the trees around it. If anything, it was a surprise that the cabin was visible at all, given how well it had been constructed to blend in.

There were several hutches out back. I could see motion inside, moving fast, like something that wasn't accustomed to being trapped. My eyes narrowed. When Sarah and I had come here, we had been expecting to find a breeder, someone stupid enough to believe that wild animals could be domesticated in a single generation. Instead, we had a trapper.

Humans don't react well to things we didn't know about before they started biting us. If the tailypo was found this way, a lot of them were going to die.

Keeping my steps as light as I could, I made my way around the side of the cabin to the hutches and peered inside. Two were full of tailypo. Another held two jackalopes, their antlers filed until they were little more than stubs. They huddled in the corner of their cage, watching me mistrustfully. The fourth hutch was empty, but the feathers in the bottom told me it hadn't been that way for long. This was where they'd been keeping the frickens.

Frickens weren't designed to be crammed in this sort of enclosure. On a hunch, I crouched and poked through the mud under the hutch. There was straw scattered there, presumably to soak up the droppings from the animals above. I didn't have to dig far to find the layer of dead frickens. Like all amphibians, they had dried out quickly, becoming withered, wasted versions of themselves. I picked one up. Most of the feathers fell away in my hand. I scowled.

Killing people is wrong and I know that, but damned if sometimes I don't wish my parents had raised me with a looser set of ethics.

Setting the fricken gently back down in the muck, I straightened and turned toward the nearest occupied hutch. It was time to set a few things free.

ELENA

I exercised extreme caution following the man's scent. I had the twins with me—I couldn't stalk a stranger to satisfy my curiosity. I considered taking them back to the others. They'd stay if I insisted on it. But if there were people out here digging pit traps and scaring the local wildlife—wildlife that shouldn't exist—I wanted to keep Kate and Logan close.

I was trying to stay downwind and keep my distance as I

figured out what was going on here. Before long, though, I caught another scent. The woman from the pit. Who was, apparently, no longer in it.

The woman was closer and moving through the woods in roughly the same direction as the man. I turned her way and whispered, "Stay close," to the kids, which earned me dual eye rolls. Of course they knew to stick close. But as an expert at finding loopholes when Jeremy had been Alpha, I knew better than to presume an implied "Don't take off" would be enough.

Soon we saw a cabin through the trees. The woman's scent came from there. I stopped and assessed. Then I glanced at the kids.

"It's *less* safe if we stay here while you get closer," Logan said before I could speak.

True.

We continued until we were around the side of the cabin. Then we all stopped, noses wrinkling.

"What's that?" Kate whispered.

Death. That's what I smelled first—the stink of carrion. It was faint, though, some creature recently dead. The stronger scent was the one Kate meant. And it was . . .

I had no idea what it was. I smelled the creature from earlier. Or others like it, the smell mingled with dirt and feces and rotted food. But there were other scents, too, creatures I didn't recognize.

When Kate started forward, I laid a hand on her shoulder. That was all it took. She glanced back with an apologetic nod.

As tempting as it was to focus on those smells, there was

a more important one coming from the same direction: the woman. I eased forward until I could see her back. She stood in front of hutches. Animal cages. That's where those smells were coming from.

We had a creature of legend—the tailypo—and more animals with scents I'd never encountered despite years exploring the forests of upstate New York. In one of those cages I could see what looked like . . . well, a feathered frog. I wouldn't know for certain without closer inspection, but I accepted that the other beast had been a tailypo and I smelled others in those hutches. Someone had captured at least one creature found only in folklore and was keeping them in cages. From the looks of the run-down hunting cabin, this woman wasn't a scientist who'd made an incredible new discovery. The smell seconded that—the stink of neglect and, yes, death, and my hackles rose as I watched her fussing with the cages.

I backed up, waving the kids with me. Even Logan followed with obvious reluctance and kept glancing toward those cages. I was about to tell the kids I needed them to stay back while I figured out what to do. Then I heard a click. I stiffened, my hands going to their shoulders, ready to shove them to the ground. But the click came from the hatches. The woman was opening them.

We crept back to where we'd been and saw her reach into one cage and take out what was indeed a feathered frog. Then she set it free.

I exhaled. Well, that made things easier. I'd had no idea what I'd do about this, only that I'd have been compelled to do something, that I couldn't leave those creatures in those cages to die . . . and more importantly, couldn't do that with my children watching. If she was setting them free, then I could skip what might be a dangerous—

Another noise sounded deep in the forest. Footsteps. Heading in this direction. I inhaled deeply and caught the scent of the man from earlier. The one who'd frightened the tailypo. Now, I know as well as Logan that we can't jump to conclusions, but it was a safe bet the man was the one who'd put those creatures in those cages. I circled around the cabin, the kids at my heels, and got close enough on the other side to confirm that his scent trails ran all around the place.

Those footsteps were coming fast. And the woman freeing the creatures was taking her time, checking them out before she let them go. She couldn't hear or smell the man. And he wasn't going to be too happy when he returned to see what she was doing.

I whispered a quick plan to the kids, and then watched as they took off to find a tree to scale, getting out of harm's way. Once I saw them going up, I went after the man.

VERITY

There had been a few frickens left alive and clinging to the roof of their hutch, terrified out of their tiny amphibian minds. The rest were either sold or dead; I was going to have to let Alex know that he needed to watch the reptile communities he belonged to for people talking a little too enthusiastically about their rare new acquisitions. The jackalopes were in better shape. They were more accustomed to being hunted, and had long since evolved a "run when you can, give up completely when you can't" approach to predation. Maybe that wasn't healthy, but it meant they did better in this sort of situation.

I was placing a large buck on the ground and trying to encourage it to run away when I heard one of the few sounds that were guaranteed to get my attention, no matter what the situation: a man, screaming like he'd just learned the true meaning of pain. The jackalope heard it too, and went bounding wildly off into the underbrush. Well, that was one problem solved.

Straightening, I relatched the hutch—I needed to finish checking these animals out before I released them—and drew the gun from my belt, holding it low to my hip as I slunk toward the trees. Maybe I was gonna get lucky, and that asshole poacher was at the bottom of one of his own pit traps.

The asshole poacher was not at the bottom of one of his own pit traps. The asshole poacher was, instead, in the process of being punched in the throat by a tall woman with silver-blonde hair in a shade that couldn't possibly have come out of a bottle. She had the build for the tango but moved like she was dancing capoeira, all shifting balance and brute force. It was impressive.

It was also disproportionate as a reaction to a poacher, or seemed that way, until I saw the knife in his hand, a big serrated dealie that would have had me going for the takedown as fast as possible, just for the sake of keeping my insides from becoming my outsides. Something rustled in one of the nearby trees. I slanted a glance in that direction, trying to be unobtrusive about it; if it was tailypo, that was fine, but if it was another poacher, I was going to have to get involved.

Instead, there was a flash of hairless skin, too pale to belong to a Bigfoot, if there were even any in this area. A kid. The lady had a kid with her. That explained the footsteps I'd heard before, and the speed with which she'd gone from zero to throat-punching. No parent in the world would hold back when their kids were nearby.

The woman punched the poacher one more time. He went down like a sack of wet laundry, sprawling on the ground. The knife skittered from his hand, shooting across the forest floor to wind up near enough to my feet that I stepped on it to stop its progress, only realizing as I moved that I should have kept still. The woman—human, dragon princess, whatever—was clearly a predator, and one with a child, to boot. Attracting attention was the last thing I should have done.

Her hair wasn't black. She wasn't a cuckoo. I might survive this. And so, as she turned to look in my direction, I plastered on my best reality television smile and offered a sunny, "Hi."

ELENA

When the guy went down, the knife went flying. I turned, ready to kick it out of the way, in case he rose. That's when I saw the woman from the pit. She stood there with her foot on the knife, and she smiled—a big, bright smile, as if she'd happened upon me enjoying a forest stroll.

"Hi," she said.

I resisted the urge to look up and check on the twins, but I must have glanced in that direction because Kate gave a soft birdcall, telling me they were all right. I looked back at the woman. Then down at the blade under her foot.

"That was his," I said.

"I saw that. Nice work. You meet some real creeps out here."

Her accent suggested she wasn't local. She kept smiling, as if she saw absolutely nothing odd about me trouncing some potential predator lurking in the woods. Behind that smile, though, there was a touch of unease. Completely justified considering what she'd witnessed. She was probably wondering if the guy on the ground wasn't the only dangerous one out here.

I was about to say something when a noise sounded in the treetops, and I looked up before I could stop myself. It was just the tailypo—or one of them—racing along a branch. From where we stood, we could only see the general shape and that incredible tail.

"Huh," she said. "Weird-looking raccoon."

"We get them up here," I said. "A regional variation, I think." I looked at the knife again. "You'd better keep that, in case this guy wasn't alone. He looks as if he'll be sleeping for a while, but you might not want to hang around. There's a ranger station that way, I think." I pointed.

She picked up the knife. "Thanks for the tip. It's easy to get turned around in these woods."

"It is," I said. "Well, take care. And watch out for the mosquitoes. They seem to be out early this year and they're nastier than usual."

"Oh, I'm sure there's an ecological reason for that. It'll sort itself out."

I said goodbye and left, picking a path that took me into thick brush. When I was sure she could no longer see me, I stopped to wait. A few moments later, the kids came, running silently. We continued on until we were out of earshot. They kept looking back. Not at the woman—they'd probably forgotten her already—but at the cabin.

"Can we come out tomorrow, Momma?" Logan asked. "She emptied all the cages but there were things in them . . . We'd like to look around more."

I ruffled his hair. "We'll do that." I glanced into the forest, peering around, trying to catch a glimpse of something new, something wondrous. Then I turned back to them and said, "We'll definitely do that."

VERITY

Killing people is rude and bad and wrong and leads to lots of paperwork, which is why I didn't kill the poacher. I just stuffed him into one of his own hutches, where his friends would eventually find and release him. Assuming he *had* any friends. This was the sort of thing that led to stories about monsters in the woods, which discouraged poachers from coming around. The local ecosystem had been damaged, but it would all work itself out, given a little time to regenerate.

Sarah was sitting on the bed when I returned to the motel. She had her laptop on her knees, and was typing rapidly, her eyes fixed on the screen.

"How's Artie?" I asked, easing the door closed behind me.

"Antimony dragged him to roller derby practice. He's never leaving the house again." She turned in my direction, and blinked. "Why are you covered in mud?"

"Pit trap."

"Oh."

"Is there a Nest near here?"

Sarah blinked again. "Maybe. I don't know. I don't keep track. Why?"

"Because I'm pretty sure I just met the world's first MMA-qualifying dragon princess."

"Oh. And the poacher . . . ?"

"She kicked his ass." I held up my souvenir. "I got his knife."

"Oh." Sarah paused for a moment before she brightened, and asked, "Does that mean we can skip the Pet Expo tomorrow?"

I laughed. I couldn't help myself. I was covered in mud and I'd just shoved an adult man into a rabbit hutch, and there were beautiful blonde women with incredible roundhouse kicks running around in the woods, protecting their children from poachers. It was a wonderful world.

"Yes," I said. "We can definitely do that."

Sweet, Blissful Certainty

STEVEN SAVILE AND CRAIG SCHAEFER

Eddie Sunday was accustomed to dealing with dead men, but there was a proper time and place for that kind of job. Not on his doorstep in east Las Vegas, and not at two in the morning. He balled up a fist and rubbed his knuckles across his sleep-crusted eyes.

Eddie wore a pair of boxers and a ratty old terry cloth robe that hung low off his slack skin and very noticeable bones. His visitor, standing across the threshold, opted for a tailored black silk suit with the artfully folded puff of a blue silk handkerchief poking from his jacket's breast pocket.

Eddie rubbed his eyes again. No luck. The man was still there, flashing a lazy smile edged with hunger and the threat of casual cruelty.

"Daniel Faust." Eddie's voice came out softer than he wanted it to. "Heard you were dead."

"I heard that, too." He glanced down. On Eddie's side of the doorway, a thick line of salt ran from edge to edge across worn, bare floorboards. "You gonna invite me in?"

Eddie swallowed. "Are . . . are you a vampire now?"

Faust stepped over the salt and into Eddie's apartment, rolling his eyes as he sidled past him.

"Vampires aren't real. And Jesus, Eddie, how do you live like this? Have some self-respect."

Eddie had to ask himself that same question. He shut the door, flipped the knobs on three separate dead bolts, and turned to share the view. His second-floor walkup was a wasteland of garage-sale furniture, empty beer bottles, and cigarette ash. A three-foot-tall cross made of neon tubing hung on one wall, bathing the room in flickering, sickly shades of orange.

He scurried over to the futon, stacking up a few empty pizza boxes and shoving them to one side, clearing up a space to sit. Faust ignored the gesture. He walked over to the window, slow and easy, like he owned the place.

"Hard times," was the only explanation Eddie could manage.

"I'm guessing most of your disposable income's still going straight into your veins." He looked the man up and down. "What are you down to, ninety pounds soaking wet? I feel like I should take you down to Redondo for the afternoon, just so I can kick sand in your face."

"Keeps the voices quiet." Eddie sat down and nudged a stray pizza crust under the futon with his bare foot. "Gotta do what you gotta do, right?"

"I'm not here to judge."

"It's never that simple with you, eh?"

Faust glanced out the window. Eddie lived in no-man's-land, across the street from a crumbling brick slab of shuttered storefronts, boarded windows, and an all-night massage parlor. The dazzling lights of the Las Vegas Strip rose up in the distance, a constellation of fallen stars shouting empty promises half a city away. Paradise, almost close enough to touch.

"So, uh," Eddie said, "let's just get the obvious question out of the way: why aren't you dead? Everybody's been talking about the riot up at Eisenberg Correctional. Something like a hundred people got . . ."

Faust looked at him. Eddie's voice trailed off.

"The riot I'm guessing you caused," Eddie said, finishing his thought.

Faust spread his open hands. "Call it a magic trick. I need to be dead right now. It's time to settle a few accounts, and it's better if they don't see me coming."

Eddie pushed himself back against the cheap futon mattress, his spindly fingers digging into a cigarette burn.

"That's cool, man. Everything's good. You and me," he said. "We've always had a, you know, a good working relationship. Right?"

"Sure, Eddie. We're fine. Better than fine."

"That's good to hear, man."

"So good, in fact, that I've got a little job for you, just to show there're no hard feelings."

Eddie was off the futon in a heartbeat, pacing the groaning floorboards, every muscle in the tweeker's body twitching.

"No, uh-uh. I'm retired. I am fully and officially retired from that bullshit—"

"Don't say that, Eddie. I come bearing gifts," Faust said. He showed his open palm, closed his fingers, then opened them up again with a flourish. Now a bindle of plastic wrap sat nestled in his hand, twisted around a mound of crumbly yellow-brown chunks.

Eddie stopped pacing. Eyes drawn to the bindle like a fly to an electric light.

"A cut above your usual stuff, I'm going to guess. It's yours if you want it. All you have to do is hear me out."

Eddie shook his head, but he couldn't pretend he wasn't interested. He clenched his right hand into a fist like he was thinking about hitting Faust. Maybe he was, just for a second. Some rogue synapse in his brain going off with a flash: this is a good idea. It didn't take long for the rest of Eddie's brain to shout it down. "You're a real bastard, you know that?"

"That's a no then?"

"Just give it to me, don't be a bastard and make me beg, okay?" Eddie held out his right hand. It was shaking as Faust tossed him the bindle. He looked back to the window.

"You ever hear of 'the man with the Cheshire smile,' Eddie?"

Eddie was already busy halfway across the room, rummaging inside a cluttered end table drawer.

"Rings a bell," he said. "Nothing specific, I mean, just fringe stuff. Rumors about rumors. Sounds like a bad dude. Somebody to stay away from. There are plenty of people like that in this city. Like you."

Faust looked out the window. Stared at the distant lights. They lacked the glamour of the casinos and the high-priced hotels that Vegas was famous for.

"I saw something, in prison. Brushed up against the edges of something big this guy's been cooking up. Something big and something terrible. I think I stopped it from happening. But I need to *know*."

Eddie walked back to the futon, carrying his kit. He let out a nervous laugh as he rested a zippered eelskin case on his bony lap.

"You're getting a little fortune-cookie here, boss. You need me to take you down to Madam Zee's to see if she can help you out?"

Madam Zee was a contortionist clairvoyant who had a weird little show she put on in one of the seedier theaters just off the Strip. The one thing she absolutely didn't do was see the future, though she did plenty of other tricks.

"I'm not allowed back there anymore," Faust started to explain, then paused. "You know what? Never mind why. I need your help to get a glimpse into the future." Before Eddie could object, Faust said, "Because there's a very real chance there isn't going to be a future." He worked his fingers, like the old gag where you danced a coin across the top of them. It looked like he was playing an invisible piano. There was something about Faust's expression that scared the tweeker. "It's been eating at me since I got out. I can't sleep, not without dreaming about it. It's always there, worming away inside. I can't stop thinking about it. I need some peace of mind, that's all."

Eddie quirked an eyebrow at him. "You know I talk to dead people, right? Very good for learning about the *past*, but I've gotta be honest, it's kinda lousy for learning about the future, given that the only people who'd know about that aren't dead yet. The dead can't help you with that."

"*One* dead man can."

While Eddie unzipped his case, his trembling fingers clinging to a length of coiled rubber tubing like it was plated in gold, Faust got out his phone. He tilted the screen toward Eddie, showing him the picture of a vintage theater poster. Doves flew from the outstretched arms of a man in a tuxedo, while tiny red imps capered at his feet.

The Great Damiola, screamed a splash of garish silver text. *You will be Astounded! You will be Amazed! You will witness Miracles!*

"Huh," Eddie said, squinting. "Damiola? Does he have a show just off the Strip? Could swear I saw him and The Amazing Jonathan on a double bill once."

"I don't think that's very likely, Eddie, seeing as Cadmus Damiola has been dead for almost a hundred years."

"Ah, so you want me to talk to him?"

"He was one of the last true magicians, Eddie. He had a gift. A proper talent. I've got my own suspicions how he came into his power, but to be honest I don't really care about the hows and whys; I'm all about his legacy. His last great illusion."

"Isn't that cheating? Going after a dead magician's tricks? Aren't you guys supposed to be all honor and secrecy?"

He swiped the picture away, replacing it with a grainy photograph.

"What is that? Some kind of movie projector?" Eddie asked.

"Some kind," Faust agreed. "Damiola called it the *Opticron*. It offered glimpses of other worlds, or so he claimed. It was the center of his act during his last few shows in London before he disappeared. Listen to this:

"'At first I thought he'd presented us with a doll's house, for that is exactly what it looked like; a house with countless windows. When he fed electricity into the infernal machine, a light from deep within flared to life, and with the jarring rattle of a praxinoscope's drum spinning almost out of control somewhere deep inside the mechanism, the shaft of light that speared through one of the open windows projected the most shocking spectacle onto a white sheet the magician had stretched taut across the window frame. The sky darkened with vast-winged planes, while an army walked in a lockstep parade. Maps showed the tide of war, surging once again across Europe, while a voice warned of a new threat posed by the combined forces of Italy and the Hun.'"

Eddie shrugged. He pushed up the right sleeve of his robe, bunching it up around his shoulder, and took one end of the plastic tubing between his teeth. "Sounds like a World War Two newsreel. I'm not seeing the amazing trick here? It's not like the guy invented TV."

"That extract is from a diary written in 1923."

Midway through wrapping the tubing around his scrawny bicep, baring an ant parade of needle marks down the inside of his arm, Eddie paused. He blinked. "Okay, that's slightly more impressive, I'll give you that, but still, it's like Nostradamus, right? Show enough possible visions of the future, one of them is going to have to be right—or at least look the part when seen in hindsight."

"There are others. Plenty of them. One for each window in that doll's house, I'd hazard. One report describes the Kennedy assassination, right down to Jackie O's pillbox hat. Just days before Damiola disappeared in January 1924, another audience got a real treat; they witnessed the launch of Apollo 11."

"Okay, that must have been some show the guy put on." Eddie grinned. He tied off the tubing and picked up a corroded spoon before opening the plastic-wrap bindle with all the care of a bomb disposal guy handling a primed detonator, fingers trembling, and delicately placed a few crumbly pebbles in the bowl of the spoon. "So where's this Opticron now?"

Faust slipped his phone back into his pocket. "That's the million-dollar question, isn't it? I put some feelers out. A few of those feelers got bitten. Near as I can tell, it's in London. Damiola left all of his tricks to the Magic Circle, so I figured it had to be in there, but it's not."

"You know that for sure?"

"Yep. There was a break-in the other day. Two comedians walked out with one of Damiola's journals. It was the only thing taken. No reports mentioned the Opticron so I dug a little deeper. Cashed in a few favors I probably shouldn't have. Best I can tell, if it isn't in a thousand pieces, it's in the hands of an old-school gangster family. We're talking proper East End heavies."

"Too heavy for you to handle?"

"Right now? I've got the Chicago Outfit breathing down my neck, half my crew is missing or in hiding, and Vegas is disputed territory for the first time in thirty years. Flying to Britain and reenacting a Guy Ritchie movie is *not* on my agenda, as much fun as that may sound. I figure we can do better than that. And by 'we,' I mean 'you,' Eddie. And before you try and wriggle out of it, you owe me. So, we go to the source. Cadmus Damiola built the thing. He can tell me how to build another one."

Eddie didn't answer right away. He sat snared in the spiral of an old, familiar ritual; the snap of his cheap plastic lighter, bringing the ceremonial flame. The slow, oily bubbling of the heroin in the spoon, chemical sorcery transforming solid to liquid, readying the holy sacrament for his veins.

Eddie sat, transfixed by the lighter's glow.

"Conjure Cadmus Damiola's spirit for me, and you'll be five hundred dollars richer."

Eddie glanced up at him. "Five hundred and you go away?"

"And I go away."

He set down the lighter and picked up the syringe.

"Do you think he's in Hell?"

Faust shrugged. "How should I know? Why? What difference does it make?"

The syringe, thirsty, slurped up the tar in the spoon. A tiny wet driblet drooled from the tip of the needle.

"It'd be nice, you know," Eddie said, "if just for once the dead man wasn't in Hell. Being down there does stuff to a soul. And you know, no one who ends up burning was exactly sweetness and light in the first place."

"Five hundred bucks, Eddie."

"I didn't say I wasn't going to do it. I was just making a point. You owe *me*."

"Five hundred bucks," Faust repeated.

The needle bit and the warmth flooded in, racing through Eddie's veins like the tropical surf on a white sand beach. All the filth and the fear tore away like a bandage from a healed wound, and he was a child again, safe in his mother's arms.

Sometimes, on the nod, he dreamed of the old days. The better days before everything went wrong. The days when he wore a three-piece suit the color of vanilla ice cream and preached the Gospel to a packed tent. The Minnesota heat and the summer flies couldn't slow him down, and he'd brush the sweat from his brow with a smile as his words conjured up visions of thunder and brimstone.

Elsa Mae's funeral, that's where it started. He remembered it like it was yesterday. Standing by the open casket, holding hands with the elderly woman's daughter and trying to help her through the pain.

"She's in a better place now, Norma. Looking down—no, she's *smiling* down on you, better believe that. The cancer's gone, all that weight lifted from her. She's with the good Lord now, and—"

Norma, croaked a strangled voice in his left ear. *Is that you? I can't see you.*

"Pastor?" The woman blinked at him. Eddie froze, shaken.

Norma, the voice whispered. *They put razors in my eyes.*

He slowly turned to look. A standing mirror by the altar caught a beam of sunshine, Elsa Mae's coffin glowing in the reflection.

And the bloody, disfigured crone in the glass, the one pulling her way out of the coffin with broken fingernails, turned her sightless head toward him.

That was the first time. Not the worst, though. When Eddie couldn't find solace in his faith any longer the Bible was shouldered aside by new books; books sold out of back rooms, and in dark alleys, books whose pages sprouted verse in degenerate forms of Latin and sported spidery, hand-drawn symbols that made his eyes water and his stomach twist.

He had a natural talent, he discovered, for conjuring the dead by name. The one thing he could never do was shut it off completely. The spirits he *didn't* want to summon? They were always with him. In every reflection. In every dark and quiet room. Making him a witness to their pain.

The only thing stopping Eddie Sunday from putting a gun to his head was his fear of joining them.

The back room of Eddie's apartment had been converted into a magician's temple. Octagonal walls, painted in alternating colors: garish fire-engine red and midnight black. The hardwood floors bore the ghostly white traces of a thousand chalked symbols, drawn and erased again and again.

Fresh from his heroin dream, Eddie was on his hands and knees, chalking a circle within a circle. Hebraic letters ringed the outer rim, wards and seals he only half-understood. Faust helped, rolling a standing mirror with a scalloped wooden frame to the circle's edge.

"Little left," Eddie said. "Has to be perfectly facing the southwest corner."

There were four mirrors in all, aligned to converge on the center of the conjuring-circle. Faust chuckled.

"Funny," he said, "calling up a dead stage magician like this."

Eddie squinted at him. "What's funny about it?"

Faust rapped his knuckles against the antique mirror's glass.

"You know, smoke and mirrors?"

"Hilarious." Eddie got up, dusted off his knees, and stared down at his handiwork. "Okay. That should do it. Let's get this over with."

The man stood on the steps of the old church, hating himself for what he had done. There was no going back, though. Seth Lockwood was gone and the girl with him. The scene of his great deceit, outside the old stone church, wasn't lost on Cadmus Damiola, either. She'd run to Lockwood, seeing a savior until the very last second, when the illusion had fallen away and she'd realized sickly that he had betrayed her, delivering her into the hands of the man who would own her, not the man who loved her. By then it had been too late; the halo around Glass Town was in place and she was already one step out of time, and with every passing minute falling further and further behind.

"I'm supposed to kill you now," the man beside Damiola said.

Ruben Glass.

Glass was an odd one, an entrepreneur who'd fallen in with thieves, but then greed did funny things to a man, didn't it?

"But you're not going to?" Damiola asked, walking down the steps.

"He's not here to see whether I go through with it or not," Glass reasoned.

"Funny," Damiola said, taking the note from his pocket that Lockwood's boy had delivered, setting the evening's events into motion. He offered it to Glass. "I got this about an hour ago."

The other man unfolded the paper and read the final two lines that ordered his own death.

"Well, that does put a different complexion on things, wouldn't you say?"

"Seems he wanted both of us gone," Damiola said.

"And logically, he wouldn't have trusted either one of us to go through with killing the other."

"We're walking dead men," the magician agreed.

"So what now? Are you going back to the West End? The show must go on and all that?"

Damiola shook his head. He had no intention of ever stepping foot on the stage again. If he wanted to live to a ripe old age the smartest thing he could do was disappear.

"And you expect me to just turn my back and walk away from you, now that I know you're supposed to kill me?"

"You can do what you want," Damiola said. "If you're smart you'll just get as far away from London as you can, and hope that the rest of Lockwood's twisted little clan don't come after you. Or you can stick around and try your luck. Either way, our fates divide here. This is the last time we're going to see each other, Ruben. I can't say it's been a pleasure."

"What are you going to do?"

"Eventually? Die. Between now and then, focus on trying to stay alive."

Which was a sound plan.

Damiola returned to the lodging house in Bow, cramming every last thing of worth he owned into the battered traveling chest, intending to be out of there, out of the city, and away before dawn.

The flaw was always going to be one of the random factors he hadn't foreseen, like the knock at the door.

"Come in," he called, looking over his shoulder as he hid the last of his journals beneath the folds of a shirt so it couldn't be seen by prying eyes.

Mrs. Hogarth opened the door.

She had a face like a week-old washcloth and a personality to match, but her rooms were cheap and clean. "Visitor, Mister Damiola," she said, standing aside to let the newcomer in. "I'll be downstairs if you need me."

"Please don't trouble yourself, we'll be just fine," the newcomer said, closing the door behind himself before the landlady could protest.

"Isaiah," Damiola said. Isaiah Lockwood. Seth's younger, and in many ways nastier, brother who was the heir to the empire now that Seth was gone. Isaiah Lockwood was also the man who loved the girl his brother had just disappeared into Glass Town with. Families, there was nothing more screwed up than them.

"Where are they?"

"Gone."

"That's not a good enough answer, Cadmus. I'll ask you again, where are they?"

"Gone," Damiola repeated. "I can't say it more plainly." He started to rise, holding his hands out, palms to the newcomer to show there was nothing up his sleeve.

"Bring them back!"

"There's no coming back from where they are," the magician said.

"I don't believe you. No road is one-way. That's not how it works."

Damiola looked up toward the wardrobe door, wondering if it might not be possible to show the young man and just be done with it. The boardinghouse was on the outskirts of what had been—until a couple of hours ago at least—Glass Town. Not that anyone here would remember it in the morning. It would simply be as if the streets had folded in on one another, effectively sealing the place away, the joins along the seams invisible. But for a few moments at least, perhaps he could open a window of sorts into the fast-disappearing Glass Town? He opened the wardrobe doors, standing between them, and began the invocation, barely vocalizing the words. Isaiah was across the room and at his shoulder in the silence between two heartbeats, arriving in time to catch a fast-failing glimpse of Glass Town through the doors. "See for yourself."

Isaiah pushed past him, rushing headlong into the closet as though it really were a door into another realm—only to be hurled bodily back and sent sprawling across the threadbare carpet of the lodging room floor. The air stank of magic. People had forgotten what magic smelled like; they assumed the overpowering aromas of freshly mown grass and the sickly sweet scent of baking pastries were just that, not understanding that they were sensing the last lingering traces of magic in the city.

Isaiah tried to scramble back to his feet, but his legs betrayed him.

The wardrobe was just a wardrobe once more; the fleeting glimpse he had caught of Eleanor Raines in her red dress burned onto his mind's eye forever. Isaiah stared at the wooden boards at the back of the closet and at the last items of clothing still hanging there, waiting to be stuffed into the magician's traveling chest.

"What did you do?"

What had he done? That was the question that was going to plague Damiola for the rest of his life, no matter how long or short a time that might end up being.

"What I had to," he said.

"What was that place in there? Hell? Is she dead?"

"To you, yes."

"No." Isaiah shook his head. "I won't accept that. I can't accept that. There must be something you can do. She was just here. I *saw* her."

"She's gone," Damiola said again, not unkindly. He offered a hand for the younger man to take, then helped him up. "Even if you could walk through that wardrobe door into Glass Town, you'd never end up *when* she is, even if you made it to *where*. The best thing you can do is just accept that as the truth and move on with your life. I know it sounds callous, but frankly we're both men of the world, and this is nothing more than a painful lesson: sometimes the bastards win."

That was when Isaiah drew the gun, a snub-nosed British Bull Dog. The piece was old but lovingly maintained. An heirloom from the Great War. Isaiah could smell the grease that had been used to oil the barrel recently. He was shaking—part in anger, no small part in fear. The pocket revolver had an effective range of fifteen yards. They were less than five feet apart. It would be more than effective when it came to ending the magician. "On your knees," Isaiah demanded.

Damiola sank slowly to his knees, careful not to make any sudden movement. He didn't want the young man's itchy trigger finger making a mess on the carpet if it could be helped.

He put his hands on his head and laced his fingers.

He felt the cold steel of the barrel press against the back of his head, just beneath his fingers. For a moment he thought about trying to wrench the gun from Isaiah's hand but before he could, the young man said, "I'm going to ask you again, bring her back. And if you can't do that, then open that doorway again so I can get to her."

Damiola could have lied. He could have made all sorts of promises to buy time to save his life, but for a man who made a career of deceit he couldn't bring himself to conjure up even a half-truth.

"It doesn't work like that. I can't just open a doorway. Glass Town is gone. It's history."

"It was just here!"

"And now it's not."

"I don't believe you. It's just a trick. An illusion."

"It's the single greatest feat of magic performed on this soil in centuries," Damiola said. It sounded like a boast. It wasn't. It was a fact. Magic had long since left England, lost with the arrival of concrete and steel and the revolutions of agriculture and industry. "Believe me, it's more than just a trick."

"What if I kill you? What then? Does your magic die with you? Is that how it works?"

"Pull the trigger, it won't change anything," the magician said. "I can't help you. She's gone."

Isaiah did as he was told.

"All right," Eddie said, sitting cross-legged at the circle's edge, "watch the mirrors. He'll show up inside one of them."

Faust paced around the outer rim of the warded circle. He lit the charcoal disks in the brass braziers. Before he was halfway around the circle the scent of sandalwood and the uglier aftertaste of wormwood filled the small room, conjured by the plumes of gray smoke.

"Why four, why not one?"

"To *keep* him inside. He can run, but the only place he's going is to another glass trap. Better to be safe than, well, I had one get out, once. Trust me, once was enough. You don't dick around with the dead unless you're toting some major juju."

"They call that a learning experience," Faust said.

Eddie wasn't arguing. He put his palms on his knees, upturned, and closed his eyes. "Just shut up and let me do this."

"Sure," Faust said, lingering at the edge of the room. "I'll be a right little church mouse. Pretend I'm not here."

But Eddie wasn't listening. His voice dropped to a breathless whisper, so soft it took a moment for Faust to make out the fact that he was calling Damiola's name. Again, and again, slowly rocking back and forth as he cast the name into the void, sending his words in search of the long-dead magician. He listened for an answer. Faust wasn't a fan of messing around with the dead. It had a whole *Pet Sematary* vibe to it. This guy had been gone for a long time. There was no knowing what that did to a man's mind. Even if Eddie found him, would there be enough of Damiola left inside his shade to actually treat with?

The smoke from the braziers thickened, twisting and knotting in the air like gray velvet streamers. It curled around the magic circle, becoming a veiled curtain, reflected endlessly in the standing mirrors.

The flesh of Faust's arms prickled, fine hairs standing on end, the room awash in static electricity. He felt something else, too; a gust of elemental power that left his spine crackling with pinprick fires. In his mind's eye he saw a room in a boardinghouse, a man on his knees, gun pressed to the back of his head, a chill wind blowing through the open doors of an old closet like they were cemetery gates. The intensity rose, pressure building relentlessly inside his skull, pressing on the plates of bone, crushing down on them, as though a tornado suddenly filled the room, the barometric pressure of it threatening to cave his skull in even as the incense smoke gyred and whirled, faster and faster—

"*Fuck it,*" Eddie suddenly snapped. "He's not there. I tried. Believe me. I looked in places no living soul should ever look. We're talking haunted dreams for the rest of my life, but I couldn't get a lock on his spirit."

The energy dissipated, the crackles fizzling and sizzling out like a damp squib.

"I'm sorry." Eddie sagged. "I tried, but the dead have never heard of him—"

"Eddie," Faust said, his eyes riveted on the thinning cloud of smoke.

"There's something wrong when the dead don't know you . . . It's like he's hidden from them."

"*Eddie*," Faust repeated. "You might want to open your fucking eyes, my friend."

The smoke curled lazily away from a dark shape at its core, a thousand snakes of shadow coiling around the figure of a man—no luminous spirit, but flesh and blood—kneeling in the middle of the magic circle. He had his fingers laced behind his head, waiting for the bullet that would end his life. It was as though he'd been torn out of Faust's vision from moments before.

"Okay, that," Eddie said slowly, unable to take his eyes off the kneeling man who had just materialized in the circle, "is *not* supposed to happen."

Cadmus Damiola unlaced his fingers, slowly, and looked around the room, unable to mask his confusion. He saw Faust and asked, "Am I in Hell? Or is this place . . ." He could barely bring himself to say it, and given the state of the room Faust couldn't exactly blame him. "Heaven?"

"Neither, maybe both, depending if your luck is in or not," Faust said. Damiola obviously didn't understand the joke. "Las Vegas."

The magician didn't look any the wiser.

"It didn't exist when you died. Or . . . more accurately, when you *didn't* die. Tell me, what's the last thing you remember, before you showed up here?"

"The barrel of a gun pressing into the back of my head, on my knees, waiting for the bullet . . ." Damiola felt the back of his skull and the obvious lack of a hole. "He couldn't have missed, it's impossible, not from that distance. So he killed me and I ended up in this Purgatory."

"What year is it, right now, this second?"

"Nineteen twenty-four."

Eddie pushed himself up to his feet and began anxiously pacing around the edge of the circle, wringing his hands. "Aw shit, man. Shit. This is *bad*. Shit. This is really bad. Faust, we didn't grab his spirit, we grabbed *him*. Just before he was supposed to take a bullet."

"Then I guess it is his lucky day."

"Jeez, Faust, don't you get it? We just completely fucked the space-time continuum. Who knows what happens now? A zombie horde out on the Strip? Aliens? Fuck it, man, we've completely changed the history of the world."

Faust walked over and offered Damiola his hand, pulling him to his feet on unsteady legs.

"I wouldn't worry about it," Faust told Eddie.

"Wouldn't worry about it?" He spun around to face Faust, his face a mix of panic and manic fear, as if the ax had just come slamming through the door and Jack was poking his grinning face through the wound. "When you fuck with time the Nazis *win* World War Two and everything we know and love unravels. Happens *every* time. We're gonna look out of that window and there's gonna be, like, a swastika flapping in the wind."

"And Hitler riding a dinosaur," Faust said with a wry grin. "You'll have to forgive my friend," Faust told Damiola. "He's watched too many B movies. Curse of a misspent youth. I'm Daniel Faust, by the way. And to answer the question I know you're burning to ask, I'd guess you're about ninety years past your sell-by date."

Damiola took a halting step backwards, shaking his head. "Ninety years? How is that even possible? Or—" Something seemed to occur to him. "Perhaps it is. Your friend here has the medium's gift, doesn't he? That would make sense. I'd been immersed in the flow of time. Up to my elbows in it, having just brought the halo into place, slowing the passage of time within Glass Town, effectively lifting it out of time . . . It is conceivable, and judging by the fact that I am here now, likely, that your friend's call reached me while there was still the residue of that great working in my bones . . ."

"Presto!" Faust said. "Excellent timing, too."

Damiola didn't disagree, pun or not. Instead he considered his next words carefully, not sure he wanted to know what the future had in store for him. Curiosity won out. He said, "You know my name. Does anyone else? It is hard to believe that the world has not moved on so much that the subtleties of my art no longer entertain the masses."

Faust just smiled.

"Eddie," he said, "do you still drive that shitbox Toyota?"

"Yeah, why?"

"Give me your keys. I think a nice evening drive might be enlightening."

And that was how Daniel Faust ended up walking on the Las Vegas Strip at midnight with a man who should have been a ghost. That was the joy of the witching hour. Anything was possible.

Damiola stared up, wild-eyed, in the canyon of blazing light. It was all so garishly bright, a world of neon that probably looked closer to Hell than any of the old masters' renditions did. He grabbed at Faust's sleeve and pointed up at a dizzyingly impossible structure ahead of them with his other hand.

"That . . . is a *pyramid.*"

"It most certainly is, though not exactly authentic. No slaves were harmed during its construction, though it probably cost more than Giza. See that spotlight at the top? Believe it or not, you can see that from outer space." He paused. "Oh yeah, there's that, too. We go to outer space now. Or we did. It's been a while since anyone walked on the moon, but we just got some pretty awesome photos from Pluto the other day. Interesting times."

Damiola turned in place, trying to take it all in, but there was so much to see, and all of it utterly unlike the London of the 1920s he'd left behind.

"And this was all built in a desert?"

"Middle of the Mojave," Faust assured him.

On the corner, a crew of guys in loud orange shirts that read GIRLS TO YOUR ROOM—CALL NOW handed out tiny slips of cardboard. Damiola reached out, taking one without thinking, and blinked at the photograph.

"This woman," he said. "This is . . . indecent."

"Indeed it is."

"How can it be allowed? There must be laws . . ."

"You can get anything you want in Vegas. Anything. Which brings me to the important part of our nocturnal perambulation."

Damiola followed Faust up an escalator to a fenced walkway that crossed over Las Vegas Boulevard. Below, an endless snarl of taxis inched by, adding their flickering brake lights to the symphony of neon.

"Take a look up there," Faust said, pointing to a distant tower. It blazed cherry in the dark, lighting up the desert from half a mile away. "You see that billboard taking up the entire side of the hotel? About twenty stories high?"

"How could I miss it?"

"Those two guys in the gray suits? They're magicians. They've got a whole custom-built theater, just for their act. I think they cleared around twenty million dollars last year."

"I assume that is a lot of money even in this new world?"

"It really is. And up there." Faust pointed to a closer billboard, almost as big, on the side of a tower lit in emerald green. "That guy in the poet shirt? Also a magician. Not a particularly skilled one, if you ask me, but he owns his own private island, so what do I know? Across the boulevard; the douchebag with the open vest and the gold chains? Him too, unfortunately."

He threw his arm around Damiola's shoulder and took in the chaos of the Strip with a slow sweep of his hand. "We're in the entertainment capital of the world, my new friend," he said. "A man-made town where you can get *anything* you want. And do you know what people want? *Magic.* To answer your question, the art is most certainly not dead, Cadmus. People might not remember your name, but your legacy is very much alive and kicking and that's what counts, right? But here's the thing," Faust added, "this might all be going away. Soon. I need something from you, to make sure that doesn't happen. That's why you're here. This whole happy accident isn't exactly accidental."

Damiola turned to face him. "What do you need?"

"Okay, don't say no, just hear me out, I know what magicians are like with their tricks. I've been looking for the Opticron, but it's been a pretty joyless quest. I'm pretty sure it hasn't survived the ninety years since you made it, but given that was pretty much yesterday for you, I'm hoping you'll show me how to build a new one."

By way of answer, Damiola gazed up at the billboards.

"Are you quite sure that's what you want?" After a moment's thought Faust nodded. "Well, then, with the caveat of being careful what you wish for, I think that I can help you."

They headed back to Eddie's place. Faust expected to find him stretched out on the couch, belt fastened around his bicep, on the nod again.

He wasn't.

Eddie—eyes every bit as feverish as when he was wasted—stood at the temple door, back pressed to the wood as it *thumped* against him. Each blow forcing it an inch wider, but mercifully not wide enough for whatever was in there to escape.

"What's back there?" Faust said, striding across the room to lend his weight to Eddie's struggle.

"*He* is." Eddie nodded at Damiola. His hands stretched out across the door, clawing at the varnish for purchase. "Or something *like* him, dressed in his skin. It came out of one of the mirrors."

"Open it up."

"Are you out of your fucking mind?"

Faust sighed. A handful of playing cards leaped from his hip pocket, riffling into his open palm.

"Sound mind and body," he said. "Now get out of the way and let the big boys play."

Eddie did as he was told. He stepped away from the door, only for it to slam into his back as he tried to get out of the way. The thing that emerged from the temple *was* Cadmus Damiola, there was no mistaking the similarities, but it was a Cadmus Damiola handcrafted by a blind and idiot god. Its features were crude, misshapen in all the wrong ways, everything a half inch off the mark or skewed on an angle as though the magician had suffered a stroke. The big difference was its runny-egg eyes. There was nothing back there but a mindless, animal rage as it charged from the doorway, hungry for the blood of the Damiola it might have been.

Two cards shot from Faust's hand, carving into the creature's chest and neck, and biting deep. The cards drew spurts of yellow ichor, but the beast didn't slow down. There was a weird moment as the creature put one foot in front of the other and seemed to step out of their reality, the air around it sizzling and stinking of burning celluloid, and then it was back in the here and now and barreling into Faust like a freight train. The impact slammed him, the beast's weight and momentum sending Faust sprawling across the floorboards, and then it was on him, drooling spittle from jagged teeth as it went for his throat.

Faust fought for his life, fingers digging into the deformed Damiola's face as he tried to gouge its eyes out. "A little help," he said. He might just as easily have been asking if anyone had a spare cigarette.

"I'll save you!" Eddie shouted, like a kid playing super-heroes. He took a swing, giving it his best shot, which in this case was a heroin needle to the back of the neck. The needle dangled uselessly.

"Maybe something a little sharper, like a fucking *knife*, Eddie," Faust grunted. "You're not trying to get the bastard addicted."

"Right, right, yeah." Eddie rushed out of sight. Faust could hear him rattling around in the kitchen looking for something sharp, turning drawers out desperately. Faust's arms burned with pain as he pushed back against the crea-ture's impossible strength. The teeth inched closer to his skin. There was no way he could hold it off much longer.

Damiola—the real Damiola—kicked over Eddie's arm-chair, wrenching against one of the wooden legs until it came away in his hands, all the while mumbling to him-self. "Time echoes. Some lesser part of me, caught up in the timestream in my wake. Echoes all the way down through ninety years of possibilities. Ninety years of almost me's. Which likely means . . ." He didn't need to say what it meant, Faust got it. He was a quick learner when he needed to be. It meant bad shit.

In the temple, beyond the open doorway, a slick black arm glistening with the mucus of some weird afterbirth slowly pushed its way out of another mirror as another de-formed alternative Damiola that had never been clawed its way into their world.

Faust twisted around under the beast, looking to his left as Eddie ran back from the kitchen nook, brandishing a pizza cutter like it was Excalibur.

"Eddie," he said through gritted teeth, "you . . . are . . . an . . . *asshole*."

Eddie looked at the pizza cutter, winced, and ran back into the kitchen in search of a bigger, sharper blade.

Damiola stumbled over to the mêlée, raising the wooden chair leg high, and swung for the fences. It crashed down on his double's head, crunching bone. A second blow every bit as brutal as the first sprayed the floor with more of that yellow ichor that passed for the doppelgänger's blood.

Faust shoved the twitching creature off of him, wiping his drenched face with his sleeve.

"I owe you," he said, grabbing a chair leg of his own just in time to see the second doppelgänger come slathering and sliding from the doorway, and behind it the shadows of a third, starting to emerge from the mirror. There were more black spots in the distance, clawing their way toward the glass that divided the worlds.

The two men stood side by side, chair legs in their hands, looking at the stuff of the pit crawling toward them.

"Stupid question: how many of these things are there?" Faust grunted, taking the moment's respite to catch his breath.

Damiola's answer wasn't exactly comforting. "The echoes of time are recursive."

"I have no idea what that means."

"Our enemy is infinite."

"Oh, just fucking great! So we stand here forever with our sticks in our hands, beating off these fucked-up versions of you until we're overrun or die of old age?"

"There's an alternative," Eddie said, coming back into

the room. "We break the mirrors, we get rid of every reflective surface in the temple where the summoning happened, and hope they can't find a way through."

"You were doing great right up until the word *hope*," Faust said. "But given the lack of alternatives, I say what the hell, let's pretend we're the Rolling Stones and smash this place up."

"There's a problem, though."

"Of course there is," Faust said. "Go on, what is it?"

"Without the original mirrors there's no way we can send him back. He's stuck here."

"And if we did send him back, he'd go right back to that second we snatched him from, right?"

"Right," Eddie agreed, fingers twitching like they were playing out a concerto on some invisible piano. Admittedly, it was probably heavy with the minor keys, filled with menace, like the theme from *Jaws*.

"So that's your choice, big guy." Faust turned to Damiola. "We shatter the mirrors to stop an infinite number of fucked-up versions of you swarming out and overwhelming Las Vegas, eventually the whole West Coast, then the world, or we don't, and we send you back to the split second before you got your brains blown out back there in 1924. What do you say? Ready to live in the brave new world?"

The third Damiola dragged itself into the room. The muscles of its twisted body were so deteriorated it couldn't stand. The fourth was halfway out of the mirror by now, the glyphs that Eddie had drawn into the floor glittering as the slime of its birth into the Prime Material splashed on them.

"There is no choice," the real Damiola said. "I have spoken with the dead and they all tell me the same thing, this life is a fine place to be compared to the alternatives."

"Amen to that," Faust said. "Okay, let's do this thing."

Side by side the three of them charged the doppelgängers, but as Faust and Eddie hurled themselves at the flesh-and-blood monstrosities, Damiola went for the glass, shattering the first mirror with a huge clubbing blow that fractured the glass into a spider's web of cracks where each crack offered a glimpse of the little black spot that was his time echo clawing its way toward ungodly life. If there'd been a single moment when he'd feared he was making a mistake, that he should have welcomed death instead of fighting grimly to stay alive, those thousands of tiny reflections of Hell crawling toward him banished it. Behind him he heard the sickly wet smack of Faust beating a version of himself to a bloody pulp, the wooden chair leg slamming into the meat of the doppelgänger's limp form until all that remained of its unnatural life was an autonomous muscular twitch.

Damiola shattered the second mirror and the third, closing the circle. He faced himself in the last one. The entire left side of his reflection's face was a mess of corruption, maggots worming away beneath the skin to make it ripple with revolting fluidity. Damiola reached out, laying his palm flat against the glass. He didn't shatter it, not at first. First he said a prayer for all of those versions of himself that would never, could never, be.

Then he destroyed the final mirror.

Two months later. Christmas Eve in Sin City. It was hard to be holiday-festive in a town that was *always* festive, but they gave it their best shot. You could find the occasional drunken Santa Claus cavorting with showgirls, and strands of Day-Glo lights dripping from the fronds of palm trees. Faust wasn't in a holiday mood. For a start he was down the price of a plane ticket to London, along with a bogus passport and a little pocket money to make sure Damiola got wherever he was going. He couldn't understand why the guy would want to leave the land of opportunity, but he figured that if he was in Damiola's shoes, he'd want to check out his old neighborhood, too.

When Faust arrived at Eddie Sunday's door, he wasn't carrying a Christmas present. He had a gun, though, holstered under his jacket, with a round in the chamber and the safety off.

He knocked, for the third time, and was weighing his options when a door up the hall creaked open. An elderly woman, her hair done up in plastic curlers, poked her head out.

"Are you the police?"

Faust tilted his head at her. "Just a friend. Why?"

"I called those jerks an hour ago. You'd *think* they'd show up by now, but no. Your 'friend' was screamin' his head off in there, so loud I couldn't hear my shows. This is a decent building, with decent people. I should be able to watch my shows without junkies bothering me."

"Sorry, ma'am," Faust said. "I'll take care of it."

She wagged a finger at him. "See that you do! I pay good money to live a quiet life here, I don't need no stupid addicts ruining my shows . . ."

She slammed the door. He dipped his fingers into his inside breast pocket, and fished out his lock picks.

He'd lost count of the amount of times he'd faked out a set of tumblers—better ones than these—who better to break in than a magician? The answer, three seconds later as the lock rolled over and clicked, was no one.

Eddie's door groaned open.

No lights in the room beyond save for the glow from the three-foot neon cross. Faust stepped into the gloom, silhouetted in pumpkin orange. He gently shut the door behind him.

"Eddie?" he called out, edging toward the temple door on the far side of the room.

He expected the worst. It was in the air, thick, heavy, cloying. He wasn't big on portents or premonitions and stuff, but he really didn't want to open that door. There were some doors, once opened, you could never close again. That temple door felt like one of them.

Faust pulled his gun, holding it easy at his side.

He could hear something, a faint ticking noise. For one sickening second he remembered that third grotesque Damiola that had come crawling out of Eddie's mirror, and the way it had moved, lurching and phasing in and out of this dimension into whatever parallel world they'd opened dragging the magician here. That sound, that flicker, like a projector at the end of a reel, celluloid slapping metal in an endless droning whir, was unmistakable. It was like the wings of a cockroach, right next to your ear.

Faust braced himself, ready to face whatever hellion waited on the other side of the temple door.

"Eddie?" Faust said, a little louder this time. "Stop dicking around, man. Are you here?"

Aside from the *slap-slap-slap* of the film reel, the rasp of his own breath was the only other sound in the apartment. It wasn't exactly a reassuring symphony.

The door to the temple swung open.

It was all he could do not to pull the trigger and put a bullet into the wood.

Eddie stood in the doorway, white light at his back, orange neon washing over him from the cross on the wall, the mingled colors turning his tear-stained face into a ghoulish mask of pain.

He looked like shit.

He had a pistol, too, a fat .45 automatic hanging limp in his hand. The way he glared at Faust, anger cutting through the tears, made Faust wonder if Eddie might be crazy enough to pull the trigger.

"Why did you make me do it?" Eddie asked.

"Do what?" Faust said, even though he already knew.

They leveled their guns in unison, neither man pulling the trigger, dropping a dead aim as they squared off from ten feet away. The neon cross, at Eddie's side, flickered and hummed.

"Why did you make me build it?" Eddie said. "You knew. You *knew* what would happen if I built it. You knew, Faust, you fucker. You knew."

"Sure I did. Once-in-a-lifetime opportunity, Eddie. You don't let them pass you by. You just don't. Even when you know the risks. That's what makes them worthwhile. Put the gun down, Eddie. I'm not here to hurt you."

"Bullshit, Faust. You already *did*," Eddie spat. "Why didn't you stop me? Why didn't you save me?"

The gun dropped, limp in Eddie's fingertips as he clawed at his tangled hair with his other hand. There would be no more killing here, natural or supernatural. Faust lowered his own weapon.

"Simple," Faust told him. "I didn't want to. In case you haven't heard, the Vegas underworld's been blowing up these last couple of months. Literally. I couldn't go toe-to-toe with the mob, protect my investments, and build the Opticron at the same time. Sometimes in this life you have to use people to get what you want. I knew you wouldn't let me down, Eddie."

Eddie laughed. A hysterical bark, tinged with grief. "This was supposed to be my redemption," he said. "My comeback: Eddie Sunday, two-point-oh! I could do it just like Damiola did. Couldn't you imagine it? Me, back in my white three-piece suit and hundred-dollar haircut, touring the country with my very own Opticron? I used to pack tents with fire and brimstone; just imagine what I could do with *that* thing. They'd come from miles around, and they'd pay. Not to see wonders, but to *know*. To know what's coming. Because we're all afraid of the future, Faust. That's the human condition. And that's the Opticron's power. Certainty. Sweet, blissful certainty. Even bad news is better than the fear of not knowing."

Eddie paused a moment. He shook his head. "That's what I thought, before tonight. Stupid. Fucking *stupid*. All I wanted was my old life back. Was that so wrong?"

"You can't go back in time, Eddie. Only forward. Time's an arrow."

Eddie's lips twisted in a grimace.

"So you came here to kill me and take the Opticron?" Eddie nodded at Faust's gun.

"I was just going to take it from you. I don't think I need to get violent, do I?"

Eddie swept his arm back toward the temple door like a carnival barker.

"Go ahead. Take it. You're more than fucking welcome, Faust. Gaze into the abyss. No one deserves that shit more than you."

Faust took a step forward. "You finished it? It really works?"

"It works. I wish it didn't. But it works. I saw the future, Faust. Just . . . just a couple of years from now. I wanted to know . . . just a couple of years into the future, not much could change, but maybe I could? Maybe I could fix myself."

The orange neon hummed and popped, filling the sudden gulf of silence between them.

"Eddie," Faust said, "what did you see?"

"I've been wondering something, tonight. Do you think I'm going to Hell when I die?"

Faust shrugged. "Man, not my place to even *guess*. You're no angel, sure, but if you look at some of the shit we're supposed to go to Hell for, then pretty much everyone in this place is going down. Believe what you want to believe, worry about what you want to worry about, but mainly save that shit for your deathbed. Don't let it fuck with the here and now."

"I've done some bad stuff," Eddie said, not listening to him. "Broken a shit ton of commandments. Never killed anybody, but I've stolen things. I've lied. Adultery? I've dabbled. I know I've hurt people. You go to Hell for that stuff. That's what the Book says, doesn't it?"

"It says a lot of things," Faust agreed. "Pretty sure it advocates stoning a guy for fucking your goat, which, come to think of it, sounds like a perfectly valid response. Why?"

Eddie chuckled. Then the chuckle became a trembling laugh, his shoulders shaking. Faust saw the tears track down his cheeks.

"I saw the future, Faust. I saw what happens next. I wish to fuck I hadn't. I was wrong. The fear of uncertainty is a gift. Not *knowing* is a gift. Because now I've seen the future." The gun swung up. He pressed the barrel to the side of his head. "I'll take Hell. Hell is better."

Eddie pulled the trigger and painted the neon cross in wet scarlet as his body tumbled to the floor. It was over in half a second, before Faust could move to stop him.

Eddie Sunday lay dead at his feet. Another casualty, another life snuffed out in Daniel Faust's wake, another name for the bill he'd eventually have to pay. Whatever horrors Eddie had witnessed in that temple, he'd take them to the grave and beyond. Faust felt like he'd been submerged in ice water. Cold. Cold as the desert night, and numb at the edges.

Only one thing left to do. He stepped over Eddie's corpse, and into the temple.

Eddie had built the new Opticron into the shell of a dollhouse, much as Damiola had described the original. It was perched on a three-legged stool. A dirty white sheet, tacked up on one wall, provided a screen for Eddie's last movie. Now it only flickered white, a dead beam strobing through one of the dollhouse's many windows. Faust knew how it worked. Each window offered a different angle of the world. He'd lied when he'd called time an arrow. That was just how we perceived it. It was much more complicated than that.

The house sat there, infused with the magic of possibility. He could feel it, like a living organism, urging him to reach inside, kindle its power, and see what Eddie had seen. It had worlds of wonder to show him. It had horrors unimaginable and all too real waiting to be exposed. It had lives not worth living waiting to be thrown into stark relief on the white sheet.

Eddie had called fear of the future the human condition. Fear of uncertainty. It was that same uncertainty that kindled hope, that sparked imagination and endless dreams of *what might be*. And here was the Opticron, promising to take that all away. To show him exactly what was coming for him—and for the entire world—in a few short years. It was tempting. Forewarned was forearmed. The machine might show him a crucial clue, or insight into the nature of his enemy. It was what he had wanted—what he needed.

But more than any of that, he needed his hope. He knew what he had to do.

A snow-white Audi Quattro idled at the curb outside the tenement. Faust climbed into the passenger's seat.

The woman behind the wheel, her long hair braided into a scarlet twist, looked his way as she tugged the gearshift.

"I heard the shots," she said in a faint Scottish brogue. "Did you find the answers you were looking for?"

Faust stared straight ahead, into the dark.

"Yeah," he said. "I got my answers."

"How much time do we have?"

"We've got tonight," he said.

"And tomorrow?"

The Audi pulled away from the curb, and the city darkness swallowed them whole. Headlight beams blazed against the night, doing their best to push back the shadows.

"We'll see," he said. "We'll see when we get there."

Pig Roast

JOSEPH NASSISE AND SAM WITT

"They called themselves the Devil's Swine, which, if you ask me, is pretty damned appropriate," Knight Commander Cade Williams said as he tossed a set of surveillance photos down on the conference room table for the other members of the team to examine.

The first several images were classic look-down shots most likely taken by a drone and showed a group of rough-looking men in leather vests and jeans moving down a stretch of highway astride motorcycles. The bikes were a mix of classic Harleys and custom choppers, the club emblem—a tusked boar—prominently displayed on several gas tanks as well as on the backs of the men's vests.

Cade went on. "Intelligence has been tracking these guys for months now, believing them to be responsible for the cross-country transportation and delivery of certain stolen artifacts moving from one group to another. Word is that they've just taken possession of a particular object known as the Eye of Horus, and we've been tasked with getting it back."

The next set of images were on-the-ground shots, taken by an undercover human operative with a long-distance lens. Surprisingly, they were grainier than the previous set of photos, making it hard to make out individual facial features despite the relative nearness of the subjects to the photographer. When Cade had first seen the photos his initial thought had been that someone should teach the photographer to clean his damn lens, but now he wasn't so certain it was the photographer's fault at all, given what he knew.

Cade's second in command, Master Sergeant Matt Riley, held up one of the photographs.

"What happened here?" he asked, turning the shot so that the other two men at the table, Sergeants Nick Olsen and Sean Duncan, could see as well. It was one of the aerial photographs and it showed the line of bikers coming around a bend and entering a thickly forested section of the roadway only to be swallowed up by a thick black mass covering two-thirds of the image. "Guy get his thumb in the way?"

"Not exactly," Williams replied, tossing a few more photographs onto the tabletop. All of them showed the same thing—a dark black mass and nothing more.

"Those pictures are why the four of us are sitting here right now," he said, as they looked through the images. "And before you ask, there was nothing wrong with the drone that took them. Tech has taken the camera off the drone and run it through every test imaginable. It works perfectly."

"Jamming, maybe?" Duncan asked.

Olsen, the stocky redhead who doubled as the team's sniper in addition to being its electronics expert, shook his head. "If it is, it's a type I've never encountered before." He turned to Cade. "Do we know the extent of the anomaly?"

Using the touch-screen keyboard set into the surface of

the conference room table, Cade called up a map of Missouri and displayed it via the wide-screen monitor hanging on the wall at the far end of the table. A section of the map in the corner of the state was highlighted in red.

"That," Cade said, pointing at the highlighted region, "is Pitchfork County, Missouri. A lovely little backwoods kind of place and home base for our motorcycle-happy friends. And, amazingly enough, it also happens to be one of the few places in the whole damned country where our surveillance equipment fails on a regular basis, even when there is nothing wrong with the equipment itself."

The others had been around long enough to pick up on Cade's sarcasm and read between the lines. There was something in Pitchfork County, something unnatural, and it was going to be their job to root it out while they dealt with the bikers and located the Eye.

The four men gathered in the room were members of the Order of the Poor Knights of Christ and the Temple of Solomon, otherwise known as the Knights Templar. Most of the world thought the Order had been destroyed in 1312 when Pope Clement V, in cooperation with King Philip IV of France, ordered its members forcibly arrested, tortured, and eventually burned at the stake. The two patriarchs had been after the Templars' vast wealth, but the treasury, as well as many of the Order's members, was never found and eventually disappeared into the mists of time and legend.

Cade and the others knew the truth, however. The Order had not disbanded but had instead gone underground, using their wealth to hide themselves away from the world while working to continue their sacred mission: protecting mankind from supernatural threats and enemies. When Hitler and his demonic allies had threatened the world in the 1940s, the Order had emerged from the shadows, reuniting with the organization that had given birth to it in the first place, the Catholic Church, and thrown all of its weight and power into the fight against the powers of darkness. In the wake of the Allies' victory, the Order became the de facto combat arm of the Vatican, continuing their mission to this very day.

Williams led the Echo Team, one of six special operations units within the Templar hierarchy, and was responsible for dealing with all supernatural activity in the U.S. They were supported by several mainline combat units, but Echo was the best of the best; when everything went straight to hell, they were the guys that got called to make things right.

Which brought them to today's briefing.

"We are to liaise with a guy on the ground by the name of Joe Hark. He knows his way around and we'll no doubt benefit from his knowledge of the locals, but we're to keep things as close to the vest as possible when dealing with him. The Preceptor was very clear. Priority number one is tracking down that biker gang and recovering the Eye before they have time to pass it on to its intended buyer. Priority number two is to make sure that the gang is no longer operational by the time we leave. If, and only if, we manage to accomplish those two objectives are we free to investigate anything that might be contributing to our inability to generate surveillance of Pitchfork County. We clear?"

The other three men nodded; they were veterans, they knew the drill.

On the other hand, they also knew their commander and not a single one of them had any doubt that he was going to do things his way, regardless of what the Preceptor wanted.

Such was life when working with the man the Templars called the Heretic.

Joe cupped his hands around the unopened can of Busch and let the chill soak into his palms. Though it was February, the temperature inside Smokey's House of Meat felt more like high summer than midwinter. The heat intensified the shack's accumulated reek from decades of smoke and spilled beer, but the burnt ends and pork ribs more than made up for that.

Joe hoped the New Englanders he was here to meet would feel the same way.

By the time a black Expedition rolled into the gravel parking lot, the unopened beer had slicked the Night Marshal's hands with a layer of condensation that had warmed to room temperature. Joe didn't wear a watch, but by his reckoning the city boys were more than a little bit late. He'd expected them for lunch and it was well on toward suppertime. He stood from the rickety oak table and hollered into the kitchen, "These boys are gonna be hungry, Smokey. Get 'em a couple racks of ribs and whatever burnt ends you can rustle up."

Joe headed out into the cold winter air, drying his hands on the thighs of his jeans as he went to greet his visitors. *They're looking for someone*, the Long Man had told Joe. *Show them around, keep them from poking their noses where they don't belong. Try not to start a fight.*

That last would be easier said than done. The men piling out of the Expedition looked like they'd seen more than their fair share of trouble and were expecting even more. They weren't displaying any obvious weaponry, which was a good first step, but their uniform gray coveralls didn't even try to hide the bulges and seams of the body armor it covered.

Joe grinned as he approached the team's obvious leader. The man wore an eye patch that covered his right eye and looked worn ragged and pissed, a combination that gave Joe pause. The Night Marshal stopped well back from the new-comers, giving them space. He shoved his thumbs into his front pockets to show them he meant no harm and said, "I reckon we've got two choices. We can tussle out here in the cold until we decide we're both on the same team and ought to work together or you fellas can get out of the cold and enjoy the best barbecue this side of Texas."

The eye-patched man kept right on scowling but jerked his head toward the door. "I don't know about you, but we missed lunch. Let's eat."

Cade didn't know what to make of the man they called the Night Marshal, but he had to agree this barbecue was something special. The five of them ate together in silence, tossing stripped rib bones onto a sheet of butcher paper in the center of the table.

Cade was irritated the trip had taken so long, and he couldn't help but feel the Night Marshal had given them inadequate directions as a way of putting the "city boys" in their place. They'd driven for hours trying to find the right combination of gravel back roads and potholed state highways to reach their destination, wasting time they couldn't afford to let slip through their fingers. But, as irritated as he'd been when they finally arrived, the barbecue had blunted the edge of Cade's temper. It was hard to stay pissed with a belly full of perfectly smoked pig meat.

He sampled one of the burnt ends, and the glazed chunk of blackened protein buried the last of his anger. It was rich and savory and sweet, like a piece of chewy candy forged from smoke and sugar and meat so tender it almost melted on his tongue. For a moment, all Cade could think about was how much he was going to miss this when he went back to Connecticut.

He needed to satisfy his curiosity, still. He sat back in his chair and stretched. "I had a hell of a time finding this place. If I didn't know better, I'd say someone didn't want us here."

The Night Marshal grinned, and Cade thought the expression would've looked more at home on a shark. "Maybe you don't know better. Pitchfork has a way of keeping outsiders where they belong."

Cade crossed his arms over his chest. "And where's that?"

"You know. Outside."

The Templar didn't want to give credence to the idea that somehow the land itself had conspired against them, but he didn't know how else to explain their trip into Pitchfork County. As soon as they crossed the county line the Expedition's navigation system lost its signal and every chance they had to take a wrong turn, they ended up taking it. A trip that looked like less than an hour on the map had taken them almost three to complete. "I guess it didn't get the job done. We're here now. Were you briefed?"

The Night Marshal nodded. "Bikers, charms, or some such bullshit, blah, blah, blah. Just another day in fuckin' paradise."

"That does about sum it up. Where do you want to start?" Cade was itching to get the case resolved and get the hell out of here. There was something about this part of the country that made him uneasy. The sooner he could get his team back to the Ravensgate Commandery, the better.

"Yeah, there's a few places we can hit up. You can ride with me, and your guys can follow us. Stick close. If you get lost, there's no telling where you'll wind up. I don't feel like spending all day rounding up lost ducklings."

Riley bristled at the Marshal's tone, but Cade checked him with a glance. "They're not going to get lost."

Joe gestured at the empty plates and the mound of bones on the table. "All right, then. Looks like everybody's fueled up, might as well get this party started."

There was something off about Cade, but Joe couldn't put his finger on it. It wasn't just his eye patch, or his scars, or the weirdo serial killer gloves. Joe'd never seen anyone eat ribs with gloves before. It was fucking unnerving. Whatever the weirdness was, it went bone deep. Joe figured he'd be able to get to the bottom of it by giving the Templar a supernatural once-over, but that seemed a little rude, so he decided to let it lie. He'd keep the conversation light. "You believe this is Left-Hand Path work?"

The Templar didn't respond at first, just stared out the window at the dense forest of leafless trees they were driving through. Then, "It's supernatural, I'll give you that. Perhaps even demonic. We'll find out soon enough."

Joe thought it over for a sec and then nodded. "Right. I forgot. You're Catholic," he said, as if that explained everything.

Which, in fact, it probably did.

He eased the truck onto a thin dirt trail, pumping his brakes to flash the taillights so the Expedition wouldn't miss the turn. He was impressed with the driver behind him; for someone not familiar with Pitchfork's roads, the man was doing a good job of keeping up.

The road wound deeper into the forest and climbed up the side of a hill. At the peak, Joe killed the truck's engine and turned to Cade. "We're going to have to hike a little bit, so we don't spook this guy. Just follow my lead, you'll be fine."

Joe grabbed his shotgun from the rack in the truck's back window and climbed out into the cold. The rest of the Templars were waiting at the front of the Expedition. Joe raised his voice to be heard over the winter wind and creaking branches. "The guy we want to talk to is down at the bottom of this hill. We'll walk the rest of the way in so he doesn't hear the cars and get spooked. I don't think we'll have any real trouble, but you might as well gear up. He's less likely to start shooting if we look like we're ready to shoot back."

Joe always thought he was a decent enough woodsman, capable of getting through the brush without raising a ruckus, but the Templars were damn near ghosts. He had to keep looking back to make sure they were still following him and always found them unnervingly close. Where his hobnailed boots made a trail of clear prints in the shallow snow, the city boys left faint tracks that would be hidden by the wind in a matter of minutes.

At the edge of the woods, Joe raised a hand to bring the Templars to a halt. From their vantage, they could see a rusted-out trailer with a makeshift shed grafted onto its side. He turned back to the Templars and drew them into a huddle so their voices wouldn't carry on the wind. "This guy knows bikers; he'll know where to find who you're hunting. But he used to be a meth cook. His brains are . . . well, he's not all there. He'll act tough and might get weird. Try not to put a bullet through his brainpan before we have a chance to talk to him."

And don't cut him in half with one of those fucking swords, Joe thought.

They crossed the open space between the forest and the trailer without incident. That made Joe more nervous than if the mad old bastard had come out onto his porch with a shotgun. Hyrum was permanently paranoid, and his lack of reaction to their presence was troubling.

Joe eased the shotgun off his shoulder and cradled it in both hands. He climbed up the short staircase and banged on the door with the shotgun's butt. At least he tried to bang on it—the first impact sent the door swinging inward.

Cade whispered from behind Joe, "Maybe he was expecting company?"

Joe rolled his eyes. Great. He'd teamed up with a sarcastic ninja from New England.

This is going to be a bad day.

Cade entered the house after the Night Marshal, with Riley and Duncan on his heels. His men swept to the left and right, covering the interior of the cramped trailer. Olsen stayed on the porch, eyes peeled for trouble. If he saw any coming, he'd put a bullet to the top of its head before it got within fifty yards.

The Templar didn't know what he'd expected, but this wasn't it. A circle of filth an inch deep covered the center of the room, its surface churned and dotted with flecks of pink and white. The stench was incredible, an earthy assault on his sense of smell. "So this is what it looks like when you don't have indoor plumbing."

The Night Marshal chuckled at that and shook his head. He pointed at the couch with a TV tray in front of it, the moldy remains of a frozen dinner resting on the plastic. "Even out here, folks don't shit where they eat."

Cade wrinkled his nose. "You think your guy pulled out and, what? Wild animals got in here?"

The Night Marshal nudged at the mess with the toe of his hobnailed boot. A filthy acorn cap rolled out in front of his foot. "Yes, on the wild animal part. I'm guessing pigs based on these acorns. No, on my guy pulling out."

The Templar looked around the place. There was a thin layer of dust on every surface and from the looks of the left-over food, no one had been there for at least a week. "So where is he?"

Joe jabbed a finger at a cluster of pink-tinged chunks half-buried in the filth. "You big-city folks would probably want a DNA test, but my gut tells me that my guy is right there. Or at least what's left of him."

Cade rubbed his jaw. "You have to be kidding."

"Nope, that's not a joke. Pretty sure that's Hyrum. Fuckin' pigs must've eaten him."

Duncan's stomach groaned in protest at the idea. Cade raised an eyebrow in their guide's direction. "You're telling me our lead was eaten by wild pigs?"

Joe shrugged. "I'm not telling you it's a coincidence. Someone knew you were coming and decided to tie up loose ends. They made it ugly to shut down anyone else who might consider being helpful and forthcoming when I paid 'em a visit."

Cade furrowed his brows. "Any idea where we go from here?"

Joe bared his teeth in a grim smile. "Yeah, but you're not going to like it."

The Templar frowned. "Mind sharing any more details?"

"Sure," Joe said as he headed for the door. "We're going to go and rustle some pigs."

Half an hour later the five men were lying on their bellies along a tree-shrouded ridgeline, peering down into the clearing on the other side where an old, abandoned slaughterhouse stood. After leaving Hyrum's place, Joe told them that he had an idea where the Swine might be operating from and had led them through a maze of backwoods roads only to arrive at a spot in the woods that looked to Cade like every other spot. The Night Marshal apparently knew where he was going, however, for after a fifteen-minute walk through the woods humping their gear with them on their backs, they arrived at the base of the ridge upon which they now lingered.

The two-story brick building had certainly seen better days, Cade noted. The glass had been broken out in most of the windows, graffiti-covered plywood having taken its place, at least on the lower floor. One section of bricks was stained black with soot, evidence of an earlier fire that had threatened to take the building down with it before it had been put out.

It wasn't so much the look but rather the feel of the place that set Cade's nerves on edge. It squatted there in the center of the clearing like a malevolent spider waiting to trap its prey, and even the air around it seemed to be tainted by its presence. He had expected a certain amount of emotional residue when Joe had told them they were headed for a slaughterhouse, but this was way off the charts.

There was something else going on here.

The first clue, of course, was the fact that the "abandoned" slaughterhouse was no longer abandoned. Several members of the Devil's Swine were hanging around in front of the place. Some were working on their bikes, while others sat around drinking beer and horsing about. All of them were armed in some manner or another; Cade could see an assortment of pistols, rifles, and shotguns being carried or lying within reach of their owners. Two men, both armed with M16s, stood about half a dozen yards away from the others, lackadaisically guarding the entrance to the only road that led into or out of the clearing.

The second was revealed when Cade triggered his Sight; that mystical ability he'd gained when the fallen angel known as the Adversary had tried to kill him, the very event that had prompted his entrance into the Order. His Sight let him see past the Veil and into the Beyond, the Purgatory-like plane between the lands of the living and those of the dead, and seeing the slaughterhouse through its lens revealed the dark heart of corruption that lurked somewhere within its depths. A gray-green miasma rolled off the place in waves, leaking from every opening like a thick fog that was pushing its way out from the inside, and Cade shuddered to think just how much black arts it had taken to taint the place so heavily.

If this wasn't the source of the electric jamming that was interfering with their surveillance, it was at least a contributing factor. If the Eye was anywhere in Pitchfork County, Cade suspected this would be the place.

A burst of movement among those in front of the building caught his attention and he turned to see a long white Cadillac coming down the access road. The guards moved out of the way and let the vehicle pass without stopping it and, given the way the bikers practically leaped to attention as the car pulled up in front of the slaughterhouse, Cade figured they were about to meet the Swine's head honcho.

Turned out he was right.

One of the bikers opened the rear door of the Cadillac and a man unfolded himself from the backseat. He was dressed in a dark suit that hung loosely on his thin frame and he stood several inches above the bikers around him; Cade put his height at six foot four or so, give or take an inch. The man was fish-belly pale and wore dark glasses, his bald head gleaming in the midafternoon sunlight.

The newcomer barked a few orders to the men around him and then headed straight for the door to the slaughterhouse.

Just before entering the building, however, the man paused, then turned and slowly looked up toward the ridgeline where Cade and the others were concealed.

For just an instant Cade felt as if a thousand insects were scurrying up his spine and into his brain, but then the feeling passed and the newcomer stepped through the doorway and disappeared into the depths of the building.

Have we been seen? Cade wondered.

They were under good cover and no one had even done so much as flinch when that guy looked in their direction, but that creepy-crawly feeling nagged at him.

Only one way to find out.

He signaled to the others and they moved back down the slope, where they could talk without risk of being seen or overheard.

"Who's the guy in the Caddy?" Cade asked, expecting Joe to have at least a passing familiarity with the dude, but the other man just shook his head.

"Never seen him before," he said, and from his tone it was clear that he wasn't any happier about his lack of information than the Templars.

"Anything we should know about the place before busting in?"

Rather than a quick reply, the Night Marshal gave the question some serious consideration before answering, something Cade respected. This guy knew his business, it seemed.

"This place was built just after the Civil War, so there's no telling what shape the interior is in. Watch where you put your feet; there are bound to be open drains and troughs all over the place in there and you might not see them clearly in the shadows."

Sound advice, Cade thought with a nod.

"All right, here's the plan."

Riley was a mere ten yards from the guards on the road and they still hadn't noticed him. He and Duncan were walking down the access road in plain view, but the guards were facing in entirely the wrong direction—back toward the slaughterhouse—and chatting loudly amongst themselves, which served to cover Riley's approaching footsteps.

Damned poor security, he thought. *If I'd wanted to gun them down I could have done it ten times already.*

But he wasn't here to do that, at least not yet. His Mossberg combat shotgun, his preferred firearm for close-in dirty work, was strapped to his back, easily reachable but currently out of sight of the men in front of him. He'd use it when the time came, but for now his mission was to delay rather than destroy.

He stopped walking and heard Duncan's footsteps come to a halt behind him a step later. Hoping the idiots in front of him wouldn't shoot them out of sheer surprise, he said a silent prayer heavenward and did what he'd come here to do.

"Ah, excuse me?" he called out tentatively.

The men jumped as if they'd been goosed with an electric cattle prod and spun around, the guns in their hands coming up in ragged surprise.

Riley held up both hands, palms out.

"Easy there, gents. Easy. Just need a little help, that's all."

To his relief the guards lowered their weapons toward the ground, apparently thinking Riley wasn't any kind of threat despite all the visual cues staring them in the face.

Thank God for blind arrogance, he thought.

"Get the fuck out of here," one of them said, waving the tip of his weapon to indicate that they should go back out the way they had come in.

Riley had no intention of doing that.

"Come on, now. Help a brother out, huh? My buddy and I were doing a little deer huntin' and our truck broke down a mile or so back. Just need to borrow a phone to call for a tow and I'll be out of your hair."

"Are you deaf or just dumb?" the other guard asked, scowling. "Turn around and get the hell out of here before we shoot your ass!"

The one on the right raised his gun again and Riley decided he'd given Cade and Joe time enough. He flicked his finger in the prearranged signal and was rewarded a split second later by the sight of the man's head exploding into pieces as a .50-caliber bullet from Olsen's Barrett sniper rifle moving at 2,700-plus feet per second tore through it with only the barest bit of resistance. The sound of the shot finally reached his ears but Riley was already in motion at that point, crouching down as he ripped his shotgun off his back, bringing it to bear on guard number two while he was still staring in horror at the decapitated body of his partner, who was only just now beginning to topple over.

Like fish in a barrel, Riley thought as he pulled the trigger and cut the other man down as quickly as the first.

Cade and Joe had moved past the stockyards and were crouched next to a plywood-covered window on the far side of the building when the sound of Olsen's shot rang out. Seconds later the air was filled with the sounds of gunfire as Riley and Duncan followed suit and the caught-with-their-pants-down bikers tried to respond.

It was the signal they'd been waiting for. Joe stood up, drew back a foot, and slammed it into the plywood, sending it bouncing away into the darkness beyond. He turned and gestured with a smile.

"After you, good sir."

Cade grunted in reply and slipped over the threshold, entering the old slaughterhouse with Joe at his heels.

The smell caught him first, a thick stench of death and decay that hung over everything like a wet blanket, and he had to force himself to keep from gagging. It wasn't just the scent of old death, either; this was fresh and close by somewhere. Whatever these guys were doing, it couldn't be good.

He gave himself a moment to let his eyes adjust and then, after a tap on the shoulder from the Night Marshal indicating he was ready to go, Cade led the way into the darkness.

They moved through room after room like a team that had worked together for years rather than two men who had just met. One of them would kick open a door, spinning to the left while the other went right, their weapons up and ready, but room after room met them with empty and open silence.

Where the hell is this guy? Cade wondered.

The bikers considered themselves to be badasses and maybe against the average Joe they actually were, but against the highly trained special operators of the Templar Echo Team, they were woefully unprepared and outclassed.

Riley's first shot took down guard number two and the man's corpse hadn't even hit the dirt before both he and Duncan were sprinting forward, firing at the bikers in front of the slaughterhouse as they came.

Normally crossing two hundred feet without cover while being fired upon would have gotten them quickly killed, but they had a few things going for them: training, surprise, and the fact that Olsen was currently causing chaos in the bikers' ranks as he took down one combatant after another from the safety of the ridgeline above.

By the time Riley and Duncan reached the protection of the Cadillac, the fight was all but over.

Things weren't going so well inside, however.

They found the leader of the gang in the next room they entered. Joe kicked open the door and Cade hustled in, the pistol in his hands searching for a target in the shadows, and then a set of floodlights came on with a loud click, bathing the room in their harsh brilliance.

What he saw in their light brought Cade up short.

The Templar commander was in a wide room with a dirt floor, facing a stage-like platform on which the Swine's leader currently stood, dressed in a robe stained nearly black with accumulated blood and wearing what Cade thought was a pig mask. Surrounding him on three sides were a dozen or more, well, demon-swine was the best reference Cade could come up with to describe them at the moment; large, misshapen creatures that looked like a cross between a human, a pig, and a demon or two—all snouts, dark beady eyes, and thick slabs of calloused flesh.

"Fuck me," Cade heard Joe whisper at his back and he found he couldn't agree more.

Fuck me was right.

Apparently the Swine's leader had seen them on the ridge.

Joe decided taking the offensive was the best move, for he stepped forward to stand beside Cade.

"We've come for the Eye, priest," Joe said. "Surrender it now and you'll be dealt with leniently. Make us take it from you and . . . well . . . ."

The pig-faced leader laughed in his face. "No, Night Marshal, the time for blind acquiescence has passed. I have no intention of surrendering my property, to you or anyone else. I rule here, not you. He told me you were coming, told me the Templar scum would be with you."

Without pause, the man turned and addressed Cade directly. "Tell me, Templar, how's that wife of yours?"

Joe said something in reply, but Cade didn't hear it. He was staring at the man on the stage in surprise, stunned by what he'd said.

How's that wife of yours?

Cade's wife, Gabrielle, had perished at the hands of a supernatural entity known as the Adversary several years before. It was the same creature that had attacked Cade and started him on the long path that eventually brought him to the Templars and put him in command of the Echo Team. He had been hunting the creature ever since. The fact that the pig-faced man in front of him knew anything about

Gabrielle suggested that the two, he and the Adversary, were in league with each other in some fashion.

Staring at the man, trying to make sense of it all, Cade suddenly realized something.

That's not a mask . . .

Cade didn't know who, or what, the man before them actually was, but there was no doubt in his mind that he was working for the other side, and that condemned him in Cade's mind as surely as if the Adversary was standing there on the platform beside him.

Enough screwing around, Cade thought. Without further hesitation he swung the weapon in his hand up toward its target.

Joe knew there was trouble the minute the porcine-priest revealed himself. This wasn't just some biker gang moving stolen artifacts as he'd been told. This was Left-Hand Path work, no doubt about it, and this guy was giving off vibes that said he had some serious mumbo-jumbo at his disposal.

Normally Joe was the type to crack some teeth first and ask questions later, but with the city boy beside him he thought it might be prudent to try to negotiate first. He'd barely started when he caught movement out of the corner of his eye and realized with a start that things were about to go from bad to worse.

Cade's first shot would have taken the priest right between the eyes if it hadn't been for the pig-demon standing beside him. The thing must have caught sight of Cade's gun coming up, for it flung itself forward just as the Templar pulled the trigger.

Dark blood and bits of brain matter splattered the face of the priest as the left side of the creature's head intercepted the path of the bullet, deflecting it from its intended target and sending the demon back to whatever hell it belonged in.

The body was still twitching when the priest pointed a finger at Joe and his companion and screamed, "Kill them!"

As one, the other pig-demons charged.

Joe's shotgun roared in response, taking down several of the vile creatures with a single shot while beside him he heard Cade's pistol blasting away. There were a lot of the damned pig creatures, but unlike other things he'd faced in the past at least these things could be killed with the application of a little well-targeted violence, and he intended to deliver quite a bit of that.

Within seconds the room was filled with the acrid scent of gunpowder, the stench of blood and feces, and the grunts and screams of dying pig-demons. When the creatures got too close for the men to use their firearms, they switched to melee weapons, Joe smashing skulls with the stock of his shotgun while Cade laid waste about him with the long sword he'd pulled out of the sheath on his back.

"He's getting away!" Cade shouted over the din and Joe glanced over the head of the pig-demon in front of him to see that the priest had torn open a door at the back of the platform and was in the process of disappearing through it.

Oh no, you don't, you bastard, Joe thought, and redoubled his efforts, forcing his way forward with a few final swings of his shotgun stock until there were simply no more demons left in front of him to fight.

"This way!" he shouted and rushed for the platform, slamming through the door the pig-headed priest had used and stumbling into a dusty, fly-specked office. He growled in frustration as the man dashed through another door on the far side of the room.

Sensing Williams at his heels, Joe charged through that door as well and into a narrow stairwell. A mélange of foul scents flowed up to meet them.

Cade grunted behind Joe. "Blood."

Joe sniffed, then added, "And pig shit."

The Night Marshal thundered down the steps, not even trying to be sneaky. If they didn't catch the priest before he rallied his supernatural defenses, they were fucked.

Crystals embedded in the stairwell's earthen walls shed pulses of asynchronous orange light, revealing flashes of the priest's back as he took the stairs two at a time.

Joe's hobnailed boots skidded at the bottom of the steps, slipping in a reeking froth of blood and mud and shit, frustrating his pursuit. He could see the priest's filth-stained robes as the man fled down an earthen tunnel, but Joe was gaining ground.

They passed arched openings as they hauled ass down the tunnel after the priest. Joe glimpsed piles of bloody bones and rotting meat and tried not to look at the sigils that flared to life atop the mounds of carrion. The priest was up to something, and they were running out of time to catch him.

Joe put on a desperate burst of speed and his fingertips

brushed the priest's robes as they exited the tunnel into an enormous cavern. Then the priest was gone, hurling himself from a muddy ledge. Joe and Cade skidded to a stop at the edge and saw their quarry splashing through the slop at the bottom of a shallow, muddy pit. Shadow forms rippled through the slop around him, forming a protective phalanx of unseen threats.

Joe rubbed his jaw. "Flip you for it? Heads, you jump down into the shit and kill him. Tails, I stay up here and watch."

Cade grimaced. "I should've brought a rifle."

A chorus of enraged squeals demanded their attention. They turned to see a growing mob of monstrosities charging down the tunnel toward them. They had the heavy-jowled heads and pointed pink ears of swine, but their faces and bodies were mockeries of the human form. Rows of slick pink nipples ran down their torsos, and their hands and feet were sharp black hooves.

Cade hefted his sword. "Locals aren't very friendly, are they?"

Joe's face split into a shark's grin, and he raised his shotgun. "You just gotta get to know 'em."

Then the pig-demons were on them, screaming and gnashing their teeth as they closed in for the kill.

Cade met the lead pig-demon with a cross-body slash that opened it from shoulder to hip, emptying its innards onto the bloody floor. The creature's death squeals sent its brothers into a frenzy and Cade suddenly found himself surrounded by shrieking demons.

He hacked a hoofed arm off one of his attackers, then pivoted to rip the tip of his long sword through the leg of another. He parried a hoof aimed at his head and counterattacked with a pommel strike that split the creature's muzzle to the bone.

Another attacker slipped through Cade's defenses and slammed its hooves into his back. The blow sent the Templar stumbling into another one of the pigs, which snapped yellowed tusks at his face. Before Cade could respond, there was a thunderous roar and he was covered with a thick coating of sticky gore.

The Night Marshal flashed a grin over the gushing stump of the demon swine's tattered neck before turning to blast a smoking crater in another monster's chest. Cade couldn't be sure, but it looked like Joe was enjoying this a little bit too much.

The monstrosities were clumsy fighters but they made up for their lack of finesse with numbers and raw strength. Cade's arms grew weary from the constant hacking and parrying. He'd lost count of how many of the things had fallen under his sword, but the numbers of those still standing never seemed to dwindle.

He tore the head from another of the beasts and once again found himself eye-to-eye with the Night Marshal. "Can't keep this up, they're wearing us down."

The Night Marshal responded by smashing in the face of a pig-demon with an elbow and slamming a fresh set of shells into his shotgun. "What's wrong, city boy? Arm getting tired?"

Cade growled and plunged his long sword into the heart

of another demon. The mob had pushed him and the Night Marshal almost back to the ledge. He glanced over his shoulders and ignited his supernatural Sight. The priest stood atop a pile of offal and bones, head thrown back, arms raised. Thrumming arcs of power surged up from the bloody ground to form a massive shape.

Cade grabbed the Night Marshal's shoulder and shouted, "We've got trouble."

Joe fired his shotgun into the oncoming horde, then glanced at Cade and asked, "What the—"

A shock wave of arcane energy blasted across the ledge and into the tunnel, tumbling the charging demons onto their backs. Cade had to brace himself with his sword to keep from falling over and saw the Night Marshal hunkering forward to do the same.

Cade turned toward the pit and felt his heart sink.

An enormous sow, easily twenty feet high at the shoulder, crouched in the center of the pit, smoking blood running down her snout and off her back. With a shrieking roar, she lowered her head and charged, murderous rage curling her lips back from enormous jagged teeth.

Cade raised his sword but knew that thing would run them down long before they could do enough damage to stop it. He and the Night Marshal were as good as dead.

Joe knew they were fucked. The pig-demons were regrouping after the shock wave knocked them on their asses and they'd be back in the fight in seconds. The hell-sow would reach the ledge before that, and he had no doubt she'd tear the damned wall down to get at him and the Templar.

He grabbed Cade by the shoulder and pointed at the charging giant. "Jump!"

Joe didn't wait to see if the Templar followed his advice. If they stayed put, they'd be crushed between the charging pig-demons and the sow behemoth. Their only hope of survival lay in getting off that ledge.

Joe's leap carried him over the giant sow's lowered head and onto her bristled back. His boots slid on the creature's bloody flesh and he crashed to his knees. His left hand grabbed a knot of wiry hairs that just saved him from sliding off the thing's back and under its trampling hooves.

Cade landed next to Joe and drove his long sword into the devil-sow's flesh to arrest his leap. Six inches of steel disappeared into the gargantuan pig's meaty shoulder. That got its attention.

The monster threw itself into the muddy ledge, crushing a handful of its demon-pig minions while attempting to dislodge its enemies. It squealed in hellish rage and shook itself with such force that Joe nearly lost his grip.

"That'll be enough of that shit," the Night Marshal snarled. He rammed the gaping barrels of his shotgun between two knobs of the hell-sow's spine and squeezed both triggers.

The shotgun's occult discharge split the air like a peal of thunder. Silver fire and acidic green smoke gushed from the shotgun and tore a blistered crater in the monster's back.

Its front legs folded underneath it and its blunt snout crashed into the filth-covered floor. It squealed like a piglet on its way to the slaughter, the sound clawing at Joe's ears and hammering at his sanity.

The Templar reared back and drove his blade into the exposed gristle of the demon-pig's spinal cord.

The blade sank home with a meaty thunk.

It should have been a killing blow, even against a creature of the sow's size. Instead, the mortal assault filled the beast with an unholy vigor.

The pig reared back onto its hind legs with such sudden violence that Joe found himself flying through the air, fist still clenched around a clump of bristly hairs.

Fuck, he thought, then slammed into the muck-covered ground.

Cade hung on to his sword, but the weapon ripped free of the monstrosity's spine and he slid off the thing's back and into the blood and shit. He rolled on impact, which was the only thing that saved him from shattering both of his ankles.

He couldn't see the Night Marshal, and prayed his new ally wasn't dead or too wounded to carry on the fight. Cade had to figure out how to kill the damned sow without being crushed beneath the mammoth hooves that smashed down all around him.

He let his supernatural Sight slide into place as he dodged around a descending hoof. The missed attack splashed him with a foul mixture of gore and manure. Cade retaliated with a wild swing that gouged away a chunk of the beast's leg.

Blood burst from the wound, but so did a coruscating flicker of black light. It was there for the merest flash of a moment, but it showed Cade what he needed to know.

He threw himself away from the trampling devil-sow and slid on his chest and belly for a few yards. Then he scrambled forward, sprinting for the spot he'd seen the black light disappear into. He prayed he was right about this.

Because if he was wrong, he'd be dead.

Cade raised his sword and then slammed the blessed weapon into a seething vortex of power.

There was a tremendous flash and a moment of blinding agony, and then Cade was gone.

A hoofed kick slammed into Joe's shoulder, jarring him out of his daze and numbing his arm down to his fingertips. He rolled with the attack and lurched back to his feet, shotgun raised in his good hand.

The Night Marshal squeezed both triggers before realizing he hadn't had a chance to reload. The metallic click against the hollow barrels threw him off balance, and he narrowly avoided the demon's flailing attack. He needed space to reload, but knew he wouldn't get it. He could see more demons plunging off the ledge, hungry for his blood.

Worse, the sow saw him and was headed in his direction.

"Cade!" he shouted. He didn't know where the Templar had gone, but he didn't have time to find out. Joe turned his back on the demons and ran like hell.

Plunging into the Beyond left Cade blind and deaf. Before he could recover his senses, someone stabbed him.

The attack slipped between the armored plates on his right arm and pierced his bicep. Pain and adrenaline shook Cade back to his senses in time to see the priest drawing a wicked blade back for another attack.

With his sword arm injured, Cade lunged forward and

hooked the fingers of his left hand around the man's filthy throat. The priest writhed in pain and tried to gather his power.

The priest was the conduit between this realm and the devil-sow he'd called forth into Pitchfork County. As long as he could draw power from the land of the dead and funnel it into the demon, the thing couldn't be killed.

But the same didn't hold true for the priest. Cade lifted the man up by his throat. "Didn't expect to see me here, did you?"

The priest's eyes bugged from their sockets and his mouth chewed on arcane syllables that couldn't find their way past his lips.

Cade threw the priest to the floor and bore down on his throat with all of his weight.

There was a split second of resistance, then a wet crunch echoed through the gloom and the priest's eyes went glassy and dark.

As Cade got to his feet the gleam of something metallic caught his eye and he reached down, pushing aside the dead man's robes to reveal the Eye of Horus on a chain around the man's throat. With a quick yank, Cade pulled it free.

Behind him came a churning roar in response. Cade turned and watched as the portal out of the Beyond tied itself into a knot and disappeared.

Joe returned his empty shotgun to its back scabbard and pumped his arms and legs for all he was worth. His lungs burned; running wasn't his normal game plan, but the hell-sow was gaining on him. Something had changed; he could feel the demons' desperation as they closed in on him. The sow paid no heed to the pig-demons she crushed in her pursuit of Joe; their squeals of pain and fear turned the Night Marshal's stomach.

Ahead of him, the lights of the cavern grew dim and a curved wall blocked his path. Joe realized where he was under the slaughterhouse and couldn't help but grin. Maybe he'd get out of this after all.

Joe leaped at the concrete wall and climbed, fingers and toes digging into its irregular surface. Years of erosion from seeping water and more gruesome fluids had left the concrete rough, giving him the hand- and footholds he needed.

"Let's see if you fuckers can swim," he snarled.

Pig-headed spirits coalesced out of the gray fog surrounding Cade. He drew his long sword, preparing to wade into the mob before him, then thought better of it.

"Live to fight another day" was never one of his favorite expressions, but damned if it didn't make sense right about now. He held no illusions about his odds of fighting off that many of the creatures and had no intention of sacrificing himself needlessly either.

Discretion is the better part of valor, a voice in the back of his mind spoke up, one that sounded suspiciously like his dead wife, Gabrielle, and he listened to it, turning to run with every ounce of strength he had left.

All he needed to do was stay ahead of the demons long enough to find a portal back to the other side.

No pressure.

Joe was thirty feet up the side of the concrete wall when the hell-sow plowed into it. The enormous creature didn't even try to slow down, which Joe had counted on. He hugged the wall, knowing that even if this plan worked, there was a good chance he'd end up dead.

The sow's impact sent huge cracks racing up the wall's face, and a massive chunk collapsed into rubble, revealing a pillar of viscous red.

A tsunami of clotted blood gushed from the ruptured silo. The crimson wave slammed the demonic swine to the floor and washed their bloated bodies into the cavern's walls with bone-shattering, blubber-rupturing force.

Even the massive sow was shoved off her feet and hurled against a stone wall. Her legs twisted and gave way with wet cracks as bones split and burst through the skin.

The monstrous swine's wounds oozed thick black blood and her shattered legs twitched feebly. The Templar must have managed some trick to keep it down. "Thanks, Cade," he said as he stalked toward the fallen pig.

It watched his approach with too human eyes filled with inhuman hatred. Joe pulled his shotgun from its scabbard and cracked it open. He loaded two shells into the barrels and snapped the gun closed.

The sow grunted and tried to lift its head, but Joe pinned its snout with his left foot. Despite its size, the thing's strength had fled.

Joe pointed the shotgun at the creature's oversized eye. "See you in hell."

The shotgun's roar echoed through the cavern, drowning out the hell-swine's dying scream.

Cade ran as if the demons of hell were at his heels because, well, they were. They didn't move as quickly as he did, their misshapen forms making it difficult for them to get up any decent speed, but he was exhausted from all the fighting and couldn't seem to widen his lead any more than a few dozen yards. As he went, he kept looking around frantically, searching for that telltale gleam of a portal in the distance.

The Beyond was an unusual place and despite all the years he'd been traveling here he had yet to squirrel out many of its secrets. He had learned to control his passage into the Beyond via the Mirror's Road, using any reflective surface to step from the land of the living into this dark and desolate plane of existence, but he hadn't learned how to do the same to get back.

Instead, he was forced to rely on preexisting portals, gleaming spheres of energy that were mystically tied to some reflecting surface in the real world which allowed him to travel in the opposite direction back to the world of the living.

Trouble was, they were few and, sometimes, far between.

And that was in a highly populated area. He'd entered the Beyond literally in the backwoods and the chance of finding a portal in so unpopulated an area was not good.

Not good at all.

But there was no way he was giving up.

A pig-demon got a little too close for comfort and he lashed out with his sword, cleaving off the top of the creature's skull with a single blow, before turning back and concentrating on widening the distance between him and the rest of the pack.

A sudden gleam of light popped into existence about fifty yards to his right and he put on a burst of speed, angling toward it as fast as he could go. The only thing over here that shone like that was a portal, but Cade knew that it could vanish just as abruptly as it had appeared. He had to get to it before it had the chance to do so.

Faster, Cade, faster, he urged himself, and bent to the task.

Joe was standing over the carcass, wondering what the hell he was going to tell the other Templars about Cade, when he felt a faint burst of heat coming from the pocket where he kept his badge.

No sooner had he taken out his badge than it suddenly flared with heat, causing him to drop it in surprise. He was staring down at the garish red burn it left on the palm of his hand when the badge burst into brilliance, giving off a silver-white light so bright that he had to step back and shield his eyes just to see anything at all.

The light grew, flowing outward, expanding from the center of the badge until it formed a spherical platform a few feet off the ground. It reminded him of a hellgate, the kind of portal that Left-Hand Path sorcerers sometimes used to summon demons to this world, and he stepped back in preparation.

It was a good thing he did, for in the next moment something did, indeed, come flying through the portal.

Not pig-demons as he'd expected, but Cade Williams.

Cade felt that moment of chilling cold that marked the passage from the Beyond back into the real world and then landed with a mucky splash face-first in the muddy pit he'd left behind what felt like hours before.

He heard someone shout his name in surprise and lifted his head to respond, only to find himself literally face-to-face with the giant demon-sow that he and Joe had been working so hard to kill. The hideous face, so close to his own, made him cry out and scramble backward in surprise, which set the Night Marshal to laughing hysterically.

The sheer incongruity of the situation forced a laugh out of Cade, too, and the two men spent a good minute just reveling in the simple fact that they were still alive. Even better, the mission had been accomplished, which was a good thing for all concerned.

When they were done laughing, Joe helped Cade up and the two men filled each other in on what had happened since they separated. They were congratulating each other on a job well done when the rest of the Templar unit burst through a door on the far side of the room, staring at the two men covered in mud and pig shit, wondering what the hell had happened.

Which only set Joe and Cade to laughing all over again.

Joe let the Templars decompress and debrief for a few minutes. They'd all been through hell and deserved a bit of rest before they got to the end of this thing. He stood apart from the other men, giving them their space. When it sounded like they were winding down, he cleared his throat. "All right, ladies, you get what you came for?"

Cade tapped the sealed pouch on his right hip. "Right here."

"Glad to hear it. Now you get to help me with something."

Cade felt the tension in the Templars around him. Hark had proved himself handy in a fight, but they weren't going to be happy taking orders from someone outside their command. "What are you talking about?"

Joe chuckled darkly. "You're going to love this part. It's time to clean this shit up."

The Night Marshal held his badge aloft and it shed a piercing silver radiance before him. The Templars followed Joe away from the dead hell-sow and into the ruptured cistern. For a long moment, the group stood in silence and stared at the horrors before them.

Thick iron chains dangled from the high ceiling, their links glistening with congealed blood and scabbed with old rust. Each of the chains held thirteen meat hooks, and each of the hooks held a brutalized human body pierced through the neck. Cade whistled, long and low. "What the hell were they doing here?"

Joe aimed the light from his badge at the nearest body. It was a young man with a shaved head and a panoply of crude tattoos etched into his arms and legs. An incision ran from where the meat hook corrupted his throat down to his crotch. Thick black threads sealed the edges of the wound, and expertly. There were gaps between the stitches in his bulging abdomen, and through one of them a black eye stared. Whatever was in there squealed and burrowed deeper into the body to escape the purifying light from Joe's badge. "Looks like they were making piglets."

Cade turned to his men. "Haul the demolition gear down here."

Joe waited until the rest of the Templars were gone before asking, "You have enough toys to bring this whole place down?"

Cade nodded. "It won't take as much as you might think. A few well-placed charges and we'll turn this whole place into a crater."

"I just wanted to say, you know, thanks for the hand with this shit. If you hadn't come along these pig fuckers probably would have bitten me on the ass at some point." Joe scratched his chin. "But, once we're done here, it's probably best if you get the fuck out of my county and forget how you got here."

Cade stared at Joe, who stared right back at him. "What am I missing?"

"Nothing. You and I both know what happens when people like us spend too much time in the same place. Sooner or later, we'd end up on opposite sides of the fence." Joe spat, trying to erase the foul taste of blood from his mouth. "And then I'd have to kill you. Or you'd take a run at me. Seems like more trouble than it's worth."

It took the Templar team a couple of hours to wire the slaughterhouse and the cavern below it with explosives. When they were finished, they all drove a quarter mile away from the place and parked on a hill overlooking it. Joe and Cade leaned against the Night Marshal's truck, waiting for the fireworks.

Cade showed Joe a flat black slab of plastic with a single red button on its face. "You want to do the honors?"

Joe grinned and pressed the button.

Dozens of bright flashes as the charges on the surface went off, and then a thunderous roar as subterranean blasts weakened the earth. A burning cloud rose from the growing crater and bloomed far overhead.

They watched the ruins burn until they could see the flashing red and blue lights of approaching law enforcement. "Probably best if you boys move along," Joe said. "I'll handle the local law."

Cade stuck out a gloved hand and the Night Marshal shook it. "Good luck, Marshal."

Joe watched the fires burn behind the Templar, and wondered if they'd fixed this problem or just cut off one of the hydra's heads. "You, too."

The Templars loaded into their black SUVs and disappeared into the night, and the Night Marshal waited for the law and wished for a drink.

Takes All Kinds

DIANA ROWLAND AND CARRIE VAUGHN

"Turn left in . . . one . . . quarter . . . mile," said the aggravatingly calm computerized voice.

"But there's no left turn there." Kitty unfolded a paper map, turned it right side up, and accidentally ripped it almost in half along the crease. Her sigh was almost a growl. "This road just goes on and on and on."

In the driver's seat, Ben was grinning. "Go on. Ask me to pull over for directions. Just ask. I dare you."

"Where are you gonna pull over?"

They looked around at wide, flat stretches of almost-swampland, heat shimmering visibly in the sticky air. The only building in sight was a weathered cabin maybe half a mile off the road with a bunch of beater cars parked out front. It didn't look inhabited. A haze hung over distant clumps of trees, and the sky here seemed small. Louisiana was not really anything like Colorado. Their whimsical last-minute decision to take the scenic route had led them to increasingly narrower, less-well-paved roads until they ended up here, on some long stretch of gravel, trying to figure out how to get back on the highway to New Orleans. If she didn't show up on time at the Southern Paranormal

Research Conference tomorrow, would anyone notice? Would they send rescue crews? Was there cell service out here?

She thought she heard banjos playing in the distance, but was sure that was her imagination. No need to panic. Yet.

"How much gas do we have?" She leaned over, trying to look at Ben's side of the dash.

"Half a tank. We're fine."

Her husband seemed very unconcerned. He might even have been enjoying himself.

"What are you smiling about?"

"I'm just reveling in this cliché moment we've created together. It's kind of nice. Makes me feel a little more normal, you know?"

She looked over at him, affection winning out over annoyance. They might have been thrown together at the start, but oddly enough they suited one another. He was sensible to her impulsive, wry to her sarcastic. God, he put up with her, what more could she ask? He was just above average height, maybe just below average build, had bright hazel eyes, and his scruffy brown hair always seemed to need a trim, but that only made her want to run her hands through it even more.

"You're really cute, you know that?" she said.

He put a hand on her knee; the touch comforted her, as he must have known it would.

She studied the road ahead, looking for a direction sign or someplace—anyplace—to turn. Instead, a column of black smoke threaded up to the sky, billowing out as it rose. Ben saw it too; he pressed on the gas, and the car sped toward the source.

Maybe a mile ahead, a car was on fire. It hadn't been burning long; the brown finish of the older-model sedan was still visible. Ben pulled over to the shoulder. He already had his cell phone out and was calling 911. Kitty stared at the flames, which engulfed the interior. She narrowed her gaze, peering—there didn't seem to be anybody in the car. She couldn't make out the shapes of any bodies.

"Yes," Ben said at his phone. Thank goodness he'd been able to get a signal. "There's a car on fire, we're on—where the hell are we?"

Kitty grabbed their GPS navigator, even though she didn't have much faith in it after the goose chase it had sent them on. "Parish Highway 307?"

Ben repeated the information, tried to estimate their location and what was happening, and was assured that emergency vehicles were on their way.

Kitty leaned close to the phone as the dispatcher asked, "Is anyone hurt?"

She and Ben looked at each other, and his uncertain expression matched her own. "I don't know, we can't tell."

They agreed to wait at the scene to talk to police when they arrived.

Kitty couldn't help herself. She got out of the car. Maybe if she could get a good scent of the surroundings, catch the trail of anyone who might have left the area, she could reassure herself that nobody was in there.

"Kitty—" Ben called after her. Then *he* got out of the car.

They stood together in the middle of the road. Flames reached up, roaring. The heat of it pressed them back. Their werewolf noses worked, taking in acrid scents of burning metal and rubber—and blood. What Kitty had thought was oil spilled from the ruined car was actually blood, a great messy pool of it—enough to be a sign of murder. The blood wasn't all—once she got past the stink of all the synthetics, the smell of cooking meat came through. A body on fire.

Under her rib cage, her wolf-self stirred, pricked her ears, and looked for the danger. Someone had been hunting here . . .

She reached out. Ben's hand was right there to hold hers.

"Hon, back in the car," he said.

"But there's something really weird—"

"Exactly. That's why we're sitting tight and waiting for the cops."

He was right, of course. Any way she interfered in the scene would just get her sucked into a situation she didn't need to be in. They could be good citizens and report the accident, but they didn't need to do any more than that. There wasn't much more *to* do.

Ben must have been thinking the same thing. "Anybody in that car is way past saving. There's nothing you can do."

"Yeah, but—look at all that blood."

His nose wrinkled, taking in the scent of it. His wolf knew that smell as well as hers did.

"We wait for the cops."

They locked themselves in their car and waited, sweating in the heat even with the air conditioner cranked up.

Within half an hour, the remote highway turned into a

traffic jam as fire trucks, police cars, and an ambulance all tried to crowd around the scene of the burning car. One crew put out the fire, and a police car pulled up alongside Kitty and Ben. Ben rolled down the window and answered all the nice officer's questions. Surreptitiously he asked a few of his own and found out that yes, there had been a body inside the car. The officer wouldn't answer any further questions, but reassured Ben that they likely couldn't have done anything to save the victim.

Yellow police tape went up next, surrounding the car, the pool of blood on the road, and a good distance beyond. A couple more cops directed the sparse traffic around the site, and Kitty was vaguely reassured that this road actually did have people on it every now and then. They wouldn't have been *totally* stranded.

Kitty opened her window and leaned out to watch, to listen, to smell. The guy was right, they probably couldn't have saved whoever it was. But she wondered: What had happened here? Whose blood was that? She was itching to get out and have another look around. See if there was some kind of trail to follow.

"I need to stretch my legs," she announced and opened the door.

"Wait, Kitty—"

"Just for a minute."

Bystanders gathered, and the ubiquitous phones were out snapping pictures before a uniformed officer ordered people to move along. Kitty walked off the road, a ways out from the caution tape, just taking in the air. Smelling for a trail. Trouble was, she didn't know what exactly she was smelling for, and the acrid burn from the fire and the chemicals used to put it out overwhelmed her nose.

Two more vehicles arrived: a black Dodge Durango followed by a black van. Coroner's office, looked like. The grimmest work of the whole episode began and Kitty didn't really want to watch this part as the two nitrile-gloved CO personnel carefully removed the body from the car and laid it out on an open body bag. A burned lump, black char against black plastic. The thing was abstract enough that Kitty could distance herself from it. It was just a shape, nothing more. She took one last, long breath of the scene, searching for anything out of the ordinary, for another clue to go with the blood and mess—and caught something she'd never smelled before. Ever. And that was saying something.

There was a chill, an icy thread in the air that she normally associated with vampires, but this had something else to it. A fungal tang, the thing in the forest growing under a rock, simultaneously rotting and full of life. The smell made Kitty stop and tilt her head, trying to capture it, trying to track its origin.

She moved back toward the road, and unfortunately back in view of the body, which the techs were sealing into the body bag and loading onto a gurney. And there it was. Not the body; the weird smell came from the woman in the coroner's office shirt, skinny with punked-out hair and an overly pale face, like she rarely went out in the sun. She moved, lifting the bag with her partner, strapping it in place, exchanging a few words with a nearby cop—and the scent was her. Now that Kitty had it, it overwhelmed the blood baking in the sun.

The woman looked up briefly and caught Kitty staring at her. Kitty didn't look away.

Then the woman wheeled the gurney to the back of the van, and she was gone.

"Huh," Kitty murmured.

Now the whole scene was looking bleak and sad. She wandered back to the car, where Ben was leaning on the hood, arms crossed, smirking.

"See what you need to?" he asked.

"Yeah, um—I think there's something very strange going on here."

"I think you're right."

That surprised her. Ben was usually the last person to encourage her bouts of dangerous curiosity.

"I just sat here, listening," he said. Werewolves didn't just have hypersensitive noses. They had really good hearing.

"Oh?"

"The victim in the car? They're saying he was already dead when the fire started. Like something had sliced him to pieces."

"That explains all the blood. So what the hell happened?"

"Let's get out of here, then we can talk about it."

That sounded like an excellent idea. Ben waved at the officer in charge one more time, and they got in the car and steered away from the chaos. Ben had also, it turned out, asked for directions from one of the officers. They were just two turns away from a major highway that would take them straight to New Orleans.

"And this is the last time we take the scenic route anywhere," Ben added.

"Watch the arm," Angel murmured. The death investigator, Derrel, nodded and readjusted his grip, and together they carefully extracted the partially burned corpse from the vehicle and set it in the open body bag. A thin breeze wafted the gruesomely appetizing scent of cooked meat to Angel's nose and she suppressed a groan as her mouth watered. It was small comfort to know that others had the same reaction to the odor of burned human. And like those others, Angel had no desire to ever actually eat human flesh.

Well, except for the brain. But that didn't really count as flesh, right?

Angel zipped the body bag closed, sealing away the human BBQ smell, to her relief. Derrel helped her get the bag onto the gurney, then he turned back to finish getting information for his report while Angel started toward the coroner's office van with the gurney. Gawkers mingled beyond the crime scene tape, but they backed away from her and the body bag, and a few hard glares from her sent most slinking back to their cars.

A new scent rode the breeze to Angel, wild and strange—enough so that she found herself scanning the area in a primal search for the smell. Onlookers continued to trickle away from the crime scene tape, but a slender blond woman stood by the car at the front of the line, eyes narrowed on Angel.

The hell? The odd scent came from *her*, Angel realized as she locked gazes with the woman. It had been a couple of days since Angel's last brain-meal, which meant her zombie parasite was highly aware of all the juicy human brains in the area. Police. Firemen. Gawking bystanders.

And the blonde—except hers wasn't like any human brain Angel had ever smelled. It had a wild edge to it, sharp and feral, with a hint of blood and a whisper of trees and earth. Human . . . and more.

Angel pulled her gaze away and continued wheeling the gurney to the van, but as soon as she had the body loaded up, she pulled her phone out and snapped a few pics of Blondie. The job with the morgue kept Angel well-supplied with the brains she needed to keep her mental faculties acute and her body in one non-rotted piece but, most importantly, kept her from turning into a monster who'd bash skulls in for a meal.

And I know a monster when I see one, Angel thought grimly.

Her thoughts tumbled as she drove away from the scene. She'd known the murder victim. Hell, everyone knew Jimmy Nunez. Like her, he'd lived his entire life in St. Edwards Parish, Louisiana. He wasn't the sharpest knife in the drawer, but he was a decent guy who stayed out of trouble, and was always willing to help a neighbor out. Likeable. That was the word. Angel couldn't imagine anyone hating him enough to slash him up, then set him on fire.

Maybe Jimmy was just in the wrong place at the wrong time—and came upon Blondie.

At the morgue, Angel got the body tucked away in the cooler and the pertinent info logged into the computer. There was no valid reason to be suspicious of the blond woman—other than the fact that she wasn't from 'round these parts and smelled funny. There hadn't been any long blond hairs conveniently draped around the crime scene, and she hadn't been spattered with blood. But Angel couldn't shake the sense there was something unpredictable and dangerous about her.

She was still mulling it over when Derrel walked into the morgue.

"Who was the tall, blond chick out at the scene?" she asked.

Derrel set his notepad on the desk and dropped into a chair. "She and her husband called it in. Her name's Kitty Norville." He glanced at Angel as if waiting for her to recognize the name. When she merely looked at him blankly, he went on. "She's a radio DJ. Has a show called *The Midnight Hour.*"

"Never heard of it," Angel said. Hell, it'd been ages since she had a car with a working radio.

"Supposed to be a radio show for supernatural creatures, like vampires and ghosts." Derrel snorted. "Her schtick is that she's a werewolf."

Angel's pulse stuttered. "A *werewolf*? Are you shitting me?"

"I'm not shitting you, but Kitty Norville certainly is." He shrugged. "Crazy what people will believe. A while back she did this big publicity stunt that was supposed to reveal how werewolves and other supernatural creatures were real. Even got picked up by some of the big networks."

Angel clamped down on the urge to press him about Kitty Norville's werewolf-ness. Derrel didn't believe it was true, but then again he probably didn't believe in zombies either.

"What's she doing in bumfuck Louisiana?" Angel asked, doing her best to sound casual.

"Road trip, on her way to a conference in New Orleans

with a bunch of other crazy whackadoodles." His phone beeped with an incoming call, and he excused himself and stepped out. Angel waited for his footsteps to retreat down the hall, then scooted over to Derrel's notepad and shamelessly snapped pictures of his notes—including Kitty Norville's info and statement.

Derrel didn't believe, but Angel did. Maybe Jimmy hadn't been sliced up.

Maybe he'd been clawed.

Kitty and Ben checked into their hotel at the edge of the French Quarter and a couple of blocks from the convention center where the Southern Paranormal Research Conference—a nice polite gathering of scientists and commentators hoping to share notes and drag some of their work into the light— started the next day. Kitty had wanted to get into town early, walk around, see the sights, and eat her body weight in seafood. But she and Ben ended up sitting on the bed, still pondering what had happened on that back road.

"So this woman," Ben asked. "From the coroner's office— *what* did she smell like?"

"That's just it, I don't know, she didn't smell like *anything*." And Kitty had been around vampires, fae, Navajo skinwalkers, djinn, and a few other things besides. "She wasn't human. Did you get her scent?"

"I must have been upwind. Is she not human enough to have something to do with tearing up that body?"

"And setting the car on fire to cover it up?"

"I did hear the firefighters talking about accelerant. So yeah."

"The next question: Is there anything we can do about it?"

Probably not. As one of the scheduled guests at the conference she had a couple of presentations she was supposed to be preparing for and an increasingly agitated inner wolf to keep calm. Best thing would be to forget about the whole thing. Let the police do their jobs.

Unless the police didn't realize they had some kind of supernatural being working for them. A being who maybe had that job because it got her close to crime scenes, maybe even let her cover up crime scenes . . . Stranger things had happened. Much stranger.

Kitty said, "We can maybe do a little digging. Just a tiny bit of digging. Minimal. Right?"

Ben gave her that skeptical look, the one that meant he knew exactly where all this was going but he wasn't going to say anything about it. He got out his laptop and cell phone. He was a criminal defense lawyer, and even though they were in Louisiana and not Colorado, Kitty bet he'd know exactly who to call and what questions to ask.

She started her own internet search. You could find *anything* on the internet. The name of the road, the accident, and then further afield: articles from underground magazines, fringe blogs, forums on supernatural dealings in Louisiana, whether New Orleans really was the popular haven for vampires its reputation made it out to be—she had it on good authority that the city had no more and no fewer vampires than any other city of its size. It had its own Mistress, but she kept a low profile and her followers did the same. Kitty was secretly hoping to meet her, confident her reputation as the host of America's premier talk radio advice show for the supernatural would get her an in—on the other hand, her reputation might just piss off someone like the Mistress of New Orleans. No way to find out until she asked.

The city had a lot of other threads she was hoping to follow after talking to some of the locals at the conference: Marie Laveau and her voodoo legacy, rumors of were-alligators, and any real hauntings at the famous local cemeteries.

She'd been through these online backwaters before, and ninety percent of the time she couldn't trust a thing they said. But that still left ten percent. That fascinating ten percent.

Ben interrupted her race down the online supernatural rabbit hole.

"They've released the victim's name," he said. "James Nunez, twenty-three, sporadically employed. Nothing about what he was doing on that road. The car was borrowed, though—didn't belong to him. I can call in a favor and get info off the plates. Maybe the car's owner knows something. You find anything?"

"There was a string of murders here last year—a serial killer was going around cutting people's heads off." She wrinkled her nose. "There are rumors about some kind of underground organization that's covering up . . . something. I would say that one's just the usual conspiracy nonsense. Except for that smell."

"You can't find anything about weird-smelling coroner techs?"

"Now wouldn't that be something? Google search for

smell? Like, 'What does Greeley smell like?' so when people from out of town hear that when you can smell Greeley you know it's going to snow, they'll know what you're talking about?"

"Imagine the cat memes that would come out of that," he said, but his tone wasn't wistful at all. Kitty suppressed a shiver. "The coroner doesn't list staff on their web site. We could hang out there, try to spot her, maybe try to talk to her—"

"Unless she's some kind of monster that loses control and tears people apart?"

"What are the odds?"

Kitty shrugged innocently. "We *are* werewolves."

"Fair."

"I could just start walking around, see if I catch that scent anywhere else."

"That's random. Police procedure would be to track down the victim, trace his whereabouts before the accident, see if any of his friends or family know what might have happened."

"Do we know anything about him?"

He tapped a few keys on his laptop, something pinged, and he donned a thin, predatory smile. "Actually . . . turns out the car belongs to a Dwayne Fontaine. Friend, maybe? Ah, look at this."

He turned the screen around so she could see it. He'd googled their names together and come up with a local community newspaper story from several years ago about some high school event. The picture featured both men— boys, here—their names side by side in the caption, their arms over each other's shoulders. Smiling in happier days.

Nunez had been a burly white kid, with a mop of hair and a friendly smile. His friend, the car's owner, was lanky and cocky, his grin crooked. Kitty sighed a little. Those two had no idea what was coming up for them just a few years on. It made her sad.

Ben continued, "If he's up for it, Fontaine might be able to tell us if Nunez was into anything weird, why he might have been on that road."

"We really shouldn't be getting involved in this, should we?"

"So, you're going to talk to the car's owner and I'm going to see what I can find out about that serial killer and this weird mafia stuff you dug up?"

"That's right," she said, and kissed him. She almost changed her plan, staying behind to spend more quality time with her husband this was the whole reason they drove and made a vacation out of the conference. But the sooner she got this bug out of her system, the sooner she could focus on him and him alone. She grabbed her phone and the car keys and headed out.

Angel crouched in the middle of the road and peered at the scorched and blackened gravel. The burned car had been hauled off to the crime lab for processing, and the section of road had been photographed, videoed, measured, and sampled to kingdom come before being opened back up to traffic. She'd assisted in the gruesome autopsy of Jimmy Nunez only a couple of hours earlier, which left her with even more questions. The fire hadn't killed Jimmy, which was one small blessing. The pathologist had counted over a dozen slashes across Jimmy's arms and torso. Though not terribly deep—a half inch or so at the most—the gashes would've needed a helluva lot of stitches had Jimmy lived. And he probably would have, if not for the one that raked across his upper chest . . . and caught his throat right above his collarbone, in the frighteningly perfect spot to open up the vein.

"That shit ain't right," Angel murmured. Someone—or something—had gone nuts on Jimmy. But why? Rage? Revenge? Angel scowled at the darkened swath of road. Monsters didn't need reasons to hurt and kill. That's what made them monsters.

She'd known Jimmy since junior high. He'd been a year ahead of her—a sweet boy with round cheeks and a smile for everyone. His daddy had run off before he was born, and his mama had worked two jobs to keep a roof over their head and food on the table, but Jimmy never seemed to notice or care that they were dirt poor. More than a little naïve, he'd been a prime target for bullies until Dwayne Fontaine had stepped up to his defense. The two became fast friends and close as brothers—and when Jimmy's mama passed away a few years later, Dwayne's folks took Jimmy in so that he could finish up high school.

He was harmless, damn it. And he hadn't stood a chance against his killer.

The sound of tires on gravel pulled Angel from her musing. She straightened and stepped off the road as a battered yellow car approached. But instead of passing by, the car screeched to an unsteady stop on the opposite shoulder. The door flew open, and a woman with red hair and a billion freckles stumbled out.

Damn. Maylene McKelvey—Dwayne's fiancée. Angel

sprinted across the road as Maylene's eyes fell to the burned patch, then filled with tears.

"Maylene, no." Angel grabbed her by the shoulders and spun her around. "Don't look at it."

The tears spilled over. "Oh god, it's true. I didn't want to believe it, but . . ." She started to turn, then caught herself. Her face was blotchy, as if she'd already done her fair share of crying. "Angel, I don't understand. Why would anyone want to hurt Jimmy?" Her lower lip quivered. "He was the sweetest guy in the whole world."

Angel sighed. "I don't know, Maylene, but I promise I'll do my part to make sure whoever did this burns in hell."

Maylene's legs folded, and she plopped onto her butt in the grass. "I saw the smoke earlier and didn't think nothing of it. I figured it was Mr. Estes burning trash again even though he done been told time and time again that he's not supposed to. But then Dwayne came by to tell me. Guess it's a good thing I missed him with the flowerpot."

"Er, missed who?"

"Dwayne." Maylene sniffled. "He pulled up on that dumb noisy four-wheeler, and I ran out and threw a flowerpot at him."

Angel gingerly sat in front of Maylene—after checking for fire ants. "Y'all had another fight?" The woman had a temper to match her hair, and she and Dwayne had broken up and gotten back together at least a dozen times in the five or so years they'd been dating.

"Well, yeah. Why else would I chuck a flowerpot at him?"

Angel spread her hands. "Y'got me there."

Maylene stole a look over her shoulder at the scorched

ground and shuddered. "I figured Dwayne was coming by to do the whole I'm-so-sorry-I-love-you crap, and I just wasn't in the mood for it. Not after last night and him telling me that he wanted to elope to Vegas right then and there. Elope!" Her cheeks flushed. "Can you believe it? After all the time I done spent shopping for dresses and flowers? And just last week we put a deposit down at the Motel Deux Banquet Hall." Her face crumbled. "But then he told me about Jimmy, and I about died right then and there on my front step." With that she dissolved into sobs.

"I'm so sorry, Maylene," Angel said, awkwardly patting the other woman's shoulders. After a moment Maylene lifted her head and wiped her eyes, smudging her mascara.

"Thanks, Angel. I never lost anyone close to me, so I guess it hit me extra hard." She took a shaky breath. "Jimmy didn't have no family. D'you know if it'd be okay if I arranged his funeral? I was thinking of taking up a collection. After all, everybody liked Jimmy."

Well, somebody didn't, Angel thought. "If there's no next of kin, I don't see why that would be a problem," she reassured Maylene. "Maybe Dwayne could help with—"

"I don't need Dwayne's help," she snapped, the fire returning to her eyes. She pushed to her feet. "We are *over*. Do you know, I was sitting there on my front step crying on his shoulder, and he starts trying to kiss me and feel me up? I got mad and told him to cut it out and how the hell could he think of sex at a time like this, and he's telling me how we should celebrate life. Ugh!"

"People grieve in different ways," Angel said as she stood. "But as far as the funeral arrangements go, you probably need to call the coroner's office and find out what you need to do to get permission. Ask for Derrel. He's cool." She staggered as Maylene threw her arms around her in a hug.

"Thank you so much. Jimmy'll have the best send-off a guy could ever want!" She released Angel and dove into her car, then sped off, leaving a cloud of dust in her wake.

Angel watched Maylene's car retreat into the distance, unsurprised that she'd offered to handle Jimmy's funeral arrangements. Maylene had started dating Dwayne when they were seniors in high school, and Jimmy had—of course—always been around. As far as anyone could tell, Maylene simply thought of Jimmy as part of Dwayne's family. If Maylene had ever resented Jimmy being a constant third wheel, she hid it well.

Then again, maybe that was part of why she and Dwayne broke up so many times?

Considering, Angel shifted her gaze up the road—the direction Maylene had come from. Another two miles and Mule Ear Road forked off to the right. A half mile up the road was Maylene's place and not much else. Jimmy had borrowed Dwayne's car—as usual, since he didn't have his own—and was headed to see Maylene, Angel was positive. To plead Dwayne's case and get the two back together? Jimmy was a natural-born peacemaker who just wanted people to be happy. Dwayne was always miserable and angry during the breakups, and Jimmy loved him like a brother. It made sense that he'd try to mend fences.

What if Maylene got sick of Jimmy butting in? Angel shuddered at the ugly thought. Maylene had a temper, but it was hard to believe she'd slice Jimmy up and burn him. "Yeah, much easier to believe Jimmy got himself ambushed by a werewolf," Angel said with a roll of her eyes. Besides, if Maylene murdered Jimmy, the cops would find out soon enough. They really did know what the hell they were doing—at least when it came to normal, mundane crimes. Yup, the St. Edwards Parish Sheriff's Office knew how to close a case. Yessirree.

Angel climbed into her car, drumming her fingers on the steering wheel as she headed home. Of course, if it *was* something more than an ordinary murder, there'd be no way for the cops to find the real killer. In fact, if there was even the slightest chance Jimmy was killed by something not completely human, then Angel had a civic duty to get involved. Right? Maybe she would take a couple of hours and head into the city, drop in on the Southern Paranormal Research Conference and check out this Kitty Norville up close.

Her eyes dropped to her gas gauge. Crap. And her bank account was damn near as empty. So much for a drive to New Orleans. *Talk to Dwayne instead?* His house was about a quarter mile up the highway on the right. What if Jimmy had called in to Kitty Norville's radio show and somehow made himself a target? Dwayne might know if Jimmy was into that sort of thing. It would only take a few minutes to drop by and chat him up.

Angel grimaced. Of course, dropping in on him might be a little too pushy considering Jimmy wasn't even dead twelve hours yet. As messed up as Maylene was over Jimmy's murder, Dwayne was surely a hundred times worse. Maybe it'd be best to wait until—

What the hell? Angel slammed on the brakes, then yanked

the wheel to make the turn onto the long gravel driveway. She narrowed her eyes at the car parked in front of Dwayne's house, pulled in behind it, then checked the pictures on her phone. It was the same car that a certain werewolf had gotten into at the crime scene.

Why on earth was she *here*?

Dwayne Fontaine—and wasn't that a good Southern name, straight out of *The Dukes of Hazzard*?—lived in a run-down house in a neighborhood full of run-down houses, fifty-year-old cottages with porches that might have been cute once when the area was full of middle-class suburbanites. But the place hadn't been kept up, and now paint was peeling and the lawns were mostly scrappy weeds. This told Kitty something about Dwayne, and it made her sad all over again.

She carefully made her way up the creaking steps of the front porch, and wrinkled her nose at the smell of mold that had seeped into the fiber of the wood around her. She didn't encounter that smell much in semi-arid Colorado. She could spend a day cataloguing Louisiana smells.

Quickly, firmly, she knocked on the weathered front door before she could change her mind. If the guy answered with a shotgun in hand, she was fully prepared to run. Her werewolf healing meant a shotgun blast wouldn't kill her. But it would still *hurt*. Likely Dwayne was a perfectly reasonable, grief-stricken young man. No need to go inventing horror stories around here.

A white guy in his twenties opened the door. She recognized him from the old newspaper photo. He wore a gray T-shirt, scuffed jeans and sneakers, and had a cautious gaze.

He held on to the edge of the door as he looked Kitty up and down. He did not appear to be holding a shotgun.

"Yeah?"

"Hi. Are you Dwayne Fontaine?"

"Yeah?" His caution deepened; he probably didn't like the idea of strangers showing up knowing his name.

"I'm sorry, I just wanted to offer my condolences. I'm really sorry about the loss of your friend."

"What?" the guy said, apparently startled.

"Your friend, James. The car fire. My husband and I reported the accident, and I found out it was your car he was driving, and I'm really sorry."

"Oh. Um. Thanks. Who are you again?"

"My name's Kitty Norville, I host a late-night talk radio show." She offered a business card. She always kept a few in her pocket for such occasions. A nice card with the KNOB logo on it lent a startling amount of authority. "I don't really know how to explain this, but I think something weird's going on with your friend's accident. Some things about the scene—well, they didn't make a whole lot of sense. I thought I'd track a couple of things down. You know, for my own curiosity. Was he into anything weird? Or, like, supernatural?"

"I don't know what you're talking about." And he didn't. His brow was furrowed. "Like, ghosts or some shit?" He had a strong Southern drawl that didn't seem to fit with the expletive.

"Can I come in?" she said and proceeded to push her way in. As she hoped, Dwayne stepped aside and reflexively closed the door behind her.

The house's front room was that of a typical midtwenties bachelor: secondhand sofa, worn coffee table bearing a few scattered beer cans, hardwood floor that was probably a decade past needing a good refinish. The large flat-screen TV was by far the nicest, most expensive thing here. She was betting the house was a rental. An air conditioner rattled out back.

"Thanks for talking to me," she continued quickly, trying to win him over. "I know this is intrusive. But I'm kind of serious. Did the police tell you that James had been killed before the fire started?"

"What?"

"Just based on some things I saw there"—no need to explain to him that she'd actually smelled it—"and I can't leave stuff like this alone, my husband's always getting after me about sticking my nose where it doesn't belong, but I figure if I can help—"

"What are you tryin' to say?"

She took a deep breath. "Was he into anything that might have gotten him killed in a . . . weird way?"

Dwayne's expression shut down. He started sweating, a thick tang of fear rolling off him, and his heartbeat sped up. What was he scared of? Was the thing that killed Nunez after him as well? Had the thing gone after the car, and not Nunez?

Kitty remembered the strange woman, and all the hideous signs of murder.

But Fontaine was done talking to her. "I reckon you oughta get on out of here and talk to the cops about this."

"Why? Is there something the police should know?"

"I don't know anything about it, ma'am." The guy was nervous. Like, really nervous. Sweating buckets, even in the air-conditioning. His lips were pressed in an angry line. There was a story here; she could always tell.

Frowning, he stepped past her to open the door. And a scent from outside intruded, more than the damp and the mold and the background of swamp and vegetation. That cold, living dead smell that made her hackles jump. That same smell from the car fire.

Well. This was going to be interesting.

"Thanks again for talking to me," she said. "And I really am sorry."

She stepped out and Fontaine slammed the door after her, muttering curses under his breath.

Which left her looking across the dirt drive to the skinny, punked-out woman from the coroner's office, leaning on the hood of Kitty's sedan, her arms crossed, and a look of joyous murder in her pale eyes.

The front door opened and Kitty Norville stepped out. Her gaze locked onto Angel, strong and sure. Angel tensed for an attack—whether physical or verbal—but Kitty simply gave her a bright smile.

"Hi!" Kitty said as she descended the steps.

"Er, hi," Angel replied, scowling at herself for being caught off guard by congeniality, of all things. This was the South, for chrissakes. Then again, there was caution in Kitty's eyes, so it wasn't all fun and games.

"My name's Kitty," she said, still smiling though it was

clear she was sizing Angel up. She tilted her head. "And you are . . . ?"

"I'm Angel." She folded her arms over her chest. "Do you get teased by the other werewolves with that name?"

"I do actually," Kitty replied without a flicker of hesitation. "They're just insecure."

"Uh-huh." She gave Kitty her own once-over. "I saw you out at the crime scene."

"Yeah. We called it in." Kitty's smile didn't change, but a note of caution laced her voice. "But you already know that, given your job." Her stance shifted, back tensing. "A lot of bodies in your line of work."

"Yeah, I've seen lots of dead people." Angel stepped closer. "Y'know, I thought at first you might've done it."

Kitty didn't sprout fur in response to the accusation, but a subtle change came over her bearing. Her smile widened to show teeth, and her shoulders lifted, giving the impression of raised hackles.

Yep, she's a werewolf, Angel thought, pulse quickening.

Kitty held up her hands, fingers bent like claws. "Wanna check my fingernails for blood?"

Angel held her ground and returned a tight smile. "I figure you'd have licked them clean by now." She casually pulled a packet of protein gel from the side pocket of her cargo pants. If this was going to turn into monster vs. monster, she was going to need a little help. "Why are you here?" She gestured toward Dwayne's house, kept her eyes on Kitty as she sucked the contents of the packet down. The best kind of protein: pureed brains, and exactly the

175

boost Angel needed in case this bitch decided to go full werewolf.

Kitty's eyes widened on the "protein gel." "What is that? What are you—that's *human*! Oh my god, you're . . . What the hell are you?"

Angel blinked. "Huh. Thought your doggie nose would've figured it out by now."

"Wolf, thank you."

"I'm a zombie." Angel shrugged. "Why the hell do you think I work in a morgue?"

Kitty stared in disbelief. "Zombie?" She shook her head. "The last zombie I met was the Haitian voodoo slave kind. You're saying you're like the brain-eating shambling kind? I thought that was only in the movies."

"Yeah, well I thought werewolves were only in the movies. And I only shamble when I haven't had brains in a while. Or coffee." Angel scowled and tugged a hand through her hair. "Look, did you kill Jimmy or not? Because if you did, that's way uncool. And if you didn't, I wanna find out who did."

"I thought maybe you did it. I mean, you don't exactly smell . . . right," Kitty replied. "Then you set the fire to cover it up."

Angel laughed. "Oh, no. His skull was still intact. If I'd done it, I'd have taken the brain. 'Waste not want not,' and all that shit."

A pained look swept over Kitty's face, and she put a hand to her head. "So you eat people. Should I be worried?"

"Nah, your brain smells funny," Angel said, wrinkling her nose. "Besides, I get plenty from the morgue—after people are legit dead. You're safe from me."

"Coffee," Kitty said as if seizing a lifeline. "You mentioned coffee. Is there anywhere around here we can get some and maybe hash this out like normal people?"

"I know just the place," Angel said, then grinned. "Good thing you didn't want a beer. Sounds like a bad joke. A zombie and a werewolf walk into a bar . . ." She stopped at Kitty's look and cleared her throat. "How 'bout you just follow me."

Angel eyed Kitty over her mug. The "monster" took her coffee with lots of cream.

"Does Maylene often throw flowerpots at Dwayne?" Kitty asked.

"Only when they fight," Angel said, then gave a wry smile. The two women had spent the last ten minutes exchanging notes, and were now trying to make sense of it all. "Which means at least once a month. Though it's not always flowerpots. Just whatever's closest and throwable." She snorted. "Welcome to the deep South."

"Oh, it's not just the South," Kitty said. "We have plenty of redneck drama in Colorado. My husband's father's in jail on weapons and conspiracy charges."

"Good to know it's universal." Angel wrinkled her nose. "You said Dwayne was a fidgety wreck when you talked to him?"

Kitty nodded. "He was afraid. Sweating. He didn't like that I was asking questions." She tilted her head. "Is it possible he was involved in some sort of illegal activity? Jimmy was driving Dwayne's car . . ."

"You think maybe Jimmy was killed by mistake, and it was supposed to be Dwayne?" Angel tugged a hand through her already rumpled hair. "Shit. I guess anything's possible, though Dwayne's always seemed like a real straight arrow."

"Even straight arrows get blown off course," Kitty pointed out.

"True." Angel shifted in her seat. "I, uh, can put out some feelers about what kind of stuff he might've gotten into." She swirled the coffee in her mug before taking a sip.

"There are rumors of an . . . underground mob-type organization around here," Kitty said.

Angel spluttered her coffee, then grinned as she grabbed a napkin. "You sure dug deep to hear *those* rumors." When Kitty merely gave her a bland look, Angel continued, "Trust me, Dwayne's not involved with them."

"You're sure?"

"Completely." Angel met Kitty's eyes. "They're my version of a wolfpack. I used to call them the zombie mafia. We look out for each other."

"Huh. Well, how about that?" Kitty said.

"That said, there are plenty of other ways Dwayne could've gotten in over his head," Angel said. "God knows he ain't rich."

"And doesn't Maylene want a big wedding?" Kitty sat back and gave the waitress—"Hazel Lou" according to her nametag—a smile as she refilled their coffee.

Angel made a face. "Ugh. Yes. Six bridesmaids—so far— and a couple of weeks ago I heard that she was angling for a string quartet and live doves."

Hazel Lou *hmmf*ed as she dropped fresh sugar packets into the bowl on the table. "Live doves? Guess now I know why she up and decided to have an outdoor wedding in the middle of July."

Angel looked up with a frown. "Wait. I thought she was using Motel Deux Banquet Hall. She told me she gave them a deposit last week."

Hazel Lou set the coffeepot down. "Uh-huh, and three days ago she asked for it back. Lucky for her Jimmy Nunez— rest his soul—had just called asking if the Turkey Club could have their annual dinner there that same day she'd reserved, otherwise I can't imagine Mr. Emmet would've given her any of her money back."

Kitty and Angel exchanged a look.

"Could we have the check, please?" Angel asked Hazel Lou. As soon as the waitress walked off, both women leaned in and lowered their voices.

Kitty said, "I've only been in Louisiana a couple of days and I've already sweated through my entire wardrobe. Maylene *can't* have an outdoor wedding in July here."

"Right. No one is that insane," Angel agreed.

"So she asks for that deposit back before Dwayne runs over wanting to elope . . ." Her brow furrowed, making her look less monstrous.

Angel tapped her hand on the table, thinking hard. The timing was so close—one event had to have triggered the other. "He must have gotten wind that something was up. Thought maybe she was getting cold feet."

"And he was hoping to rush her into getting married before things fell completely apart. So I'm guessing Jimmy wasn't really going over to her house to patch things up between her and Dwayne, was he?" She got this narrow focus to her gaze, like she'd put puzzle pieces together.

It was like she figured out this sort of thing all the time. "What's your radio show about again?" Angel asked.

Kitty donned a sly grin. She handed over a business card from her pocket like it was a habit. "I offer relationship advice to supernatural creatures. Like, if your vampire boyfriend is a pain in the neck? Turns out a lot of these problems are universal."

Angel arched a brow. The card had a radio station logo on one side, and the show title on the other: THE MIDNIGHT HOUR: TALK RADIO WITH BITE. Well, it took all kinds . . . "Werewolves, zombies . . . rednecks?"

"Exactly."

"Then what happened? Maylene got tired of Dwayne's shit and set her sights on Jimmy?"

"Or Jimmy set his sights on her. This might have been going on a long time and Maylene just couldn't bring herself to break it off with Dwayne."

"And Dwayne found out," Angel said, expression darkening. She had a sudden urge to get her hands around his good-ol'-boy neck.

"And now he's spooked," Kitty said.

"Grab him before he runs?"

"Damn straight."

The two women lurched up from their chairs, threw bills onto the table, and ran for the door.

Angel drove. Angel the zombie. Kitty still had a hard time wrapping her brain around that one—and wasn't that the pot calling the kettle black? This second trip to Dwayne's house went a lot faster than the first one, and she was ready to hunt.

The crunch of their tires on the gravel driveway gave them away. Dwayne dashed from the back of the house in a sprint for the tree line when they were still a hundred yards from the house, and disappeared into the marsh before they were out of the car. It might have been Kitty's imagination, but he seemed to be holding something that looked like a machete. Something anyone in these backwoods might own to hack back encroaching vegetation. Or, you know, to take out one's frustrations on an old friend.

Angel let out an impressive stream of curses. "We lost him!" She turned a worried look on Kitty. "What if he goes after Maylene now?"

"I can track him," Kitty said, also thinking of Maylene, who might have been confused and flighty but sure didn't deserve what had happened to Jimmy. This Dwayne was an angry guy.

"Wait. What?"

"I mean, I'm pretty sure I can track him. I've never hunted in a swamp before, and I gotta tell you it smells kind of rank. But his trail's fresh, he's in a panic, shouldn't be too hard." In fact, she was already tracking. She'd gotten a pretty good whiff of the guy before. That scent formed a strong trail behind him. She pulled off her shirt and zipped down her jeans while Angel looked on, startled. Well, she'd just have to be startled.

"You mean like some kind of a bloodhound?" Angel tugged a "protein gel" from her pocket and sucked the contents down. And there was another thing Kitty couldn't quite wrap her brain around. Her head itched thinking of it.

"Um. Sort of not really? Keep my clothes dry, would you?"

"Sure thing. Got your back. Even if it's . . . furry."

Kitty's bra and panties came off, and she folded the items neatly with the rest of the clothes. She placed a chain with a ring on it—a wedding band—carefully on top of the pile, patting it gently, fondly. She was unself-conscious, moving gracefully across the front yard, hands at her sides, poised on the balls of her feet like she was ready to run. Some kind of prehistoric hunting goddess, her blond hair loose and eyes gleaming. She loved the feeling of strength. Her vision was blurring into Wolf's heightened senses.

"You might not want to watch, this really squicks some people out," she said. "Oh—and stay back. We wouldn't want to confuse her."

"Her?"

Despite the warning, Angel watched as Kitty's skin seemed to blur. A million needle-pricks itched along her skin, fur sprouting. Pain clenched her limbs, bowed her back, and she grunted. Experience taught her that this hurt less if she let it wash through her, let the Wolf out of its cage in her gut, let it roar through her—

She shakes off her skin and runs, four legs stretching, sinuous body reaching. She hunts, and the hunt feels good. Even if this isn't home—home is hard ground, granite hills, endless pines, and air that smells of old ice. This place is wet, mud seeping up around the pads, making her feet itch and her gait stiff. The air here smells of moss and a million crawling things.

None of that matters. This is a hunt, and through the thick mess of foreign smells, the prey's scent is fresh and strong: tobacco smoke, alcohol, old rubber. Steel with old blood on it. She flies after the creature, sure of little but that he must be stopped.

She is fast. Even splashing mud up on her belly, even with it caking on her fur and pulling at her, she flies. Her nose is up, depending more on the air than the ground to show her the trail. The smell is strong; the prey is so close she can hear it now as well as smell it: splashing along the path, knowing it's being hunted, panicking.

"Oh, Jesus! Gawdalmighty!"

It changes course, like prey always does at this stage, angling as if it can distract her, dodge her. But she anticipates and zigs to keep pace, cutting off its new path. The prey screams. Cornered now, it turns to face her and lashes out, slashing with a weapon, sharp metal. She ducks. It catches her shoulder. She hardly notices. It's not silver, so it doesn't matter. Mouth open, tongue hanging out to taste air, she prepares to leap, mouth around throat, anticipating the wash of blood—

"Kitty!" The name, the sound of it, rattles her hearing. Her stride breaks, ears pricked forward, tail up, all awareness bent toward learning what's wrong. "Kitty, back down! It's okay!"

Her mate speaks. His voice is a wash of warmth and comfort, even as she is annoyed at his two-legged self.

They should hunt together; he should be four-legged, fur-covered, like her.

"Get it away from me! Get it away!"

She would strike it down just to make it quiet.

"Drop that machete or I'll tell her to go for it!"

The blade falls.

"Kitty. The police are coming. Angel's here. We got this, you can rest now."

She paces, whines. She wants the prey's blood. As long as the prey is still moving, the hunt's not finished, and this creature is dripping fear, ready for her to take it–

"Kitty."

She droops, tail falling, ears flat. This is her mate, standing in front of her, and his scent means home and safety. If he says the hunt is over, she'll believe him. But only him. He's low to the ground, and she pads over to him, rubs along his body, pressing herself to his warmth.

"I need you to sleep now. Okay?"

Maybe. Only because he's with her.

"Oh, Jesus!" the terrified voice cries again, and her hackles go stiff, her muscles tensed for attack. A growl burrs in her throat.

"Shh." Her mate's hand flattens her fur, strokes along her flank. In spite of herself, she settles.

"Why don't you kill that thing!" Its screaming is desperate.

"Why don't you shut the hell up!" another voice intervenes, as angry as Wolf feels.

But her mate murmurs, wraps her with his warmth, and she lets her weight go, leaning into him. He holds her. She's safe.

"So, is she gonna turn back human now or what?" this other voice intrudes. Angel, her two-legged self murmurs.

"She has to sleep. It'll take a little while."

She is already fading, already slipping away, feeling like she has left a job unfinished . . .

The wolf loped off into the woods with giant, graceful strides, and disappeared. Angel couldn't hope to follow her on foot, not even with the fresh jolt of brains fueling her. Dwayne had a dumpy four-wheel ATV that he used for hunting critters around here somewhere. It said something about how panicked he was that he hadn't fled on that thing. Since it wasn't out where she could see it, it was likely parked in the locked Tuff Shed around back. Breaking the lock? *That* was something her zombie strength could handle. She yanked on the door, and the dead bolt ripped through the cheap plywood. She rolled her head on her shoulders. Yeah, that was kinda satisfying!

She was about to fire up the ATV when the distinctive roar of a Harley-Davidson powered up the driveway. She'd recognized the rider from the crime scene—the thirty-something man who'd been with Kitty. Probably her husband, Ben. Angel decided not to ask why the hell he was on Jessie "Snake" Crowe's bike. It was sure to be a long story.

"She's out there," she yelled to him, and before the sentence was fully out of her mouth, Ben leaped up behind her on the four-wheeler.

"That way," he said, pointing.

They roared off like a couple of unlikely knights on an even more unlikely steed. Angel tried to follow in the direction she'd seen Kitty run; but it was Ben, evidently also a werewolf, tracking with his nose, who ended up finding Kitty and Dwayne.

The wolf had Dwayne cornered. With her smoky gray and tan fur fading to a pale belly, sharp ears flattened and all her fur standing on end, she did sort of bring to mind the image of Kitty with her shoulders bunched up. Dwayne held a machete—what he'd used to kill Jimmy, Angel was sure. She had no doubt the crime lab would match it to the cuts in what was left of Jimmy's body.

Kitty looked like she wanted to rip into the man, and Angel was inclined to let her. She realized now that the slashes on Jimmy couldn't have come from Kitty's claws. Those cuts had been a lot cleaner than what was about to happen to Dwayne.

Ben jumped off the ATV and yelled at her to stop. Unbelievably, she did and, just like that, it was all over. Angel found duct tape in the ATV's cargo bag and approached Dwayne, who was curled up on the ground in the fetal position and weeping outright.

"You're a fucking worthless piece of shit asshole," was all she could find to say to him. He simply huddled and sobbed. He looked as if facing Kitty's wolf side might have given him a few nightmares. Good.

She finished duct-taping Dwayne's wrists behind his back, yanked his shirt over his head so he couldn't see what was going on, then watched in morbid fascination as Kitty became, well, Kitty again. Fur retreated into flesh. Limbs shifted, and bones melted and reformed. A moment later Ben cradled a mud-spattered human woman in his arms, gazing down at her with such tenderness that Angel had to look away, abruptly feeling as if she was intruding.

Using a ratty tissue she'd had stuffed in one of her pockets, she retrieved the machete from the mud and carefully set it in the cargo bag. The police would want to see it.

Back at the four-wheeler, Angel retrieved the clothing from where she'd stuffed it into a storage compartment, and by the time she made it back to Ben, Kitty was awake and more than ready to get dressed.

Ben rose to his feet and gave Angel a grateful smile, but it flickered as his gaze dropped to her left forearm. "You, ah, have a . . ." He trailed off, wincing.

Angel looked down to see a long ribbon of flesh dangling from her wrist. "Crap." She sighed. "All those damn branches whipping at us. And my lunchbox is in my car." She flicked a gaze toward Dwayne. Nice human brain right there . . .

Angel realized that Ben and Kitty were staring at her with matching looks of horror and consternation. "Relax," she said with a laugh. "I'm not *that* hungry." Mostly. She flopped the strip of flesh back into place and duct-taped it down. "But I'd better get to my lunchbox before the cops come."

With Dwayne draped across the back rack, they managed to arrange themselves on the four-wheeler so that no one had to walk through the muck. Kitty stayed uncharacteristically quiet, and another creature still seemed to look out of her eyes. Dwayne had managed to cut her with his machete; the wound had already healed.

Angel darted to her car even as the first cop car pulled into the driveway, and managed to gulp down the left parietal lobe of a recent heart attack victim before the deputy parked.

She wiped her face, checked to make sure she was all in one piece again, and stepped out of her car in time to give the deputy a wide grin. "Hey, Billy Roy! Me and my new friends got a present for y'all."

Well, that had been a little embarrassing. Sort of not really. Wolf was feeling pretty great—they'd gotten to go on a real hunt for a real bad guy and had maybe even done some good, bringing a murderer to justice.

But they hadn't gotten to actually *eat* him.

Unlike Angel, Kitty didn't need to eat people. She didn't *want* to eat people. She got a little queasy thinking about it. But Wolf could almost feel the blood sliding over her tongue, and the flesh coming apart between her teeth . . .

"You okay?" Ben asked.

He was driving them back to New Orleans—he knew exactly the way to go this time. No GPS shenanigans for them. Kitty was hunched in the front seat, cleaned up and back in her clothes, reminding herself that she had arms and hands and not four furry legs ending in deadly claws. Her fingers itched.

"Yeah. Just . . . restless I guess. People can be so . . . *shitty.*"

"Yeah," he agreed. And he should know; he saw some of the worst in his line of work. "But not all of them."

"Angel ended up being pretty nice."

"For a zombie."

"For a zombie, of course. And I wonder if she's out there thinking we're pretty nice for werewolves."

"Well, we are. I think. I mean, you didn't actually *eat* that guy. So that's good."

"Yeah," she said, but it came out a little wistful. That last bit of her Wolf still lingering on the surface. "And neither did Angel."

Ben gave her a look and shook his head. "Someday we're going to take a trip where *nothing happens*. No murders, no vampires, no zombies, no conspiracies. Nothing. Just relaxing by the pool or something."

"Or something," she murmured, raising an eyebrow.

He glanced over at her, returning the suggestive look. And the car sped down the highway just a little bit faster, getting back to the hotel that much quicker.

The Lessons of Room 19

WESTON OCHSE AND DAVID WELLINGTON

ONE

Grief can take on many forms. Sometimes it's a granite headstone in a cemetery. Sometimes it's a shrine by the side of the road. There's a noble sort of grief in the elderly man sitting alone on a park bench. There's the respectful grief for a soldier, his boots resting atop his coffin as his unit files by, reverently saluting. Grief can be a source of fuel someone can tap into to accomplish something they wouldn't have ordinarily been able to accomplish. Grief can actually be a power for good. Or grief can just be a crazed man wielding a bloody coat hanger, beating the shit out of a ghost hanging on the wall who won't stop moaning in the voice of his dead girlfriend.

Jack Walker let the coat hanger fall to the ground and grabbed the almost-empty bottle of Jameson sitting on the dresser. He tilted back the bottle and let the last two inches of warm bitterness rush through him. He gasped as the alcohol hit him, wobbling him back on his heels. He closed his eyes and imagined her blue eyes sparkling, red hair caught in an ocean breeze, the light winking off Coronado Bay behind her.

Then he opened his eyes and beheld the mewling pathetic thing on the wall, blue glimmers sheening off it like visible static, and how it hung like a saggy red skin-suit. But if he touched it, when he touched it, it became Jen. He'd spent the first day and a half leaning against the wall, touching it, speaking to it and letting it speak back at him. At first he was sure it was Jen, able to channel herself from wherever she was in the afterlife, into this piece of Amish-made ectoplasm.

But then he'd fallen asleep and when he'd awoken, it wasn't Jen. It was someone else. Someone he didn't know at all. And no matter what he did, he couldn't get Jen back. So he'd begun his cycle of beating the thing into submission until it finally capitulated and brought Jen back. Sometimes it would pretend to be her if only to make him stop. But he could tell the difference. After all, they'd been engaged to be married. He knew her better than anyone.

Jack shoved the empty bottle into the box and pulled out another from the case he'd bought when he'd left Philly. He unscrewed the cap and took another gulp. But this time he was in front of the mirror and what he saw stopped him.

What the hell are you doing?

He let the question hang there as he stared at himself, hating himself. The unkempt hair, the bloodshot eyes, and the unwashed clothes couldn't be his. After all, he was part of a unit that was at the very spear tip of America's supernatural defense. He was a US Navy SEAL. He was the best weapon his country could create.

If you're so good, why'd you let her die then?

He snapped his gaze away from himself. For a brief

moment, he thought about breaking the damn mirror. Instead, he grabbed a sheet from the bed and draped it over the glass. Out of sight, out of mind.

The thought gave him a heartless giggle.

Out of mind.

He was surely that.

Out of mind.

"Jack, are you there?" came the words like a sizzle from a pan.

He averted his gaze from the ghost, went into the bathroom, and washed his face and hands. The cold water was a shock and helped shove some of the alcohol aside so he could actually think.

Somewhere down deep he knew that this wasn't the ghost of his dead girlfriend, but it could sometimes look and sound just like her. The Amish man behind the motel counter who'd sold it to him said that the ghost was capable of channeling Jen, but that it would also be like a shining light, drawing any ghost capable of noticing. Like now, it sounded like an old man, voice barely registering, cracking at the end of life.

When SEAL Team 666 had returned from their mission to England, Jack had buried himself in books about ghosts and mediums. He'd needed to speak with Jen one last time. He'd needed to apologize for not being there. To tell her that he'd wait and never go with another woman again. Laws had offered to help, but Jack hadn't felt like being part of Triple Six at that moment. He'd needed time to mourn . . . to be alone.

He'd managed to stumble across a story on one of the

conspiracy websites, an Amish legend about people who not only could harvest ghosts, but could channel the spirits of the dead. He'd done additional research and found that there were several blogs pointing toward southern Pennsylvania. He cross-referenced the locations with the Triple Six mission logs and found that as early as the 1920s, the team had been sent to investigate the disappearance of a state senator. Ultimately, Triple Six was able to track down a family living in the town of Gainesboro who'd kidnapped the man, then killed and harvested his ghost in order to get information about disputed land titles. These witchbillies, as they'd come to be called, were able to cast spells to include reading the future. The family was rounded up and put to work by the War Department, divining future attacks to American interests. That's where the information got skimpy.

So Jack had taken a few weeks' leave, flown into Philadelphia, and rented a car. He'd headed west and was soon in cow country; houses and barns clustered far apart from the others, as if beneath the looming ridges and the deep, shadowy valleys they could remain alone, isolated, to do whatever they wanted.

On the edge of Gainesboro he'd spied a two-story motel with a hex sign painted on the side. The White Deer Forest Travel Lodge. He'd decided to park and spend the night. Now five nights later, he'd yet to leave. If it wasn't for food delivery, he'd have long ago starved. He'd been lucky enough to stumble into witchbilly central. After an exchange of two months' pay he'd been saving for his and Jen's wedding, the motel owner had come into the room, hung a thing like a white deer hide on the wall, and bowed out smiling. That was all.

Jack wiped his face with a hand towel, tried to smooth back his hair, which was seriously out of regulation, and then found a clean shirt to put on—his last.

"Jack, is that you?" came the voice again, this time female, younger. Still not Jen.

He picked up the hanger from the floor and approached the ghost.

"I want Jen. Bring her back," he commanded.

Eyes formed in the skin and regarded him. *"Oh no, look at the man with the coat hanger."* A smirk formed, then vanished. Still not Jen.

"I know you're keeping her from me."

"Coat hangers make for great abortions, Jackie," came the voice of his mother, long dead.

"Stop it," he shouted.

"Stop it," it mimicked. Not Jen.

He grabbed at the bottle, knocking it over and onto the floor. He fell to his hands and knees, pulling it from beneath the bed where it had rolled. He sat. Laying the coat hanger on his lap, he opened the bottle and took a deep draft.

"You know what you need to do, right, little Jackie?" said the voice of a Filipino child Jack knew had been run over by a cement truck. Not Jen.

He knew what he needed to do. Hell yes, he did. He got to his feet, drank three huge gulps of anger fuel, then sat the bottle back on the dresser. He turned to the ghost and held up his coat hanger.

"What do you know about abortions?" he growled.

The ghost seemed about to respond, but Jack wouldn't let it. Instead he unleashed his own fury, slashing and hacking at the vile thing hanging on the wall. He screamed at it while he beat it, the words lost in his incomprehensible sobbing. Pieces of the ghost flew from it with each strike. The wall was scarred from where he'd hit it. But still he struck it. Over and over and over, until he was out of breath, his arms tired, his soul stained with what he knew he shouldn't be doing.

But finally his pathetic tantrum was rewarded.

"Jack, is that you?" Jen.

He fell to his knees and let his head rest against the wall beneath the ghost. He struggled to control his breathing . . . his emotions.

"Yes, yes, it's me. It's your Jack."

"I'm sorry I wasn't here. They wouldn't let me."

He nodded and let the hanger fall to the carpet. "I know, Jen. I know. But I fixed it."

"That's good, Jack. Now tell me," the ghost purred in the voice of Jen. *"Where were we?"*

"I don't know," he sobbed. "I forgot."

"We were talking about how much you love me, Jack."

He felt the bottom of his heart drop away. "Ah, that. Yes, we were, weren't we?"

They talked long into the night until daylight streamed through the dirty windows, afternoon light burning the eyes, and two more bottles of Jameson littering the carpet like headstones of shattered dreams.

TWO

Laura remembered when Patience was twelve, and how seriously creepy her special talent was back then. Now that the girl was nearly twenty, it was . . . still creepy, actually.

Patience Polder wore a white dress, very plain in design, that buttoned all the way up to her throat. Her hair was covered by a white cloth.

She might have been an Amish girl, dressed like that. She definitely wasn't. Patience was the leader of the witchbillies, a little community of people who dressed simply and lived simply in the backwoods of Pennsylvania, keeping their own ways. Like the Amish, they were wary of technology, but for a different reason. Because they'd found something better. Magic, for lack of a better term.

Patience sat on a dark wooden chair, one leg up over one of its arms, her bare foot kicking back and forth. Her eyes were closed.

She was a seer. Not some kind of phony medium speaking with the spirits of the dead and handing out empty platitudes. Not a fake psychic claiming to know where the bodies were buried. Patience knew things she couldn't possibly know. She saw them as clearly as Laura saw the nose on her own face. She would talk about things that wouldn't happen for years as casually as people talked about yesterday's news, because for her, there wasn't any difference.

"He's in a motel near Gainesboro," Patience said. As if she'd read it somewhere on the internet. "He's already lost."

There was no computer in the farmhouse. There was a

telephone about a half mile away, in a trailer at the edge of the valley. When it got dark in the farmhouse you lit a kerosene lamp, or you just went to bed.

Laura had worried about the Polders, once. What would happen if there was a fire, or someone broke into the farmhouse? They couldn't call 911. Now she knew the witchbillies were perfectly capable of taking care of their own problems.

Just not in a way anyone outside the valley would ever call normal.

"You'll need to hurry," Patience told Laura. "By the time the sun sets, it'll be too late for him." The girl studied her short-cut fingernails.

Laura nodded and rose from her chair. She'd come to Patience because she'd been asked to find some kind of Special Ops guy who'd gone rogue. She'd been given very few details. A name, Jack Walker, and the fact that this US Navy SEAL was somewhere in southern Pennsylvania. This from an anonymous voice calling her cell phone on an untraceable number. A voice that knew another name, the name of her probation officer. A voice that could make very believable threats. The voice hadn't identified itself, hadn't even responded when she demanded to know more. The voice had not specified why she had been chosen. Certainly there were better people for the job. All it said was that if she didn't find this guy, didn't "exfiltrate" him, she was going back to jail.

"Why me?" Laura asked, now, because she might actually get an answer from Patience.

"It has to be you. You need to go, now. Every minute you

waste is going to make this harder. And Laura?" Patience asked.

"What?"

"Get him out of there. By sunset. Or it'll be too late for you, as well." Patience turned and looked her right in the eye, then lifted a hand and waved it in a shooing motion.

With an exasperated sigh, Laura headed out of the room, back into the daylight outside. After the dusty gloom of the farmhouse, the world dazzled her, half-blinded her. She put on a pair of sunglasses and jumped in her car.

She sped all the way to Gainesboro. It wasn't far. She opened up the maps app on her phone and set it to search for local motels.

The app zoomed way out, to show her a motel on the edge of Lancaster. Twenty miles away.

Laura cursed and pulled over to the side of the road. She zoomed in on the map again and scrolled around, looking for any sign of the place Patience had mentioned. Nothing turned up. She zoomed out a little more and saw a big patch of green. White Deer Forest, one of those patches of land reserved for hunters. There were a lot of hunters in Pennsylvania. People would come from miles around to hunt in that forest, and they needed a place to stay. There had to be some kind of motel nearby, but where?

Laura Caxton had grown up in this part of Pennsylvania. She'd spent years on these roads as a state trooper, doing highway patrol back when she was a solid citizen, not an ex-con. She knew how this land worked, could read volumes in the way the ridges ran, how the shadows folded into the hollows between those long, high hills. In a place like this, you would build near running water, where the local creek met the highway.

Laura had no psychic talents, at least none that were actually helpful. She was a hell of a detective, though, when she set her mind to it. She drove another two miles, deeper into the woods. The light danced as it filtered down through the rolling waves of leaves over her car. Up ahead she saw a general store and a pizza place. She pulled into the lot they shared and waited until somebody came out, a middle-aged guy in a stained T-shirt holding a large pie, shifting it from hand to hand as it burned his fingers. She rolled down her window. "Hey!" she called.

This was rural Pennsylvania. The people were friendly. He smiled and walked over to her car. Set his pizza on her hood.

"You know of a motel around here?" she asked. "Some place hunters go?"

"T'ain't season yet, not for months," he said, with a shake of his head.

"That's all right, I'm not hunting." Not for deer, anyway. "Listen. I'll level with you," she said, "I'm looking for somebody. Somebody who probably doesn't want to be found. I heard he was holing up around here." Maybe the guy with the pizza would mistake her for a cop. Even years after she'd lost her badge, it happened all the time. She still had the cop look. You couldn't shake that once you learned it.

The guy smiled, one of those nasty grins that meant he thought he knew more than he was letting on. "What happened, your husband run out on you? Give him a couple days, I'm sure he'll come home on his own."

Okay, so much for the cop look. Whatever, she could work with this. "He took my ATM card and I need to buy groceries," she said.

The man shrugged. That stupid grin was lingering on his face like it was painted there. "There is a place, but if he's there . . . well, maybe he ain't comin' back after all." He nodded as if he'd just decided something, worked through some moral quandary. "Ayep, you head down this road another two miles. Look for the hex sign on the side of the place, you'll know it. I'm sorry, honey."

"Sorry?" she asked.

"If he's there, maybe you don't want him back."

She thanked the man and got back on the road.

She found the motel soon enough. It was the only building on that stretch of road that hadn't collapsed under its own weight or rotted down to nothing where it stood. It looked like there had been a decent-sized town here once, but the motel was all that remained. Not that it was in great shape, except by comparison. The white paint was all peeling and the hex sign had faded in the sun. A bunch of cars sat out front, several of them rusted out so they would never run again.

The hex sign on its side wall was a work of art. You saw a lot of hex signs in this part of the state—round panels of wood, colorfully painted with designs of birds and stars and hearts. They were an old folk tradition, brought to Pennsylvania by German settlers. Most of them were just for tourists now, souvenirs to take home from your visit to Amish country.

Typically they were the size of a dinner plate. This one

was ten feet across, and so packed with symbols it must have taken days just to design, much less paint.

The witchbillies—Patience Polder's people—could make hex signs that had real power. They could protect a house from intruders, or help crops grow. This looked like one of those. She wondered if it functioned to keep people away, those who weren't invited, at least. She wondered if that hex sign was why the motel didn't show up on maps.

There was a little office to one side of the motel, with an attached restaurant that looked out on the road. The main bulk of the place was two floors of rooms, all of them facing the same direction, each one fronted by a plate glass window. Every single room had its curtains drawn, but she saw a flicker of blue light through a crack in the drapes of one of the first-floor rooms. She walked across the parking lot, her shoes crunching on the gravel. She wanted a better look.

Not that she didn't know already. She knew that particular shade of blue all too well. As she got closer, she started to hear her father's voice calling out from behind her. Still faint enough that she could pretend it was a trick her mind was playing on her.

As she got closer to that blue light, it was like her father was standing right behind her.

"*Laura,*" he called.

She heard it with her ears. It was as real as the crunch of the gravel, the chirping of the crickets out in the woods.

"*Laura,*" he said. "*We need to talk about Mom.*"

She clamped her eyes shut, terrified she would see him if she looked. He'd been dead for twenty years. It wasn't fair.

Laura Caxton might not have any psychic talents but she did have one nasty psychic liability. She was sensitive to ghosts. "Susceptible" might be a better word. Vulnerable. She couldn't resist them.

Whoever that voice on the phone had been, the person who sent her on this manhunt was a real bastard. A jerk of the first order.

"Laura, she's suffering. She's just hurting every day now," her father said. *"The doctors say the cancer's in remission, but I think they're wrong."*

She started hammering on doors at random, shouting for the people inside to come out.

But no one came out. Twice she saw haunted faces peer at her through a gap in water-stained curtains, but that was all. Then she saw the rental car. A pristine Detroit pearl in a lot full of rusty crap. It was parked in front of room 19. She ran and banged on the door.

No answer, but she could hear someone inside. A deep voice, babbling. Drunk, by the sound of it.

She glanced both ways. Seeing no one, she raised her leg and kicked open the door. It slammed into the wall. She caught it on the rebound as she strode into the room. She saw the thing on the wall for a brief second before she averted her eyes. Even that little time created a longing, a yearning she was barely able to control. She was desperate to be out of the place. But first she had to get her guy away from the ghostskin.

She couldn't see him at first. She took in the ruin of the motel room, the carpet strewn with garbage, wet towels mildewing on the side of a bed that had probably never been slept in. The blue flicker of the skin on the wall kept pulling at her, demanding her attention.

"She's hurting, Laura. Not just her body. Laura? Young lady, this is serious. We need to talk about your mother."

Already the skin was changing. Taking shape. A wedding ring glinted on a hand that only had three fingers. As she shoved her way through the garbage-strewn floor, the skin grew a fourth finger, and then a thumb. It would start growing her father's face next. It would look like he was walking out of the wall. Coming back.

She had to get out of this room before that happened. She forced herself to look down and saw what she'd come for. The guy she'd been sent to save must have been something once—he was built like an athlete. His face was covered in greasy stubble, though, maybe a week's worth, and his hair was a rat's nest.

There was no way she could carry him. "Get up," she said. "Come on. You need to help me."

"Fuck off," he moaned. He wasn't even looking at her.

No, of course not. He was looking at the skin on the wall. The skin that had started to form her father's arm, his shoulder. The thick cords of his neck, that special place she remembered hiding her face on the Fourth of July, when the fireworks were too loud and scary. That same place she'd buried her tears when Mom died.

Laura punched herself in the thigh, hard enough to leave a bruise. The pain helped clear her head. She looked down at the man on the floor and wondered if maybe he could use a little of that spur, himself.

So she kicked him.

Tried to, anyway.

He might be a drunken shadow of himself here in this dead-end place, but his reflexes were hardwired. His hand shot out and grabbed her ankle, hard enough she worried he might break it. "I said fuck off!" he shouted.

At least there was still some fire in him. "Get the hell up, sailor," she said. She tried to make herself sound like a drill sergeant. "Get up right now or I'm leaving you behind. Orders or no orders."

"Just . . . just give me a second. Gotta talk to somebody first," he said, struggling to get to his feet, his hands unable to grip the bed enough to help him up.

On the wall the skin started growing hair. Her father's thinning hair. He'd never tried to comb it over. Never worried too much about how he looked, though Mom always talked about how handsome he'd been, back when they were courting. Mom always said—

"No time," she told the sailor. She looked around and found an ice bucket that was half-full of what she thought was stagnant water.

It wasn't water. He'd been so locked into the skin's trance that he hadn't been able to make it to the toilet.

He came up at her, howling like an animal, ready to kill.

She could work with that.

"Come on!" she said. "You want a piece of me? Then come and get it, tough guy!"

He chased her out of the room and halfway across the parking lot. Then suddenly his face changed and he looked at her like he had no idea where he was or what he was doing there.

"Hey," he said. "Hey, I'm sorry about that. I thought you were . . . I thought . . ."

"I know," she told him. "I know what you've been up to for the last week."

Big tough sailor guy he might be. Still he turned his face away in shame.

"I know. And I can help," she said.

THREE

He needed to clean himself up, but she couldn't let him out of her sight. They headed over to the little restaurant attached to the motel, all grimy tables and mismatched chairs. "Restroom?" Laura asked, when she spotted the lone waitress leaning on the counter.

The woman pointed behind her, barely looking up. Until she realized Laura was taking the sailor into the bathroom with her. "No, no, no," she said then, chasing after them. "This is a family place, you can't—"

Laura slammed the door in the waitress' face. That seemed to do the trick.

She sat down on the lid of the toilet while he leaned hard on the cheap porcelain sink; hard enough the bolts holding it to the wall creaked.

"What's your name?" she asked, though she already knew.

He took a while answering. Like he wasn't sure she had security clearance. "Jack," he said.

She nodded. "You've got some powerful friends, Jack. People who want you back. That's not enough, is it? Just knowing that somebody worries about you, it's not as good as what you had in that room."

"Listen, ma'am," he said. "I'm going to apologize for this in advance. But you know shit-all about me."

Laura let it sit like that while he washed his face, ran fingers through his hair. She could see the discipline in this man, the iron in him, like she was looking at the bones under his skin. She could feel his shame radiating off his back. He pulled his shirt off over his head. Reached for his belt buckle, then stopped and glanced her way.

"Don't worry," she told him. "I'm not going to get any ideas. For one thing, you look like something that got snaked out of a drain right now. For another, you aren't my type."

"Right," he said, drawing out the word.

"Let me put it this way: you have any sisters?"

He laughed. It wasn't much, just a quick chuckle, but at least it was something. If he'd chosen to be a hard case, he could have made this impossible.

He scrubbed himself down with paper towels and pink liquid hand soap. Only when he started dressing again did she say what she needed to say.

"Jack, I do know one thing about you," she told him. "There's somebody—somebody who means more to you than your friends do. Somebody you can't live without. And they're dead."

She saw every muscle in his body tense up. His hands balled into fists and she wondered if she would have to fight him, right there in the bathroom.

Instead he punched the mirror.

In prison, the mirrors were just polished steel. You could

punch them all you wanted and they would just dent. Sometimes she had trouble remembering she was outside now, a place where things shattered. She cried out a little as fragments of silvered glass, long triangular shards, cascaded down into the sink and onto the floor.

He turned and stared at her. His hand was bloody, bits of mirror sticking out of his skin.

"I'm done," he said, his voice empty, as he slid to the ground, his back to the door. "I'm done. Just leave me here. I'm done and done."

She had no idea what to tell him.

They sat together in the bathroom, staring at each other, staring at nothing.

FOUR

Eventually, Jack pulled himself to his feet, cleaned his wounds as well as he could, then exited the bathroom.

The waitress didn't seem particularly surprised when Jack came out of the restroom with blood streaming down his arm. She grabbed a towel and wrapped his hand for him, tying it in a knot. "Happens more often than you'd think," she said.

No demand that he pay for the damage. No insistence that he leave *right now* and not come back. She took one look at an injured man and she tried to help.

He'd forgotten there were people in the world who weren't trying to kill each other.

"Let's get you some food. You too, Miss, you look like you could use a good meal. Burgers and fries okay? They're frozen, just take me a second to defrost them and heat 'em up."

The woman, this strange, short-haired woman who had dragged him away from Jen, nodded and then she led him over to a booth and sat him down. She never stopped staring at him.

"We call them ghosts but they're not the spirits of the dead. Don't think of dead people haunting the living because they have unfinished business, they're not like that. I don't know if that kind of ghost even exists, really."

"They do," he said, though he shouldn't have. Maybe all these people trying to help him were making him soft. "They exist. And they're bad enough."

She didn't seem surprised to hear it. "This is different. Don't think lost souls. Think ectoplasm, maybe," she said. Laura. Her name was Laura. That one fact had actually penetrated the swamp that his brain had become.

"They're not dead. They're living creatures, I think. Not flesh and blood, and not from around here. Some other . . . Jeez, I know how this sounds, but they come from another dimension or something. Mostly they just pass through our world, barely touching us. Maybe you hear a whisper from behind you, maybe catch a glimpse of something in a window, and that's it, they're gone. Somebody, somewhere along the line, figured out a way to trap them. And skin them."

He looked up at her. How did she know all this? Most people in his experience were more than happy to ignore all the crazy stuff. The monsters and the magic. Who wanted to live in a world full of zombies and werewolves, right? So much easier to pretend it was all myth and forget about it and let SEAL Team 666 handle it.

In his experience people who knew, who lived in the world where the bad things roamed, had to be broken; so fucked up by what they'd experienced they could never go home again. So what was this woman's story?

She was still talking, and he knew he should listen. Much as he wanted to go back inside his own head.

"Skin them," he said. "Like raccoon pelts."

"Exactly like that," Laura told him. "That thing on your wall—it's a ghostskin. Maybe the first person to make one of those just thought it would be pretty. Shimmery and blue, right? Might make a nice cocktail dress. That probably didn't work out so well for them. The skins are psycho-reactive. That's a fancy word for saying they can read your mind. That skin you were looking at, it's not intelligent, it's not self-aware. It *is* hungry. It feeds off your energy. It knows one trick to help it get its food, that's all. But it's a hell of a trick."

"Listen," he said. "I know it isn't real. I know it's not—" Damn it. He would not say Jen's name out loud, not here. "I know it was just showing me what I wanted to see. Saying what I wanted to hear. Okay? I know it's just an illusion. So . . . thank you. Thank you for pulling me away from that thing. Job well done, yeah? You got me out of that room and clearly I needed help with that. I owe you."

She leaned back in the booth, her arms folded across her chest. He knew that posture. She was waiting him out. Eventually the food came. She picked at her fries.

"I think I'm going to be okay, now," he said. "I fell down, sure. But now I'm back on my feet. You can go home. I'll be okay."

"It's not real," she said. Repeating his words.

He looked down at his plate. He couldn't imagine eating that greasy mess—he might as well have been served a plate of wood chips doused in kerosene. Probably would have smelled better.

"Yeah. Exactly. Now I know that. I can shake it. So thanks. For telling me it's not real."

"A heroin addict will tell you they can feel the drug in their veins, feel it climbing up their arm, even though there are no nerve endings inside your blood vessels."

"I don't understand," Jack said.

"What that addict feels, is it real? Because they'll do anything to get it again. It feels pretty damned real to them. You say you're okay, Jack. You say I can go home. Because you know once I walk out that door, you can head right back to room nineteen. Back to that ghostskin."

He gave her a nasty look, then. Jack Walker had some pretty good nasty looks in him. She didn't flinch.

"You're wondering how I knew that," she said. "Can't you guess? I'm addicted to ghostskin, too. Just like you."

"Addicted—" He shook his head furiously. "I'm not addicted. I haven't even been here a week."

She laughed hoarsely. "Yeah. That's a good one. Make no mistake about it. If that room was full of needles and heroin, it would be easier to walk away." Seeing his doubt, she asked, "Are you going to tell me you don't want to go back? Are you thinking right now you can *just say no*?"

Instead of answering, he looked away.

"When I walked into your room, it reacted to me. It started taking on the shape of my father."

"What? No, it looked like—"

She shook her head. "It shows each person what they want to see. We could look at it at exactly the same time and see two different things. I miss my dad, a lot. I would give anything just to see him again. The ghostskin knows that. Like I said, just one trick, but a really good one."

"You're not going to leave me alone, are you?" Jack asked.

"No. I'm going to shove you into my car and drive you someplace safe and let you sleep this off. Then maybe we talk about how you get rid of me."

He shoved his plate away. He found his wallet in his pocket and pulled out a crisp hundred-dollar bill and slapped it on the table. He couldn't look at the waitress on the way out. Couldn't so much as thank her. He felt worthless, desperate, stupid. He glanced at his car in the parking lot. The keys were snug in his pocket. He could just drive away and get lost somewhere.

Instead she pointed toward her own car, a little Japanese car like the one Jen had driven.

Maybe, though.

Maybe there was still a chance for him.

Maybe.

As he reached for the passenger door, he couldn't help but look back at the motel. Looking was okay, right? If you didn't look too long, maybe.

For the very first time he actually *saw* the motel, its run-down decks, its rows of rooms. For the first time he noticed all the drawn curtains. Saw the faint blue flicker coming from every room.

"Oh hell," he said, letting his hand fall away from the car door.

"Don't. Just get in the car," she told him.

"No," he said. "It's in every room." He glanced up at the motel's sign. NO VACANCY. "Shit, there are other people in there. Other people like us . . . like me," he added, the words sour in his mouth.

"They're not your problem," Laura told him.

Jack Walker didn't operate that way. It was in his DNA to be heroic even if doing so could get him killed . . . even if being a hero was the last thing he needed to be doing. What had Commander Holmes called him that first day with Triple Six? Impetuous? Dangerous? Impulsive? All of those were still true, except he'd learned to rein them in. But that was before an asshole motel owner had created a prison for those in need, a place where the desperate became the damned, wasting away their lives talking to a ghostskin, pretending to be someone they couldn't possibly be.

No. If he was ever going to get past this, if he was going to look at himself in a mirror again, ever, there was something he needed to do first.

She tried to grab his arm. She weighed probably half what he did.

He shrugged her off and made a beeline for the motel's office.

"Jack!" she called after him.

He heard, but he was on mission now, and he wasn't going to stop until he was done. He was like a man on fire as he burst into the office, the bell above the door heralding his coming. No one was behind the counter, so he tried the door on the left, which he remembered had access to the back office. It was locked. He opened it with his size eleven shoe key, shattering the cheaply made doorframe. The room had a desk, a chair, and a file cabinet, but no person.

He exited the room and kicked down the other door, which was to the manager's apartment—nothing more than a glorified suite, with a living area and a bedroom, both of which were empty also. As he approached the closed door to the bathroom, he noticed that it had a hex sign painted on it. He had no idea what it meant, but knew that something important had to be inside.

As he reached to open the door, Laura's voice came from behind him. "I'd be careful opening that if I were you."

"What's it going to do? Explode?" he snarled.

"You see hex signs all over this part of the country. People paint them on their houses to keep their kids safe. For them, the signs are about as effective as nailing up a horseshoe. Just a quaint old custom."

"I'm guessing this one's not so quaint." It didn't look like a lot of the hex signs he'd seen before, actually. It wasn't as colorful, or as complex. It looked like a pentagram made of bird wings.

"If you actually know what you're doing, there's real magic you can put in those things. That one," she said, gesturing at the door, "for instance, is the hex for a safe haven. It protects whoever is inside."

He turned to regard the hex once more. "Safe haven from whom?" he asked.

"When you start messing with psychoreactive stuff like

ghosts, it has a tendency to draw attention. Think of the ghostskins like a magnet. Bad things are drawn to bad things."

"So you think the owner is inside? Hiding from us?"

She cocked her head. "Could be. But we need to be careful. Whoever it is has been using witchbilly magic. It can get dangerous."

"So I shouldn't touch the door?"

"I wouldn't."

"Okay, then." He went to the side of the bed, cleared the surface of an end table with one sweep of an arm, and hefted it. He turned, took three running steps, and threw it at the door. The door shattered inward and the table immediately burst into flame.

He heard Laura run out of the room, but he wasn't about to leave.

He grabbed the bed cover and threw it on top of the burning table. Covering his mouth with his left hand, he leaned into the bathroom.

Empty.

Where was the manager, the man who had given him the ghostskin?

Laura came back inside lugging a fire extinguisher. Good thing she did, too. The last thing he needed on his conscience was a motel's worth of burn victims as a result of a fire he'd caused.

When she was done, she turned to him. "Don't go throwing things at hexes. You never know if it might throw something back at you."

He understood, but could barely contain his frustration. He needed to do something. Anything. She seemed to notice.

"It appears that we have three choices. We can either search for the guy who put the hexes in place and created the ghostskins or we can go into each and every room and try and bring the victims to safety."

After a beat he said, "I thought you said there were three choices."

"Or three, we do nothing and get the hell out of here. It's actually the one I like best."

He suddenly felt exhausted. How long had he been in the thrall of the ghostskin, and what had it taken out of him? He could just leave—just pack up and get the hell out, go back to Coronado and do a mission, leaving all of this behind him. He could do it. He could absolutely turn his back on all the people enthralled by someone's sick joke of a soul leech. But then the real voice of Jen asked him from a faraway memory—*But at what cost to your soul?*

Who was he kidding? He could no more leave than he could give up. His eyes brightened a little as he set his jaw. "Let's find this wizard and see if we can't find an 'off' button for these damned ghostskins."

If he'd had his team with him, he'd have either requested overhead sat imagery or considered using a man-packable UAV to survey the area. But since he wasn't with his team, he was forced to do it the old-fashioned way. The front of the motel and the parking lot were to the right of the manager's office, so they peeled off left. He was in front, with Laura behind him. He could have sworn she rolled her eyes at him, but he couldn't be sure.

About halfway around the back, they saw a worn path leading into the thick Pennsylvania woods that abutted the back of the motel. The last of the daylight was failing, and the shadows under the trees were thick with darkness. Not the best time of day for recon, but they didn't have much choice. He glanced back once at Laura, who gestured impatiently for him to proceed. He went into a slight crouch as he moved, ready to react to any signs of threat. The path wove through several trees and knee-high ferns. After about thirty feet, he spied a mark on a tree that had to be man-made. He crouched and searched the ground until he found a pressure plate in the middle of the path. What it might set off he didn't know and unlike with the bathroom door, he didn't want to know.

He silently communicated his discovery, then pointed to the thick brush and made a walking sign with his fingers.

Laura raised an eyebrow, but made no other comment.

Walker left the trail and began paralleling it on the left. The going was much slower. Not only was the brush thick enough that he needed to push his way through, but he also had to be concerned for additional traps set to get those who left the trail, although he hoped the motel manager wasn't that sophisticated.

Tripping, sweating, and cursing as they pushed their way through the brush, they made it another fifty feet before they saw a worn wooden shack leaning lazily against the side of a hill. Hex signs had been drawn all over the sides and the door in various colors and patterns. Walker didn't recognize them, but their totality made him itch, indicating that they indeed held a lot of magic.

"You're the Special Ops guy. What do we do now?" Laura said in his ear.

"About now we'd generally send in Hoover."

"You'd send in a vacuum?"

"Hoover's our dog."

"Why'd you name your dog after a vacuum?"

He stared at her for a moment, then shook his head. "It's a long story," he said. "We can either make our way through the hexes or we can wait to see who comes out."

"That is if anyone is in there," she added.

"There is that," he agreed. "I don't suppose you've got a piece on you?"

"What, a gun?" she asked. "No."

"You came out here unarmed?"

"Bullets can't kill a ghost," she explained. "Plus . . . I'm on probation."

He cursed silently to himself. He hadn't brought any weapons to the motel, either. He'd been too worried he might do something irrevocable, so he'd left them behind.

Great.

They stood in the brush staring at the shack for about ten minutes, when Walker couldn't take it any longer. He began to move forward.

She grabbed the back of his collar. "Where do you think you're going?"

"I want to see the other side of the shack. Make sure there isn't another way out."

"Be careful," she whispered.

Aren't I always? he said to himself, knowing it to be a colossal delusion. Still, it was his delusion so he held fast to it. He checked the ground before each foot landed and made his way quickly across the path and into the dense vegetation on the other side. Sidestepping around a bush, he found himself face-to-face with a shimmering blue ghostskin, its flat misshapen surface even now changing into that of his dead fiancée.

He squeezed shut his eyes and gritted his teeth as an impossible voice crackle-whispered, *"Don't leave me, Jack. It's cold in Hell. I need you to keep me warm."*

He spun back around the bush and fell to a knee. He tried desperately to clear his head. It sounded so much like her. What if she was in Hell? What if she was there because of something he'd caused her to do, like in the mission to Mexico where she'd been forced to commit murder to save him?

No! Stop it! he told himself. This was exactly what it wanted . . . to get under his skin.

He stood, determined to get beyond it. He kept his eyes open, but focused. He spun around the bush again and saw where the ghostskin was hanging from the tree like a profane sheet. He stepped past it, his eyes on the shack.

Still, it spoke to him. *"Jack. So cold. Jack. Don't leave me."*

He felt his eyes burn as he continued to step through the brush. When he made it another ten feet the feeling disappeared, and his tears evaporated. He took a deep, gasping breath and beheld a cave opening that had been previously blocked from view by their position on the other side of the path.

Walker examined the perimeter for any sort of early-warning devices, but couldn't see anything. Entering the shack was absolutely out of the question. But the cave, on the other hand . . . if that's where the warlock was hanging his magic hat, then that's where Walker wanted to be.

He found a path through the forest that would take him closest to the hillside. It took him fifteen minutes of stealthy walk-crawling to follow the path to where it ended, six feet from the hillside, and ten feet to the right of the opening. He checked again for any type of surveillance, but he couldn't even detect any power lines, much less any electronic devices.

Keeping low with his back to the hillside, he slid toward the opening, until his shoulder was about to edge into the open space. He stuck his head into the opening for a brief second, taking in everything, then returned to an upright position.

The cave was deeper than he'd expected. From the muted rays of twilight, he was able to see a few tables near the entrance with some arcane instruments laid out upon them and the telltale blue glitter from ghostskins hanging farther back. A well-worn path ran through a stack of waist-high boxes nearest the entrance.

If he could make it to the boxes, he could use them for concealment as he checked out the rest of the cave. With luck, he'd find the warlock before he'd need to traverse to where the ghostskins hung. He could almost hear them now, a chorus of false voices, begging and breaking his heart. The fact that he now dreaded to hear Jen's voice made him angry. He grabbed on to that rage and used it as his weapon.

He cautiously edged around the corner, trying to limit the amount of time he was backlit by the opening. He almost made it to the boxes before he heard a faint click, then the sound of a generator coming on inside the shack. Before he could even move, he was speared by a shaft of blinding light. It was as if someone had turned a spotlight on him, except this spotlight kept him from moving. He was completely frozen. Nothing moved at all. Not even his lungs. He panicked, but it did nothing to change his position. It was as if he was locked out of his own body. Without breath, his body would cease to function in a matter of minutes, if not seconds.

Then he saw it. Coming out from a light embedded in the ceiling of the cave in front of him was a hex sign. Not a hex sign drawn on the ground or on a wall. Not one of substance. But one made of light, one projected upon him trapping him as surely as if it had been a physical restraint. A light as deadly as a bullet to the brain.

FIVE

What the hell was taking Walker so long?

The sun had set and night had fallen across the woods and still there was no sign of him. Laura crouched low in the undergrowth, wondering what her move here ought to be. She was only supposed to rescue the jerk, not back him up on some kind of mission of vindication. Sure, she felt bad for the other people in the motel—she was a ghost junkie herself. Maybe she would have come back for them later, once she had Jack somewhere safe.

Yeah. She would have. She would have done exactly what Walker had chosen to do, she knew. She just would have been smarter about it.

She peered through the darkness, trying to get a better

look at the shack. Somebody really wanted to protect it. Typically even somebody who knew what they were doing would paint a single hex sign on the eaves of a barn or a house, and that would be enough. This shack was protected from every possible direction. Whoever had done that—and presumably, whoever had collected the ghostskins and put them up in the motel rooms—wasn't just some amateur witchbilly.

They were the real deal.

Walker might already be dead if he'd tried to break into that shack. Hex signs could protect, but they could also cast powerful curses on anyone who tried to interfere with them. They could turn your bones to custard, or dry up all the blood in your body.

She couldn't wait any longer.

Moving as carefully and as quietly as she could, Laura moved to the shack, looking for any way inside that wouldn't trigger one of the hex signs. She knew it couldn't be that easy, and it wasn't. She saw no sign of Walker, nor did she sense anything moving inside the shack. She fought back a strong urge to grunt in frustration.

Then the shack began to rumble.

She backed away, expecting a legion of hexenmeisters to burst from the hoary hex-laced wood, but there was nothing.

The rumbling continued, but it wasn't like something magical. This was something mechanical. She stepped to the right as she tried to figure out what it could be. In the dark she almost missed the cave entrance—probably the entrance to an old worked-out coal mine—but a flash of light clued her in and when she went to investigate she nearly stumbled into the trap herself.

Walker stood perfectly still in the middle of the cave mouth, bathed in a waterfall of light, facing away from her. Not moving so much as a muscle. He looked like a man who'd stepped on a land mine and knew that if he lifted his foot again, it would go off.

Then she noticed something strange. There was a breeze blowing out of the cave, cool air from inside the earth. It ruffled her clothes. But Walker's hair wasn't moving at all, as if it was held down with a whole bottle of Aqua Net.

She looked around him, knowing there had to be a trap. When she saw the hex sign glowing from the projector embedded in the ceiling, she swore under her breath. It was a simple repeating geometric pattern of snowflakes being projected into space, freezing anyone within its grasp in place. If it was strong enough, it might stop his heart, too. But if she tried to touch him, if she tried to save him, she would get stuck in the same hex.

There was no time to think about what to do next. She found a wooden crate that was half-rotten; it must have been back here a long time. With her foot she broke off a piece of it about two and a half feet long, mostly just a worm-eaten plank.

She wound up like it was a baseball bat and smacked him across the back of his knees. But it did nothing other than shatter the rotten board. She went and found another one, this one a little stouter. She hit him hard enough in the legs that the board cracked. But it also caused Walker to stumble and fall backward, out of the hex sign's influence.

He gasped for breath and she then realized he would have suffocated if she hadn't broken him free. He crawled toward her on the ground, avoiding the nimbus of hexed light, his apparent need to curse her out overwhelmed by his need for oxygen.

She crouched down next to him and checked his eyes. His pupils were huge, but then again, it was dark in the cave. That about exhausted her knowledge of how to check somebody for brain damage. "Can you talk?" she asked. "Can you get up?"

"Yeah," he muttered, still wheezing. He pulled himself up to his feet, hobbling on a game leg, and stared at her. "You didn't have to hit me so hard."

"Yes I did," she snarled. "I told you not to mess with this shit. Now, can we please get out of here? Before one of us gets killed by your stupidity?"

He bridled at that, but, good. Maybe if she got him pissed off enough he would actually start thinking. Then he opened his mouth and proved her theory wrong. "Not," he said, between heavy breaths, "until we . . . finish this."

She sighed in exasperation. She couldn't just leave him here, as much as she might want to. The voice on the phone, the one that sent her on this mission, had made that very clear. She needed to save this guy or she was going back to prison.

So she took her time getting out of the cave. Letting him stagger after her. When she reached the cave mouth she stopped and looked out into the night, making sure nobody had noticed them stumbling around.

Too bad somebody had.

Blue light filtered through the trees, and her first thought was that dawn must be breaking, even though it was hours away. Hadn't it just been twilight? Then the light moved and she saw it had the shape of a man. She glanced over and saw the door of the hex-protected shed standing wide open, the sound of the generator louder and no longer muffled. She had no doubt that she was looking at the manager of the motel, the hexenmeister, to use the technical term, who had skinned all those ghosts. Who had nearly killed Walker.

Not that his identity was immediately discernible. He was dressed in a suit that covered him from head to toe, a suit made of ghostskin. Dozens of skins, in fact, held together with loose stitches of coarse black thread. Like a patchwork doll.

A hell of a lot more dangerous, though, than any doll.

"Jack," she whispered. "Jack, maybe you should just run."

He was still doubled over, with his hand rubbing the back of his leg where she'd struck it. He managed to give her another one of his nasty looks.

He had no idea what was about to happen to them.

It was hardly the first time since she'd left prison that Laura wished she still owned a gun. Ghostskins weren't bulletproof. Even though she'd told Walker they wouldn't do any good, if she got close with this asshole, she might be able to shoot him, getting past his protective suit.

She thought desperately, trying to figure a way out of this, even as the flickering blue man came closer. Unfortunately, before she'd come up with anything, Walker decided to act.

He grabbed her shoulder and held it for support for a few brief seconds, then pushed past her—maybe he thought he was going to protect her—and shouted out, "Hey! You, fucker—you've got a lot to answer for." Then he rushed forward in a crouch that a hundred terrorists had probably witnessed right before they'd gone on to meet their maker. Only the hexenmeister was a terrorist of a different sort and no US Navy SEAL, no matter how tough, could go against him unarmed.

"No!" Laura shouted, but it was no use. She chased after him—then came up short.

"*Caxton?*"

"*Laura?*"

"*Is that you, pumpkin?*"

"*Ms. Caxton?*"

"*Trooper? Were we in a car accident or something?*"

She squeezed her eyes shut but she couldn't keep out the voices. They were all around her, close enough that it felt like she could reach out and touch them. Every person she'd ever betrayed, or failed, or disappointed. Old bosses. Old lovers. Cops she'd gotten killed in her crusade against the vampires. Innocent civilians—kids—who'd died because she had been a few seconds too late.

"*Laura?*" Deanna asked. Deanna, who'd killed herself because Laura couldn't see how bad her depression had gotten. Deanna, who came back as a vampire.

"*Baby,*" her mother said, coughing up her last breath.

"*Laura, we need to talk,*" her father said.

"*Caxton. Didn't think I'd see you again.*"

That last voice—she couldn't face it. Couldn't face the memories that came with hearing it again. She forced herself to open her eyes, to look around.

The night was blue with them. Bright enough to hurt

her eyes. They stood between the trees. Some right at her shoulder. Others farther away, gesturing for her to come to them. Not just spectral hands, not disembodied voices. They were there, as real as life.

"Jen, please, honey. Stop this." This time it was a real voice. One that wasn't just in her head. Walker was pleading with somebody, somebody Laura couldn't see.

It wasn't that you thought they were real—you knew, the whole time, that it was just an illusion. Psychic nonsense pulled out of your head and shown to you like a movie of somebody you couldn't bear to see. Somebody you couldn't let go.

The thing was that knowing the truth of it didn't help much.

"Walker," she shouted. "Walker, stick with me! We have to—we have to—"

"Pumpkin. It's my birthday. Why won't you come kiss me?"

"Hey, gorgeous. Long time no see!"

"Baby. Baby, just look at me. Just talk to me."

They pressed in close around her. Reached for her with cold, flickering blue hands. She pushed through them.

She had to stop the hexenmeister. She might not be a cop anymore, but she still went looking for the bad guys who broke the rules.

She lashed out at the ghosts, all around her, punching and kicking, and yet they weren't there—when she should have connected they were just . . . somewhere else, effortlessly escaping her, taunting her. Mocking her.

"Laura."

"Laura."

"*Laura . . .*"

"*Caxton. Thought I taught you better than this.*"

And there he was. Not the motel manager, not Walker. It was Jameson Arkeley. The man who'd taught her everything she knew about fighting vampires. The man who'd turned himself into a vampire to save her.

The man she'd thrown down a crack in the earth, into a burning coal seam.

She saw his jowly face, his long coat. His hands, cracked and scarred from a lifetime of fighting. His dead fish eyes that stared right through you. Judged you before you even had a chance to defend yourself.

He'd been a good man, once. They'd even loved each other, in a certain way. Then that stopped.

"No!" she screamed. "No, you bastard!" and before she could even think about what she was doing she swung her hand out, her fingers curled like claws. She knew what would happen, that he would just dance backward, recede every time she got close.

But this time it didn't happen that way.

Her fingers found something soft and yielding and then it tore, it tore away as she completed her swing. Arkeley's face ripped right off and he was still standing there in his coat, with his old hands but his face was different.

It wasn't blue. It didn't flicker.

She'd found the manager, torn through his ghostskin suit and revealed his true face. Watery eyes, soft chin with a fringe of beard. He looked scared.

"*Trooper, I wish I didn't have to say this.*"

"*You're off the team.*"

"I did this because I knew you couldn't finish things yourself. You're not strong enough."

Arkeley again, Arkeley all around her. Dozens of him. Fangs growing from between his lips. His iron-colored hair falling from his head, cascading down across his face. His skin losing all color, but his eyes burning red, red, so red and he was lunging for her, his mouth opening wide enough to tear out her throat, he was going to drink her blood, steal her life—

Walker was next to her, suddenly, and his massive arm was up, moving. She saw it in slow motion. His hand was flat as a blade, moving past her, smashing into the hexenmeister's face. She saw the sorcerer's cheek ripple with the impact, saw blood spurt from his nose.

The bastard fell hard to the ground. She dropped down next to him, tore open the flickering blue suit he wore. It had to be there, had to be—

"I was just using you as bait."

"You're weak. You're too vulnerable to their lies."

"You're never going to be a fighter. You're soft."

Arkeley, again. Cutting her with his words. Looking deep inside her, finding where she was softest. Attacking her there. Her doubts, her insecurities. Her sure and certain knowledge that she'd never be good enough. Never be a real cop, like him.

"Shut up," Walker shouted next to her ear. "Just shut up!" He placed a hand over the manager's mouth and nose, causing him to kick as he began to suffocate.

Laura had to find it. She had to find the focus. If you were going to summon ghosts like this, you needed a way to control them. To keep them from sucking you in. There had to be some hex against them . . .

There! Around the manager's wrist—a bracelet of woven threads, with little bone charms hanging from it. Carved knucklebones and vertebrae from a small animal. That had to be it. She yanked it off the man's arm and jumped up, holding it over her head. She spoke the words, the spell Patience Polder had taught her once, words that made her lips bleed, that made her throat sore. Witchbilly words.

The ghosts all turned to stare at her in horror, pleading. But their words were gone, she'd forbade them to speak. Their hands went next, their faces. The blue light streaked away into the wind, twisting and evaporating like toxic smoke.

And then they were gone.

Just Laura, and Jack, and the goddamned motel manager, struggling to breathe, albeit weakly now, lying on his back dressed in a patchwork suit of dead skin. Soon the skin began to dry out, shrivel. Fall away.

She looked over at Jack.

"They're gone," she told him. "All of them. Don't."

He ignored her. Pain, agony, confusion, and dread, battling across his face.

She grabbed his wrist and tried to pull it away from the manager's mouth. "Don't, Jack. It's done."

He turned to her and didn't seem to see her at first. Then his eyes cleared. He glanced down at his hand and jerked it away in shock. He staggered to his feet. He ran his hands through his hair and across his face.

"Jack, it's done. They won't be bothering us again."

But he was already running toward the cave, toward the

last flicker of blue light in there. Several ghostskins still hung from the walls of the cave, lingering there, still clutching to this world, just a little. They would be gone in a minute along with all the others in the motel.

SIX

"Remember what I said," Laura told Walker, two days later, as she drove him up to the top of a ridge, a place so far back in the woods there weren't even any power lines. "These are good guys. The witchbillies don't hurt anybody. They just want to be left alone."

"Sure," he grunted. Jack felt like he needed a shower. He needed to soap out the inside of his head. Like the worst hangover he'd ever had. Jen—Jen was gone. He knew that now. She'd been gone since that moment the Wild Hunt had taken her at Stonehenge.

Sometimes when he closed his eyes he still heard her voice. Not her ghost. Just memories. That was normal, right? To remember the good times?

After he'd had one last word with the ghostskins in the cave and watched them rot away, he and Laura dragged the other guests out of the motel. It hadn't been too hard—once Laura had found the focus, the spell she'd used to disperse the ghosts had destroyed all the ghostskins in the motel rooms as well. The men and women in those rooms could barely walk. Some of them were so lost to the ghosts that they cried like babies as they were led away, sent home to their families.

None of them fought.

All of them held their shame closely, a shame Jack knew intimately.

Now there was just one last thread to tie up.

They pulled up in front of a big farmhouse that might have been two hundred years old. The paint on the slatted wood was new, though, and there were flowers lining the path to the door. The two of them got out of the car and headed up the walk.

A girl came out of the house, dressed all in white, her wrists and even her throat covered. Jack was a little surprised she wasn't wearing a bonnet. She gave him a smile that felt just plain wrong, though it was warm enough.

"You'll never forgive yourself," the girl told Jack. Not like she was giving him advice. It was just a statement of fact. "For all the good you do. All the people you save. You'll never truly be at peace. I'm sorry."

Her smile didn't change.

Jack shook his head, unwilling to accept her proclamation. "Do I know you?"

Behind him Laura laughed. "Jack Walker, meet Patience Polder. I'd say you get used to it, but I'd be lying. She's got a gift."

"Whatever." Jack opened the trunk of the car. The motel manager—wearing street clothes now—was in there, tied up and gagged. Jack had almost killed him back at the cave entrance. It had been close. Even afterward, he'd considered meting out the justice no governmental system would be able to replicate.

But Laura had other ideas.

"He's one of ours," Patience Polder said, with a nod.

"Hello, Alvin." The girl went over to the trunk and reached down, touching the manager's face. To Jack, she said, "My father taught him how to skin ghosts. The skill was never supposed to be used this way." She loosened the gag. "Tell me, Alvin. Tell me why you did it."

She said it as if she knew already. As if she just wanted to hear it from his mouth.

"Money." His voice was raw. "That's all. I was sick of being poor."

Patience Polder nodded. Turned back to Jack and Laura. "We take a vow when we learn the old ways. Never to profit from suffering, only to aid and comfort. He broke that promise."

Jack had taken a similar vow and understood. "What are you going to do with him?"

"He will be shunned."

The way Patience said it, it didn't exactly sound like he'd just be given the silent treatment. It sounded pretty final, actually. Maybe a lot worse than what Jack had been thinking.

He decided maybe he didn't want to know.

They left the man to his fate with Patience and drove back down the ridge toward civilization.

Laura took Jack back to the motel so he could get his rental car. When he got out, she did too, and walked him to his car.

"Are you going to be all right?" she asked.

"I'm fine," he told her.

"You don't have to act tough for me. I've been through what you have. I know what it does to your soul."

"I'm fine," he repeated.

He wasn't, though, but he was closer to being fine than when he'd arrived. As crazy as it sounded, communing with the ghostskin had helped him. He'd been able to say the things he'd needed to say, even if he hadn't really been speaking to Jen. It was a type of closure. Then, as he'd almost killed the motel manager, he'd realized another thing. The ghostskins had been used as well. Jen had died after her body was transformed into one of the beasts of the Wild Hunt. The ghosts in the motel might not be human, but they'd never asked to be skinned and hung on a wall.

Jack stared at Laura for a while, not sure what else there was to say. They were two of a kind, he knew that now. Tough mothers. Maybe he was a sailor, maybe she was a cop, but they had something in common. Sand, grit, whatever you wanted to call it. A need to serve something greater than themselves, even if they didn't want to. A grudging responsibility that only a damned few were haunted by.

He didn't have to say anything. One look in her eyes and he knew that she knew. With nothing to say, he held out a hand. She shook it. Then she turned around and walked back to her car and drove away.

He glanced once at the motel, then reached into his pocket for the keys to his rental car. As he pulled them out, another key fell to the ground. He crouched down and picked it up. It was the room key, the number 19 stenciled on the green triangular plastic key fob. Flickering blue memories slammed into him, the sickness of communing with the ghosts, and the terrible hole he still had in his soul from losing Jen. He found that he'd been squeezing the key painfully. He reared back his hand to throw it away, but then stopped halfway through the motion. After a beat, he shoved the key into his pocket, got into his car, and drove away.

The motel receded into the distance, but he never once looked back. Instead he looked forward, past the barns with hex symbols, past the rolling fields with deep shadowed grottos, past the crowded interstate, past the rental car return sign. He had to look past these things. He couldn't *not* look forward. For to look back was too damn hard.

On the way through security, as Walker was about to walk toward his gate, a TSA agent stopped him.

"Excuse me, sir. I think you forgot this," he said, holding out a round white tray. Inside lay the room key.

Walker stared at it for a hard minute.

"This is your key, isn't it, sir?"

Walker looked into the eyes of the agent. African American. Tall. Stubble burn on his neck. Bright eyes that had never seen the things Walker had seen.

"Sir? Are you okay?"

Walker snatched the key and mumbled a thank you.

Looking forward was what he had to do, but it might be okay to look back a little. After all, it was important for one to know where he'd been, to know what he'd lost, and to know the price of it all.

Blood for Blood

CHARLAINE HARRIS AND CHRISTOPHER GOLDEN

The screaming got old by the second day. On the first day, Peter Octavian was too battered to do anything more than wish the screamer would shut up. She would be silent for maybe eight hours, but then she'd start again. He was lying as still as he could on the stone floor, the chill creeping through his bruised skin and flesh and digging into his bones. He could have sworn those were bruised, too.

Time crept by, as it does when you're in excruciating pain. Octavian slowed his thoughts to a crawl as he concentrated on his recovery. After so many years as a sorcerer, he had grown so used to being able to summon magic on a whim that he'd taken its presence for granted. Not here. In the midst of his pain, he kept searching within himself and reaching out into the world around him, but he could not feel much magic at all. Yes, he was in a strange land powered by a strange magic, but it felt as if his cell was lined with some substance that sapped his own sorcery.

Faery.

He hated the Fae. He hated Faery. He hated the mission that had brought him here. He hated the dungeon he was in, and the woman screaming next door.

He was sure it was a woman. He formed a picture of her.

She was aged, with ragged graying hair and a bony frame, and she was hurting as much as he was.

But by the third day, Octavian decided she deserved it.

Food would come at intervals, and Octavian made himself crawl to the door and consume everything they slid through the space at the bottom of the door. He needed the strength. As he was eating the second meal, Octavian couldn't help but notice that he hadn't heard a food plate being delivered under the door next to his. At first he didn't understand what that meant, but the second time he was alert enough to listen and comprehend that the screamer was not receiving food. Maybe a cup of water? It was hard to tell.

After that realization, Octavian cut her a little more slack. He wondered, *How does she have the energy to scream like that, if she's not getting any food?* But mostly, he worried about himself.

Maybe for once, he was in over his head. Maybe this would be the end of him. A strange thing after so very long, to imagine an ending.

The third day, he decided to speak to the screamer.

"Shut up long enough to answer a question. Why aren't they feeding you?"

The screaming was cut off as if he'd sawed it in two.

"Because the spell wore off," a voice said, slowly and carefully, as if she were having to remember how to speak English.

"What spell?" he asked.

"To make the smell of Fae less intoxicating to me," she said, still pausing between words.

"What are you?"

"Vampire," she said, with just an echo of pride in her voice.

Everything made sense now. The (more or less) eight hours of silence fell during the daytime, when she slept the sleep of the dead. Octavian had a long history with vampirism and vampires—he'd been one for centuries, before he'd been to Hell and things had . . . changed—but this one sounded a little different from the bloodsuckers he was used to.

"And the Fae are very good blood for vampires?" he asked. This was an unfamiliar fact, and Octavian tried to fit it into his world.

"Oh," she said longingly, "the blood is like cake and honey. I am *so hungry.*"

"Where are you from?" Octavian asked quickly, before she could start screaming again.

"I live in the Rhodes nest," she said.

"I don't understand," he said, since she couldn't see his blank look.

"What's to understand? I live in America, in the city of Rhodes. It's not far from Chicago. It's a large city. I live in a vampire nest, and Joaquin is my sheriff."

She might as well have been speaking Greek. Which was what she did next. It seemed as if she didn't expect him to comprehend, and given the string of insults she was hurling at him, he decided to go along with that presumption.

"I've never heard of vampires living in nests or having sheriffs. And Rhodes isn't on my map of America."

She fell silent. Then she said, "What are you?"

"I'm a sorcerer," he said. "Peter Octavian."

"A sorcerer." She said it slowly, thoughtfully, as if speaking the word for the first time. "I know there are witches. Do you know the legend of Circe?"

"I have heard of it."

"I killed the last Circe," she said. "For murdering my husband." She was absolutely matter-of-fact.

"Understandable," Octavian said. "But I haven't murdered anyone belonging to you, and I don't intend to."

"Are vampires citizens, where you come from?" she said.

"For a time it looked like they might be, but no. That's never going to happen now."

"And yet, in the United States where I live, we are," the woman said. "And by the way, other-worldling, my name is Dahlia Lynley-Chivers." She sounded proud she'd remembered it.

"How long have you been down here?" Octavian asked. He was chewing over the implications of her being from another world.

"I came in two days before you. I was charged with a mission by my sheriff. I was armed with a spell so I could resist the blood of the Fae until my mission was accomplished. But just as I found my target, the spell wore off and I am now the pitiful and ravening thing you hear." Her self-contempt was scorching. This was a proud woman.

"You could say I came here on a mission, too," Octavian said slowly. He pressed his face against the bars and looked to his right as much as he could. He was in a corner cell. The corridor stretched to his left five more cells. He had heard a faint moaning coming from that direction, and once he'd heard a man cursing, but other than that, nothing. He looked at Dahlia's cell, the first one to the right, at a forty-five-degree angle to his. Though it was awkward, he could catch a glimpse through the bars of the next cell, just enough to tell Dahlia Lynley-Chivers was short—much shorter than he'd envisioned. And young, very young. At least in appearance.

"What was your mission?" she asked. She was pressed forward, too, and their eyes met.

Octavian felt a jolt down to his bones. She was old and strong beyond anything he'd anticipated. Though Dahlia looked perhaps twenty, her eyes were centuries old. She was also, undoubtedly, standing on her tiptoes to reach the barred aperture. Octavian found that amusing. Almost.

"I don't see any point in keeping it a secret, considering it's looking fairly likely we'll die here," Octavian said after a moment's thought.

Dahlia waited without speaking, her large brown eyes curious. Octavian was glad that the curiosity was keeping the screaming at bay. He also suspected that her pride had been piqued, now that she had met the prisoner beside her. She had a face to keep, now.

"I was sent to extricate a half-demon, half-Fae portal traveler named Ripley," he said.

He hadn't expected the shock and suspicion that transformed Dahlia's face.

"You're a plant," she said, snarling, and she vanished from the barred window. Seconds later, the screaming resumed.

It was another day before he could persuade her to talk to him again.

Three more meals of grilled meat and a salad pushed under the door. Hours of listening to her weakening voice.

"Peter Octavian," she said, on what had to be the moment darkness fell outside. She was whispering.

"Dahlia," Octavian said. "I'm guessing from your reaction that you were sent here on the same mission?"

"I was," she said. "And unlike you, I was very close to success when I was captured."

Octavian bristled at her needling, but he had to admit that if she had gotten close to the objective, she *had* gotten further than he had.

"Do you know where Ripley is?"

"I do."

Octavian waited until it was obvious Dahlia was not going to say anything else.

"What is your price?" he asked.

"Your blood."

Octavian sighed. There was no way out. He could not reach her to force her to speak. Though he felt stronger now that his body was healing, and he could feel the power in him beginning to regenerate in a small portion, his magic was not as strong here in Faery as it had been in his own world. Not by a fraction. It might not have been the cell he was in after all; it might have been Faery itself.

"How?" he asked.

"Our cell doors are close together," she said. "If you lie on your back as close to the corner as possible, and reach out through the slot at the bottom of the door, I think that your arm might be close enough for me to bite."

"How do I know you'll let go?"

"For one thing, I'm too weak to hold on to you," she said. "For another, I have honor."

This was the last word Octavian expected to hear from a vampire. Octavian was still doubtful about Dahlia, and he thought if she died—as she might, perhaps, after prolonged starvation—he would at least have silence. But he had to begin taking some kind of action, however dubious, because he was sure it wouldn't be long before the Fae decided to make an example out of him. And from what he knew of the Fae, that wouldn't be a pleasant process. The Fae were universally beautiful, strong, and pragmatic. Cruelty didn't seem to be a fault from their perspective. They had their own brand of honor, but it wasn't the sort that included keeping their word to outlanders. They cared only about their own kind.

Resigned to the experiment, Octavian lowered himself to the floor. Instead of the traditional slot jailers used to slide plates under, the whole door was raised about four inches. Octavian lay on his back and worked his arm out through the gap. He could hear that Dahlia was on the floor too, and he heard her crying. She was doing everything she could to suppress her hunger, but it was overwhelming her.

"My mouth can't reach your wrist, Peter Octavian," she said. "I am going to puncture your arm, and the blood will flow to me. I'm sorry. This will hurt."

And it did. Her thumbnail was like a knife, a dull knife, and it took all the self-control he had to stay still while his blood flowed out. He could hear her eating, the eager, urgent sounds of her lapping up his blood as fast as it ran over the irregular bricks of the corridor floor.

When the dull ache had gotten to be more than Octavian could endure, he said so. "Wait for a second," Dahlia said, and he made himself stay still. Then he felt pressure on his wrist, and moisture. "All right," she said.

He pulled his arm back under the door and looked at his wrist. It was already healing.

"How did you do that?" he asked.

"My saliva," she said. "Now that I have some. Thank you. That was so good."

She sounded almost dreamy with delight. After a moment, she added, "Stay on the floor for a while, wizard. You will regain your strength."

"Probably lucky for me that you aren't free," he said.

"Yes, lucky for you," she agreed. After a few seconds in which her relief practically hummed, she said, "Ripley is up two floors. He's the only hybrid demon-Fae, and though the Fae find that abhorrent, they also think there may be a use for him. They are putting him through whatever paces he has, but at any moment, they may decide that he is worthless."

"How far did you get?"

"I came in through a portal in the backyard of a house in Louisiana. A woman Niall is fond of lives there. I had heard there might be a way through, someplace close to her."

"Niall?"

"The king." Her voice added silently, *You idiot.* "Niall is strong and ancient, but there has already been one attempted coup, and who knows how much longer he will last?"

"And why do you want Ripley?" As long as she was answering, he might as well ask another question.

"We want his blood, of course. Not even all of it! A few vials full. It's terrible being a slave to the smell of the Fae. Now that they have retreated to Faery, for the most part, it's not as much of a problem—but to have immunity, that would be best of all."

"The Fae have retreated in my world, too," Octavian said thoughtfully. "In fact, maybe that is where our worlds join . . . here."

"And you need Ripley because?"

He hesitated, then shrugged. "Medea's Disease."

"What is that?" He could tell she really didn't know.

"It's a sickness that targets the magically gifted."

"Like you?"

"Yes. Like me. And other sorcerers. And witches. For centuries, magicians thought it had been eradicated, but now it's reappeared. It's spreading. Ten people have already died. The last time it was active, the blood of a creature half-fairy and half-demon was used to cure it, but nothing like that exists in my world now. A group of sorcerers and witches came together to search for something comparable. The most powerful seer I've ever met had a vision of this guy, Ripley. Sensed his blood from a world away. Even she doesn't know if it will work, but he's the closest we're going to get, so we have to take the chance."

Dahlia went quiet for a bit, and Octavian could practically hear her ruminating.

"Do you need all of his blood?" she asked.

"Not necessarily, though we'd like to have him alive so he could keep producing blood, in case the first attempt to make a cure doesn't work."

"My sheriff would also like Ripley alive. But he doesn't require it."

"Then maybe we can work together." Octavian felt a flash of hope, which was more than he'd had so far.

"Yes. Maybe." She was doubtful, but interested. "I feel better already. If I can get back to my full strength, and you can regain some of your magic, maybe we can survive to escape. Though I would rather get out of here with Ripley in tow, dead or alive."

"Me, too." Octavian didn't like to think how many other magic users that he knew might have sickened since he'd been down here.

That night, Dahlia didn't scream. Instead, he could hear her move. He was tempted to ask her what she was doing, but he was so tired from his blood loss that he slept instead. He was terribly thirsty, and when she slid her cup of water over to him, he drank it as well as his own.

The guards who came through the corridor that day seemed suspicious, and Octavian wondered if they could smell his blood. But he took care to lie still at the back of his cell, and of course since it was daytime, Dahlia was silent in hers. He could hear the two guards, a man and a woman, muttering to each other in their own language. The woman said, "Maybe she caught a rat," and the man laughed. "That's appropriate," he said. Then they continued on their way.

The Fae were negligent jailers. They almost never came into the cell. Octavian's waste bucket was noxious, but once he fell asleep and when he woke up it had been swapped for a clean one. The sleep had been induced. That was the only time someone had opened the door or actually looked at him.

For two more days Octavian and Dahlia followed the same procedure. He fed her; she healed him. Though Octavian had feared he would get weaker and weaker from the blood-taking, that didn't happen, maybe partly due to the extra water Dahlia gave him to drink, and her immediate healing of the puncture. Octavian also recovered from the physical punishment he'd received when he'd been captured as he entered Faery.

The portal he'd used had obviously been watched. In retrospect, it seemed likely that Dahlia's break-in had made the Fae suspicious.

Octavian thought it was strange the Fae guards seemed to show no interest in the two of them besides giving them food and water. The next night, that changed.

And not for the better.

Though the door never opened, he became aware that he was not in his cell alone. A beautiful woman was there, and she bore a heartbreaking resemblance to someone he'd once loved. He just couldn't quite recall who that someone was. But she was so familiar, her eyes just as he remembered, and her breasts, too, because she was quite naked.

He was not surprised to hear an exclamation in another language from Dahlia's cell. She had a visitor, too.

"My love," said the woman. "I am so glad to see you, so happy."

"My God," he said, knowing what he was seeing could not be real, must be magic . . . but still, it was intoxicating to see her again. "You're stunning," he said falteringly. Breath-less. "I don't believe it."

"You don't believe this?" She smiled as she took his hand and put it on her breast.

Octavian frowned. "You don't smell right."

"What do you want me to smell like?" she said, with the teasing smile he remembered so well.

"Honey and cotton," he said, though he hadn't wanted to speak.

Her smell changed.

"There, my darling, is that better? I'm so anxious to hear why you came to me here. Why am I having the pleasure of being with you again? Please tell me how you came to find me."

It was harder and harder for him to cling to a shred of reality—*I'm in a jail cell, she couldn't really be here, she would never ask me for my secrets.* After the bleakness of the cell and the pain of the past few days, her flesh and sweetness were absolutely compelling. He might have succumbed to the vision entirely, but then the screaming from the next cell began, and it wasn't Dahlia's familiar voice that was making all that noise.

The woman in front of him glanced toward the wall of the next cell, and in that second, the illusion was broken. It was a woman, yes, but she was Fae, not his beloved, and she was at least a foot taller than the woman he'd adored. She was naked, yes, but her body was not at all reminiscent of the one he'd made love to.

When her gaze returned to him, she could tell her spell had broken, and she instantly slammed him into the wall with such force that she knocked him out. When he came to again, he was alone.

Dahlia was laughing in her cell.

He went to the door. The corridor, as far as he could tell, was empty.

"What happened?" he said. He could hear Dahlia moving closer to her door and caught a glimpse of her.

"Killed him," she said proudly. "He made himself in the image of my husband, but I knew it could not be Todd, and I killed him."

"You should be full of blood," Octavian said.

"Drained him dry," she all but chortled.

"I'm going to go out on a limb and say this would be a good time to break out," Octavian said. "You know they're going to retaliate."

"Yes, they'll kill me," she agreed. "But it was worth it."

She was suspiciously cheerful.

"Did the blood make you high?"

She jumped up and down so he could glimpse her grin and bloody clothes. "As a kite," she said. "Have you regained any of your magic?"

"A bit." He wasn't sure how much, but he could feel the magic flowing in his blood and will. Maybe the flow was a trickle rather than the usual torrent, but it was there. In every conscious moment, he had been tapping into the magic at his core and using it to reach out into Faery. Accessing the magic here, drawing on it to bolster the magic inside him, was like learning a new and very difficult language. But he could feel the connections beginning to be made; the translation taking place.

"Hopefully enough," he added.

"Then now is the moment." She laughed and Octavian thought he'd never heard such a mad and excited sound. If this was the effect Fae blood had on vampires, he was surprised they'd let her live at all.

"Now," she said, and a terrifying strength was in her voice. "Octavian, weaken these bars."

He would have helped her anyway, but he felt compelled to press his face against the bars of his own window. He felt his slender thread of magic furl itself around the bars crossing Dahlia's. He pulled, and he saw Dahlia's tiny fingers wrap around the bars as she pushed. They both strained. She was growling, though he didn't think she realized it, and he was aware that he'd been holding his breath, which really wouldn't help at all. Octavian thought his brain was going to pop from the pressure he was putting on it. He closed his eyes to focus more intently, only to open them when he heard a groaning sound that had not come from a human throat.

The bars were bending outward.

"I've got it now," Dahlia said, and the bars popped out and flew across the corridor, to *thwang!* into the opposite wall.

Octavian said, "Oh, that's not going to attract any attention."

But Dahlia leaped forward and kicked her door, and the wood splintered outward now that it was not reinforced. She pushed through the gap, and for the first time he saw Dahlia in her entirety. She was a lot like a very short Barbie doll, and she was wearing boots with very high heels and the remnants of what Octavian, in his male ignorance, would have called a cocktail dress. At least, it was short and tight. It had probably been aqua once upon a time, before grime and blood made their own random patterns. Her tight, wavy black hair was in a sort of Helena Bonham Carter state.

Dahlia was beaming as she grabbed the bars of his window, her hands covered in something messy and smelly. She leaped up easily and braced her feet against the door while she pulled with her arms. The bars smoked and hissed against the substance covering her hands, and Octavian pushed on alternate bars. When the whole barred frame gave way he thumped against the door, then staggered backward.

Dahlia delivered one of her kicks to the wood, and he was out of the cell. From being captive to being free had taken about two minutes. Dahlia gave him a resounding kiss (which tasted of blood and metal) and pointed to her right. They began to run. Octavian wanted to escape the cellblock as swiftly as possible. "Anywhere but here," he said, and Dahlia nodded.

Even in the boots, she could keep up with him, and Octavian suspected she might have passed him if she hadn't been trying to stay at his side.

They heard voices just in time to flatten themselves against a wall.

". . . what happened with Bronwyn and Eigar?" one of the Fae was asking. He was tall with long brown hair and a pair of pants that looked like snakeskin. His companion was shorter, blonder, and even more ethereally beautiful than the first. Octavian was too smart to be envious, but he noticed that Dahlia was smiling.

Maybe she was thinking about how good their blood would taste.

"Bronwyn said she made an exact copy from his memory, but he still detected it," the shorter Fae said.

"And the vampire woman ate Eigar," the first Fae said. "Foolish of him to let that happen."

"Hard to believe Eigar is gone. And he owed me money!"

"More fool you." And they went on their way. They had not noticed the two escapees. Octavian, who was feeling stronger by the second, became aware with a thrill of pleasure that he had cast a concealment spell over them without conscious thought. He kindled the embers of magic inside him, reached out and felt a more solid connection to the power in this world than he had before. The magic he knew and the magic of the Fae were beginning to communicate with each other—to translate. He thought of cell phone signals and how frustrating it could be to have only one bar. This felt like three bars, now. Not great, but better.

Nonetheless, they needed to proceed with great caution.

The corridor came to a nexus where several others also met, a roughly circular space with a ramp leading up on one side and what appeared to be an elevator on another. The idea of an elevator in Faery seemed odd and somehow funny to Octavian, but now wasn't the time to ruminate on Fae architecture. There were several Fae in sight, some traveling up and down the ramp, and a pair emerging from the elevator. With a growing sense of urgency, Octavian whispered, "Our guards."

Dahlia nodded. "Elevator," she whispered back.

After a second, Octavian nodded. The ramp was obviously a major thoroughfare. People moved along it in a steady stream. Octavian couldn't understand why anyone would choose to be below the surface when they could be under a real night sky. He pushed the idea away and took Dahlia's hand to keep them in sync, reinforcing the glamour that kept them invisible with a gesture of his hand and a muttered phrase.

The elevator was similar to all elevators Octavian had ever used, except the doors did not close from the sides but from the top and bottom. He and Dahlia pressed against the rear of the box, which had room enough for eight people, more or less. The doors opened again after one level.

Three Fae got on. One had a crutch and a bandage on his leg, and he was complaining loudly that the fight had been thrown. The other two, both women, were skeptical about this and began to jibe at the male Fae.

Octavian was just beginning to relax when the paler of the two women said, "What is that smell?"

The man swiveled on his crutch and said, "I smell blood. Are you having a human menses, Adelphi?"

"Watch out or you'll lose your other leg," Adelphi said. "Seriously, what is it?" She began to examine the floor, perhaps looking for drips of blood. "That's weird," she said. "I can't see . . ."

And then her throat wasn't there.

The male Fae bellowed, the woman shrieked, and Adelphi fell dead to the floor, only to be yanked back up by invisible hands and to be held, moving, at about the height of a small vampire's mouth.

Octavian killed the male with a spell that paralyzed his breathing, and then used the same magic on the remaining female, but not before she drew a dagger and made a determined effort to cut his throat. She might have managed, if only she'd been sure where his throat was.

They arrived at the final level. According to Dahlia, this was the level where Ripley was being held. Dahlia dropped the corpse she'd been drinking from, beamed at Octavian, and stepped over the other two as she left the elevator. With some disgust, Octavian followed her, pushing a head back into the elevator and punching several buttons on his way out to stall their inevitable discovery. The guards should have reached the demolished cell doors by now, in any case.

Still weak from days of feeding Dahlia his blood, Octavian had been operating on adrenaline up to this point. Now to his chagrin he stumbled and would have fallen if his companion hadn't gripped his shoulders.

"Shit," she muttered. "Shit. Hold the illusion, sorcerer!"

Octavian struggled to maintain his consciousness and to hold their invisibility. There were Fae around, he knew; he could sense movement and hear voices, though dimly. He heard a little fleshy sound, and then Dahlia's grimy wrist was at his lips.

"Drink this, now!" she said in what he could only think of as a commanding whisper. To his astonishment, he obeyed. The second the blood hit his own bloodstream, his strength surged, and he felt smarter and faster and more wonderful than ever before. He was truly a great sorcerer, and he knew he would succeed. And he was moving so fast he thought anyone watching would only see a blur. He was also bouncing up and down.

What the hell did she just do to me? he thought. But really, he felt so damned good that it hardly mattered at all.

The thoughts nagged at him, though. When he could bring himself to stop drinking from her, he said, "I feel you influencing me. You have some kind of power over me?"

"Just a little mental influence because I've taken your blood a few times," she said. "It's going to wear off, Octavian. Don't worry, you're not my human puppet," she said as she took off the ridiculous boots.

"Where are we?" With her blood buzzing in his head he had been in a kind of fog.

"We're in a bedroom of the residence of Niall, the king," she said.

"What?"

"Yeah, I know, dangerous. But we were in a public place, and I knew someone would hear us or smell us again," she said, in a rapid whisper. "Pay attention! You are strong enough now even without your sorcery to blow these Fae out of the water, but it won't last long. They're inherently magic, while you acquired yours."

Octavian nodded.

"So we've got to move while you've still got the extra strength I just gave you. We have to get Ripley out of here and to the portal. The thin place. In my Louisiana."

Octavian still buzzed but his thoughts were not so clouded that he was blind to how that scenario would likely end. "No. To *my* thin place. The one I created on my property in Italy. It opens right in the courtyard in front of this palace."

"Which is why you ended up in the dungeon with me," she said, waving her hand. "And I'm betting they've shut it down by now. But let's worry about step two after we've accomplished step one, which is to get the bastard out."

"Agreed," said Octavian, with deep distrust. "Where is he?"

"He's three doors away. But we are in Niall's palace, and if we encounter the king, we are dead. Niall is cold and incredibly strong." Dahlia was a fan, it seemed. "There are guards at Ripley's doors and windows. They want to keep him sweet until they decide what to do with him."

"I thought they were going to kill him?"

"Or they might use him. They might decide to sell him to us. Or to you."

Octavian threw up his hands. "We can't wait for them to decide. We're here. Let's get him."

"Oh, sure," Dahlia said. "If you take care of the guards inside, I'll take care of the guards outside the window of Ripley's room. We have to be quick, and we have to be quiet. If I am killed, you will find my portal to the west. Run three miles due west through the forest. You won't encounter many Fae in the forest at night. After that, you'll pass through a thick gray mist and you won't be able to see anything around you. That's their buffer zone. But if you follow your nose, and let's hope your nose is good for a human's, you'll smell roses and vegetation if you keep going west. That's the garden we need. There's a spot in the mist that looks almost like a picture frame, and the picture will be a rosebush. That's the portal. Just leap through with Ripley, if you still have him by then."

"It took days to weave the spell to create my own

portal . . ." he said. "I didn't know where it would lead in Faery. When it opened into the courtyard I knew I was in trouble. They had me the minute I came through. The shift from my world's magic to the . . . I guess the wavelength of magic in this world had me disoriented and they swarmed me, beat me unconscious. But it's right there, so much closer. Are you sure they'll have closed it? I think I'd have felt it."

"Bad luck," Dahlia said briskly, "but yes. Almost certainly. The portals are all supposed to be sealed forever. So when you created one, it probably set off some kind of alarm."

"What about the one you came through?"

"Ha! That's Niall's only remaining portal, his personal one," Dahlia said. "And if I told you how I found out about it, I'd have to kill you."

It didn't make any difference to Octavian how she'd found out about its existence, he realized. "Okay," he said. "So I end up in another world, in Louisiana, but still not home."

"Better than being here," Dahlia said.

He couldn't argue with that, and there was no time to come up with a different plan.

Dahlia nodded at him as if he'd agreed out loud. Without further ado, she turned and went to the windows, which had curious handles shaped like hands. She gripped the hand on the right window as though she were going to shake, turned it, and the window opened inward. Then she did the same with the left. She gave Octavian a brilliant smile and stepped over the sill gracefully, looking to her right.

Octavian knew she would be visible to others the moment she left his proximity and he waited for the shouts of discovery. Apparently, when you were as fast as Dahlia, invisibility wasn't at such a premium, though. He heard a deep moan, realized Dahlia was doing her part, and shook himself. The surge of power he'd felt still rode him. Octavian took a deep breath, opened the bedroom door, and entered.

Two male warriors in leather pants stood on each side of the door. These weren't the casual guards of the prison level. These Fae were sharp and wary, and they drew swords at the sound of the door swinging, but it took an instant for them to recognize Octavian as an enemy. He'd already summoned the magic inside him, magic bolstered by the strength of Dahlia's blood. He hit them with a blast of percussive force that knocked them unconscious on impact, then caught them with a levitation spell before they could slam to the ground. He lowered them gently and soundlessly to the floor.

He didn't have such luck with the young Fae woman who stepped out of a room farther down the hall; she caught sight of him and let out a piercing scream, waxing and waning like a siren. Screams in Faery attract just as much attention as screaming anywhere else. Octavian could hear the sounds of doors opening and voices exclaiming; the noises echoing over what felt like a huge area. Maybe one of those voices was Niall's, and that would be bad. Even Dahlia was afraid of Niall.

Octavian stepped over the guards to open the door of the room with a little flick of his hands, stepped inside, and resealed it with a spell that might keep the room tight until kingdom come. He couldn't remember ever feeling so confident, so determined, in his use of magic. He wasn't at all surprised to see Dahlia holding a knife to the throat of a burly man in his twenties. Octavian didn't know where the knife had come from, but that was not what surprised him.

"Ripley?" he said.

"Uh. Yeah," said the burly man.

"I confess, I'm disappointed," Dahlia said.

"Everyone is," said Ripley. He sounded as philosophical as a man can with a knife to his throat.

The tumult outside the room was growing louder, and Octavian said, "We have to move." He found himself trying to estimate how many liters of blood a big man like Ripley might contain, and was not proud of himself. But when he thought of his dead friends, and those who were dying, he knew he needed Ripley's blood, all of it. Dahlia's needs were frivolous compared with his.

"Here, I'll carry him," Octavian said.

"Are you serious?" Dahlia snorted, a strange sound to come from her haughty little nose. "I could carry a rhinoceros."

Octavian realized that was true, and he also realized they had to leave two minutes ago. "Out the window, then," he said. "I'm tethered to my magic and I'm sure my portal is still open. It's closer than yours in the woods."

"That's no guarantee. Even if it's open, your portal in the courtyard is undoubtedly surrounded by a million Fae," she said, and he could tell she was barely holding on to her temper. To stop the argument, she leaped through the window with Ripley over her shoulder and took off running like a deer. It was a ridiculous sight, but Octavian, hard-pressed to keep up with her, did not feel like laughing.

Ripley was bouncing in great discomfort on Dahlia's little shoulder, and he bellowed in protest. At the sound of his cry, Octavian felt a hush fall over Faery momentarily, and then he heard the pursuit.

Ripley, who did not seem to want to be rescued from Faery, bellowed louder. Octavian used some of his free-flowing power to knock the demon-Fae out, and he saw a mad grin spread over Dahlia's face when Ripley fell silent.

"Throw something behind us," she yelled, and Octavian, thinking quickly, cast a spell that turned the leaves of all of the low-lying brush on the path behind them into razored metal.

He felt he'd been running a marathon by that time, but the screams he heard as the foremost Fae hit the spikes encouraged him and he managed to muster the speed to run abreast of Dahlia and her burden. "How much farther?" he gasped.

She seemed to be calculating. "Probably another mile. Or two," she added without pity. "I am so glad I got to drink the blood of more Fae." She shot him a wicked smile. And she accelerated. "Otherwise the smell of the bleeding ones behind us would have rendered me useless with hunger."

Eyes wild with the scent of Fae blood, she put on another burst of speed. Octavian ran even faster. He would keep her in sight or die.

He quickly began to believe he would die.

But the thick mist she'd warned him about came into view and that gave him the strength to keep up with the little vampire for one more spurt of speed. The sounds of pursuit had not abated. In fact, he was sure he could hear voices calling closely. He was right behind Dahlia and her bouncing burden when they went into the mist, which was the thickest fog he'd ever encountered.

It was obviously magical in origin, and he opened himself to it. Dahlia had the strength that came with being what she was, and that had been amped up immensely by the Fae blood. But he had the magic that powered the existence of the Fae, and for the moment he could tap into that. He listened to the magic, and it told him where to go.

The portal created and maintained by the king of the Fae was ahead and to his left, and he was just in time to see the faint oval in the air outlining a landscape view into a yard— without the sunlight or roses Dahlia had described. It was raining and it was night. *Of course*, Octavian thought, and dove through after her.

He turned and threw the magical equivalent of gray paint over the portal, confident that would conceal the shape of it and render the portal opaque to the pursuers . . . at least for a while.

He sat down abruptly, his legs having simply given way. Yes, it was raining, and luckily for Dahlia, it was night. They were sitting in a backyard, as best he could tell by the one security light that shone over the screen door on the back porch. The house was old, but not dilapidated. From what he could see, it was a farmhouse that had been added onto, but not significantly remodeled. No vinyl siding or hot tubs here. Just rain, and roses. Dahlia had been right about that.

Dahlia was sitting on the ground a yard away, even her strength temporarily exhausted. Ripley sprawled beside her, struggling to sit up.

"Listen," the demon-Fae hybrid said. "I appreciate you all helping me, but you didn't ask me what I wanted to do."

"We don't care," Dahlia said. Her voice was so cold that a shiver went up Octavian's spine. Absurd, because the rain was warm. Evidently, it was summer here, and summer in Louisiana meant the same thing as it did in Octavian's world.

"It's not fair," Ripley said, with a surprising amount of passion and in too loud a voice. "Dammit, I liked being with the Fae!"

"Too many people were counting on you getting out of there," Octavian said. "People are dying, and you can help."

"I don't have a clue what you're talking about," Ripley said angrily. "Even if that's true, why should I sacrifice what I want for a bunch of people I've never met?"

Octavian felt an old, savage anger rising in the back of him, the vampire he'd been once upon a time. The vampire who'd lived for eons in Hell.

"We need you, Ripley," he said. "But we only need parts of you. Think about that before you speak again."

"What?" Ripley's eyes went wide and his round, stubbled face grew alarmed.

"He means your blood, idiot," Dahlia said, sounding almost bored. "The doctor should be here at any moment."

"We're going to do this here in the rain?" Octavian asked.

"There are people asleep in that house," Dahlia told him. "They're not all completely human. Let's keep our voices down . . . if we don't want to imperil them. And we don't, do we?"

"No," Octavian agreed, though he was tired of Dahlia having the last word. She was an infuriating woman.

A small figure limped past the house and into the backyard. As it drew nearer, Octavian was able to see it was a tiny (even tinier than Dahlia, who was normal-small) hunchbacked woman who was at least in her sixties. The years had been harsh for her, and she was not happy. Nodding toward Ripley, she said, "Is this lump the one I take the blood from?" She put down the heavy case she'd been carrying. "And fuck all of you for getting me out on a night like this."

Even Dahlia seemed taken aback. "Dr. Ludwig? I thought I would have to call you," she said.

"I knew when you came through," a voice said, and another vampire followed the little doctor into the security light. He looked like a contemporary of Dahlia's, and to Octavian he had the same feel of age. He was Asian and slender and obviously quite fond of Dahlia.

"Fujimara," Dahlia said, with every evidence of pleasure, "you are such a welcome sight."

"As are you," he said, and bowed.

"If you can get this lovefest over with, hold his arm," Dr. Ludwig said.

Octavian moved behind Ripley's shoulders and gripped them. Fujimara took his right arm and held it out for the doctor's examination. Dahlia held a flashlight to help Dr. Ludwig find the right spot to put the needle.

Ripley struggled, but he gave up after a moment or two. "What are you going to do with my blood?" he asked fearfully.

"There's a disease that's killing witches and sorcerers in my world," Octavian said. "Your blood can be used as a cure, as soon as I get home." Now that he had a moment to think, he began to figure out how he'd do that in time for the blood to still be viable. He'd created a portal into the land of the Fae and he should be able to create another leading from Dahlia's world into his own. Since he could visualize his own home exactly, the weaving of the appropriate spells would take much less time.

"Curing a disease, that's good," Ripley said weakly. It was evident he didn't want to look at his own blood flowing out. "What about you, pretty vampire?"

"I will take this to doctors who work for my sheriff," she said. "We hope to become immune to the weakness we have for the Fae."

Ripley shuddered as the fourth Vacutainer was sealed. Dr. Ludwig, who was muttering to herself, had two waterproof pouches. So far, she'd put two Vacutainers into each one. The rain pattered down around them, and Octavian was glad of the continuous sound of it. He hoped the people in the house would not wake up. In fact, he cast another spell to keep them deep in sleep, for their own protection.

By then each pouch contained three vials of Ripley's blood, and the big man looked close to passing out. Surely the loss of the blood could not be that serious? Was he just queasy because he didn't like to see his own blood leave his body?

"He's going to faint," Dahlia said, and her companion let go of Ripley's arm. But Octavian could feel the new tension in Ripley's shoulders, and he said, "No!"

It was too late. Octavian lost his grip on the wet man and Ripley tore himself away and leaped through the place where the portal had been. None of them had anticipated how easy it was to see the portal in the human world, since it was still gray and opaque. Dahlia and Octavian had been too preoccupied with moving their agenda forward.

"You let him go," Dahlia hissed at Octavian, and then she was on him, her hands seeking his throat. Octavian reared back and punched her in the head, then got a hand up and hit her with a concussive burst of magic that knocked her backward. He was wet and hard to hold on to, and she went flying.

He crouched and braced himself, but her vampire companion simply said, "I don't think he let Ripley go, Dahlia. I think Ripley fooled us."

"Since the patient has left, so will I," Dr. Ludwig snarled. "Tell your sheriff to expect a very high bill in the mail, and he'd better pay it on the nose." She trudged off, her case clutched in her hand.

Dahlia retrieved one of the pouches so swiftly that Octavian could only see a blur. She reached for the second one, but Octavian snatched it up first. "Mine," he said. "This is an even and fair divide, Dahlia."

Her companion looked at Dahlia, one black eyebrow raised.

Dahlia looked angry for one moment, and then her face smoothed out into what Octavian thought of as vampire mode. Cool impassivity.

"It would be better if I took all of it," she said. "But we did help each other get out of the Fae dungeon, and we did find Ripley, though that was mostly me."

"We did elude the Fae pursuit, though that was mostly me," Octavian countered.

The Asian vampire seemed to be quite good at letting Dahlia solve her own problems. "You appear to be even," he remarked calmly.

"Yes, you're right," Dahlia said, giving him a genuine smile. For the first time, Octavian realized she was beautiful, though he thought he would just as soon have a wolverine as a buddy.

"Then we can go home? Joaquin is waiting."

"Can I have one of your vials?" Octavian said. He didn't want to think of it as begging, but he would have felt wrong if he hadn't even asked. "I am trying to save lives."

"Don't push it, magician," Dahlia said. "We are not doing something as noble as you think you are, but great things may happen if we don't feel the impulse to slaughter every fairy we come across."

"Fae blood. *Mmmm*," Fujimara said, his eyes closing in delight.

"So we'll go," Dahlia said. "Goodbye, Octavian. I hope you don't die."

"Goodbye, Dahlia. Try not to kill anyone who hasn't earned it."

He could hear her laugh as she and her companion vanished from sight.

Octavian felt he could hardly get any more sodden, so he sat in the garden for a few more moments gathering his strength. Any place would do, though he'd rather be dry and he'd rather gather a few supplies. He got up, and stuffed the waterproof pouch inside his shirt.

He began walking, identifying the driveway mostly by feel, and he could tell it would be a long time until he got to the road. But when he did, he saw headlights. Hesitantly, he went to the driver's side. The window rolled down. The dome light came on.

"Hey, you Peter?" the driver said. He was old and grizzled and had a thick Cajun accent.

"Yes," Octavian said cautiously.

"Then hop in, I'm taking you to New Orleans," the man said.

"I'm glad," Octavian said. "But who asked you to? And I don't have money on me."

"Don't worry about it," the man said. "I got hired by the vampire sheriff in Shreveport. He got a call a few minutes ago, some vamp business. He's doing a favor for some sheriff somewhere else. All I know is, I was supposed to show up here and wait for you and take you to the Big Easy. Oh, and give you this." The grizzled man handed Octavian a wad of bills.

Surprised, Octavian climbed into the vehicle, which was a clean pickup truck, and said, "I didn't expect this."

"I heard them arguing about it," the man said. "But the Asian dude, he spoke up for you."

Octavian smiled. "Then let's be on our way," he said.

I have lives to save.

Spite House

C. E. MURPHY AND KAT RICHARDSON

The ad had said *Do you believe in the SUPERNATURAL!?!* in a woo-woo font that would make anybody credible roll their eyes and turn the page. A few years ago that's exactly what I would have done. But being reborn as a shaman—a calling that included exciting benefits like healing and shape-shifting—had somewhat changed my perspective on what was and wasn't possible, so despite the cheesy font, I was intrigued by the fine print's proposal of visiting a genuine haunted house.

The even finer print mentioned a reward of ten thousand dollars for "plumbing the mystery," and as I'd been unemployed a fair stretch of time now, that was even more intriguing. I was not ashamed to admit that my anemic bank account was why I marched right through the front door of a tiny late-Victorian house on Queen Anne Hill without even knocking. A couple of seconds later I *was* moderately ashamed to admit that I hadn't kicked on my Sight—the thing that let me judge the spiritual aspect of a situation—before I did so. On the other hand, it wasn't like whatever I had seen would have stopped me, so at least I looked confident before I swept in.

There was an uncomfortable shift as I passed through the

door, like I'd stepped into a place I didn't quite belong. The Sight slipped on, giving me a double-layer of world to see. The regular world showed me a strangely narrow but beautifully constructed house: dust and cobwebs and century-old furniture suggested it hadn't been lived in for decades, but neither was it ramshackle beneath the grime. Ordinarily I would expect a building like this one to glow green, showing pride in its ability to safely house its occupants.

Instead it shone so black that it had weight, as if the color itself was trying to drag the house into the very earth below me. Spikes of deep crimson rage held it in place, keeping it from sinking, and I didn't think I imagined a moan of agony reverberating through the floorboards. The warring colors swam into my skull and spun around there, trying to pull me into the fight. I put a hand on the wall to steady myself, breathed, "Whoo," and the door opened behind me.

Harper hadn't realized she missed Seattle's rain, but after staking out the house on Queen Anne for a few days, she still reveled in the pattering hush of it and the scents of wet cement and wetter grass. It hadn't blinded her to the comings and goings—mostly at high speed—of people willing to brave the rain to get inside the old place. Most hadn't made it past the front door and the few who had ran back out as if they'd narrowly avoided being shot and weren't sticking around for more. *What some people will do for money* . . . Whatever lurked inside the house was apparently not worth ten grand to most of them after all.

Harper wouldn't turn up her nose at the money, but that wasn't what had brought her up the hill—this was work she needed to get back to. *Rather not have the Guardian come down like a hail of bones and fury just to get my butt back in gear.* So she'd checked out the ad—a legacy paid for by an estate law firm that had refused to give any further information. Then she'd waited. There was something distinctly odd in the mix. The house looked a bit weird, with a psychic brilliance like it existed in several planes at once, but not solidly in any one. Then a woman in a long white coat had waltzed in with no problems, and, while she looked like a live person, moved like a live person, she wasn't quite *there.* She almost seemed like a repeater—the ghostly recording of an event that had happened long ago and continued to play over and over. Yet the woman had an aura and a presence in the Grey that no ghost had. *There's a first.* Harper buttoned her black wool overcoat closed and eased out of the car. *Let's see if "the most haunted house in the Pacific Northwest" is going to let me in without a fight.*

Once out of the car, she saw a picket of true ghosts lining the path to the porch. Her injured leg was stiff and she leaned harder on her cane than she liked. The shaft with its winding silver patterns passed through the phantoms, stirring and disrupting them as she approached the front door of the narrow house wedged defiantly between the larger houses on each side. The dead stared in silence or stuttered through endless loops of their truncated lives. Most ignored her, but their presence sent a chill right through her vintage coat. The front door with the brass knocker opened to her touch and she limped through to the candlelit foyer. The house hadn't the size to carry off a grand entryway, but it had gracious lines—under the grime and cobwebs. A bunch of objects had been laid out on the small hall table and the woman in the white coat stood leaning with one hand against the wall nearby.

Harper lifted an eyebrow. *Huh, it's a bit like seeing the darker, prettier edition of me—more buff, and maybe an inch or two taller, though that could be the shoes. But the general description could be either of us,* she thought. *Don't meet too many women over five foot ten. Damn, that's unnerving.*

The woman in white looked her over with a professional fast flicker common to cops and con men and straightened. "Hi," she said. "Are you with the house?"

"No. My name's Harper Blaine and I don't reside here, but you could say it's my side of the street."

Harper cocked her head and glanced a bit sideways through the Grey. The woman was bright—and it wasn't just the white leather coat. Her energy corona reached out in all directions and twined around her in iridescent blue and clear amber with twists of spring green, stabbed here and there with small black thorns, like reminders of passing death. An assembly of spirits stood with her. *Interesting.* The house's energetic form was as dark and dense as a coal mine delineated with flickers of red and white energy that shone through billowing smoke. *Whatever they are, her shining companions aren't haunts.* "You're not with this house either," Harper said. "Got pulled in by that 'solve the mystery and win money' thing?"

Harper Blaine was nearly my height, dressed far more professionally than I, and, as far as I could tell, in desperate need of a sandwich. Or three. Possibly seven. I considered her limp, her silver cane, and her location in a haunted house, and wondered if she needed a sandwich because she was recovering from using too much magic, which I had personally found tended to eat the flesh right off my bones. Except I would have liked to think I'd have noticed if somebody was wielding that kind of power in my town, so maybe she was just a very thin person.

"Joanne Walker. You can call me Jo. And yeah, kind of. I mean, who doesn't need ten grand? But I'm working on getting a private investigator's license and this could be the last step I need for qualifying. And I didn't think anybody else serious would be here. But you're serious."

I mashed my lips together before they let any more idiotic-sounding words escape. By *serious* I meant Ms. Blaine had a fricking fascinating aura, unlike anything I'd ever seen before. She looked connected to the spirit worlds in a way I hadn't encountered, like she could step in and out as easily as breathing. There was a soft greyness to it that made my eyes want to slide right off her and not quite see her, almost like she was a ghost. I didn't do ghosts, by which I mean I couldn't See them, so she wasn't one herself, but she was . . . *something*.

"I am serious," she agreed while I was trying to figure out what else she was. "I'm also a PI."

Cold lumped in my stomach and drew it downward, like the house had gotten inside me after all. I needed this gig, not competition on it, or I was going to be living off my boyfriend's goodwill forever, which was a perfectly horrible idea. I opened my mouth to plead my case, but what came out was a belligerent "Wait, what? You're a female supernatural PI in

Seattle who's nearly as tall as I am and I've never heard of you before? That's not even possible." My hostility faded as the truth of that struck me. "Wait. It really almost is *not* possible. The world kind of took a nasty-feeling dip to the left when I walked through the door. Did that happen to you?" I took two long strides to the door and yanked it open.

Or that was the plan, anyway. What really happened was I took two long strides, put my hand on the knob, and got a white-hot shock that threw me halfway down the hall. I landed on my tuchus, stared in offense between the door-knob and my throbbing hand, and said, "I'd say try the door, but, uh, ow. Uh. Okay, look. This house is a big sucking black spot on the spirit world's property value, and I gener-ally give the city a once-over every week or so to make sure this kind of thing isn't *there*. And it wasn't here, but it's not new, either. And you're . . . not new, either, except to me. And your aura is weird. Not evil-weird," I said hastily. "Just weird-weird. And . . . look, do you have any experience with parallel universes? Because I have a little, and I don't think we're getting home until we fix this haunted house."

Harper let out an unhappy laugh. "First job back and it's a death trap. Goody." *Parallel universes? Why didn't I bring Quinton?* She narrowed her eyes and ground through the possibilities; then she reached for the door, but pulled her hand back at the last second. "No . . . that would be stupid of me, wouldn't it?" *And that door does not look friendly.* It had sprouted ugly crimson spikes as soon as Walker touched it. Harper poked it with her cane and the door emitted a sizzle and a fountain of sparks, but gave no way. *Definitely not.*

"Something's very not-right here. A planar shift of some kind could explain why neither of us has any prior knowledge of a place this strange." She glanced at Walker, whose aura increased in intensity, then faded back to normal as she shook her burned hand. Her *formerly* burned hand: it looked fine now. Harper's eyebrows rose. "Interesting trick. And since you're not trying to kill me, my guess would be we both fit some requirement of this ten-grand puzzle. But there have to be clues . . . What about those things on the table?" she asked, limping closer. The table's surface shone with an oil-slick radiance. *Hrm?* "Wait. Give me a second."

She eased closer to the Grey, getting a bit ghostly in the here and now, to look at the room from another perspective. It didn't look better. The grid of magic's warp and weft seemed very distant and the house was as impenetrable in the world between as if it had been built of paranormal cement or sat in a rift of nothingness that howled and keened. Even the temporaclines—planes of frozen time that piled up like sheets of ice—weren't quite right here and shimmered with a fire-limned silver edge. The furniture seemed spun of ghostlight and the air was crushingly cold in this mode. She felt dizzy, suffocated, and electrified as the dense black walls began to bleed. *Not good, not good!*

Harper backed away from the fringe of the worlds, coming back up to the normal like a swimmer gasping for air. She stumbled and had to catch her balance with the cane, though she hadn't moved. Something shrieked, rushing in a storm of light toward them from the narrow stair at the back of the room. The sound seemed to push into the air with the palpable force of a bomb blast.

"Jo! Get down!" Harper yelled, reaching for the sharp silver edge of the Grey as her hand slipped on the cane's handle. *Oh shit!*

Get down **was great advice. I heard it right about the same time** a blast of ice slammed into my spine and shoved me out of this plane of existence and into another.

That sort of thing used to happen to me all the time, before I had any kind of decent control over my shamanic gifts. Lately it hadn't happened at all, so taking a sharp breath in the red-skied, yellow-earthed super-saturated colors of the Lower World—a place where spirits took physical form—was a shock. And dangerous: getting yanked between planes was a good way to wake up dead.

There was a presence there, an anger so old it had rooted in the Lower World's earth and grown up, tall and sharp and narrow. It had entrapping walls that tried to squeeze closer together, as if it could capture me. The soil beneath my feet was blood-blackened with obsidian blades of grass growing from it, and as I watched, a broken, twisted human form cracked the earth and reached clawed fingers toward me.

I hauled myself back into the regular world, double-time.

I hadn't been gone more than five heartbeats, but when I came back Harper looked like she was also sliding out of the world we were sharing. The soft greyness of her aura enveloped her, and I remembered she'd just said *first job back*. I yelled and stretched my hands toward her, casting a psychic net. I honestly didn't know if I was trying to catch her or the cold blast she'd warned me about, but I was determined to catch *something*.

Except I didn't. My net, which was typically very good at snagging things with physical form, passed through Harper like she was a ghost and never stood a chance of catching the ethereal explosion. I bellowed, "What the actual—" and considered that I had no idea how my new friend here felt about swearing. She seemed like she might be the type to get uptight over it, so I ended on a flaccid ". . . heck . . ." and scuttled on hands and knees to see if Harper was okay.

Harper couldn't reach Walker to pull the aegis over them both before the other woman seemed to . . . blink out for a moment, without actually going anywhere at all. With the shield barely pulled, Harper got bowled over by the blast of icy energy. Then something warm touched her and she flinched unconsciously, rolled, and went a little Grey, stifling the urge to scream as her leg gave notice of its disapproval. She reached for the bright chill, hoping to get ahold of it or at least a feel for what it was. *Black, red, spiky, ice, pain, fire, fury, I-hate-you, why-don't-you-die—*

"Holy crap," she spat and let go, sprawling on the floor as the hot-cold searing of the thing's energy whipped away into the blackness. *Ass over teakettle like a godsdamned amateur and landed on my gun, to boot. And I didn't even help the woman. Embarrassing.* Normally, Harper restrained her language in front of clients and people she didn't know, but at the moment a fit of blue words seemed entirely appropriate. "I am going to take you a-freakin'-part, you nasty bit of paranormal shit," she muttered. She reached for the cane and grimaced at Walker, who didn't look like she needed much help, to be honest. "Sorry—I don't mean you. I'm not usually so foul, but that . . . thing has pissed me off. I'm supposed to be good at this shit and here I am on my back like a bug." She slapped the floor in frustration. "Fuck. Ow."

Walker snorted a giggle. "And I was just thinking you might be a bit of a stiff."

"Only if I die again. I think I'm all out of rebounds." Harper sat up and clutched the cane, trying to push herself upright.

Walker got her shoulder under Harper's armpit and lifted as she muttered, "Die *again*? Do you make a habit of it?" in a tone that somehow accepted that the answer was yes.

Upright again, Harper propped herself against the wall for a moment. She blew out a breath and pushed her hair out of her eyes with her free hand. "That was a complete lack of fun. Thanks. I'm still pretty clumsy with this thing and I really don't want to land on my ass again before that bundle of ire and bad news comes back. Damn, I'm out of shape."

Walker looked her up and down, her aura gleaming a little brighter in the dim room. "Yeaaaah. You know, I'm a shaman. A healer. I could do something about that injury . . ."

Harper smiled. "I appreciate the offer, but the problem is that I heal *too* fast. The doctors were a little weirded out by the wound knitting up without a bone in place—an intact leg without a shin attracts surgeons like a corpse attracts flies. It's doing all right—I'm just not used to it yet."

Walker actually brightened. "Oh. It's like that, is it? I get that. Okay. So how'd you lose your, uh, shin?" Her brightness faded into a cringe, although Harper thought it was from imagining what losing a shin felt like more than any other consideration.

"Oh, you know . . . mages, monsters . . . bit off more than I could chew and had to chew it anyway. And I assume you *do* know," Harper added, eyeing the evidence of deaths that marked her aura. She shrugged. "So . . . what's your take on our brush with whatever that thing was? Because I'm getting a distinct whiff of ghost—but not your garden-variety repeater or low-level haunt—something a lot bigger and meaner."

"Lady," I said with genuine feeling, "when we get out of here I'm gonna buy you a drink. We can get tanked and exchange mystical magical war stories." My mouth shut off long enough for my ears to hear what she'd said, and my eyebrows rose. "Ghost? No, a ghost wouldn't have knocked me into the Lower World, and besides, I saw a—well, it felt like it had been human once, so maybe demon but eh, no, the closed-in walls, the rage, the ambition, probably a sorcerer. Blood magic shamanism is sorcery. Evil," I added helpfully, in case I hadn't made myself clear so far. "Bad. No-good yucko stuff."

Honestly, I sounded like I was twelve, and Harper's increasingly controlled expression suggested she thought so, too. I muttered, "I'm gonna shut up now," and hoped to God I would. To help myself, I went to have a look at the table of artifacts, now scattered halfway down the hall.

An ivory bracelet, an iron key, a faded photograph of two beautifully kept Victorian houses with a narrow strip of lawn between them, and a heart-shaped locket, opened to show the portraits within had both been scratched out with something sharp. I let the locket dangle from its chain, so

Harper could see the ruined pictures as they spun. "Betcha one of these pictures is our shaman. Wait, sorcerer-ghost, not shaman-ghost. Ghorcerer. Or does that sound too much like the guy you buy your groceries from?"

Harper did her best to keep a straight face. She favored silence and distance as her own defense against nerves, but that didn't mean she couldn't appreciate Walker's approach—this house would make anyone nervous. She moved to follow and peer over the other woman's shoulder. Her view of the artifacts was partially blocked by Walker's crouching body.

The photo seemed ordinary enough, but the others— key, bracelet, and locket—wore the remnant colors of blood, darkness, and acts of evil intent. The clinging energy didn't seem to bother Walker. It would have bugged the shit out of Harper, and she screwed up her face as she wondered exactly how a shaman worked. She'd have asked, but her attention was caught by the locket, spinning as Walker picked it up. The defaced portraits gave off flashes of silvery ghostlight torn by slashes of scarlet ire. Harper winced from the sharp stabs of light. *Damn. Well, if it doesn't bug* her, *maybe it's not really a dark artifact . . .*

"Ghorcerer," Harper agreed, steeling herself against the glare. "That works. From my perspective, energy lingers, and the stronger and more terrible it was to begin with, the more likely it is to hang around, whether it manifests as an entity or something else."

I beamed at her. "That's how it works for me, too. We're totally simpatico here. Awesome." I picked up the key—old-fashioned, heavy iron, large, but not otherwise special—and along with it, the bracelet, which was tangled in the key's teeth. The bracelet was made of narrow strips of hollow ivory, strung on a silver chain and kept apart from one another by silver beads. I handed the locket to Harper and disentangled the bracelet from the key, glancing up at her as I did so.

Harper growled and her face became a crone's, lined and hollowed and full of ancient rage. I knew that face, as if I'd seen it in the mirror every day of my life, and I hated it with every inch of my being.

I didn't even need a weapon. I just flung myself up out of my crouch and drove my shoulder toward her gut, screaming my loathing at the top of my lungs.

The locket had come into Harper's hand as cold and heavy as guilt and she staggered a step to the right as it seemed to weigh her down. A growl of foreign fury rose from her throat and her vision darkened as if blood dripped from her brow. *No, that's not right* . . . She wrenched her gaze sideways at Walker just as a barbed coil of blackness lashed from the bracelet and encircled the other woman's head like a crown.

Walker lunged for her with a scream of hatred, coming in low and hard. Harper planted the cane and pivoted aside. Walker rushed past, close enough to shove Harper back a step; then she spun around, her expression twisted with revulsion. Without a thought, Harper put her weight on her right foot and swung the cane toward Walker's knees with both hands, the locket tangling on the handle. The silver scrolls imbedded in the dark wood sparked and gleamed as the cane's shaft cut the air like a scythe, and words forced themselves from Harper's mouth in hard jolts. "No. You. Don't. Alma." The four words wove around the part of her mind that was screaming *No! What are you doing?* like the long strands of a net, choking it off.

"You can't stop me again, Mae—!" Walker lurched for the cane and the bracelet flew from her hand, striking a singing spark as it bounced off the wood and metal to skitter across the floor. Walker's eyes went wide, all vestiges of rage vanishing as her empty hand closed over the metal tracery. The iron key dropped from her other hand. She jumped at the sound and yanked on the cane.

The locket slithered down the shaft, arcing a trail of red and blue sparks as it slid. The sensation of being trapped fell away and Harper hauled backward on the cane, pulling it from Walker's grasp. Then she flicked the stick sideways and the delicate necklace cleared the cane's tip to soar across the room and rattle to a distant halt.

Harper stumbled against the nearest wall and leaned clumsily into it. "What the fucking hell? Are you out of your damned mind, or do you make a habit of picking up bits of solidified evil without checking from a distance first?"

"What? What! You swung at me—!"

"You jumped me first," Harper replied, breathing a little harder than mere exertion accounted for. "I thought you were going to kill me. You certainly looked like you had it in mind."

"Not *my* mind! I mean, that's not what I was thinking at all because it wasn't you I wanted to kill! Or not kill, or . . .

wait. Who the hell is 'Alma' anyway?" Walker pressed the heel of her hand to her forehead, eyes closed.

"I have no idea," Harper snapped.

"But that's what you called me. And you were—you were Mae. I can almost—almost hear them. Feel them. Mae really doesn't like Alma." Walker's eyes popped open to focus on Harper's cane. "What's with that thing? I mean, it's silver, I figured there was something hinky about it, but what'd it do? Where's it from?"

Harper had the feeling she'd forgotten something and it pissed her off. "Gift from a friend. Minor bit of spell disruption imbued into the silver inlay. She figured I might need an extra hand in my current state."

"Well, it's *awesome*. I think it just saved our lives. I wonder if I could get something like that put on the swor no, he'd kill me." Walker brushed her thought away.

Harper frowned, trying to scrape together an elusive memory. *Wasn't I just angry at Walker? Why? Or was I . . . ? The electricity isn't the only thing that's off in this house.* She scowled and glared at a spot to Walker's left with a snort of self-disgust as she put the past five minutes back together. "Damn it. Those things came with the house." She peered at Walker. "You can't possibly have wanted to hurt me—you haven't known me long enough. And I have no reason to try and knock your head in."

"Knees."

"What?"

"Looked like you were aiming farther south than my head."

Harper gave it a moment's thought and shrugged. "I never was any good at baseball."

I stared at Harper a few seconds, then giggled. A sharp overwrought giggle, to be sure, but a giggle. "I guess not. And to answer your question, yes, I usually do pick up bits of solidified evil without checking from a distance first. I don't generally get—there's a word for that kind of thing, where you touch something and it gives you information."

Harper said, "Psychometry," a bit dryly, and I snapped my fingers at her in thanks without looking her way. "Right. I don't get psychometric feedback. It's not how I work." I stared at the once-more scattered bits and pieces and leapt to a conclusion. "It's how *they* work, though. Alma and Mae. Oh! Shit. It's not *a* ghorcerer, it's ghorcerer*s*. There's two of them. Sisters. Twins, maybe. I saw your face and knew it as well as my own."

Saying it aloud made me flinch upright and look hard at Harper. We weren't twins, but between our height, relative slenderness, and psychic gifts it wasn't too far a stretch. Pennies were dropping like crazy inside my head and I was afraid to blink or even breathe for fear of knocking them out of line, so I kept staring at Harper and talking, this time in hope of getting the words out before the idea fell apart. "I'm wrong again, it's not ghorcerers. You were right. But so was I. There's a ghost and a sorcerer, and a—a blood vendetta? They hate each other," I said, sticking with the obvious. "And this house is their . . ."

I ran out of speculation, but Harper didn't. "Their war zone," she concluded. "They're the haunts. Maybe this space is what they started fighting over, or maybe it's just been poisoned by them. It's—"

"Even if they're *not* the haunts, the house is used to their shapes," I blurted. "To their magic. And we almost fit those shapes. So we pick up the artifacts and the house pours them into us." My fingers twitched. "If I had ten minutes and an internet connection I could look it up and find out the house's whole history. I could know everything we're up against."

"I have my phone." Harper took her phone out, started to toss it my way, then looked disgusted. "No signal. Of course there's no signal in a haunted house."

"That would be too easy." I made a face that caused Harper to crack a smile. I got the impression she wasn't the world's best at making friends, which was something I could sympathize with, although I'd improved a lot lately.

"I have an idea." I paused. "It's probably a bad idea. Most of my ideas are."

Harper assumed the expression of one waiting for the other shoe to drop. I smiled as brightly as I could. "We let them inside us and work this thing out the old-fashioned way."

"With torture and bloodshed?"

I cleared my throat. "I was more thinking of 'with rational minds familiar with similar power sets in control.'"

"Ah," said Harper. "You're right. That sounds like a really bad idea."

"Da-hah!" I waggled a finger in the air. "I have a *plan*. We switch it up. You take the sorcerer, I'll take the ghost. That way they don't know how to utilize the power set they've got. It might give us time to talk it out."

"Are you always this hopelessly optimistic, or is it a special performance just for me?"

"A little bit of both. Got a better idea?"

Harper sighed. "Not really. But how are we going to keep them from just straight-up trying to kill each other? I have this," she said, gesturing with the cane, "and you have *those*." She nodded at me, leaving me to peer down at myself in confusion. "The shoulders," she said. "I got a good look at their width when you tried plowing me down a minute ago. I'm guessing you've got the arms to match."

I flexed my biceps beneath their white leather sleeves without really meaning to. Truth was, she was spot-on. I had the size and strength to choke most people out, and I'd been a scrappy kid, so I knew something about fighting. "Fortunately," I said cheerfully, "I have a plan for that, too. Do you know anything about power circles?"

"I've seen wards and workings, but only from an observer's position—I'm not a mage of any stripe. I can't cast a spell."

"Oh, no," Walker said hastily. "Mages—hey. Mages *do* cast spells. My mages do that too, I mean. Me, I don't do that. Well, hardly ever. Power circles are more just building connections. With magic. As you do. Except *you* don't. Oh God, I'll stop talking now."

Harper laughed. "Mostly I hunt things down and tear them apart—more of a demolitions expert than a construction engineer. Or at least that's how I've always thought of it," Harper replied. "Though I guess they are two sides of the same coin."

Walker's eyes lit up a little. "That sounds cool. I kinda

like breaking things apart." She shook herself, and carried on with explaining the power circles. "Anyway, these are pretty simple. Keep things in, keep things out. I'm gonna keep things in this time. Can you use your magic silver stick to drag that bracelet so it's near to you or will you fall over? Oh good! No falling over. Stand there."

Harper, the bracelet safely at her toes, took up position in her assigned space. Then, at Walker's request, she extended one arm fully. Walker stood just beyond her fingertips, glanced upward like she was checking for something, nudged Harper around a few inches, and murmured something that initiated a wave of sparks in her own aura. "You're aligned to the north right now. Don't move until I'm done. Well, you can put your arm down." Harper lowered her arm, leaning heavily on her cane as she watched sparks tumble like an eager puppy after Walker, who paused every quarter-circle to murmur again. When she'd returned to where she started, a glimmer shot to the ceiling, then fell again, though the air took on a fine-grained texture that spoke of, but wasn't exactly, the Grey's silver and smoke. Harper gave it a curious prod with a fingertip, feeling resistance that shimmered and rippled in hues of determined green.

The contact sang a reassuring note in her mind. *Oh, that's Walker. An extension of her powers, like a tethered thread from the Grid.* "Sorry."

Walker straightened an extra half inch at the poke and shivered. "How intimate. But it kept you in, which is good. I've never tried to encircle a . . . whatever you are."

"Greywalker."

"Well, that clears things right up. No, it kinda does, if I think of your Grey as the Dead Zone. Where ghosts go before moving on," Walker clarified before she, too, moved on, building a secondary circle that encompassed Harper's and left room for another small one.

"I think so . . ." Harper replied. "It's like an interference fringe between one place and the next, fairly raw, pretty cold." The larger circle closed and Harper winced a little as a bright ringing pierced her inner ears, as if subsonics had been turned on all around her. A deep oceanic green shot through the circle before fading and taking the thrumming with it.

"That's actually an almost weirdly accurate description of the Dead Zone." Walker made the third circle with herself and the locket inside it, and as it sealed, the Grey itself seemed held at bay—even more so than in the steel-and-glass cage of the Land Rover. In spite of the setting, the world almost felt . . . *safe*. Harper snorted at herself—any sense of safety in the world had been lost long before she'd entered the Grey. And then the momentary, warm respite and sudden silence of the Grid's constant singing came like a shock of sensory deprivation and the echo of a half-forgotten life. As it settled on her, Harper gasped. Her blood was too loud in her ears and the world was *ordinary*, as it hadn't been in years. "What was *that*?"

Walker, already crouched to pick up the locket, glanced at her and then the circles. "They're walls, basically. Walls like to keep the things inside them safe. That's their job. What, did they get a little overzealous? Are you ready for this?" she added before Harper could answer the first question.

Harper muttered, "No, but that's never stopped me." Walker gave her a rueful smile, and they picked up their artifacts at the same time.

If the Grey had faltered before, it failed entirely now: a world of hard colors rose in its place, red sky and yellow earth, the sun a blue-white ball that threw sharp shadows from thick blades of purple grass. Pain rose, strangely recognizable. Under the harsh glare of mismatched colors Harper thought, *I'm dying.*

"Dead! No, dead *again*," burst from her throat, a stranger's words in a familiar voice. Her hands clawed of their own volition, turning palms-up so she could stare at them, and a second shriek erupted: "*Mae!* Mae, what have you done?!"

The words filled the air, not muffled or softened by the Grey's constant babble, but thrown into relief, almost visible as sharp stabs of rage across the crimson sky. Shadows hung from them, darkening them into slashes that rent open, gaining depth and power. Shapes appeared within, black light bending itself into well-known forms: a bear, a badger, an owl, all of them twisting into bone-breaking distortions of themselves. Alma's words ripped from Harper's throat again, a terrible melding of triumph and rage. "I told you! *I told you!* This is the world after death, bright and broken colors! Not your *grey*," she spat. "Not your 'singing silence' of ghosts and 'living light.' There's true life here. *Life!* Mae, *where are you?* See that I'm *right!* After all this time, after drowning in your arms, after your lies and hysterics, *see that I was right!*"

The voice rang and tore and Harper's hands flew to her

head, clutching her temples; for an instant she didn't know who had commanded the action, herself or the rider inside. But it was herself. Harper wasn't surprised, half a breath later, that she could stand here in this mis-colored place without her cane, without pain pulsing through her leg. The taut, furious energy within was and *wasn't* like carrying the remnant of the unlamented Reggie Lassiter—it burned and ached, but with cold and hate instead of hot agony. "Drowned." Harper's own voice, speaking to Alma with a stab of understanding. "Did you and Mae drown together?"

Dying had drawn Harper into the Grey, and Walker had, earlier, wondered if dying was something Harper did a lot, as if it was familiar territory for her, too. *Must be—those little black slivers of death don't lie.*

"Cold." Alma stole Harper's voice back in a whisper. "Winter ice, so thin, so cold, so black. We fell so far. We held on, we tried to breathe, but the black, the cold, the ice, it stole our souls." The whisper cracked back to a scream. "And when they drew us out she told *lies*! Lies about where we had been, what we had seen, about what death itself *was*! She lied about the magic . . ."

Power stuttered in Harper's hands, a flare that reminded her of the wash that had healed Walker's burned hand in the hallway. It felt alien and beautiful all at once, an extraordinary sense of connection to the strangely colored world around her that spread wide, unlike the narrow, vibrant streams of the Grey's energy grid as it rushed through the blackness between. This she could fall into and it would catch her, cushion her, accepting her as if she belonged, and make her whole again—

—until Alma ripped it free, confident in its use instead of gently exploratory. The flow of healing magic grew ragged, sharp edges tearing into her until its only purpose was pain and the survival of self. Of Alma's self: Harper was to be subsumed, just as Mae ought to have been. Mae, the lying, betraying sister; Mae, who—

—who was not there. That thought crystallized in Alma's mind, more powerful than any ideas that Harper could hold in place. Were this the Grey, it would be all right; there she could clutch and tear at singing skeins of energy, twist them into shapes or pluck them apart, but this was Walker's type of magic and the strange beauty of it was drowned by Alma's corruption. Walker had said shamanic magic gone wrong was sorcery, hadn't she? In the Grey, Harper could have torn into the shape of it—of Alma herself—but sucked down by this choking filth of unfamiliar sorcery, she didn't know how to fight back. She couldn't see the Grid, hear its muttering or the ring and hum of Seattle's constructed soul. There were no bright coils of living energy to touch, no shapes of magic like neon tracery in fog . . .

The cane, the silver deeply steeped in incantations—those were her weapons here. *If I can reach them, if I can hold this bitch off long enough to find a way* . . . Harper wrenched control back, looking for the cane, hoping it had come with her into the color-rich shamanic world. It was hard enough to hold any corporeal thing in the Grey, but she'd thought the cane would have enough affinity, even in such a foreign place . . .

A nasty laugh erupted from her own throat as Alma, sharing the confines of Harper's own thoughts, latched onto the idea of the cane. It wasn't there; a ghost of Alma's knowledge hinted to Harper that it wasn't part of Harper's own self-image, not enough for it to travel into this other world with her. The knowledge was like a knife—her strength had always lain in her ability to take her own body into the incorporate world, to be safe within the citadel of it and reach for the strands of magic like burning threads. But now, that too had failed. Here, *Alma* knew how to move, *Alma* knew how to draw things to her.

Or to vault upward again, out of the red-sky world and back into the haunted house. Harper staggered, disoriented and stunned by the harsh transition, while Alma forced their shared body into motion, seizing the cane that lay at Harper's feet, within her shamanic circle.

Two vicious slashes with the magic-disrupting cane, and the circle fell. But this was the house—multi-planed, corporeal and magical at the same time—and Alma had just made a big mistake.

The circle closed around me with a chime and a bright pulse of silvery light. Then the whole world went sideways, like I was trying to walk with one foot on the ground and the other on an escalator. The world filled up with chilly fog—but not fog really, more like the cold steam that comes off a frozen lake in a sudden beam of sunlight. It boiled and churned into shapes that were nearly recognizable—human faces, bodies, creatures that swam through the endlessly bright mist like sea serpents. And it all muttered and whispered in wind-chime voices, punctuated with the clack of bones and silver bells. I could see the house as lines of charcoal and red drawn in the restless fog of the Grey.

A shape like a tangled wad of colored light writhed around just in front of me—angry red and bitter green all twisted through with stiff bits of black like burnt twigs caught in a messed-up ball of yarn. The shape bloomed into something kind of human, wrapped in the cold fog that billowed into a face that peered at me, then dropped toward me like an anvil. I flung up a shield, gunmetal blue, and flinched as the thing slipped right through it and into me.

A twist of real anger and fear coiled through me. My shields were damn near impenetrable, at this point. I'd lost a lot, learning to keep them that way. That this *thing* could slip inside me so easily was bad with a capital B. I would have spent some quality time getting truly upset about that, if the misty world hadn't lurched like I'd fallen through the floor as the cold dove into me.

My stomach felt like it stayed at floor-level while I fell down, and the silvery fog-world lit up like the neon grave-yard outside Las Vegas. Every color I could ever have imag-ined raced up and down, north and south, east and west . . . but not quite at random. There was a system to it, almost like the animistic colors I normally Saw, and equally entirely unlike them. Some colors ran toward the poles, others side-to-side, and a few just rose up and curled like springwater bubbling into the air. They were myriad and gorgeous, like the northern lights gone wild, and I thought I could make sense of them, given a little time.

I wasn't given time. Instead I was given *voices*. The Grey *talked*. It whispered, it chattered, it babbled like a brook and sang like an endless choir in the fog-bound distance. Brilliant streams of light outlined the whole world like one of those crazy wire-frame simulations in some computer game. There was the house, as heavy and dense as the worst depression, seeming to float on the steam and speeding lines of colored fire.

"Alma . . ." I could hear the voice from my own mouth, but it was a floating stream of cold fog, not air. "You see? I *told* you! Can't you feel it now? Racing through you like a torrent? It's so beautiful! So much more beautiful than that nasty yellow earth and bloodred sky of yours."

"Mae?" I asked, and it was me asking: it didn't ride the air the way Mae's voice did. "What happened to you?"

But she didn't care about me; she was focused on Alma and on proving to her, somehow, that her own way of seeing the world was the real way to see it. Conviction and anger dripped icicles from the breathy fog as her voice grew more strident. "How could you lie about this? How could you, when we sank into the cold together? We used to be *together*! Together, together . . . like sisters ought to be, but you couldn't let the world be right! No, no! You had to *lie*! To say that *I* was the liar! To keep it for yourself! This is where the power is—shaped in the living mist—"

The living mist, I thought under Mae's rant. How could Harper stand it? It was fucking cold, to be honest, and while it was pretty, it was also disorienting and empty and terribly full at the same time. Which might have been bearable if the *muttering* would shut *up*!

My hands in Mae's control reached out and drew the light and fog into shapes familiar and strange—wire frames clothed in silver mist like the projection of a black-and-white film someone had left running in a steam-filled room. "Look what I can do—and you couldn't understand how I could take all your little toys apart! Look, look, *look*! I told you this was how it was. I *told you*!"

I could *feel* the shape rendering from Mae's thoughts inside my head, the force of her imagining pulling the power forth and clothing it in the smoke-and-silver of the Grey. She/I held the colored energy in our hands just like threads or ropes and the power just . . . flowed into shape like some wild woven creature with a burning heart of light. "If I could only bring you here, Alma . . . Then you'd see, then you'd know. And I'd pluck you apart . . . just like this!" Then she tangled my hand in the unburning heat of the thing and yanked the blazing core out, tearing it apart. I almost screamed from the burn of it, but as the thing fell apart, the heat turned back to cold . . .

"You held me down, you let me drown, you kept me in the cold and ice, and you took everything for yourself—everything, everyone! You told them such lies! *Such lies!* And this is all there is, forever and forever . . . Now we'll see . . . now we'll see how your bright colors and wild animals can protect you, liar!" She turned us and through the mist I saw a bright shape of light—no, two: a fury-red knotted up with spikes of bleeding black that tangled in and through another shape that flashed colors like light through a prism. That had to be Harper—containing Alma.

Mae plucked the thought from my head and shrieked, "Alma!" She tore through the swirling mist toward the black sketch of the house, and plunged our hands into the sparking shape of my power circle, which she definitely should not have been able to do. I felt it like electricity up my arms as she grabbed hold of it and tore it open.

A brief *holy shit!* that was definitely all my own popped out before we were spat into the last of my circles. Harper hadn't been kidding about tearing things apart, if she—or working the Grey—could do that to one of my power circles. *Nobody* could do that to one of my power circles.

Except me. And I was me and I was Mae and, oh God, that got complicated.

What was not complicated was that we—Mae and I—were now free to roam that small enclosure.

Free, in her mind, to attack.

But I wasn't in the chilly Grey now, and Mae wasn't a shaman.

Harper was in no condition to run, even with the cane in one hand, but Alma didn't know that. She forced Harper's legs two or three staggering steps before the half-healed shin and joints couldn't take any more. Alma's shock was even greater than her own pain as the next step sent them tumbling gracelessly to the floor: the hard landing came mostly on Harper's shoulder, sending a blunt throb deep into the joint. *I'm gonna be a bloody mess by the time this is over . . . Quinton's going to read me the riot act.*

Harper's hands were already moving under Alma's volition, fingernails preparing to scratch open a vein—blood magic to heal the inconvenient wounds—when Walker ripped apart her own small power circle and landed on Harper like a massive cat pouncing on its prey.

All of Harper's breath wheezed out, stymieing not just her, but Alma, too. Walker, with a rictus nothing like her own expressions, pushed her knee deeper into Harper's diaphragm and coiled her hands in an all too familiar fashion. Harper could see the intent, how the Grey surged to answer her, its ephemeral silver and burning colors ready to bend and yield, to let Mae plunge her hands—the tools of her intent—into their combined coil and tear her and Alma to glittering shreds. *Is that how I look? Is that how the ghosts and monsters see me?*

Deep in Harper's mind, Alma shouted with fear-edged outrage, summoning her own bloodstained shamanic magic. Words burst forth, a torrent of wrath and denial. "Not again! Not again, Mae! You killed me once before—!"

"I killed *you*?" a voice unlike Walker's howled from her lips. Harper could have laughed at the echo of her and Walker's earlier fight—if she hadn't been sick with dread. "You killed *me*, with your lies, with your filthy foolish animal magic, you—" Her grasp on the subtlety of the Grey failed under the heat of her invective, and rather than snatch through the streams of magic, she locked her hands into a double fist and slammed them down like a hammer.

Harper twitched her head just far enough to the side, a part of her wincing as Walker's knuckles smashed into the floor. But the part powered by Alma's hatred swung the cane upward, catching Walker's cheekbone and knocking her aside. Walker tumbled, her weight leaving Harper's chest, and Alma forced Harper upward a few inches to strike with the cane again, even as Harper herself locked her arm to keep the blow from landing true. It slammed into Walker's upper arm instead of her neck, and a host of conflicting emotions danced over Walker's face: pain, offense, gratitude, frustration. Harper felt Alma's spike of black humor through an equal blur of emotions that were—and weren't—hers.

Before Alma could strike again, Walker rolled backward and dropped into a crouch, putting a little distance between the two of them. Her jaw worked, and her voice grated, but it was *her own* voice now. "I propose we get this done with before these two beat us to death with our own bodies."

Still too winded to waste breath, Harper contented herself with, "How?"

"Give them what they asked for." Walker locked eyes with Harper and spoke very precisely, but then her grin turned feral again, the madness plain in it: Mae spread her hands, sliding closer to the Grey, gathering herself to dive deep and rip into the gleaming energy, but with Walker's benediction behind the gesture. Ice slid down Harper's spine. She pushed to her feet, weight heavy on the cane, and felt a disorienting sluice of power as Alma, unchallenged, sought the shamanic sorcery that she commanded so naturally.

Give them what they asked for. Harper ran the phrase through her mind, keeping it deep and quiet. Walker had picked her words this time, instead of her usual rough-and-tumble voicing of whatever came to mind. *Give them what they asked for.*

Harper breathed, "All right, Jo," and hoped like hell that Walker knew what she was doing.

The Grey felt like a weaponized web rising under my—Mae's—hands. I couldn't do what she was doing, couldn't push it and pull it and force myself through to take something apart as she could, but I could give her the freedom to *do* that. The threads she reached for turned crimson, and I could feel her shifting around inside of me, trying on my body for speed and size.

I was a lot bigger than Mae had been when she was alive, and much, much stronger. Her delight at being given this vehicle to end her sister with became palpable, and brightened further as she began to appreciate how Harper moved clumsily, putting weight on the silver cane. Alma was in a lesser vessel; that was Mae's conclusion, and I was okay with her thinking that.

Lesser vessel or not—and while I was inclined to bet on *not*, I also didn't want Mae picking up on that thought—the shamanic sorcerer Harper carried inside her was strong enough to have broken out of my power circle, albeit with an enspelled silver cane. I couldn't handle Mae's grasp on the Grey, but I could certainly see Alma's awakening of sorcery in Harper's narrow form. She didn't *heal* the leg wound; she just shored it up with power, pouring magic into Harper's body until the half-built shin became whole with blood-spattered sorcery.

Harper's body language changed, and I didn't think it was just her sudden ability to walk easily again. She looked like someone else had settled into her bones, just as Mae had settled into mine. Alma's posture was more rigid, her steps smaller, unnatural with Harper's height. She danced her hands around each other, calling black magic into them. Sparks of grey and gold, colors that I imagined had once been Alma's natural aura, guttered through the blackness, lending it just enough light to have shadows within.

Armed with equal and unique magics, the two sisters faced off for the space of a breath. Alma's loathing made Harper's face gaunt and unforgiving; I expected I looked no more pleasant. We sized each other up. Mae was more confident than I; I *knew* how much havoc shamanism gone bad could wreak.

I didn't know which of us moved first. I went at Harper like a fencer lunging for the kill, reaching for power that flowed through my arms and stabbed forward, seeking to rend the form ahead of me into shards of scattering light. She came on like a bull, arms spread wide, fire-licked black sorcery stretched between them.

In the absolute last moment before we clashed, I hissed, "My body. My rules," at Mae, and changed the game.

Harper slammed her hands together, boxing Walker's ears and letting shamanic sorcery burst into the other woman's body. Mae's Grey thrust ripped into Harper at the same time, piercing and tearing at the shape of her life. Harper welcomed the slicing cold sizzle and burn. She snatched the energy, twisted and pulled it wide into the aegis—the cold edge and flood of colorless purity—and instead of turning it aside into a shield as she usually did, she let it inundate her body. Alma—the consciousness and memory, thoughts and soul, that shared Harper's body—couldn't refuse the reality of the Grey's singing, vibrant electricity of raw magic as it washed them both. Extraordinary awe swept over Harper, too, and her thoughts tangled up in Alma's: *This cold, this light! It is so much better than dying . . . so grand, so huge, kind* *and colorful, living and raw and full! It is the same power that spins the shamanic worlds, just . . . different.*

Across from her, Walker took in the shamanic power the same way, guzzling it down as if she'd become greedy for it. Rage and disbelief and understanding flashed through the other woman's eyes in an instant, so fast Harper could never have named the emotions had she not been experiencing the same roller coaster herself. If *Alma* had not been experiencing them, just as Mae did.

All each sister had wanted, from the beginning, was for the other to believe that her power was *real*.

It was visceral now, as true as if they had gone into the icy water together and emerged sharing magics as well as sisterly bonds. The knowledge undid them for an instant, shattered the way they'd seen the world, and rebuilt it.

An instant was apparently all Walker needed.

Gunmetal blue healing power exploded across both of them. All of them—Harper didn't know how to count them, anymore. It wrenched through Alma, burning a century of hatred from her heart. Harper gasped and staggered aside; when she caught herself, Alma stood where Harper had been, gazing in weary bewilderment at the dark walls around them.

Mae surged out of Walker as though she'd been pushed, and looked around with as much confusion as Alma. Neither spoke or moved; they hardly seemed aware of one another, and were instead drawn toward the bleak walls of the little house.

Walker blurted, "Quick quick quick quick quick, unpick

unpick unpick," and Harper, with a hoarse laugh, was surprised to understand what she meant.

The sisters had been tied to the house for far too long, and the Grey was good for taking things apart—even things that had physical form so long as the power was what held them in shape. Harper plunged her hands into the searing black and pulled. The walls shuddered, shattered, and tumbled, as the ghostlight sinews of anger and pain that had for too long bound together the very bones of the spite house tore apart, piece-by-piece. The healed spirits sighed with each crack of the walls, drifting not farther apart, but closer together, until as the house fell to bits, they embraced in lambent light, and faded into nothing.

Green grass, neatly cared for and faintly immaterial, appeared beneath Harper's feet. Walker took half a step toward her, kicked something, and said, "Ow," as she bent to pick it up. The lockbox from the hall table. Harper barked a warning too late, and Walker, box in hand, looked up with a laugh. "I never learn, do I? But it didn't bite this time."

"I should have realized it wouldn't." Harper caught a glimpse of the key and crouched to collect it, too. She handed it to Walker, noticing that her leg took her weight and movement with less complaint. It wasn't yet at full strength, but . . . "This is . . . ah . . . better," she said.

Walker looked abashed. "A little, yeah. Sorry about that. Kind of. I mean, I know you don't want to explain magically regenerating bones to the doctors, but that healing blast kind of—it wasn't very focused. I was trying to get everything out of the twins, and one of them was in you . . ."

"Hey, I was just going to say thank you." Harper shrugged and gave a crooked grin. "We'll call it a medical miracle and the docs can have a field day arguing about it." Her leg was still imperfect, but it felt like it would have less of a weather-wise ache now and she was grateful. "What's in the box?" she asked.

Walker fitted the key and opened the box. A fragile newspaper clipping lay inside; they both peered at it without daring to touch.

Miracle Twins! the boldface headline proclaimed. *Three days ago, Alma and Mae Lindsey plunged through thin ice on Lake Washington and were miraculously pulled from the water, still alive, twenty minutes later.* The story went on, but the accompanying photograph drew Harper's attention: two young women with strong jaws and long noses, sternly corseted and, despite the formality of the photograph, still clearly holding on to one another for support and comfort.

Harper smiled. "They looked a little like that at the end, didn't they?"

"Did they? I can't see ghosts. But I'm glad."

"You can't—" The ground underfoot was growing more solid. Harper frowned at it. "I've got a thousand questions for you, but I think the planes that the house held together are returning to their rightful place."

"Yeah. We're running out of time here." Walker scuffed her foot against the grass, watching it bend beneath the pressure, then looked up and offered a hand. "Well. It sure was interesting meeting you, Harper Blaine."

"You, too, Joanne Walker." They shook hands, and Harper, still testing her weight on the half-healed leg, turned and started away, the cane more jaunty and less necessary in her grip.

A moment later Walker's voice followed her: "Hey, Harper."

Harper turned back, curious. Walker, looking almost a ghost herself now, twisted something off a bracelet—Harper hadn't even seen it under the sleeves of Walker's white leather coat—and tossed it her way. It landed solidly in Harper's hand: a small copper lynx charm. She looked up at Walker questioningly.

The other woman shrugged and smiled. "Who knows? If you're ever in trouble, rub it, click your heels together, and say 'There's no one like Jo,' three times, or something."

"I think that's *there's no place like home*," Harper replied pedantically, and Walker, laughing, disappeared from the Grey.

The lynx stayed solidly in Harper's palm, though, and after a moment she held it in her fingertips, examining it in the light. It glimmered and Harper, smiling, tucked it into her pocket. "I wonder which one of us is going to get paid?"

Crossed Wires

JEFF SOMERS AND STEPHEN BLACKMOORE

"I got a problem, Lem."

I glance up from my cards and take him in: Gabby Monke is a flabby blimp of a man who always wears the same linen suit, a study in increasing alarm. Each finger of both hands is wrapped in a piece of white gauze, red stains leaking through. The effect is of a fat man with marshmallows stuck on his fingers, removing that scrap of dignity that Gabby had left.

"You don't have a nickel to your name, Gabs," I say, "so I'm not sure where I come into this."

My poverty is famous. I glance at Mags, who is squeezing drops of blood from one thumb and holding a match in his other hand, muttering a *mu* that was supposed to light the match spontaneously. A fucking useless bit of doggerel, but I could see where it could be beefed up with a few extra Words and made into something forceful. Studying the seams of his sports jacket, which spread and creak over his huge shoulders as he hunches over his project, I amend my thought: *Our* poverty is famous. Mags is basically my property by now. Hiram made it clear: The moment the huge bastard followed me out of his apartment, he was mine to water and feed.

"C'mon, Lem," Gabby says in a ridiculous stage whisper, as if there were anything like privacy in a bar filled with *idimustari*. Tricksters cast eavesdropping cantrips instinctively, automatically. "I just need a consultation."

I sigh and look around my table. I've been playing for three hours and I'm up exactly five dollars from where I started, which means I have seven dollars to my name. It's rough when you can't use a little bit of gas and cloud people's judgment, but the easiest way to get barred from Rue's Morgue, I'd learned, was to cast a spell in a room full of Tricksters who could smell blood.

"Fine, Gabs," I say. "Buy me a drink and tell me your sorrows." I stand up. "Cash me out," I say, pushing my chips into the center of the table. I look at Mags, who has fallen in love with me and can't bear to be away from my comforting presence. "Stay!" I command. "Sit!"

Mags is just a huge dog, deep down. He offers me a sad face, but settles back into his seat.

"You ever worry that boy's gonna roll over in his sleep and crush you to death?" Gabby asks as we head for the bar, where Sheila is swaying in misery, blind hungover and green-faced. She manages a smile for us, though, a true professional.

"Yes," I admit. "Among other things."

Pitr Mags is dumb as a post and strong as a fucking angry bear, and he breaks things by looking at them, by simply sharing space with them. He still thinks he will one day be a bona fide *ustari*, bleeding to cast spells and mastering the universe, even though so far he's learned about six spells, five of which he fucks up regularly. He also seems to think

I am his *gasam*, that Hiram has transferred him to me. Pitr Mags lives his life under a lot of misapprehensions, but I've grown to like the guy. He is completely honest, totally loyal, and useful in a fight.

We order shots of bourbon, clink glasses, and down them.

"Oh that's it," Gabby says breathlessly, signaling, to my amazement, for two more. We let those sit.

"So, tell me," I say, scratching my head. I haven't showered in a few days, and feel like New York City has been grated directly onto me.

He sighs. Gabby has no specialty. He's one of those *idimustari*, one of those Tricksters who discovered the Words and found his way to us, learned precisely four spells and sat back, satisfied to survive on four dollars a day. But then again I am good with the Words and I am broke and faced with the daunting task of feeding Pitr Mags later. I am in no position to judge another mage's successes.

"You know I lost my mother last year," he says, and I have to control myself. Gabby has been lamenting the loss of his "mawmaw" every day for a year now, a rail-thin, bitter woman who could not possibly have once housed someone as huge and inflated as Gabby Monke.

"So, some *ustari* set out her shingle as a medium," Gabby continues, picking up his whiskey but just holding it, staring. "Straightforward enough, no mumbo-jumbo: A C-spot, and some bleeding, and she'll let you talk to anyone who's passed on. So I go. This townhouse down in the Village, skinniest fucking building I ever saw. I pay my tithe, I bleed her a pint, and five minutes later I'm talking to Mawmaw. Like *really* talking to her, Lem!"

His eyes are shining, and I have a horrible moment of thinking he is going to fucking burst into tears on me. "You got conned, Gabs," I say, retrieving my own shot from the bar in case I upset him and he decides to regret buying it for me. "Oldest one in the *book*, practically." I think how I would do it: a light Charm, to make things friendly, a bit of Compulsion to control the reactions, a lot of Glamour to make the special effects land. It isn't like it's impossible to contact the dead, but it takes a lot more blood than a pint.

"No." Gabby reaches out and grabs my arm, making me slop whiskey everywhere. "No, Lem, I swear, this shit was *legit*. It was Mawmaw. It *was*." He grimaces. "The first time."

I tip the shot back before the miserable bastard can spill it all. "So, the second time?"

"Same thing. A hundred bucks, a pint of blood, but when she went through the spell, it wasn't my mother. It was my *father.*"

I nod, waiting.

"My father ain't dead, Lem."

I wait again, and then lean forward. "Gabs. You. Got. *Conned.*"

His hand tightens on me. "Listen, Lem, help me out. Go down there and check it out, bust that bitch, get my loot back." He licks his lips, lizard-like, and I flinch away from the sight. "Look, get back my dosh and I'll split it with you. A hundred bucks. What do you say?"

I ball my feet inside my shoes and feel the paper-thin spot on the sole that will soon be a hole, letting in tiny rocks and puddles of water. I consider my personal fortune of seven dollars, with which I will have to feed myself *and* Pitr Mags, a man who makes hot dogs disappear in one bite and then spends five minutes licking his fingers in sad remembrance of the meal that was.

"C'mon, Lem," Gabby pleads. "You know every scam, every angle, every damn trick there is. Whatever her game is, you're the one to spot it."

I sense this is a compliment. Flattery doesn't mean anything though. I calculate how many hot dogs a hundred bucks will buy Mags.

I nod. "Fine."

I'm sitting in an overpriced bar in Manhattan full of ghosts and the wealthy. The rich folks are three kinds of rich. Investment rich, old rich, or drug rich. They're all equally boring.

But the ghosts, well, they're all kinds of interesting.

Haunts who've been stuck in the building since the 1800s, Wanderers who've come in off the street to check me out, a surprising number of Echoes, psychic recordings repeating their deaths like a skipping record.

I've seen six so far and there are more hiding in the background. Two gunshot wounds, three stabbings, and I can't be sure, but I think one with a face torn off by a monkey.

To look at the place you'd think it wasn't that kind of bar. But one thing all bars have in common is people get into fights, sometimes they die. Sometimes they leave behind ghosts.

None of the other patrons can see them, of course. They're all normals near as I can tell, regular people with no magic. And even if there is another mage in the crowd they probably wouldn't see them, either. Every mage has a knack, one thing they're really good at. Divination, illusions, whatever.

My thing's necromancy. Rare enough to be exceptional, creepy enough nobody wants it. Kind of like winning a lifetime supply of fast-food cheeseburgers.

Looking at the dead in the bar I can say I'm not looking much better than they are. I've got a bruised rib, black eye, split lip, a gash on my arm I stitched together with dental floss and butterfly bandages the night before.

I should be in bed with Vicodin and a bottle of vodka. I stand out like a sore thumb in this crowd, and a nice circle of space has opened up around me since nobody wants to be near me. At least I'm wearing a tie.

"Eric Carter?" I look up from my scotch to see a young black woman dressed for a night of clubbing. She has skin the color of teak and hair pulled back into a bun on top of her head. Her dress is a short, shimmery silver number and her nails are immaculate with plum polish.

But it's the eyes that do it. They're more gold than brown, with flecks of green and orange speckled through them. Look close enough and you can see the colors dance in them like motes of dust in a sunbeam.

Easy eyes to get lost in. Which is the point.

"You Miranda?"

She sticks her hand out and I shake it. She has a grip like ice. Like literally ice. When I pull my hand back it's like I stuck it in a freezer. I rub my hands together to get some warmth back into it.

"Sorry about that," she says. "I haven't eaten tonight."

"I hear they make awesome fries here," I say. She indulges

the joke with a smile. We both know what she eats and it isn't bar food. Well, I suppose it depends on your definition of bar food.

"Thank you for coming to meet me on such short notice," she says and slides onto the stool next to me. "And for meeting me here. I don't get that it's really your scene."

"What gave it away? The rumpled suit? The bad haircut?"

"The black eye, bruises, and cuts, actually," she says.

"I'm trying a look."

"It suits you."

"Thanks. Why are we meeting here?"

"I need to eat tonight," she says. "Soon. This is a good place for it."

"Ah. Let's get to it, then. I understand you need to talk to a dead man."

"I'm hoping to. There are . . . concerns in my community."

"So it's not an ordinary dead man."

"Well, yes and no. He's ordinary. His death not so much. His name's Bill Pear. Local homeless man. Nice enough guy, didn't cause trouble. About a month ago he wandered off. Nobody thought anything of it until his body turned up two days ago. Bled to death."

Miranda's "community" is made up of supernatural creatures like herself who live in Manhattan. Every city's got them. Vampires, Gwisin, Pombero, Wendigo, things like that. They do what they can to blend in. Sometimes because they want to be left alone. Sometimes because they prey on humans. They're never quite what the stories say, though there's always a grain of truth in them, somewhere.

Miranda's a Lamia. She doesn't have a snake's tail, or

lion's feet as far as I know, but she does feed off the life force of humans a couple of times a week. She doesn't usually kill her meals, that'd draw unwanted attention, but she does shave a few years off their lives.

When you live in the shadows like Miranda you pay attention to the others who live there, too. The junkies, the hustlers, the homeless, the grifters. And when something unusual happens to them it pays to get answers before the same thing happens to you.

"Vampire moving in?"

She shakes her head. "No. He was bled, but the blood was just spilled, not taken. We don't know what this is." She pulls her phone from her purse and brings up a set of photos and hands it to me. I scroll through them and I get what she's talking about. I don't know what the hell this is, either.

Male, late sixties, probably younger. Homelessness does a real number on people. He's naked, tied upside down by his feet to a fire escape. He's been bled, all right. Messily. Instead of one neat cut across his throat there are dozens of smaller ones all across his face and body. I zoom in on one to get a better look. They're not just random cuts, they're runes. Somebody was writing on him with a knife.

"Anyone ID what the runes are? I don't recognize them."

"No," she says. "Not that any of the local mages who might be able to read them are interested in helping us."

"That's mages for you." Bunch of shortsighted sociopaths, the lot of us. If the homeless are a harbinger of trouble for the supernaturals, the supernaturals are the same thing for us. "Speaking of which. Why me? I can't be the only necromancer around here."

I haven't been in New York for very long, only about a year. I'm an L.A. boy. I left eight years ago under a bit of a cloud and haven't been back. Been wandering here and there ever since. I like New York. City of a thousand smells, none of them what I'd call good.

New York magic is city magic. Tastes like hot metal, poured concrete. A mélange of all the cultures and beliefs that have passed through it. Hopes and shattered dreams, fortunes and downfall. The magic in an area takes on the flavor of the world around it the way wine grapes take on the flavor of the soil.

New York magic is good for creating things that last. Golems and constructs, for example. Curses that really stick. Compare it with L.A., where you can't pin it down. L.A. magic is good for reinvention, making something new and burying the old.

Not that you can't use a place's magic for anything else, of course. It just makes some things easier. It's like wine with food. Pair it right, you have something special. Pair it wrong, you'll still get just as drunk.

The thing about New York is that it isn't big, there are just a lot of people in it. And that includes mages. We're a rare breed, but out here there are a shit ton of us. With this many in play there should be one or two necromancers around.

"There was one we used to work with, but she was in the Towers when they went down. A few others have moved in, but they're . . ." She searches for a word.

"Racist fucks?" I say.

"That's one way to put it. I'd heard you were more open than most."

"For the right price, I'll do just about anything."

"Hence the black eye?"

"That's more a wrong place, wrong time kind of thing. Jersey Devil."

A look of fear passes over her face and just as quickly disappears. "In the city?"

"Morristown. Sniffed me out and thought it could get a quick meal." Nasty fuckers. Up here they're Jersey Devils, down in Mexico they're El Cucuy. I hear the Russian mages call them Baba Yagas.

Whatever you call them, they're bad news. Magic eaters. They love to eat mages. But they'll go after just about anything that uses or is magic. Like Miranda here.

"You got off light."

"It wasn't very big. Anyway, where'd you find Hobo Bill? And why isn't he in the papers?"

"Behind a restaurant on Bedford and Commerce. Around three in the morning. Peter, one of our ghouls, got the body. He still has it if you want to see it. Thought it would be better than letting the police get involved."

"You sure this wasn't just some nutjob writing gibberish occult nonsense on the corpse?" I turn the phone in my hand trying to get a better view of the runes. Doesn't matter the angle; I can't tell what these are.

"I know it's unlikely, but I have to ask—"

"If Peter did it?" she says. "No. He's a scavenger, not a hunter. Very conflict avoidant. Lot of anxiety. He's been on Paxil for years. It's definitely not one of us. It can't be one of us. We'd like to find out if this is something we need to worry about."

She's scared. Her whole neighborhood's scared. I get it. Some new beastie's walked in that they don't understand and tossed everything sideways.

"I'll check the scene and see if he left a ghost. With this kind of thing they usually do. If there's enough of him left I'll ask him what happened."

"We would really appreciate it."

I keep turning the phone, trying to pick out the runes. Some of them are almost ones I recognize, but there are differences that don't match up. Like seeing a mix of different languages that don't make sense, letters mashed together to form new ones.

"This ghoul, Peter, he live near where you found the body?"

"Yes. I can give you the address. Do you want to see the body? I can let him know you're coming. He runs a butcher shop a few blocks away."

Of course he does. "Thanks. If I see the body maybe I can tell if these markings are just bullshit nonsense. Then I don't have to talk to Bill. Save you guys some money."

"Such magnanimity."

"More laziness, honestly. He hasn't eaten the body yet, has he?"

"He promised he wouldn't," she says. "For a few weeks at least. Wants to age the meat a little."

"Great. A connoisseur."

There's so much fucking gas in the city. We ride the subway downtown and there is just gas in the air, someone on the car bleeding under a bandage, under their clothes, somewhere. Not a lot, but enough for a *mu* or two, something small, if you were willing to bleed someone else. Plenty of my fellow travelers do that, paying kids or hookers or drunks for a bleed, and plenty of others don't even pay.

I'd done that once, and every time I thought of it, my skin crawled and my heart started pounding. For me and Mags, we cast off our own gas, period. I'm light-headed all the time, but I sleep at night.

At 75 1/2 Bedford Street we find the skinniest fucking house I've ever seen. Standing in front of it, Mags stretches his arms out, punishing the cheap seams of his jacket even more, and if he were inside he might have touched both walls. The neighborhood has so much money it makes me itch. I feel shabby, standing on the street in my thin suit and my fading shoes.

And then I feel something else, because there is something wrong with the house.

Mags feels it too. He turns to look back at me with the wide-eyed expression he reserves for the Unknown, for anything he isn't sure he should be afraid of. It makes him look like a kid, some monstrous six-foot-five Indian kid with hands like shovels. Mags could casually knock down walls, but he is scared of everything.

Something is . . . missing. Something I normally feel, swim around in, breathe, but never think about. But it's just a house.

"C'mon," I say gruffly, giving him a little shove as I step past him. For a hundred bucks I am ignoring my instincts. This has never gone well for me in the past, but then paying *attention* to my instincts has left me with exactly seven dollars and a man-child companion who is more stomach than brain. The lessons the universe is trying to teach me are vague, at best.

As I approach the front door the sense of wrongness gets stronger. With a furtive look around to ensure privacy, I tug up my sleeves with a practiced motion, pull my switchblade from my pocket, snap it open, and drag the blade across my forearm. The usual sting, the usual uncanny delay, and then a thick line of red blood. I taste the gas in the air and hold my arm up, touching my forefinger to my thumb to make a circle. Six Words, a *mu* of my own creation, designed to reveal truths and dispel Glamours.

I close one eye and squint through the circle formed by my fingers. The townhome is gone. Everything else is exactly as I saw it, but in place of this ridiculously skinny building there is an alleyway running between the two buildings, grass and trash.

I flex my hand and the spell snaps. The familiar wave of mild dizziness passes through me, and then I'm back to normal, and the wound on my arm is already a raw, scabbed memory. The universe is hungry for blood, but it's polite about it.

"Still doesn't make sense," I say.

"Gabs said he was *in* the house," Mags says quietly.

He's right, which is unusual enough to make me look at him in surprise. If the building isn't really there, then it's a Glamour. But if it's a Glamour, then Gabby couldn't have walked into it. And if it's a Glamour, that doesn't explain the sense of *nothing* I get from it.

"Mags," I say. "Can you give me a bit of the witchlight?"

He grunts. Teaching Mags a new spell generally means he forgets one you taught him last week, but the witchlight was one of the basics every single *idimustari*, the Little Magicians, could cast. You might never become an *enustari*, an Archmage, but you would be able to light up hidden runes and other magical markings. Not quite as useful as a solid Charm cantrip or a fireball spell, but useful enough.

He opens his palm, crisscrossed with faded white scars and newer pink ones, lines on a map. He produces a fucking steak knife, nicked, I thought, from Hiram's place when we made our unceremonious and humiliating departure, and I am fucking mortified. Hiram already thought I was an idiot to walk away from his apprenticeship—and the old man *still* hadn't released me from my magical oath of *urtuku*, which meant I was still under his thumb—but if I had to crawl back to return his fucking cutlery, my ignominy in the world of mages would be secure.

Mags slices his palm with a wince and a tiny, childlike sound. Then he clenches his fist, speaks the Words, and his hand is engulfed in a sputtering blue-white light.

"Crank it up," I say.

He settles himself and concentrates, lips moving, and the ball of light grows larger and brighter until it throws the townhome and everything around it into sharp relief. No one not in our grubby little guild of magicians could see it. All they would see was two disreputable assholes apparently doing interpretive dance on the sidewalk.

I lean forward and concentrate, but there is nothing. Not a rune, not a mark, no sign at all of any sort of spell—which is impossible, because my own spell has just revealed the skinny building to be a fake.

"All right." I wave Mags down, and with a grunt he flexes his hand and the witchlight vanishes with a splutter. "Let's go in."

I meet Peter Manelli in his butcher shop off Bleecker Street, a few blocks from where Bill was found hung out to dry. He's a sallow, snaggletoothed man with a limp and a comb-over that makes him look harmless, dismissible. The easiest of easy marks. A guy muggers and pickpockets can take in a dark alley on a moonless night.

Poor bastards.

Manelli's a ghoul. Not quite human, not quite not. He likes the taste of his fellow man. Craves it, needs it. Without it he'll wither and die.

If you really look at him you can tell that his weird, lumpy body is from muscles attached in strange places, bulging with superhuman strength. I've seen ghouls deadlift cars. And throw them.

Some ghouls are hunters. I don't get that vibe off this one. He's nervous, twitchy, doesn't know what to make of me. He avoids eye contact. Either he's a good enough actor to fool all the other supernaturals in his neighborhood, or he's legit.

He's not going to scavenge so close to where he lives and works. Which makes his butcher shop the perfect place. He has a refrigerated truck. He can head over to Brooklyn or Jersey or some backwater where he's not going to step on some other ghoul's toes, grab a body to eat and toss him in the back. I don't know how ghouls find them. They just seem to have a knack for it.

"You're Carter? The necro?" His voice sounds like he's gargling marbles. He has an esophagus that stretches like a balloon to accommodate bigger pieces of food, and teeth inside that to make sure the stuff going in keeps going in. If you're devouring your meat live I figure that must be an asset.

"Mister Manelli," I say, not shaking his hand. It's not rudeness, it's practicality. On top of everything else, a ghoul's palms are like sharkskin. "Good to meet you."

Really, nothing about ghouls is appealing.

"Yeah, sure. Miranda said you were coming by. You want to see Bill? I got him in the freezer."

I look behind him at the freezer door behind the counter. He catches my look.

"Oh god no. Not that freezer. The normals would shit kittens if I did that. I got him in the basement. Made special. Secret doors and everything. Come on, I'll show you."

Normally I make a point of not going into the basement with strange ghouls, but I'm on the clock and if things go south I can take him. Maybe.

I follow him downstairs, where he slides aside a pile of dusty junk that's all bolted together to look exactly like a pile of dusty junk. Then he hits a series of hidden catches on the wall. It pops open and swings aside to show an industrial freezer lit with bright fluorescents. Bodies hang from meat hooks.

"Nice setup." I try not to judge, but half a dozen naked

corpses hanging in a basement freezer like something Ed Gein would cook up is a little much.

"Thanks. Anyway, there he is. In the back. You need anything? I have to get back to cutting up pork chops."

"Nah, I'm good. Just leave the door open if you could. I'd hate to have to blast it off the hinges if I got stuck in here."

He frowns at me, not sure if I'm joking or not. Decides I'm not. "Yeah, sure. Just don't take too long. This meat gets too warm it's gonna be a problem." He backs out of the freezer and leaves me alone with his meat.

"All right, Hobo Bill, let's see what you got here." He's been stripped naked and hung with the hook through the back of his neck, making it easier to see the marks.

Hobo Bill is fat, balding, and gray. His blood poured out of him from cuts in his neck and wrists. He's heavily marked up with these runes. Some of them are drawn on, some of them carved on.

Up close and personal I still don't know what the hell they are, but I think they're real. People who don't do magic use the same recognizable bullshit as everybody else. Barrett's *Magus*, Crowley's *Magick*, Agrippa's *Books of Occult Philosophy*. This is none of them. It doesn't even look like any of them.

And the thing is, some of them are legit. Or near to legit. I may not be able to recognize the runes, but I can tell big magic when I see it. Even if I can't get a whiff of any magic coming off the body.

That's weird, too. I should be able to feel something residual if his death was used to fuel a spell. Something I can taste, feel. But there's nothing.

Whatever this was for, it's about the blood. The runes are too precise, too orderly. They're over his chakras, carved in the skin at the bleed points.

I'll sometimes bleed for a spell, but that's to feed ghosts, use it as bait. Sometimes it's a trigger for anything I'm doing death related. Don't ask me why, it just works that way.

Knacks are like that. I know a sex mage in SoHo who does her best work getting raw dogged in a fetish bar. Scryers who can't divine a goddamn thing without getting high as balls first. Amazing the number of mages who are heroin addicts.

Was this the same thing? Did whoever did this use the blood the way I might? I've never used this much. Can't conceive what kind of spell would even need this much blood. With a tablespoon I could summon every Wanderer in a ten-mile radius and pull in Haunts who haven't been visible in three hundred years.

But a whole person's worth? Jesus. That's some ugly magic right there. If someone dies as part of a ritual they give off a flare of energy that a mage can tap into. It's why human sacrifice was so popular when we could get away with it.

But if it was just to kill him and collect his energy to fuel a spell, why bleed him? That's just more work. Too many questions, not enough answers.

High time I asked the man himself.

Each floor of the place was basically one room. Standing in the foyer, the hairs on my arms stand on end, and I try to put my eyes everywhere. The feeling of strangeness is like static electricity. I can't sense anything: no gas in the air, no magical energy. And yet I'm standing in a space that shouldn't be there, that has to be magical.

"Welcome."

A woman; she must have come from the doorway directly in front of us, a few feet past the narrow, steep stairs rising up to the second floor. She's older, fiftyish, with gray-black hair pulled back in a sloppy bun. She's heavyset, but moves with grace, bracelets and rings tinkling. Her eyes are gorgeous: deep, clear eyes, the kind of eyes you try to drag over to you, the kind of eyes you perform for.

"I am Celine Meridia." She pauses as if this name should have an effect on us. After a tick of her head, she reassesses. "Walk-ins? Were you referred?"

I shake my head. I don't know what kind of scene Gabby might have made, so I don't use his name. "We've heard stories."

She smiles, and waves us toward her. "Come then. Don't be shy."

A few steps in and the stairs rise up on our right, and Mags has to hold his arms in close to squeeze down the hall. Even I feel crowded and crushed. The next room is a little better, though; it feels subterranean from a lack of windows and light, but the ceiling is high, crowned with an elaborate old plaster rose and a spectacular old-school chandelier made of crystal, and the space spans the full nine feet, which is a relief after the tightness of the foyer.

It's filled to bursting with a huge wooden table. Candles and tiny pieces of art line the shelves on the walls, and the floor creaks and moans as we shift our weight, the ancient floorboards wide and gnarled, chewed up and cracked. After the initial sense of freedom from the slightly larger space, it suddenly feels choked, filled with scented candle wax and smoke.

"Sit," she suggests. "You have come to be read? You know our policies: The price is one hundred dollars and a . . . sacrifice. A very personal sacrifice."

I'm sweating. I feel like it's taking secret energy for me to remain in the room, as if some force is trying to pull me away, throw me out, and I have to exert myself in some invisible, unknowable way to remain. "We don't have any money," I say, feeling lame.

She smiles. "Arrangements can be made," she says, looking at Mags. "Perhaps a more substantial . . . sacrifice."

I study her. Magic takes blood, fresh and hot and still full of life, and it can't be stored, can't be preserved—although a few enterprising *enustari* have "stored" blood by the simple expedient of imprisoning people until they could be bled at the proper time, and in the proper sequence.

Mages. We are not good people.

She smiles wider. It has every superficial resemblance to a warm, reassuring smile. "You have come in pain, as all do, seeking comfort. Do not hesitate. I take only what is necessary for the ritual. Only what is needed to make contact."

One hundred dollars. I can get as much bleeding for someone like Heller—or even Hiram, if he would have me. But something is so wrong here I can't walk away. It nags me, tugging at my sleeve.

I look at Mags. "You up for a donation, Pitr?" I swallow, feeling dirty. This is dangerously close to bleeding some-one else, I think. Dangerously close to taking advantage of the big guy, who sometimes seems confused by the simplest things.

But he looks at Celine, then around the room, then right back at me. "Yes," he says, and begins rolling up his sleeve again. I nod, not feeling any better, and turn to look at her. "All right."

The space behind the restaurant on Bedford where they found Hobo Bill is more courtyard than alley. The block is a triangle of Bedford, Commerce, and Seventh Avenue. It's boxed in by brownstones on two sides and an iron gate and brick wall on the third, an old locksmith shop sitting between them. Thick trees give a lot of cover. A good place to murder somebody if you can keep the noise down.

From the number of ghosts hanging out back here, I'd say I'm not the first person to have that thought. Except these are all Wanderers. No Haunts, no Echoes. Something's attracting the Wanderers but I can't tell what.

I find the spot where Bill was hung up pretty easily. The blood has been washed away but it's left a lingering stain on the concrete, the walls. From what I can tell he squirted out here like a juiced lemon and nobody bothered to catch the blood.

Did he use it to attract the Wanderers? Done right, spilling blood will pull them in for miles. But I don't see what's keeping them here. If it was a spell to trap them, I should feel it.

I don't see Hobo Bill anywhere among the ghosts, and I can't tell if he's hiding. There are too many here and it's all just noise. Time to sort through them all.

I sit cross-legged on the cement, check to see that no-body's watching, then roll up my left sleeve and pull out my straight razor and a small silver bowl.

I have tattoos all over my body, but I keep an empty patch on the inside of my forearm for bleeding. It's scarred and covered in little Band-Aids. I peel one of them back to get to the scab and quickly run the razor over the spot to let a few drops of blood drip into the bowl. It doesn't take much. They feed off the life in the blood, crave it like a junkie craves smack. As soon as I put some power into it I should have their attention.

Only I don't.

The Wanderers pay no attention to me. No attention to this offering of life I've spilled.

"Okay, what the fuck," I say. I cover the small wound back up with the Band-Aid and fling the blood out from the silver bowl. "Come on, take it. Chum in the water, people."

Nothing. I'm starting to get a little creeped out here.

Is it me? I cast a small flame to dance around my finger-tips. No, I can still do spells. And I can still see the ghosts.

I watch the Wanderers milling about and after a few min-utes I notice a pattern. They're all clustering more or less around a ridiculously thin house stuck between two brown-stones. Each time they pass it they turn their heads to look. Aside from it being stupidly small, I don't see anything unusual about it.

So what are the ghosts seeing?

There's only one way I know to get a view of what they're seeing and I really don't want to do it. It's a pain in the ass, and with this many ghosts around it'll probably get me killed.

I know a spell that will flip me over to the ghosts' side of the veil. It's a pretty shitty place. It sucks the life out of you, drains you away. Stay too long, you're not coming back.

And that's the upside.

The downside is you won't last that long because the ghosts will eat you. They'll chew through your soul like a fat man at a Vegas buffet. I go over there they'll swarm me like piranha.

Or maybe they won't. They don't seem to be paying attention to anything besides the house.

This is a really bad idea. Nobody ever said I was smart.

I expected mumbo jumbo. Whatever odd feeling I'm having—and I am undernourished, poorly rested, and bleed every day for small spells—there is no other reason a mage would be working people for gas and money. It has to be a grift. So I keep my eyes open.

She dispenses with the tourist bullshit and just bleeds us, slicing us each on the forearm and launching into her spell. She speaks in a twisty, bullshit-laden patois, though, clearly designed to obfuscate what the spell actually does. To the untrained ear it's merely pretty. To the stupid, which includes just about every other *idimustari* I know and *definitely* includes Gabby, it makes no sense, Words dropping like useless anvils, never coalescing into a grammar that directs the universe on how to use the gas we're feeding it.

To *my* ear, it isn't a spell that has anything to do with

summoning spirits. And yet the spirits come. Or, one spirit.

Heya, laddie, the voice says. That's all. That's enough. It's the familiar Jim Beam rasp, the four syllables that more or less defined my childhood.

"The *fuck*," I hiss, standing up. Celine blinks at me in sudden surprise. A moment later Mags surges up, copying my body language and movements, and Celine is much more alarmed, standing up and backing against the wall.

"I must *warn* you—"

I stare at her for a moment, and she shuts her mouth with a click. I have a feeling poor old Gabby isn't getting his money back, after all. My father is gone, but he'd been there, the one voice I never needed to hear again. But the spell—the spell Celine had spoken hadn't been about spirits. It hadn't been about the afterlife. It had been all about the *blood*.

It takes a few minutes to get the spell going. This is like swimming with sharks. It's not something you want to fuck up.

I hang back from the milling crowd of Wanderers. Popping over to the other side in the middle of them would be a remarkably bad idea. Over here, if they notice me, I might be far enough away to shift back before they eat me.

I close my eyes, let the void soak into my mind, put out my senses. I don't strictly need to bleed for this one, but it helps. I run the straight razor against my forearm, the blood welling up from the cut. I shake some onto the ground and will myself over.

Jet engine burst of sound. Screaming wind. Frozen air

sucks at my lungs. The world of the living shifts into a dim shadow, gray and empty, goes silent.

Architecture here is made of memory and time. The longer a thing stays in one place the more it imprints on the psychic landscape. Old buildings like these brownstones, even ones that have been torn down, have a solidity that's more than physical. Cars, streetlights, trees—anything new—are nothing but indistinct outlines bleeding over from the living side.

I made the mistake once of doing this in a new high-rise building, materializing into an empty void fifty stories up. I fell three floors before I managed to shift back. Broke my leg, collarbone, two fingers.

But down here the buildings have the weight of a hundred years or more. Rooted in time and place. Cobblestones instead of pavement, decorations on the buildings long gone. Over time the landscape will shift again as today takes over the past. But it will be a while.

The Wanderers come into full view, flickering past like badly threaded film. Their attention pulled to the narrow house stuck between the two brownstones. On the side of the living, the house is a blank wall, new construction. Over here there are two windows and a back door.

But what really takes the cake is the giant phosphorescent bubble surrounding the whole goddamn thing. It's as high as the building, stretching outward. I can see it pulsing, shifting color, intensity. I'm not sure but I think it's growing.

For the life of me I have no idea what it is. Or how it's even possible. Magic works on this side, but mages are disconnected from the pool of power we tap into to cast big spells. All we have is whatever we bring over with us. Most people it's not much. Even if Hobo Bill had been gutted for his magical potential it wouldn't be enough to do this. It would have sputtered and drained away in minutes, hours at most.

And that's not even the weirdest part. I can see now why the Wanderers are giving the house such intense stares as they mill past it in a slow circle. As they pass by wisps of their essence are being pulled off of them like smoke, funneled in through the keyhole in that spectral door.

Is it using the ghosts to power it?

I was hoping this would be simple. But then when has anything ever been simple. I'm going to have to go inside. And that means wading through the ghosts.

I edge in closer, get ready to pop back as fast as I can, waiting for them to pounce. Even at this distance they should sense me, come at me in a stampede. But they don't.

Ten feet, five. Nothing. A break in the mob opens up and I hurry through, taking care not to let them touch me. They don't pay any attention to me at all.

I step up to the bubble. No helping touching that. I stand there for a minute watching it creep slowly toward me. I step through it and . . . nothing happens. I don't burst into flame, my soul doesn't get sucked out my asshole, nothing. I feel fine.

Next step is the door. It isn't really here, not in any physical sense. It's a memory of a door. For the door to be here on this side, but not on the other, means it's recent construction.

The only way in through the back without a sledgehammer is to come to it from the dead side. Clever or coincidence, I'm not sure, but I'm leaning toward clever.

I focus my will to grasp the doorknob and turn it. It's like trying to grab hold of a greased weasel, but eventually I get it open. Inside the room is bare. I can make out the faint outlines of furniture on the living side, but there are no clues on this side as to what's going on.

I pull myself back to the land of the living. Experience that jet engine noise, the rush of colors slamming into me as the world takes shape.

At first I think I've just lost my bearings. Sometimes that happens. Dizziness washes over me, but I get control of the vertigo. But there's something wrong. It takes me a second to place it and when I do I realize I'm probably screwed

I can't feel any magic.

"You *sure* about that address?"

I nod, worrying about mold spores. The basement space that had once been Olyphant Books (the plate glass still reads USED | NEW | ESTATE SALES; the old shelves are still lined with ancient, crumbling books) feels damp and smells damp, so it's easy to imagine all the hungry single-celled organisms of the world breeding like mad, releasing cancerous spores into the air, killing us all.

Digory Ketterly looks at me from under his white eyebrows and over his square black glasses, his salt-and-pepper hair a little too long to be reputable. He glances at Mags and dismisses him; so far, Ketterly hasn't spoken a word to Mags, regarding him as a temporary anomaly in his world.

"You know that's where they took down Aednat Deasm-humhain, right?"

I blink. I have a flashback to my time with Hiram, my estranged *gasam*. He liked to start his lectures with a question I couldn't answer, too, the miserable bastard.

Ketterly sighs. "Maybe a century ago. Deasmhumhain . . . she had ambition. Wild *enustari*, dressed like a man—short hair, three-piece suits. Bled men exclusively—*that* shit got the attention of all the male *ustari* out there, believe me. She never made it onto the global stage, but for a few years there she basically ran this city, and squeezed a lot of innocent blood out of it. Until every mage of any status in the whole state came down here and put her down."

I picture the skinny house, trying to imagine a war on that spot: fireballs and golems and spells that warped reality—I flash to the way the house seemed to be there but *not* there at the same time. I tell Digs about the house and what we experienced. He leans back and rubs his face with one hand.

"That place is like *radioactive* from all the spells spoken and blood shed there, soaking into the ground. Kind of out of my league, Lem Vonnegan. You need someone with some heft, some experience. *Saganustari*, maybe. Ask your *gasam*."

I shake my head, turning to watch Mags straining to reach a thick, dusty book on the top shelf, up on his tiptoes, his hand outstretched like a kid reaching for candy. "Me and Hiram aren't on speaking terms, Digs."

He snorts. "Still? You're a stubborn bastard, Vonnegan. That old thief ain't *ever* releasing you from your bond." He sighs. "I can put you in touch with Volker, you hear of him?"

I think for a moment. "Maybe. The guy with the cats, right?"

It's an ancient townhouse up in Harlem, like deep up embedded in Harlem, where money used to be, has left and come again three or four times. It's weathered like a stone formation, made from pieces that were monumental on their own. I have Mags stand a few steps down in order to appear smaller and less likely to break everything in sight, and ring the bell. I can't smell any magic or any blood, but Digs swears this guy is *saganustari*, maybe even *enustari*. Deep magic.

The door cracks open, and a unique smell creeps out from the house and wraps itself around me, temporarily paralyzing my brain, which dedicates 110 percent of its processing cycles to identifying the components.

"What do you want, *idimustari*?"

It always bothers me how the more experienced mages can always tell I'm a shitheel, a Trickster. Maybe it's the scars, because I won't bleed anyone but myself. "Digory Ketterly sent us."

The old man cracks the door open a little more. He's tall, like inhumanly tall, maybe seven fucking feet, with a long oval face that seems to sag off the skull and a shag of white hair that hangs to his shoulders and looks to have been chopped short by a dull knife. His squinted eyes flick to Mags. I stop myself from turning to glance back, but even so I'm pretty sure Mags has just waved and smiled.

Volker looks back at me. "One of Ketterly's projects, eh?" He steps aside, opening the door. "Come in, then, come in."

I don't want to. The smell is something that will attach

itself to me and follow me everywhere for the rest of my days. It's musty and earthy and *thick*. After a moment I follow, gesturing behind me that Mags should stay put. I can't do much for the big idiot, but I can spare Mags this smell.

Inside, there is barely room to move; piles of newspapers and cardboard boxes fill everything except a space near the door that allows them to be cracked open, and a narrow lane that leads deep into the shadows of the house. I glance down; two large—like, overly, unexpectedly large—cats are peering up at me, sitting there with their orange tails curled around their paws. Their stare is steady and intelligent, yellow eyes and fierce, thick whiskers.

As I stare, one of them yawns, showing me its teeth.

I follow Volker down the lane, sidestepping cats along the way. They're all huge, coming up to my knees, and they all could not be less impressed with me.

I find myself in the kitchen, similarly stuffed full of boxes and junk, except for the lane and small areas around the appliances. Volker is standing at the small sliver of counter that isn't covered in stuff. He has a pile of dead rats there. He follows my eyes and turns back, unsmiling.

"Like you, I avoid bleeding humans," he says, his voice deep, his words slurry, like he doesn't do much talking. "My Pride hunts for me, brings them alive."

I nod as if this is perfectly reasonable. Mags and I have nothing against rats, either. A sleek black cat, even larger than the others, leaps up onto the counter and sits there next to Volker, grooming itself while somehow appearing to keep one eye on me.

"Ketterly told me you might be able to help me with

information about Seventy-Five and a Half Bedford Street and Aednat Deasmhumhain," I say, watching the cat.

He purses his lips and looks happier. "Yes? An interesting subject! You have seen the house, yes? The building that is not really there? I have made a study of it."

I nod. "A Glamour. A *very good* Glamour."

He shakes his head. "No! Not a Glamour at all! It is an extrusion of reality. It is one of the greatest spells ever cast, and it was cast under such pressure! *Ustari* come to kill and destroy Deasmhumhain, and she not only resists and counterattacks, she manages *that*." He snorts. "They were right to resist her, to come in force. Deasmhumhain would have destroyed us all if she'd been allowed to prosper!" He sighs happily. "I have studied Bedford Street for my book."

I am instantly terrified he'll start telling me about his book. "What do you mean 'extrusion of reality'?"

Volker is getting excited. "Pancakes!" he shouts, and the black cat leaps off the counter, startled, and zooms past me, making me flinch. "You must think of different realities as pancakes stacked on top of each other. The barrier between them is *thin*, but difficult to pierce. When you break through, it is like a cone: You pull some of your own universe in after you, create a bubble. Deasmhumhain may be one of the only *ustari* to have ever managed this."

I blink. This is way above my education.

Volker holds up a hand, sensing my confusion. "Imagine: A rubber sheet. You poke your finger into it. It distends into the space beyond, but does not break. That's what you have at Bedford Street. Realities overlapping, and bringing their own rules with them."

I am suddenly glad Mags is outside, because if he asks me to explain this to him I'd have to resort to threats and abuse.

"My advice?" Volker says. "Stay the fuck away from there. If Deasmhumhain did something to cause this, there's a plan behind it, and you don't want to find out what it is."

I sigh, a cold bubble of dread in my belly. "I know what it is: She's siphoning gas from us, one bleeding idiot at a time. But I don't know *why*."

Volker smiles again as a gray and white cat the size of a Greyhound bus leaps onto the counter and then onto his shoulders in what looks like one graceful dance move. "You could ask her. If she's on the other side, as you say, *siphoning*, you might contact her."

He clearly thinks this is a ridiculous, terrible idea. But then my whole life, from the moment I showed up in New York looking for a magician to teach me about magic, has been a long list of ridiculous and terrible ideas. I nod. "I think I will."

I try to call fire to my fingertips. It's one of the first spells every mage learns. It's a good test to make sure everything works.

Nothing happens.

I've heard of shit like this before, but this is the first time I've run into it. Places covered in runes and spells where magic flat-out won't work. It's like a Faraday cage. Nothing goes in, nothing comes out. Nothing works inside.

They're great mage prisons. Or mage traps. I'm not sure which one this is.

The room itself is done up like a nineteenth-century salon. Guttering gas lamps on the wall, crushed velvet seats, a wooden table, the veneer worn through until bare wood is visible. Real antiques. How the hell they got gaslight in here when nobody's used it in a hundred years is beyond me.

There's a door leading to the rest of the house and the windows and door leading outside are here, but they're boarded over on the other side with the new construction.

I check the desk drawers, look for something with a name on it. Checkbook, credit card statements, gas bill, anything. The drawers have fountain pens, bottles of ink, stationery. The last drawer I hit pay dirt, a journal.

It's a heavy book, thick. A meticulously organized diary of someone named Deasmhumhain that starts about ten years back. I skim through it. Most of it's in English, but there are words I've never heard before. *Ustari, Gasam, Idimusturi, Enustari.* What is this, Greek?

As it gets closer to the present the runes I found carved on Hobo Bill start popping up. There's talk about magic in the blood. About spells that only work "over here," and not "over there." I'm not clear on what that means until I hit a passage from about five years ago that makes no sense on its own, but taken into context with everything else gets me thinking.

In this world the magic is everywhere. In the air, the water, not locked away in blood. Maddening that it's so useless to me. And outside this small bubble of my world the Words are useless. The rules here are different. But the tunnel I've created between my world and this one through the land of shades is growing. I think

I've figured out how to tap into the spirits of the dead. I'll still need the occasional Bleeder, but once I have things established I'll be able to grow the bubble faster and larger than ever before. Can I encompass all of New York? All of this world? I don't know.

But I'm going to try.

My mind races. Puzzle pieces clicking into place. If I have this right, the reason I can't feel the magic, or even cast a spell, isn't because I'm blocked from it, it's that I'm not even in my own fucking world.

I let that sink in for a minute.

This bubble I'm in is connected through the land of the dead to Deasmhumhain's original home. A place where the magic works differently. Where it's in the blood. And she's using the souls of the dead to make the bubble bigger, bring more of her reality into mine.

That's not good.

It occurs to me that I have a straight razor, no magic, and I'm in a house that's part of an alternate universe where a mage who can travel between worlds is living.

This is my cue to leave.

I open my straight razor and head to the door. I get three steps when I feel a tugging at the back of my mind. It's magic. I can tell that much. But it's nothing like any magic I've felt before.

The bottom drops out of my mind, I stumble, catch myself on the wall as everything shifts and goes wrong. I can hear a voice. Words in a language I don't understand, but there's a power to them.

I can feel a shape in front of me, forming as if from smoke. The faintest outline of a man. I haul myself to my feet, reach for it, grab something solid.

And yank.

It's representative of my low station in life that breaking into a house at night is firmly in my skill set. It doesn't even take much gas; I'm good with the Words, and all I need is a pin-prick on my thumb, a bead of red, and two syllables to make the lock on the basement entrance of 75 1/2 Bedford Street click.

"You remember her spell?"

I nod. Mags believes memory to be a superpower. I have always been able to pick out the Words of a spell, understand the grammar, and cut away the bullshit. Celine tried hiding hers with nonsense sounds, but I have a good idea of how it's constructed. I'm not feeling so strong; I'd bled for Celine earlier, and it's going to take another healthy bleed to cast her spell. I take a deep breath as I roll up my sleeve, take out my switchblade, and drag the edge along my forearm, adding a new line to the mesh of white and pink scars there.

I begin speaking the Words.

This time it feels like something invisible is opening up under me, a chasm I can't see but can definitely fall into. Vertigo threatens to take me, and I have to strain to keep speaking, to stay upright, to hang on to reality as I know it. It's a good spell: elegant, well-constructed. More powerful than it seems at first. Celine isn't much more than a Trickster herself; someone very powerful and very smart taught her this.

339

As I speak, I can feel the greedy universe pulling the gas out of me, and it gets harder and harder to speak clearly, to focus. As I bleed, I get weak.

When I finish, there's a strange sensation of *sucking*, almost similar to when Mags fucks up a spell and the magical energy collapses like a small explosion, except in reverse. It's as if something has been pierced, and all the air in the room is being sucked away. And I have the sense that I can reach through that hole, touch something, listen . . . speak.

Tentatively, I push my thoughts at it. This is all new territory for me, this invisible shit, and I'm not sure how it works.

"Hello?" I say, my voice hoarse.

Suddenly, something grabs on to me, roughly. Physically, I'm paralyzed, but the sensation is violent, like someone grabbing you by the spiritual lapels and pushing you up against a wall.

A voice, then: *You in on this? You part of this? You're fucking up my town.*

I struggle, but have no idea what to do. This spell is beyond my pay grade. I'm a con artist. I'm not an inter-dimensional *enustari*. "Who are you?" If the answer is *Aednat Deasmhumhain* it might be the last thing I ever ask.

There's a moment of hesitation. *I'm Eric Carter*, the voice says, crackling like a long-distance radio transmission. *Who the fuck are* you?

My eyes tell me I'm grasping empty air; my hands and ears tell me something different. I can feel rough cloth, the solidity of a person. Hear the voice crackling and popping like a bad mic. But I can't see anyone.

"Well? I showed you mine, now show me yours."

Lem, the voice says after a long pause. I feel him trying to pull away, and I tighten my grip. He freezes. *Lem Vonnegan. No, not my work. Not enough gas for me to pull this off. What are you? Saganustari? Enustari?*

Huh. So that's how you pronounce those words. Do I bluff? Tell the truth? If Lem is with Deasmhumhain I could be in trouble. But if he's not, then maybe I can use him to pop her ghost-eating bubble.

"I have no idea what the hell those even mean," I say, making my decision. "We don't have whatever those are over here. I'm a necromancer. And I'm going to take a big leap of faith here and say you're not working for Deasmhumhain."

I start to mold a spell in my mind. A quick fire spell in case he tries something weird. It might not do anything to him, since it seems he's not entirely here, but I bet it'll hurt. Then I remember I can't cast over here and let it fizzle before it starts.

No. Voice wary. If he's not trying the same thing on his side I'll be surprised. *I'm here to find out what the hell she's doing.*

"How much do you know?"

How much do you know?

Oh for fuck's sake. "Short version. Deasmhumhain came to this world from yours through a tunnel through the dead side and built a bubble of her universe so she could use her magic and now she's making it bigger through blood and feeding it ghosts. That about the size of it?"

Pause. *Y-yes?*

"Excellent. Now you tell me what you know."

Lem fills in the blanks. Or some of them. He didn't know about the ghosts. Didn't know how Deasmhumhain came over here. He's fascinated by the idea of a land of the dead.

Turns out Deasmhumhain's over a hundred years old. Some kind of ubermage over in Lem's world. She took a runner when a bunch of mages came after her. Part of her world came to mine, and part of mine went to hers. She's been having an apprentice bleed for her and send the power through the tunnel, plucking ghosts to convince the rubes. Only not all the ghosts are coming from the right place.

We trade tidbits on how each of our magic works. All the power in his world is locked up in blood. The more blood, the more power.

"So you have to bleed somebody if you want to cast a spell?"

Every time.

"Dude, that's fucked up."

Says the guy who talks to dead people.

"Point. I need to kick Deasmhumhain out of here."

And bring her back here? Lem says. *No thanks.*

"If she succeeds, what makes you think she won't go back to kick all y'all's asses? Anyway, I have a plan."

You have my attention.

"Now that I know there's a connection to your New York through the land of the dead, I should be able to find it. If I can find it I might be able to sever it."

You think that'll pop the bubble?

"This shit's never that easy," I say. "If I break the connection she might still have enough of her world stuck over on this side that she can keep growing it. Is there some way you can, I dunno, shove the extrusion back over onto my side? Displace the bubble here?"

Like pushing your guts back in through a hernia.

"Vivid, but yes."

Silence for a long time. I start to wonder if the connection is failing, but then he says, *Yeah. I think I can come up with Words for that.*

He says it with the capital, and it's nowhere near the strangest thing I've heard today, so I just nod. "Cool. You go do your thing, I'll do mine. If it works my New York doesn't turn into a parallel universe, you stop getting infested by ghosts, Deasmhumhain gets stuck in between."

What if it doesn't work?

"She probably shows up and kills both of us."

This is a shitty plan.

"Never said it wasn't."

All right, let's do this. Can't say it's been nice talking to you, Eric, but it was . . . educational.

"Likewise, Lem." I let go of him and the feeling of his presence, a background hum in the back of my head, disappears. I wonder if there's a version of Lem on this side. Or a version of me on the other.

I don't go down that rabbit hole. It's time to get to work. But I can't do anything until I get out of this house. The door opens up to a narrow room with a steep staircase on one side and ends in a foyer with the front door and two close-set windows. Out that door and across the street and I'm home free.

But, as I am constantly reminded, the universe is an asshole.

The front door opens and a tall woman with pale skin and red hair cut short and slicked back freezes at the threshold, surprise on her face. She's wearing a deep green three-piece suit. The crimson tie around her throat knotted in a Windsor.

"Nice tie," I say, lifting my tie for her to see. "I can never do better than a four-in-hand. Sloppy, I know, but I just can't seem to get the hang of it."

"What— Who the hell are you?"

"You're Deasmhumhain, right? From that other New York? I've heard about you. They didn't tell me you were such a snappy dresser. I really like the suit."

The surprise grows on her face. I'll take confusion over her blasting a hole in me. I need to get out of here and the first order of business is not dying.

She pulls a switchblade from her pocket and flicks it open, cutting into her hand with a smooth, practiced motion. From what Lem told me her magic is blood and words. She's got the blood, but she hasn't opened her mouth, yet.

So I tackle her. She's surprisingly solid and I almost bounce off of her. Probably has defensive spells etched into her skin like I do. But inside the house hers actually work.

She goes down more from losing her balance than anything I've done to her, but hits the cement outside hard enough to knock the breath out of her.

I resist the urge to bounce her head on the doorstep. I doubt it'd hurt her and there's no point giving her more blood to work with.

I leap off her and bolt for the street. Behind me I can hear her muttering something unintelligible. A quick glance shows me a gout of flame leaving her fingers toward me. Once I hit the threshold of the bubble the magic should fizzle.

It doesn't mean the fire will, though. If I throw something with magic it's still got momentum. Light the air with magic, it's going to stay hot.

I feel the magic slam back into me. It's a feeling like my ears clearing after a weeklong cold, only all over. I spin and throw out a spell at the fire, forcing it to split down the middle as it comes near, dissipate into the air behind me.

Deasmhumhain is furious. She stands, starts to come toward me. It would be nice if she made this easy, crossed the threshold where I can do my thing, but she catches herself before she takes two steps.

We're at an impasse. On this side of the bubble I can counter anything she throws at me, and likely vice versa.

Not that that stops her from trying. She says some words and flicks some blood in my direction. A flash of light hits the bubble, making it temporarily visible from the living side, and sputters out. Whatever she just threw at me was probably pretty nasty.

"That has really got to suck," I say.

"I am going to fucking murder you," she says, a slight Irish lilt to her voice.

"I dunno about that. A little bird told me somebody's trying to dismantle your little pocket kingdom here from the other side. It'd suck if all this work you did went away. You might want to check on that."

It's a dick move, I know. I'm essentially siccing her on Lem. But it might get her out of my hair for a bit so I can find the connection to Lem's world and try to cut it off.

It works. She glares at me, her mouth twisting to say words she knows won't work against me. I press my thumb to my nose and waggle my fingers at her.

She slams the door closed. Time for me to get to work.

For a second I ponder the existence of Eric Carter. He sounds like someone I might like. Or at least someone who might not want to fuck me over at first chance, which is almost the same thing. I wonder if there's a . . . version of him on this side of things.

I look over at Mags. No time for social networking cross-dimensional doppelgangers. "I need your help, buddy."

He perks up, like a dog who has learned the word *treat*, and I feel like an asshole. It's easy to talk him into things, and I try not to take advantage of that.

"What happened?" he asks.

I shake my head. "I'll explain later," I say. It's too much. I can barely comprehend what I've just experienced as it is. Trying to verbalize it would be impossible. "Right now we got work to do." I take a deep breath. "And I need you to cast."

Mags shakes his head. "I'm no good, Lem," he says. "I'll mess it up. *You* do it. I'll bleed."

I don't even have the energy to be angry. I just shake my head again. "We don't bleed anyone but ourselves, Mags," I say, struggling for consciousness and clarity. This has taken more out of me than anything I'd ever done. It feels like spells that carry over into the other universe take twice as much gas, maybe more. "You bleed, I'll give you the Words. Come on, we don't have much time."

Mags, his face a mask of worry, begins pulling off his jacket, his arms getting caught in a complex web of sleeves. He tries to stay cool, and keeps working it without looking away from me. "What if I screw it up, Lem? No one says the Words like you."

I nod. It is my one and only skill and talent, and so far it has brought me poverty, humiliation, and Pitr Mags. "I'll be right here. I'll walk you through it. We have to do this, Magsie. We don't, something bad is gonna happen."

He rolls his shirtsleeve up and fumbles for his knife. He holds it poised over his arm, shaking slightly.

"All right, Lem," he says with calm, horrifying trust. "Tell me what to say."

A couple across the street are staring at me. "The fuck are you looking at?" Like they've never seen weird shit in New York. They put their heads down and hurry past.

I try not to do magic in front of the straights, but sometimes you can't help it. More than likely their minds will fill in the blanks with some rationalization. Say somebody had a flamethrower on Bedford.

I don't know how much time I've got. If Deasmhumhain can actually do anything to Lem, probably not a lot.

More Wanderers come by, entranced by the trap Deasmhumhain has set for them. Now that I know what it looks like I can see their essence coming off of them like smoke as soon as they get near. The rate that they're coming in, and dissolving, seems to be accelerating.

I sit down on the sidewalk and concentrate on moving to the other side. Focus on the darkness and the cold, emptiness, void. I tie the spell together and my mind wrenches as I shift over to the other side.

The sounds of the street disappear to be replaced by an uncharacteristic wailing, a banshee shriek that fills my head. It's almost too much to bear, but I grit my teeth and push past it.

It's the Wanderers. The ones that are still self-aware enough to realize what's happening to them. Screaming as they try to hold on to the last shreds of their souls. The bubble has cranked up its feeding frenzy and ghosts are draining away into it like they're being flushed down a toilet.

Once she saw me, Deasmhumhain must have sped up the process. I don't know enough about this magic to tell if that's going to do anything to my chances of disconnecting the bridge between worlds, but I'm going to have to assume it is. The clock is ticking. I just don't know what time it is.

I didn't see anything besides the bubble on the back of the house, so it should be connected somewhere here in the front. But I don't see anything. I run from one side of the house to the other. Nothing.

It's not in the front; it's not in the back. Does it go through the houses on either side? If so, shouldn't I see something poking out as the block ends? I don't even know what it looks like, but I'm pretty sure it's not here.

Then I kick myself for thinking like the living.

I look for a manhole cover in the street. Hope I find one that hasn't been in the ground too long. They don't get moved often, or replaced. But just because something's solid over here doesn't mean it's heavy. They're just hard to get a grip on. It's all willpower.

I find one a house down and pry it out of its hole. Sewers are some of the most solid structures over here. Most of them have been around for centuries. People don't think about the actual tunnels much, so get too far out and they sort of disappear, but around manholes and homes folks pay enough attention that I can walk around them.

I jump down into the sewer tunnel. I can see the bubble of Deasmhumhain's magic extending down below the street and into the ground. Nothing as prosaic as dirt is going to stop it.

And not far over there's the connection, a pulsing silver cord as thick as my forearm connected near the bottom and extending down to fade away into nothing.

I wonder if I have time to go get a chainsaw.

The bubble shudders, flickering with a strange static, then stabilizes. All right, that's a no on the chainsaw.

I pull my straight razor and open it. I wonder how good it is for sawing through magic pipes.

I stagger a little, and Mags feints toward me, his brow wrinkling in concern, but I wave him back. He doesn't stop speaking, which is amazing. I've seen Mags break off a spell because a butterfly danced across his field of vision, the spell collapsing around us like an invisible explosion. He settles back, blood seeping from the deep wound across his forearm, sizzling and burning off, taken by the greedy universe.

I shouldn't be as exhausted as I am. I feel like I've been bleeding for ten minutes, like I'm trying to cast some complex *biludha*, some ancient world-changing ritual. I'm ready to fall over after a spell that should be a walk in the park. Whatever Deasmhumhain had done here, folding two realities together, poking through into Carter's and dragging mine after her, it made casting much more difficult. Like walking through deep mud, the ground sucking at every Word.

I give the Words to Mags. His pronunciation leaves a lot to be desired, but so far the Universe seems to be buying it. I can feel him taking hold of the . . . tunnel, the extrusion, whatever it is, and pinch it shut. It isn't enough to close it. We'd have to bleed someone—several someones—dry to manage that. We're just trying to distract her, give Carter, whoever he is, a fighting chance on his side of things. Because the brief taste I was getting of *his* universe told me I never, ever wanted to go there.

I give Mags the Words, and Mags speaks them, and we pinch at the portal. I sway on my feet, slurring. Mags, big as a fucking mountain, doesn't seem to feel a thing.

And then, again, someone is on me, from the other side. Pulling at me, violently, and trying to drag me across, into Carter's world. Where I would be powerless, exhausted, and, in quick order I have no doubt, fucking dead.

It's painful. I feel like I'm being pushed into a three-inch pipe, skin flaying off and soul squeezed out of me like I was a tube of toothpaste. If I break off feeding Mags the Words, the spell will collapse and blow us into the air. And I'm not sure I have the gas to do anything substantial anyway.

But I'm good with the Words. And I'm a Trickster, a con artist, a grifter. On the fly, I alter the Words I'm giving Mags, grinding them out through gritted teeth and clenched throat. My slim experience with *enustari* like Deasmhumhain is that they are ready for nuclear bomb–level spells, but they never see a dirty trick coming.

I'm sawing through a tube of magical energy I barely understand with a straight razor. It's like cutting through bad steak with a butterknife.

Unlike the psychic impressions of the buildings the cord has an actual physical presence. And yet it doesn't. It's slightly spongy, and bends away from the blade as I cut, while at the same time dissolving like smoke, the blade biting into nothing. I can't tell if I'm making any progress.

A swell of energy shoots up the connection and the bubble shudders again, flickering into nothing and then back strong as ever. A thin thread of light snaps under my blade, fraying from the rest of the cord. The shuddering happens again. Another thread pops off.

Great. That only took all of five minutes. Now in about four hours or so I should be through the whole thing.

The wailing above me of the Wanderers being torn apart to feed Deasmhumhain magic rises to a crescendo, a high-pitched keening that threatens to split my head open. Then it stops.

I can still feel the Wanderers up there. They're not gone. But they're not being tortured anymore. If they're not destroyed and they're not feeding Deasmhumhain's magic, that means one thing.

I'm standing below a sea of pissed-off ghosts who have just been set free.

I saw faster.

I feed Mags the Words, and he speaks them.

It's easy to twist the spell, keep it inflating, keep it fed and orderly. All it requires is a shift in grammar, including Deasmhumhain as the object as well, so we're pinching *her* as well as the extrusion. It's strange, though. I can sense the spell. It enters the extrusion, the portal between universes, strong. And then . . . fades. When it hits her, it's weakened and slippery, like trying to grab hold of smoke. But it's working.

This is a gray area, morally. I always tell Mags: We don't bleed other people. And we *aren't*. He isn't bleeding for me. I'm not casting on his gas. We are, I realize, a single organism. Mags came to me as a burden, as this monosyllabic, monobrowed pet who costs more than a small country to feed. But Mags is mine.

Every Word tightens our grip, squeezing, and I can feel it, the flow of gas from Mags into the hole. It's like building a complex machine with Words, each syllable putting another component into place. I'm making the spell up as I go, and the effort to keep all the threads in place, all the balls in the air, has me sweating freely, my head buzzing with exhaustion.

And then she takes hold of me.

I know it's a *she*, somehow. Deasmhumhain. How she knows to ignore Mags and come after me I can't figure, except to remember what everyone told me about her: *enustari*, so powerful all the Archmages had gathered in New York a century ago to put her down. What I feel is a savage, cold hatred—as fresh and active as if someone had recently revved her up and pissed her off—and a force that's reaching *into* me. It feels like nothing I've ever experienced. It's more than a physical sensation, it's a psychic one, like a hand chopping down into my thoughts.

I stumble on the Words, dropping to the floor. Mags freezes, staring at me, and for a second I can feel the spell hovering in a quantum state, waiting a moment to see if this is Mags taking a breath or a spell broken off. And with all the gas Mags has put into it, a collapse will blow us through the wall.

Tensing, I push another Word out, and Mags speaks it. Deasmhumhain tightens her grip, agony crushing me. It's like I'm being torn apart—*me*, my existence, shredded, my thoughts and memories splintering and atrophying.

I push out another Word, and Mags speaks it, and the universe remains patient. But I don't know how long I'm going to be able to keep it up. Or how long I'll continue to exist. My new invisible friend and I have picked a fight I am suddenly uncertain I can finish.

C'mon, Mr. Carter, I think, pushing out another Word. *Hurry the fuck up.*

Another strand snaps. This thing is less a cord or a pipe and more like braided cable. I keep sawing and the strands keep popping, flares of light snapping around it with each break. But it's not going nearly fast enough.

I can feel the Wanderers nearby getting closer. They've got my scent, or whatever it is they track by over here, and I don't have a lot of time.

I dig into my jacket pocket with my free hand, not daring to stop sawing. I pull out a leather cord with six Chinese coins knotted into it. The coins are old, the metal brittle. I snap one between my fingers and drop it at my feet. There's a muted pop and one of the coins begins to burn to ash. When that's done, the next coin will go, and the next. The magic in them should hide me from the ghosts for a few minutes. Maybe.

Another strand of the cable goes, then another. The bubble shudders, contracts in on itself, grows larger. I edge away from it like I'm dodging a wave at the beach.

I was able to use my magic on the dead side when I was inside the bubble to flip to the living side when I went into the house, but I don't know what it will do to the coins if it grows large enough to touch them. Right now, they're the only things keeping me hidden from the ghosts.

Another contraction, unsteady this time. It wobbles, turns an angry shade of red. Whether that's my doing or Lem's I can't tell. It shrinks down to the size of a basketball. For a second I think it's all over.

And then it explodes. The bubble expands to envelop me, the coins, the entire sewer tunnel. The coins all pop at once, burning to useless ash in the skip of a heartbeat.

And just as quickly the bubble contracts again to its original size, but now I don't have anything blocking the ghosts from finding me.

They pour down the manhole into the tunnel, a waterfall of grasping hands, screaming faces. They seethe and roil around each other, filling the tunnel, crawling along the walls, the ceiling. One single, writhing mass pouring toward me.

I have a sudden panicked idea. I stop cutting the cord,

grab it in my hand. I focus my will, my panic and fear, primal energies I can tap into, amplify. Focus on the world of the living, breathable air, sun and stars, not this empty wasteland of the dead. I squeeze the glowing cord and throw myself to the living side, taking the cord with me.

The sewer tunnel solidifies around me, color and sound crashing in. The stink of shit, rotting garbage, and dead rats. New York.

The ghosts are nothing but shadows now, rushing headlong at me and passing harmlessly through. They wheel around grasping for a meal they'll never get.

The glowing cord is still in my hand, bucking and twisting between my fingers. It extends a few inches above and below my hand and then fades into nothing. At the edges I can see a crackle of energy and one of the ghosts tries wedging its fingers through this gap between worlds.

Then the strands making it up snap like a ball of rubber bands and the entire thing collapses. Light bounces off the sewer walls, the brackish water. The gap I pulled it through seals up, closing hard on the ghost trying to get through. A wisp of ectoplasm dissipates like smoke in the air as part of his soul severs.

The ghosts are furious or moping. Running through me, surrounding me and glaring. That last spell did me in, drained my own reserves. I tap into the local pool and pull in more power.

"Beat it, you little bastards. You're not getting me today." I lash out at the ghosts with a spell, flinging them away like trash in a hurricane. In a moment I'm alone in the sewer tunnel.

Vertigo washes over me. I stumble through the tunnel until I get to the ladder leading to the street. Of course on this side the manhole cover's still firmly in place. And it's heavy as fuck. I heave myself out onto the street. Late-night traffic is light and I don't have to dodge any cars.

The house is destroyed. Broken lumber, shattered glass. The entire structure has imploded, collapsing in on itself and bringing some of the adjoining brownstones with it.

I don't feel my magic disappearing when I get to the doorstep. I pick my way through the debris searching for that sudden cutoff in the magic that will tell me the bubble is still there.

I don't find it. I don't find Deasmhumhain, either. She's in her own world, trapped in limbo, or she took a runner. She's dead, gone, or huddled powerless in an alley somewhere. Whatever it is I don't have to worry about her anymore.

I slump against the torn-up wall of one of the brown-stones, sewer water in my shoes, my pants soaked through with the effluvia of New York. Tasty.

Thank fuck that's over.

I give Mags the last Word, and Mags speaks it. I open my eyes. I'm on the floor. On the *ground*, actually; the townhouse is . . . gone. Like it had never been there.

"Lem?"

I peer up at Mags. There's still a fishhook in my head, a persistent tugging, weak and fading, but there. I can still feel her, Deasmhumhain, fading into the background, but clinging to me like a drowning woman, grabbing on to a piece of flotsam. She's caught between universes, her portal to both closed. Carter drop-kicked her out of his, and I pinched the extrusion into mine closed, and she has only the thread of connection to me left. And she's trying to pull herself through. Through *me*. She would split me open and step through my intestines.

I feel her give another tug, inching closer to me. It *hurts*. Her grip on me is weak, but she isn't giving up. I've never felt such willpower. Such sheer will to survive.

"Mags," I croak. "One more Word, okay? You got it in you?"

I can't see him. My vision is white and blank. His voice is hoarse and heavy with exhaustion. Casting into another universe takes a lot out of a guy. "Sure, Lem."

I give Mags one final Word: *taku*. To push, to abandon. He speaks it, and with a silent scream, I feel her torn from me, the hook ripped away. For one final second I feel her, and then she's . . . gone.

My vision clears. I look around. We're in an alley between buildings, broken bottles and trash, dog turds and one stray cat peering at us from a small fortress of old cardboard boxes. Mags is sprawled on the ground next to me, and we look at each other. He smiles shyly.

"I did good, huh?"

I nod. I realize I've just adopted Mags for life, but I'm okay with that. "You did, buddy."

"What now, Lem?"

I take a deep, shuddering breath. I wonder what happened to Celine, Deasmhumhain's *urtuku*, or disciple. Whether, after saving the world and almost certainly not getting any credit or reward for it, we have any responsibility toward a two-bit Trickster who is likely nothing without her Mistress.

Fuck it. "Now we go find Gabby," I say. "And punch him in the nose."

Weaponized Hell

LARRY CORREIA AND JONATHAN MABERRY

1

CAPTAIN JOE LEDGER
DEPARTMENT OF MILITARY SCIENCES
Iraqi Desert near Mosul

They say that in times of mortal peril your life flashes through your mind. Ideally, those memories are not accompanied by shrapnel or bullets.

For me it isn't usually my childhood or images of my family or my ex-girlfriends. I don't have flashes of chances taken and chances missed. None of that stuff. When my life is about to fall apart, what flashes through my head are the details of how in the wide blue fuck I got into this mess in the first place.

Case in point . . .

First, you have to know that the ideal combat mission starts with solid and very detailed intel, with time for training your team, for putting boots on the ground with all of the equipment you need, and to have local assets on hand to smooth the way. An ideal mission has close-range and long-range tactical support, and the cavalry is cocked and locked and ready to ride over the hill to save your ass if things go south.

Yeah, that would be nice.

So nice.

Never fucking going to happen, though. At least not for guys like me.

I run the Special Projects Office for the Department of Military Sciences. Sounds like a bunch of nerds sitting around dreaming up cool gizmos. It's not. The name is boring and there's some misdirection built into it. And, sure, we have geeks and nerds working for us, but they're support. The truth is that the DMS is a covert rapid-response group. We run a couple of dozen small teams of first-chair shooters. We go after terrorists or criminal groups who are using bleeding-edge bioweapons. We are a zero red-tape outfit. If they've sent us in then the shit has already hit the fan.

The tricky thing is that this means we have to start running the moment we hear the first rumble of that avalanche. Prep time is what you can manage on the fly. Field support is usually a voice in the earbud I wear; real-time intel that the science and tactical teams are scrambling to acquire while we're running headlong into the valley of the shadow.

I'm sure I mixed a couple of metaphors there, but I actually don't give a cold shit.

I was in Iraq, in a twenty-year-old Humvee going bump-thumpity over a road that was pocked with wagon ruts and blast holes from IEDs. My driver, Rizgar, was a friendly, a Kurd with knife scars on his face. Four of his buddies were in the back. My own crew, Echo Team, was in a fast plane somewhere over the ocean. Too far away. Rizgar drove like his lifelong dream was to die in a fiery crash. My balls had climbed up inside my chest cavity and I'd found religion five separate times during near misses with boulders, craters, and the burned-out shell of an old Bradley. Rizgar had to swerve to keep from hitting a goat and—still at high speed—leaned his head all the way out the window and yelled at the animal, who was now fading in the dust behind us.

"Kerim bimzha, heez!"

I understand enough Sorani to know that it was a vile thing to say, even to a goat.

I was yelling, too, trying to have a conversation with my boss, Mr. Church. He'd snatched me away from the mission he'd sent me over here to handle—taking down a black-marketer named Ohan who was selling recovered Soviet chemical weapons left over from the Afghan war in the eighties. Church said he'd catch up to me in motion. I was, in fact, in motion.

"What's the damn op?" I demanded. "My guy in Baghdad said he could put me in a room with Ohan and—"

"We've been following a false lead," said Mr. Church. "Ohan is not in Baghdad. We have reliable intel that he is in a village outside of Mosul."

"It was reliable intel that said he was in Baghdad."

"Nature of the game, captain," said Church. "We have very high confidence in this sighting."

"What's the source of that intel? Our friends in the Agency? Another of those hotshot Delta gunslingers? Everybody's seeing Ohan lately."

"The identity of our source is classified."

Even though Rizgar could hear my end of the conversation, the feed into my earbud was filtered through a 128-bit cyclical encryption system that God couldn't hack.

"Declassify it," I growled.

Church—being Church—ignored that request. He said,

"Operatives on the ground have confirmed the presence of Ohan heading into the village. We believe he is going to meet an ISIL team to hand off a bio agent recovered from an excavated burial site."

"Whoa, wait . . . repeat that? Someone's using a burial site as a lab—?"

"No," said Church. "Sketchy reports indicate that a biological weapon has been harvested from the burial site."

"What kind of bioweapon? Are we talking mycotoxins or bacteria?"

Graves and tombs were famous for all kinds of dangerous spores, molds, fungi, and similar microscopic monsters. The whole curse of King Tut's tomb was a prime example. Lord Carnarvon, the Englishman who backed Howard Carter's expedition to find Tutankhamen, died of a mysterious illness after entering the tomb and being exposed to a fungus that had been dormant in the tombs for thousands of years and reactivated by fresh air. Other recently opened tombs in different parts of the world revealed pathogenic bacteria of the *Staphylococcus* and *Pseudomonas* genera, and the molds *Aspergillus niger* and *Aspergillus flavus*. Very nasty stuff. Obtaining and weaponizing diseases so old that modern humans have no acquired immunity for them is a popular hobby for the world's mad-fucking-scientists. Of which there are way too many.

"The nature of the threat is unknown at this time," said Church. "I need you to make an assessment and to keep it out of the hands of the ISIL team operating in that area."

I was still dressed for plainclothes infiltration of the Baghdad hotel where I was supposed to intercept Ohan. My cover was that of a South African mercenary acting as a go-between for a party wanting to buy some of Ohan's nasty toys. I had my Sig Sauer and a Wilson rapid-release folding knife, but I was not in full combat rig. I was dressed in khaki trousers and one of those canvas shirt-jackets with lots of pockets. No helmet, no long-gun, no grenades. None of my favorite toys. And not nearly enough body armor. And, more to the point, no hazmat suit or even a Saratoga Hammer Suit. Nothing to protect me if this was an active biological agent, particularly an airborne one.

"Sure," I said, "I'm on it."

I hate my job.

Rizgar pointed to a small cluster of buildings visible through the heat shimmer a couple of miles up the road. Even from that distance we could see that things had already gone to shit. A fireball suddenly leapt up from amid a group of parked vehicles, lifting them, tossing them away with fists made of superheated gasses. Over the roar of the Humvee's engine we could hear the rattle of gunfire.

2

SPECIAL AGENT FRANKS
UNITED STATES MONSTER CONTROL BUREAU

Iraqi Desert near Mosul

Special Agent Franks of the United States Monster Control Bureau was not known for his patience—especially when he had a mission to complete—but having random terrorist assholes flip his armored vehicle with an IED really put him in an even fouler mood than usual. His driver and interpreter, assigned to him from the Iraqi Army, had been killed on impact. From the noise of gunfire and bullets striking metal, the rest of the convoy was taking fire. Annoyed, Franks had crawled out of the upside-down flaming MRAP, in order to vent his frustrations on whoever had been stupid enough to ambush him.

Quickly assessing the situation, Franks realized it had been a really big bomb. It took quite a few buried artillery shells to toss an eighteen-ton vehicle on its roof. The explosion had flattened several of the houses at the front of the village. There was a blackened crater where the road had been. The enemy appeared to be a bunch of goons wearing ridiculous black pajamas, armed with AKs and looted M4s. It was an L-shaped ambush. They were firing from prepared positions in the village and from a ravine that ran parallel to the road. Their Iraqi drivers, rather than push through the ambush zone, had hit the brakes. Now they were taking heavy fire. It was another example of why Franks preferred never to work with locals, but he'd been overruled. His superiors didn't like his idea of diplomacy.

Four hostiles, one armed with an RPG, had moved up on Franks' vehicle to get a better angle on the rest of the stopped convoy. The hostiles hadn't been expecting survivors, let alone a giant killing machine who was completely unfazed by the blast. Franks killed the first hostiles before they'd even realized he was there, another two before they could react, and the last one as he was trying to run away.

And Franks hadn't used a weapon yet.

The rest of his convoy was made up of MCB personnel and their Iraqi Army escorts. It appeared that most of their vehicles were hit, though none as badly as his had been. Intel had said this area was under ISIS control, but they'd not been expecting resistance away from the dig site. As usual, their intel was wrong. He had to act fast or his strike team would be rendered combat ineffective, and they still had a mission to complete. His men would clear the ravine. His rifle had been crushed in the wreck, so Franks took the rocket-propelled grenade launcher and an AK-47 from the men he'd beaten to death and went into the village.

They'd set up a PK machine gun on the second floor of a mosque and were raking it over the convoy. There had been something in the briefing over the rules of engagement about not damaging religious buildings and blah, blah, blah, but Franks never bothered to read those things. So he blew up the mosque with the RPG. Then he went house-to-house, shooting every hostile he saw. Since Franks had reaction times that made most normal humans look like sloths, clearing out their firing positions was a piece of cake. He only had to gun down a dozen of them or so before the ambush broke and the remaining scumbags were running for their lives.

His radio had been broken in the crash, but from the noise, it sounded like his men had the road and ravine under control. Franks had seen a lot of casual barbarity in his life, but he knew ISIS were overachievers. Chasing them down was not his mission, but Franks really didn't like them. Sure. He liked hardly anyone, but these assholes were special. So he picked up another weapon and went looking for trouble.

He found it.

The ISIS fighters regrouped in a small market. Their leader was rallying the troops, shouting in Arabic—one of the many

Earthly languages Franks had never bothered to learn—so the motivational speech wouldn't have been noteworthy except this human had the stink of demons all over him.

So their intel had gotten one thing right. The insurgents had made a pact with demons. *Now this is more like it*, Franks thought as he flipped the Kalashnikov's selector to full auto and hosed down the market.

3

CAPTAIN JOE LEDGER

I made a pushing motion with my hand. Rizgar grinned and obliged by pushing the pedal all the way down to the floor. He steered with one hand and beat on the roof of the car with the other. The signal for his team to get ready.

We were driving straight into the heart of a full-blown battle, and it was going south on the good guys really damn fast. I could see a knot of men in American BDUs hunkered down behind a shattered convoy of bullet-pocked vehicles. They were taking heavy fire, but they were still in the game. Bloody bodies littered the ground around the vehicles, most with weapons still clutched in dead hands.

All around the convoy, crouched down behind cars, using broken stone walls for cover, stretched out on rooftops, and even kneeling in the street were fighters in the distinctive black of the Islamic State of Iraq and the Levant. ISIS, ISIL, call them what you want. Sons of bitches who seemed to come out of nowhere and were cutting a bloody swath across the Middle East. Well-armed, well-provisioned, and dishearteningly well-trained. Maybe thirty of them alive and twice that number dead or wounded. This battle had clearly been raging for a while. The contractors in the convoy had fought like heroes, but there simply weren't enough of them left to win this.

Rizgar, his four shooters, and Mama Ledger's firstborn didn't seem like a big enough crowd to make a difference. But let me tell you, shock and awe comes in all shapes and sizes.

Rizgar had picked the right angle for our approach. The contractors could see us but we wouldn't be in their direct line of fire. The ISIL fighters had to turn to fight us on their quarter, which decreased the suppressing fire on the convoy. Distract and weaken. Rizgar slewed around to allow the maximum number of our guns to fire at once and we hit them real damn hard. Two of Rizgar's men came out of the Humvee with RPGs on their shoulders. One targeted a building on the corner of the square, a spot where half a dozen of the black-clothed figures were grouped. They saw the grenade coming at them, they tried to move, but feet don't move fast enough to dodge rocket-propelled explosives fired from fifty yards. The explosion killed four of them, tearing them to rags; and it turned the building into deadly debris. Every man inside the blast radius went down. Some dead, some dazed.

The second RPG struck an old Ford Falcon behind which three shooters knelt. The blast lifted the car and dropped it on them. And that left a clear line of approach for me. I ran up the middle like an offensive fullback, my Sig Sauer held in a two-handed grip. I am a very good shot because

SpecOps soldiers who are bad shots get killed. I hit everything I aimed at. Might not have been the highest scores on a gun range, but men went down.

Rizgar and the others fanned out, firing automatic weapons at the ISIL team. As soon as the contractors saw what was happening they shifted their focus from defensive fire to a fresh assault. Clearing the way for us. One of them came out of an open door firing a Kalashnikov. He was a brute, a bull. Six-eight if he was an inch, and he looked like Frankenstein. But the son of a bitch could shoot. ISIL fighters spun away, blood exploding from faces and throats and chests.

They say war is hell. Sure. It absolutely is. Even if you like combat. Even when the sound of gunfire is your lullaby—which, for the record, it isn't to me. But there is a part of me—my shrink and I call him the Killer—who shares my head and my soul with my other aspects, the Modern Man and the Cop; and the Killer loves it. In times like this he is fully alive. And maybe so am I.

I hate that it's true, but it is true.

When I burned through all three of the magazines I had for the Sig, I drew my rapid-release knife and took the fight to close quarters. Using the men I killed as shields while I cut them apart, shoving them into their comrades, taking the long reach to do short, ugly cuts, going for effect rather than finesse. Slashing and slicing because stabbing will get your knife stuck and get you killed. There is a balletic quality to knife fighting when you do it right. You cruise on that edge between total awareness and a kind of Zen zero mind.

The ISIL team fell apart. Rizgar's men were brilliant,

savage, and merciless. The Kurds have old scores to settle with the kind of men who join ISIL. And the contractors, buoyed by our arrival, took the fight to the bad guys in terrible ways.

We won the fight.

Until . . .

Until the whole day changed.

I cut the throat of one of the last ISIL fighters and saw that there was a teenage girl crouched down between two of their vehicles. Not armed, not dangerous-looking. I moved in close, hoping to grab her and pull her to safety. She cringed back from me, arms wrapped around her head, and at first I thought she was a captive, maybe someone from the village being used as a hostage, or one of the unfortunate ones who would be dragged off and used savagely until her mind or body snapped.

Then I saw her eyes.

They were dark and filled with madness. Total, absolute madness.

And then they weren't.

The brown irises changed as I watched. The brown swirled like paint being stirred. Dark brown, then a medium brown flecked with gold, then sparks of red, and then they turned completely yellow. Cat yellow. Fire yellow. Her face, which had been contorted in terror at the madness and destruction around her, twisted, reshaped, became something else. Not another expression . . . it became another face.

Another *kind* of face.

Still a woman's face . . . but not a human woman's face.

URBAN ALLIES

It's impossible to describe, even now, even thinking back on it. There are things the human mind cannot process. Or refuses to accept.

The girl rose to her feet and in doing so stopped being a girl at all. Her spine curved into a monstrous hump, almost like a camel's hump; her leg bones broke with gunshot sounds and then reformed, taking on the knobbed angles of a goat's legs. And her arms grew long, the fingers splaying and stretching, the nails extending as they tore through the nail beds in splashes of bright blood, then thickened into black talons.

But her face.

Good god, her face . . .

The nostrils flattened and flared, her eyes sunk into shadowy pits so that the hellish light burned like real fire. Her cheekbones cracked and shifted, forming sharp ledges, and her jaw stretched as she smiled at me. Smiled. So incorrect and stupid a word for what was happening. The mouth grinned wide as row upon row of new teeth ripped their way from her gums until she had the dripping maw of a shark.

All of this in a few seconds.

All of this as the last pocks of gunfire tore the air.

I stumbled backward from her—from it.

One of the ISIL fighters lay dead at her feet, his throat sliced open by the knife held limply in my hand. The woman seized his wrist and with a jerk like someone cracking a whip, snapped the arm loose and then tore it from its socket. Blood and bits of tendon splashed on me, and in a moment of truly bottomless horror I watched the woman raise the severed arm to her mouth and bite. Bones crushed between

370

those rows of teeth. Meat burst and blood ran down her chin as she fixed her eyes on me.

"Jesus Christ," I breathed, and for a moment I was frozen in absolute horror.

4

SPECIAL AGENT FRANKS

Franks didn't know who the new arrivals were, but one particular man could certainly fight. He'd been doing pretty good slicing up black pajama–clad assholes until he ran into a possessed woman. When she shed her face, he froze. It wasn't a surprise. Most humans choked when they saw real demonic possession for the first time. Franks would have stepped in to save the man, but he had to duck to avoid getting shot in the head by a terrorist. A 7.62x39 rifle bullet at close range had a decent chance of penetrating his armored skull and might have rendered him temporarily combat ineffective, and thus unable to complete his mission. In other words, getting his brains blown out would have been inconvenient.

Drawing his Glock 20, Franks put a controlled pair into the shooter's chest, then turned back to face his demonic target. Franks figured the newcomer would have been torn limb-from-limb already, but surprisingly, the man had snapped out of it and gotten right back in the fight. He was staying ahead of the claws, and even managed to counter-attack and slash the creature.

Not bad, Franks thought as he went over, grabbed the demon by her hair, swung her around in a blur, and hurled her through a mud brick wall. Bones splintered and the wall collapsed in a spreading cloud of stinking dust.

"What the fuck was that?" the man shouted.

"Demon."

From the accent, he was an American. From his skillset, he might be useful. He looked up, and up, at Franks. "Who the fuck are you?"

"Special Agent Franks. MCB."

The man scowled like he'd never heard of the MCB before, but they were both Americans getting shot at in northern Iraq, so it was obvious they were on the same team. "Captain Joe Ledger. DMS."

Department of Military Sciences personnel were probably cleared high enough to get read in on this one. He'd do.

"That's nice," Franks stated as he walked toward the pile of rubble. The bricks were shifting as the demon struggled free. This was a tougher strain than expected—

THWACK!

The rifle bullet smacked into Franks' leg. It punched a neat .30-caliber entrance hole, deformed as it struck his hardened femur, and burst back out the side. Blood sprayed everywhere. Franks immediately picked out the shooter, who had appeared on a nearby rooftop, aimed, and shot him before he could get off another round.

"You're hit. Get to cover!"

But Franks just looked down at the fist-sized exit wound in his thigh and frowned. That was what he deserved for stopping to have such a lengthy conversation with Ledger. He lifted the dangling flap of skin and meat and shoved it back into the hole. "Just a scratch."

Ledger seemed a little put off by that.

That wound was going to drastically slow him down, and he'd probably need a replacement leg when he got home, but worst of all, getting shot had cost him several precious seconds he could have used killing things. The demon shook itself free from the rubble. It took one look at Franks and Ledger standing there, realized it was outmatched, and fled.

Without any hesitation and armed only with a knife, Ledger went after the monster.

This one has style, Franks thought as he limped after them.

5

CAPTAIN JOE LEDGER

So, okay, this is me running through the Iraqi desert with a guy I am pretty goddamn sure isn't human, chasing something I'm absolutely positive is a demon. Yeah. Actual demon. Psychologically speaking, I am seriously fucked. I mean . . . demons!

Shit.

The thing fled from us, running like the wind out of the village and onto the sands. Franks ran well for a guy built like a bridge support. Well, but not fast. I ran faster, outpacing him. I'm over six feet and I go about two-twenty, but I'm built like a ballplayer. If I had even a smidge of talent I could have played third base. I can run my ass off, and I pulled ahead.

Here's the thing. Running faster meant that I was going to reach the apparently unkillable desert demon sooner than the definitely unkillable guy who actually stood a chance against this thing. As plans go, that sucks ass. But the Killer was in gear and he didn't give much of a fuck what the odds were. He'd tasted blood and he wanted more.

So I ran.

The woman—thing, whatever—cut right behind a ruined wall and fled into the open desert, heading for a clump of palms clustered around a goat pen. The goats screamed and panicked, crashing into the rickety slats of the corral, leaping over the bars as they fell, jumping on each other to escape what was coming. The demon leapt the fence with ease and crashed among them, slashing right and left to clear her path. I saw heads and legs and red chunks fly into the air. It was as if the goats had run into a threshing machine. Their screams sounded like the terrified shrieks of children.

I was five paces behind her. Even though she tore through the goats it still slowed her. When she raced to leap over the rear wall of the corral, I was there. My Wilson has a 3.75-inch blade, which is great for fighting people—the weapon was so lightweight that it allowed my hand to move at full speed. But when cutting at a fleeing target it was inadequate. The tip of the blade drew a seven-inch line across her upper back, but the cut didn't go deep enough to destroy the muscles. Droplets of red-black blood spattered me and all my cut accomplished was to make her stumble. Her left foot caught the upper fence rail and the demon fell face forward into the dust on the other side.

Fell . . . and rebounded, rising into a crouch, spinning

around to hiss at me, eyes bright with madness and blood-lust, claws slashing the air. I launched myself into the air for a diving, slashing tackle.

And then something hit me like a thunderbolt, slamming into my side, driving me at a right angle to the demon. I fell hard and badly, smashing into the fence post, spinning amid a cloud of splinters, feeling fire explode on my side as something tore at me. Then I was down, rolling over and over with a second woman.

A second demon.

—
6

SPECIAL AGENT FRANKS

Another possessed woman was on top of Ledger, trying to gouge his eyes out. The two of them were rolling through the mud and shit, trying to kill each other. As entertaining as that was, Franks wasn't in the mood to dick around, so he aimed carefully and shot the creature square between the shoulder blades. The silver 10mm blew a hole through her heart, but rather than die, she screeched and reared back. Ledger reached up with his blade and slashed her throat wide open, half a second before Franks shot her through the side of the head. The demon rolled off of Ledger, thrashing and spraying.

Well, these things were proving to be obnoxiously tough. Franks grabbed one of the kicking legs and dragged the monster away from Ledger while the first demon circled back through the pile of dead goats. Ledger would just have to deal with that one while Franks figured out just how much of a hellacious beating he had to administer to finish an Alghul for good.

7

CAPTAIN JOE LEDGER

I fought the demon the way I'd fight a wild animal. I've had some experience there. Wild animals and genetically modified animals. Years ago I faced down mastiffs that had been transgenically altered to give them scorpion tails. I've faced genetically engineered vampire assassins and some other rude and nasty shit. This was my first encounter with something supernatural, but if it existed and if it could bleed, then some of the laws of nature had to apply. That was useful, that gave me a firm piece of ground in this shit storm where I could stand. And Franks had bought me a moment. So I used it.

The demon tried to end it fast by rushing at me with those claws.

Fool me once, motherfucker . . .

As she darted in I twisted and marked her from wrist to shoulder with picks—short, hard taps with the wicked point of my knife that opened bleeders and ripped apart nerves—and with quick, circular slashes to the muscles for reaching and grabbing. The demon howled in pain and darted back. Tried again, got cut again, and darted back once more. Blood the color of red bricks flowed from a dozen cuts.

If this was a person, I might have used the effect of a pick or slash to close to killing distance, but the wounds were hurting it—just not enough. Those arms still reached, still moved with obvious speed and power.

"Stop fucking around," growled Franks.

"I'm. Not. Fucking. Around," I snapped as I dodged a series of vicious slashes.

"Don't you have a big-boy knife?"

"Fuck you."

He laughed a cold, heartless, mocking laugh and tossed something to me. A knife. A Ka-Bar USMC Mark 2 combat knife whose blade flashed in the sunlight. I faked left and lunged for the blade, snatched the handle, dove into a roll to give myself time to grip it properly, rose and spun. I did a fast swap so the Wilson was in my left and the much bigger Ka-Bar was in my right.

"Silver," barked Franks, then he had to concentrate on his own battle.

Silver. Did that work on demons? I had no fucking idea. What do I know about any of this shit?

The demon, though, she stared at the blade and hissed.

She knew.

Yeah. She absolutely knew.

I felt myself smile.

The Ka-Bar was bigger and heavier, but I've fought with them many times. You lose a fraction of your speed, but when you reach out and touch someone they get the message. I switched my grips on both knives so that I held them with the blades spiked down from my fists like the claws of a praying mantis.

"Come on, beautiful," I said to the demon. "Let's dance."

Okay, it was corny but I was having a moment.

So was she.

With a banshee howl the demon flung herself at me.

$$\overline{8}$$

SPECIAL AGENT FRANKS

He hated when demons were strong enough to warp the flesh of the possessed. They always seemed to sprout claws and fangs, just to be pricks about it. This one had scratched him and tried to bite a hole through his armor before he'd slugged her in the head enough times to crack her skull and turn her brains to mush. Franks hoisted the dazed demon high overhead, and with a roar, flung her down, through the fence, and against the packed earth so hard that the snapping bones could probably be heard back at the convoy.

The Alghul lay there twitching, beaten, glaring at him with eyes filled with hatred. She opened her mouth and hissed at him in the Old Tongue. *"Traitor."*

"Yeah, whatever," Franks said as he reached down, got a handful of blood-soaked hair, and cranked the demon's head brutally to the side. He'd been planning on twisting her head clean off to shut her up, but simply snapping the neck seemed to do the trick, and he felt the ancient malignant spirit driven from the possessed flesh.

9

CAPTAIN JOE LEDGER

The demon tried to end it by driving all ten claws into me like a storm of daggers. I pivoted and parried, using the little Wilson to push the outside of her left arm to one side while also hooking and trapping her wrist. I used the Ka-Bar in a hard, sweeping overhand slash that sliced through scalp, ear, left eye, cheek, and mouth. I put muscle into it, using my inverse grip so that it hit like a heavy punch as well as a slash.

It drove her to the ground. Hard. Dark blood exploded upward, and everywhere a drop struck my exposed skin I could feel it burn.

Even hurt she tried to turn, but I stepped on her elbow, pinning it and her to the ground to spoil the turn. I stabbed down into the base of her skull to sever the spinal cord. The silver-coated knife bit deep and hard.

The demon screamed so loud that it knocked me back. She screamed so hard that blood burst from my nose as I lay there, hands clamped to my ears. The scream made the palm trees shiver and tore fronds off of them. Debris rained down on me as the scream rose and rose and . . .

The silence was immediate and intense.

For a terrified moment I wondered if my eardrums had simply burst.

But, no.

No.

I got shakily to my knees and immediately vomited into

the dust. Then I sagged back onto my heels, pawing blood from my lips and chin, blinking past pain-tears in my eyes.

Franks stood there, wide-legged, chest heaving only slightly, sweat glistening on his skin, eyes dark and intense and amused.

"What," I said, "the fuck was that?"

His expression was ugly and unfriendly. "I told you, Ledger. Demons."

"First—and don't take this the wrong way—but fuck you and your demons."

He shrugged.

"Second—since when are demons an actual thing?"

"I thought DMS knew all this stuff."

"No, we goddamn well don't."

There was a twinkle in Franks' eyes. "Your boss does. What's he call himself now? Mr. Church? You should ask him."

I tried to get to my feet, failed, and he caught me under the arm and jerked me upright. I slapped his hand away and stepped back.

"Who are you? How do you know about Church? How do you know about demons, for Christ's sake? And, just in general, what the fuck?"

"The fuck," said Franks, "is that ISIS has gone old-school."

"Meaning what?"

He pointed into the desert. "The answers are out there. If you want in, you need to come with me now."

"No, first I get answers." I stepped away from him and

tapped my earbud to get the channel for the tactical operations center. "Cowboy to Deacon."

"Go for Deacon," said Church.

"Two words," I said. "Franks and demons."

He said, "Ah."

He gave it to me in bullet points, but they hit like real bullets. Agent Franks. Monster Control Bureau. A group that responded to supernatural threats in the same way that the Department of Military Sciences responds to terrorists with high-tech science weapons.

Real.

All real.

If there was a note of apology in Church's voice for not having read me in on this earlier, I sure couldn't hear it. As I listened, Franks stood apart, checking his weapons and trying to look as casual as a towering freak of a monster killer could look.

"Franks is in the family," said Church. "You can trust him. He's one of us."

"One of us? Is he even human?"

Church paused. "At this point, captain, would that even matter?"

10

SPECIAL AGENT FRANKS

"How do you know Mr. Church?" asked Ledger.

"We've met," Franks said. "He offered me a cookie."

"Yeah. He does love his vanilla wafers. We have a pool going that there's some kind of code in that whole cookie thing. What he eats, how he eats them, what he offers to other people."

"You're overthinking it."

"Pretty good chance," said Ledger. "Equal chance we're not. He's a spooky bastard."

They walked. The sun was an open furnace.

"Most soldiers, even SpecOps, would have died," Franks told him.

Ledger cut him a look, but only shook his head.

"You fight okay." By Franks' standards, that was a huge compliment.

"I intend to go home and cry into my pillow," said Ledger. "Maybe wear sweats and eat a whole thing of Ben and Jerry's. Or get drunk. Drunk is a real contender for how I intend to process this shit."

11

CAPTAIN JOE LEDGER

I'm a big, tough manly man, but there are times I just want to go and hide. Like when I'm in the middle of the Iraqi desert, having just waded through a brutal firefight and some Frankenstein-looking cocksucker tells me that demons are real and we have to go chase one of them.

It doesn't help one little bit for me to remind myself that no one drafted me. I signed on for this stuff. Well . . . maybe not *this* stuff, but a good soldier doesn't get to choose his wars.

But, really, man . . . demons?

There is not enough bourbon in all of Kentucky to make that fit into my head.

Franks asked, "Have you heard of Alghul?"

"Sure," I said. "It's a monster from Arabian folklore."

"They're more than that."

I glanced over my shoulder in the direction we'd come. "Oh," I said. "Shit."

"*One Thousand and One Nights* has some truths. Alghul exist. They're mostly female demons who haunt grave-yards, digging up fresh corpses to feed on. They lure men to remote spots and attack them. Like mermaids." He cut me a look. "Yes. Mermaids are real. They love human flesh."

"Jesus. Disney got that wrong."

"Alghul are ferocious, but rare. Most were imprisoned. Until now."

"So . . . ISIL is doing what? Recruiting desert demons?"

"Of course." He said it so matter of-factly that it jolted me. I studied his brutish face, looking for some trace of humor or even irony. Nothing. He was as frank as his name.

"Okay, okay, so they *are* recruiting desert demons. How, though? If these Alghul are so vicious that they were impris-oned, why don't they chomp on the ISIL dickheads? I'm sure they're every bit as tasty."

"I don't do cultural evaluations," he stated. "Dark magic probably."

"And they can shape-shift? When I saw the first one she

was an ordinary girl. Sixteen, seventeen, maybe. Then suddenly she wasn't a girl."

He nodded. "They prefer to use virgins as hosts. Demons enjoy corrupting the pure."

There had been a lot in the papers about ISIL fighters kidnapping women, forcing them into marriages with their people, or consigning them to rape camps. As insane as it was, I could see the ugly shape of it. ISIL was fierce but it wasn't massive. It did not really have a home country. It couldn't put a million-man army in the field to oppose the growing coalition of international forces. Even though many of ISIL's leaders were former Saddam officers and the equipment they used was stolen advanced tech, they were still comparatively small. They could fight a guerrilla war but there was no way they could achieve a decisive win or hope to hold their territories for very long. They needed a wild card. I was dealing with some of this stateside with ISIL teams stealing technologies like portable EMPs and drone tech. This was new, and if it was something they could repeat over and over again, then this was a game changer.

<hr>

12

SPECIAL AGENT FRANKS

The sun beat down on their heads, and then the rocks beneath them radiated the heat back upward. They were traveling cross-country to avoid being spotted. It was a brutally hot day and he was sweating profusely beneath his armor. Franks didn't mind. Discomfort was one of those mortal concepts he had never really grasped. Compared with the endless void of Hell, a little mortal suffering was a small price to pay to have a body.

Captain Ledger was human and must have been dying in the agonizing heat, but he didn't seem like a complainer. They'd set a tough pace across rugged terrain, as fast as Franks was willing to risk without further aggravating the bullet hole in his leg, but Ledger had kept up. In fact, he seemed to enjoy the challenge.

So Ledger could fight extremely well, hadn't been scared of an Alghul, and was tough. It was too bad he was with a different agency, because Franks found himself thinking that he could use a man like this . . . But unfortunately, it turned out Ledger was also a smart-ass.

"So, Franks," said Ledger, "my people tell me you saved the world once."

"I heard the same thing about you."

Ledger shrugged. "Hasn't everybody?"

"No," Franks stated flatly.

But Ledger was undeterred. "That sea monster off the California coast with the nuclear sub. That was one of yours, wasn't it?"

"Classified." Franks had been working with tough guy secret agents of the US government since Benjamin Franklin had performed his first exorcism, so Franks was used to the inevitable dick measuring to see if an agent's rep was legit. "How'd you like the Red Order?"

"No comment."

"Thought so."

They made it less than half a kilometer before Ledger

tried to make conversation again. What was it with mortals and their need to break perfectly good silences?

He was a little out of breath from the climb, but he kept pace. Ledger tapped his earbud. "I'm getting a lot of nice backstory on you, Franks. Here's a fun fact. My intel guy says that people who work with you have a tendency to die horribly."

Franks snorted. If Ledger wanted to talk, they might as well talk about the mission. They would be there by sundown. "We're only a few clicks from the target. The ancient Assyrian city of Nimrud."

"I heard ISIL bulldozed it. I guess that's the sort of thing psychopaths do." Ledger snorted, seemingly disgusted by the thought. "They're destroying priceless historical relics because they think it's an insult to their skewed view of their religion. The word 'fucktard' comes to mind." He paused. "Though, I suppose something out there raised a flag, otherwise my boss wouldn't have sent me here."

Franks thought that Ledger was probably talking about intel pinged by the DMS's fancy secret super computer, Mind-Reader. The DMS used it to predict problems by looking for patterns in the massive information streams gathered by the various covert intelligence networks. Franks wasn't sure how well that actually worked for them, but it had brought Ledger here, so maybe there was something to it.

"MCB got a tip. Terrorists found the lost Prison of Shalmaneser. It was built in 1240 A.D. to house the king's enemies." Franks snorted. The mortal ones had turned to dust a long time ago. It was the immortal ones he was worried about.

"Which is why you're here, I suppose. Church tells me he intercepted communications from an ISIL tactician who'd cut a deal with someone at Nimrud for a new super weapon. You know, man, we gunslingers in the post-9/11 federal agencies are supposed to share information about stuff like this."

Franks just grunted. He'd never been good at sharing.

"Let me guess," Ledger persisted, "this lost prison holds more of those Alghul. How many are we talking about?"

Fourteen thousand corpses of the desolate plains, an unholy army that was legend among all the jealous Fallen, until King Shalmaneser had found a way to cast them from their physical bodies and entomb them in the Earth, but Franks couldn't tell Ledger that or how he knew about it, because there was classified, and then there was *classified*.

"A lot," said Franks.

"So much fun hanging out with Chatty Cathy," Ledger sighed.

13

CAPTAIN JOE LEDGER

We reached the ancient Prison of Shalmaneser just as the sun began sliding toward the western horizon. Long fingers of darkness seemed to reach out toward us from the shattered rock walls, broken trees, and parked vehicles. Our approach was cautious and circumspect. I reached Bug at the TOC and asked for whatever an eye-in-the-sky could tell us.

"Read forty heat signatures, Cowboy," he said, using my combat call sign. "Thirty-four are steady, six are variable. One minute they're normal, then they shift from low-temp to really hot. Not sure how to read that. Maybe they're underground and thermals can't get a solid lock."

I told Franks and he shook his head. "As the Alghul takes over, they burn hotter. The variations in thermal signature mean that the demons haven't fully taken hold. Human spirits are hard to destroy. Even assholes like these."

I had the impression that an explanation that long caused him actual physical pain. Getting trapped in an elevator for six hours with this guy would be a hoot.

We made maximum use of ground cover and came in on a line the satellites said was as close to a dead zone as we'd get. Franks never seemed to tire as we crawled over rocks and through dry washes and up sandy slopes. I felt like I was melting.

There was a small camp built inside the remnants of a medieval building that had collapsed centuries ago. The ISIL vehicles were hidden under desert camo tarps, but we saw a half dozen empty slots where the vehicles from the fight in town had been parked. We hunkered down to study the layout while Bug fed me what intel he could grab from the satellite.

"How many sites are there like this?" I asked, nodding to the Assyrian ruins.

"Too many." Franks grimaced, or maybe it was a smile. Really hard to tell with a face like his. "Most stay lost."

"So why haven't we heard about the Alghul until now?"

"We have. MCB find stray Alghul, we put them down.

They're here. Somebody hears a woman calling at night. Goes to look . . . The bodies are torn apart. Blame it on war. Nobody looks at a corpse over here and thinks 'demon.' "

"Um," I said, but I had nowhere to go with that.

"A few days ago a girl taken captive by ISIS returned to her village as a monster and slaughtered everyone. MCB found out. Intel says this is the source."

"We shut this place down, and we shut down the threat?" Franks shrugged.

"And here we are," I said. The shadows were lengthening and the heat of the day was already beginning to shift. Once the sun was down it would get very cold very fast. "So, what's the plan? Soft infil? Gather some data and call in an airstrike?"

"No. Explosives only kill the body. We need to kill the demons."

"Shit. Let me guess, only silver does the trick."

"It varies, demon to demon," he said. "With the Alghul, it is silver or the hands of a true warrior."

"Isn't that just peachy. What if there are a lot of them?" Franks shrugged again.

"Okay," I said, "there are forty hostiles in there and my team is hours out. We're two guys. So again I say, what's the plan?"

Frank handed me a Glock and two spare magazines. I still had the silver-coated Ka-Bar. Franks had taken enough firepower from his convoy to launch a frontal assault on the gates of Hell. He pointed to a pair of guards walking sentry outside of the opening to the ruins.

"Kill everything. How much more plan do you need?"

14

SPECIAL AGENT FRANKS

Franks gave Ledger a few minutes to get into position before he started walking right up to the front of the dig site. The site was a haphazard maze of crumbling ancient buildings, twisted rock, modern prefabs, and heavy equipment. It was crawling with insurgents and absolutely reeked of demon stink. He didn't know how many humans had already been possessed by Alghul, but it looked like they'd practically formed a line to wait their turn to go down into the prison. The tactician was smart, only letting one volunteer descend into the depths at a time, because possession wasn't pretty, and it might make the others lose their nerve.

Idiots.

Construction spotlights kept most of the area well lit, but there were plenty of shadows for Ledger to work in. Franks had thought about taking out the generator first, since he could see in the dark, but so could the Alghul.

There was a Toyota pickup truck with a machine gun mounted in back blocking the road. The man on the gun saw the darkened shape of Franks approaching, pointed, and began shouting something. Franks shouldered the SCAR, put the ACOG scope's glowing green triangle on the man's chest, and launched a .308 round through his heart. The guard spun around and toppled from the bed of the truck. Franks kept walking.

The sudden noise had gotten everyone's attention. Another man had been sleeping in the cab of the truck, and he bolted upright, glancing around, confused, until Franks' second bullet went through the driver's window and blew his brains all over the passenger's side. A man in black pajamas and white sneakers ran around the truck. He had just enough time to fire a wild burst from his AK before Franks shot him once in the chest. He tumbled forward, skidding to a stop on his face.

There was movement all over the front of the camp now. *Excellent.* If they were all paying attention to him, then Ledger could get a shot at the ISIS tactician before he could create any more Alghul. Just in case Ledger needed more time, Franks slung his rifle, hopped into the back of the pickup, worked the charging handle on the big 12.7mm DShK machine gun, and turned it on the camp. Franks was really good at being distracting.

15

CAPTAIN JOE LEDGER

There are times you have to nut up and say "fuck it."
So I nutted up and said fuck it.

16

SPECIAL AGENT FRANKS

THUMP, THUMP, THUMP, THUMP, THUMP.
The massive bullets tore right through the sheet metal of the prefab buildings. Lights shattered. Men died. Orange

muzzle flashes rippled across the camp as they returned fire. Franks methodically swiveled the heavy machine gun toward each one and mashed the trigger, ripping apart bodies and cover. An insurgent ran from the ruins with an RPG over one shoulder and took a knee. Franks tore him in half and the rocket streaked off into the darkness.

As the last of the belt of heavy rounds cycled through the gun, Franks heard a new sound over the pounding. The screams were unnatural, like a sandstorm processed through tearing human vocal cords. *Alghuls incoming*, Franks thought as he saw the twisted figures loping across the camp on all fours toward him. *About damned time.*

17

CAPTAIN JOE LEDGER

I moved in, low and fast, running with small, quick steps to keep my aim level, firing the borrowed Glock in a two-handed grip. The ISIL tactician ducked backward, grabbed the shoulder of one of his guards and hurled him at me. Part shield, part weapon.

I put two center mass and dodged around him to get to the tactician, but there were more of the fighters. So many more.

They screamed at me in half a dozen dialects and began firing their AK-47s, filling the tomb with thunder. But they were panicking, too. In surprise attacks panic is the sword and shield of the attacker and it bares the breast and throat of the attacked. The swarm of bullets burned the air around me.

I did not panic. I closed on them and fired, taking them in turn, shifting to interpose one in front of the other, making them pay for their fear that made them miss when I did not.

I could hear carnage and destruction behind me. Franks was a goddamn tank. I think he scared me more than what we were fighting. If he was an example of the MCB operators, then what the fuck *else* could they put in the field? I mean, I'm top of my game for what I am—a black ops gunslinger, but I'm flesh and blood. I couldn't shake off the kinds of damage he was wading through. Even so, I heard him grunt, saw out of the corner of my eye as some of the enemy fire hit him hard enough to tear chunks away, to slow his advance. Could he die?

Probably.

I damn well could.

And so could the fighters in this tomb.

Franks and I had proved that.

Then in one of those moments of combat improbability that offer proof that the gods of war are perverse sons of bitches, a heavy-caliber round hit the side of my gun. The force tore the gun from my hand and nearly took my trigger finger with it.

The tactician had two burly guards with him and they were all eight feet from me. Their guns were swinging toward me.

I had no time at all, and I gave them none. Eight feet is a long step and a jump. I leapt into the air, slapping the barrel of the closest AK aside a microsecond before he fired, and at the same time I hooked the shooter around the back of the neck, shoving him sideways. He crashed into the second shooter and I landed on the balls of my feet, pivoted, snapped out a low flatfooted kick to the second man's knee. The joint splintered audibly and it tore a shriek from him. I gave him a double-tap with my elbow, one very fast and very light hit to the eye socket to knock his head backward and a second, much harder shot to the Adam's apple. He fell, gagging and trying to drag air in through a throatful of junk.

The first shooter tried to slam me across the face with his rifle, but he wasn't set for it. I slapped the swing high and ducked low, chop-punching him in the groin, then rising fast and hitting him in the throat, too, this time with the stiffened Y formed by index finger and thumb.

That left the tactician facing me.

He did something cute. He pulled a knife.

So, what the hell, I pulled mine.

He was pretty good. Fast, strong, knew some moves.

Pretty good is great if you're fighting in a back alley or in the dojo using rubber knives. Not when you're fighting for your life.

He tried to drive the point of his knife into my chest, maybe hoping to end it right there. I clubbed the knife down and away with a fist and used the Ka-Bar to draw a bright red line beneath his chin. I whirled away to avoid the spray of blood.

18

SPECIAL AGENT FRANKS

Franks crashed through the camp, keeping up a steady stream of fire on the charging Alghuls. The contorted bodies were nearly as fast as he was, and it was taking several solid hits to put them down.

Beneath their tearing uniforms, their skin quickly dried and cracked apart, and unholy yellow light poured through the gaps. Bones twisted into points and ripped through their fingertips. As the possessed around them shed their humanity, the mortal ISIS fighters lost their nerve and fled into the desert. Not all of them made it, as overcome with bloodlust the Alghul fell on them, tearing them limb-from-limb, and painting the stone walls with blood. Franks would have shot the survivors in the back as they ran away, but he couldn't spare the ammunition.

There was a ripping noise as an Alghul tore through a canvas tent to get at him. When it appeared, the yellow glow leaking through its tearing visage reminded him of a candle inside a jack-o'-lantern. But when he knocked it down and then stomped its chest flat with one big combat boot what came squirting out wasn't very pumpkin-like at all.

"Franks! Over here!" He turned to see Ledger standing in a doorway to an ancient stone building. He no longer had Franks' Glock and instead held a Russian Stechkin automatic pistol he'd picked up from one of the dead ISIS fighters. Behind him, stairs led down into the darkness. Ledger glanced up as a shadow crossed him. An Alghul was spider-climbing up the rock above him. Ledger calmly raised his Stechkin and fired several rounds through its face. "I found the prison," he said as the Alghul landed next to him with a sick thud.

And the rest of the Alghul must have realized it too, because they'd quit tearing the terrorists' guts out and shoving them into their mouths long enough to all focus on the

American intruders. There were at least a dozen of them left, and they all ran shrieking toward the doorway.

"Whatever you're going to do, do it fast." Ledger grimaced as an Alghul swiped at his eyes with its claws. He shot the creature repeatedly as it stumbled away. Then Ledger darted forward and punctuated the attack with a deep slash from the silver Ka-Bar. The demon shrieked and crumpled to the stone floor.

Franks shoulder-checked another Alghul into the ground and then dumped the rest of his rifle's magazine into its body, sending up gouts of blood and sand. "Don't let anything past this point," he told Ledger as he shoved by him.

"I sure hope Church was wrong about your allies tending to die horribly," Ledger muttered as he got ready to hold off a horde of demons on his own.

"Not really," Franks said as he went down the stairs.

"That's not helping," Ledger shouted as he kept shooting.

19

CAPTAIN JOE LEDGER

I swapped out a spent magazine for a fresh one just as a wave of Alghuls rushed at me.

The Modern Man inside my head more or less screamed and passed out. The Cop backpedaled because this wasn't his kind of fight.

But the Killer . . . ?

Well, hell, I think he was waiting for the right moment to take the wheel and drive us all to crazy town.

And I liked it. They rushed at me. And I . . . fuck it. I rushed at them.

I let the gun barrel lead the way but I chased the bullets into the crowd. The heavy rounds punched holes in foreheads and burst eyeballs and painted the walls with dark gore. If we'd been in a wider space they could have circled me and cut me apart. This was a narrow stairwell and it worked for the kind of close-range fighting I do best. When the slide locked back I simply rammed the barrel into the screaming mouth of one of the Alghuls and then slashed her across the throat. As she twisted down to the ground I reached past and quick-stabbed the next one in the right eye and then the left. One-two shallow thrusts with the sharpened clip of the Ka-Bar. The demon staggered back, clawing at its face with black talons, and I knee-kicked it into the others, jamming and crowding them even more. I grabbed a fistful of hair and drove the knife into the socket of a throat, gave the blade a quarter turn and ripped it free.

The dead and dying monsters toppled against the others, pressing them backward, transforming their savage attack into a clumsy rout. I jumped onto them, riding the falling, tumbling, bone-snapping avalanche down the stairs. Claws tore at me, the stone walls and the stone steps pummeled me, teeth snapped at me, but I rode a magic carpet of destruction down to the bottom. This was my moment and although they were demons from some twisted corner of hell, I was the red king and the knife was my scepter.

Then something massive crashed past me, striking the last of the demons like a runaway truck.

Franks.

He was splashed with blood and there was a wild light in his eyes that was no more human than the monsters we fought. He smashed them with fists the size of gallon pails; he stomped on them. I saw him tear an arm from its socket in exactly the same way the first Alghul had done back at the village.

It was all red madness.

I was the only one down there who was human.

If you could call the Killer human. He was like a demon howling inside my head, and through my mouth and with my voice.

But I was wrong.

I wasn't the only human down there.

I saw a man standing at the rear of the chamber.

He was dressed in strange clothes, all of gold and jewels and leather, like someone who had stepped from a history book. In a flash of insight I realized that he was probably dressed as a shaman or sorcerer from the courts of King Shalmaneser, emulating everything down to his garb so that there was no chance of getting his horrible ritual wrong.

He was the one responsible for all this death. He was the one who had taken all of these innocent girls and turned them into monsters. He had participated in a kind of spiritual rape by opening them to the demons who destroyed their souls while stealing their flesh. The depth of this crime—this *sin*—was bottomless. If he lived, if he escaped, then all of this destruction, all of this pain, was for nothing. He would start it up again somewhere else. He would ruin more lives, and by doing it hand ISIL a weapon more dangerous than any nuke.

Behind the sorcerer was a doorway in the living rock of the cavern. It was open and beyond it I could see flames. Maybe there was a bonfire in there, but I don't think so.

I think I was looking straight into the mouth of Hell itself.

One after another of the Alghul came running from the flames to join the fight.

"Franks!" I screamed, pointing.

The brute had three Alghuls tearing at him and he bled from at least fifty deep cuts, but he turned, saw me, saw where I was pointing. Saw the sorcerer.

I saw him stiffen. I saw the moment when he understood what we were seeing.

Franks reached up and ripped one of the Alghul from him and used her body as a club to beat the other two into shattered ruin. Then he lowered his head, balled his fists, and charged toward the sorcerer.

Leaving the other ten Alghuls to swarm at me.

But I kicked myself backward and stepped on something that turned under my foot. It was one of Franks' guns. A mate to the Glock he'd given me. I snatched it up, vaulted the rail, and dropped fifteen feet to the floor. My knees buckled under the impact, but I tucked and rolled as best I could. The Alghul shrieked like crows and swarmed down the steps toward me. The sorcerer pointed at me with a ceremonial dagger and at Franks with a scepter.

"Kill them!"

The demons closed around me like a fist.

I raised the pistol and took the shot.

One bullet.

There was only one round left and the slide locked back.

The sorcerer stared at me. All the Alghul froze. The world and the moment froze.

The sorcerer had three eyes. Two brown ones and a new black one between them. Two of the Alghul stood behind him, their faces splashed with blood that was redder than theirs.

We all lived inside that frozen moment for what seemed like an hour. Or a century.

And then the sorcerer fell.

20

SPECIAL AGENT FRANKS

It really pissed him off when stupid mortals fucked around with things beyond their comprehension. This idiot had probably pieced the spell together out of some forbidden tome. He'd gotten the costume right but the actual magic words written in blood on the walls were the equivalent quality of crayon scribbles. The workmanship was so shoddy they were lucky he hadn't sucked northern Iraq into another dimension with this half-assed summoning spell.

Ledger drilling a hole through the summoner's brain had stopped the ritual. No more would cross over. However, they were still up to their eyeballs in Alghul, but since the path was still open, Franks had a solution to that little problem.

This next part wasn't in any of the MCB's manuals.

Franks walked to the shimmering portal, and placed his hands against the edges. His gloves immediately burst into flames. Even though they were all around them, the humans couldn't sense the disembodied, but Franks could. He saw that the Alghul's spirits were still tethered to this prison. In this place of power he could apply the might of his will against theirs.

Your invitation has been revoked, Franks declared in the Old Tongue. A hot desert wind ripped through the ruins, sand blasting the bloody marks from the ancient walls. The demons shrieked as the void ripped them from their newfound flesh and sent them hurtling back into the darkness.

And then he shut the door.

The flaming portal disappeared in a flash. Every possessed body instantly collapsed into a limp, wet heap.

Well, that worked better than he'd expected.

Ledger was panting, covered in blood, and surrounded by corpses. He looked to Franks, incredulous. "What the fuck just happened, Franks?"

"Mission accomplished."

21

CAPTAIN JOE LEDGER

I want to say that it was an easy wrap. I want to say that Franks did his magic mumbo jumbo and the world became all shiny and new and cartoon animals frolicked around us.

I'd love to say that. Just once.

The truth was that there were still some possessed ISIL foot soldiers out there.

Franks and I are alive right now because we earned it.

I'm telling you this now as I sit on an equipment box in

Camp Baharia in Fallujah. There are a lot of US military around me. Echo Team finally arrived, so I have my own people there. In that place, with that much muscle around me I should feel secure, should be able to take a deep breath.

But I think it's finally hit me.

There are demons. Real demons.

There are monsters. Real monsters.

We stopped a threat unlike anything I'd ever imagined could be real in this world. The gateway to Hell, or to wherever those demons came from, is closed, thanks to a monster that stands alongside ordinary humans like me.

That doorway is sealed, but when I asked Franks if that meant that demons could no longer come into our world, he did something that I didn't think he could do.

He laughed.

And, brother, it was not the kind of laugh you ever want to hear.

No, it was not.

So I sit here, waiting for my ride out of this place, for my ride home. The night is heavy and vast. I used to think the shadows were nothing more than lightless air, that nothing lived in them, that nothing could.

Now I know different.

Holy god, now I know different.

ABOUT THE AUTHORS

Kelley Armstrong is the author of the Cainsville modern gothic series and the Age of Legends young adult fantasy trilogy. Past works include the Otherworld urban fantasy series, the Darkest Powers and the Darkness Rising teen paranormal trilogies, and the Nadia Stafford crime trilogy. Armstrong lives in Ontario with her family.

Stephen Blackmoore is the author of the noir urban fantasy novels *Mythbreaker, City of the Lost, Dead Things, Broken Souls*, and the upcoming *Hungry Ghosts*. He has written tie-in fiction for the role-playing game Spirit of the Century, the video game *Wasteland 2*, and the television series *Heroes Reborn*. His short stories can be found online and in the anthologies *Deadly Treats* and *Uncage Me*. He cohosts the bimonthly crime fiction reading series Noir At The Bar L.A. He can be found online at www.stephenblackmoore .com and on Twitter at @sblackmoore.

Larry Correia is the *New York Times* bestselling author of the Monster Hunter International series, the Grimnoir Chronicles trilogy, the Dead Six military thrillers, and the Saga of the Forgotten Warrior epic fantasy series. A former accountant and firearms instructor, Larry lives in northern Utah with his patient wife and children.

ABOUT THE AUTHORS

Christopher Golden is the *New York Times* number-one bestselling author of such novels as *Snowblind, Dead Ringers, Tin Men,* and *Of Saints and Shadows,* among many others. A lifelong fan of the "team-up," Golden frequently collaborates with other writers on books, comics, and scripts. His collaborations with Mike Mignola have led to two cult favorite comic book series, Baltimore and Joe Golem: Occult Detective. As an editor, he has worked on the short story anthologies *The New Dead, Seize the Night, The Monster's Corner,* and *Dark Duets,* among others, and has also written and cowritten comic books, video games, screenplays, and a network television pilot. Golden was born and raised in Massachusetts, where he still lives with his family. His original novels have been published in more than fourteen languages in countries around the world. Please visit him at www.christophergolden.com.

Charlaine Harris is a true daughter of the South. She was born in Mississippi and has lived in Tennessee, South Carolina, Arkansas, and Texas. After years of dabbling with poetry and plays and essays, her career as a novelist began when her husband told her to stay home and write. Her first book, *Sweet and Deadly,* appeared in 1981. When Charlaine's career as a mystery writer began to falter, she decided to write a cross-genre book that would appeal to fans of mystery, science fiction, romance, and suspense. She could not have anticipated the huge surge of reader interest in the adventures of a barmaid in Louisiana, or the fact that Alan Ball would come knocking at her door. Charlaine is a voracious reader. She has one husband, three children, two grandchilden, and three rescue dogs. She leads a busy life.

ABOUT THE AUTHORS

Caitlin Kittredge is the author of sixteen books for adults and teens, including *Black Dog* and the award-winning Iron Codex trilogy. She created and wrote the comic *Coffin Hill* for Vertigo and writes the upcoming series Throwaways for Image Comics. Ava and Leo's story continues in *Grim Tidings*, Book Two of the Hellhound Chronicles. Find Caitlin on Twitter at @caitkitt.

Jonathan Maberry is a *New York Times* bestselling novelist, five-time Bram Stoker Award winner, and comic book writer. He writes the Joe Ledger thrillers, the Rot & Ruin series, the Nightsiders series, the Dead of Night series, as well as stand-alone novels in multiple genres. His comic book works include *Captain America, Bad Blood, Rot & Ruin, V-Wars*, and others. He is the editor of many anthologies, including *The X-Files, Scary Out There, Out of Tune,* and *V-Wars*. His books *Extinction Machine* and *V-Wars* are in development for TV, and Rot & Ruin is in development as a series of feature films. A board game version of *V-Wars* will be released in 2016. He is the founder of the Writers Coffeehouse, and the cofounder of the Liars Club. Prior to becoming a full-time novelist, Jonathan spent twenty-five years as a magazine feature writer, martial arts instructor, and playwright. He was a featured expert on the History Channel documentary *Zombies: A Living History* and a regular expert on the TV series *True Monsters*. Jonathan lives in Del Mar, California, with his wife, Sara Jo. Visit him at www.jonathanmaberry.com.

Seanan McGuire lives and works in Northern California, in a crumbling farmhouse shared with her two improbably large blue cats, a wide assortment of books, and far too many creepy dolls. Since the release of her first novel in 2009, she has published more than twenty-five books, which feels more like a lifetime achievement than the work of less than a decade. She is widely believed not to sleep (and even more widely believed to be the vanguard of an invading race of alien plant people, which would explain a lot). If you'd like to keep up with Seanan, we recommend looking for her at Disney World. Failing that, try www.seananmcguire.com.

According to friends, **C. E. Murphy**, who was born and raised in Alaska, began her writing career when she ran away from home at age five to write copy for the circus that had come to town. This is much more exciting than the truth, so she's sticking with it.

More prosaically, she is the author of the bestselling Walker Papers series, has been told that she's a crowdfunding pioneer, and lives with her family in Ireland, which is a magical place where it rains a lot and nothing one could seriously regard as winter ever actually arrives.

Joseph Nassise is the *New York Times* and *USA Today* bestselling author of the Templar Chronicles series, the Jeremiah Hunt trilogy, and the Great Undead War series. He is the coeditor, along with Del Howison, of *Midian Unmade: Tales of Clive Barker's Nightbreed*, and he also writes epic fantasy (in conjunction with Steven Savile) under the pseudonym Matthew Caine. Visit him on the web at www.josephnassise.com.

Weston Ochse is a former intelligence officer and special operations soldier who has engaged enemy combatants, terrorists, border crossers, narco punks, and human smugglers. His personal war stories include performing humanitarian operations over Bangladesh, being deployed to Afghanistan, and having a near miss being cannibalized in Papua New Guinea. His work has been praised by *USA Today*, *The Atlantic*, the *New York Post*, the *Financial Times*, *Publishers Weekly*, Peter Straub, Joe Lansdale, Jonathan Maberry, Kevin J. Anderson, Tim Lebbon, and Christopher Golden. The American Library Association labeled him as one of the Major Horror Authors of the Twenty-First Century. His work has also won the Bram Stoker Award, been nominated for the Pushcart Prize, and won multiple New Mexico–Arizona Book Awards. A writer of more than twenty-six books in multiple genres, his military supernatural series SEAL Team 666 has been optioned to be a movie starring Dwayne Johnson. His military sci-fi series, which starts with *Grunt Life*, has been praised for its PTSD-positive depiction of soldiers at peace and at war.

Kat Richardson is the bestselling author of the Greywalker novels, as well as a small tantrum of short fantasy, science fiction, and mystery stories. She is an accomplished feeder of crows.

Diana Rowland has worked as a bartender, a blackjack dealer, a pit boss, a street cop, a detective, a computer forensics specialist, a crime scene investigator, and a morgue assistant, which means that she's seen a helluva lot of weird crap. She won the marksmanship award in her police academy class, has a black belt in hapkido, has handled numerous dead bodies in various states of decomposition, once saved her family's life by grabbing a roach, and can't Rollerblade to save her life. She currently lives in south Louisiana, where she is deeply grateful for the existence of air-conditioning.

ABOUT THE AUTHORS

Steven Savile has written for popular franchises including *Doctor Who*, *Torchwood*, *Primeval*, *Stargate*, *Warhammer*, and *Sherlock Holmes*. He was a finalist for the People's Book Prize in the UK and has won the Lifeboat Foundation's Lifeboat to the Stars Award and the International Association of Media Tie-In Writers Scribe Award. He wrote the storyline for the bestselling computer game *Battlefield 3*, which sold more than five million copies in its first week of release, and his novel *Silver* was one of the UK's top thirty bestselling novels of 2011. Under the name Matt Langley his young adult fantasy novel *Black Flag* was the first original novel published by Cambridge University Press in the five hundred years since Henry VIII awarded them their royal charter. He has novels under option with CBS, Level One Entertainment, and Sony Entertainment. His forthcoming novels include *Parallel Lines*, a crime novel to be published by Titan in 2017, and *Glass Town*, a fantasy novel to be published by St. Martin's in the fall of 2016, where you'll meet Cadmus Damiola on his home turf.

Craig Schaefer's books have taken readers to the seamy edge of a criminal underworld drenched in shadow (the Daniel Faust series); to a world torn by war, poison, and witchcraft (the Revanche Cycle); and across a modern America mired in occult mysteries and a conspiracy of lies (the Harmony Black series). Despite this, people say he's strangely normal. Suspiciously normal, in fact.

Schaefer lives in Illinois with a small retinue of cats, all of whom try to interrupt his writing schedule and/or try to kill him on a regular basis. He practices sleight of hand in his spare time, though he's not very good at it. His home on the web is www.craigschaeferbooks.com.

ABOUT THE AUTHORS

Jeff Somers (www.jeffreysomers.com) began writing by court order as an attempt to steer his creative impulses away from engineering genetic grotesqueries. His feeble memory makes every day a joyous adventure of discovery and adventure even as it destroys personal relationships, and his weakness for adorable furry creatures leaves him with many cats. He has published nine novels, including the Avery Cates series of noir–science fiction novels from Orbit Books (www.avery-cates.com), the darkly hilarious crime novel *Chum* from Tyrus Books (www.chumthenovel .com), and most recently a tale of blood magic and short cons, *We Are Not Good People,* from Pocket Gallery (www .wearenotgoodpeople.com). He has published more than thirty short stories, including "Ringing the Changes," which was selected for inclusion in *Best American Mystery Stories 2006,* and "Sift, Almost Invisible, Through," which appeared in the anthology *Crimes by Moonlight,* edited by Charlaine Harris. He also writes about books for Barnes & Noble and About.com. He lives in Hoboken with his wife, the Duchess, and their cats. He considers pants to always be optional.

Carrie Vaughn is best known for her *New York Times* bestselling series of novels about a werewolf named Kitty, who hosts a talk radio show for the supernaturally disadvantaged, the fourteenth installment of which is *Kitty Saves the World.* She's written several other contemporary fantasy and young adult novels, as well as upwards of eighty short stories. She's a contributor to the Wild Cards series of shared-world superhero books edited by George R. R. Martin and is a graduate of the Odyssey Fantasy Writing Workshop. An air force brat, she survived her nomadic childhood and managed to put down roots in Boulder, Colorado. Visit her at www.carrievaughn.com.

David Wellington is the author of seventeen books, including the Monster Island series of zombie novels and the Chimera trilogy of thrillers. He is perhaps best known for his Thirteen Bullets series, featuring the vampire hunter Laura Caxton. His work can be found online at www.david wellington.net and www.grimblyhall.com. He lives and works in New York City.

Jaye Wells is a *USA Today* bestselling author of urban fantasy and speculative crime fiction. Raised by booksellers, she loved reading books from a very young age. That gateway drug eventually led to a full-blown writing addiction. When she's not chasing the word dragon, she loves to travel, drink good bourbon, and do things that scare her so she can put them in her books. Jaye lives in Texas.

Sam Witt writes dark thrillers infused with the supernatural. Informed by a rural Midwestern childhood and big-city adulthood, he combines down-home folklore and legends with a hard-hitting, take-no-prisoners writing style.

His Pitchfork County series follows the dark and twisting lives of a family intent on using their own cursed abilities to protect the place they call home from all manner of threats, from mad gods to meth cults.